HUNTING
TROPHY

A MYSTERY BY
BOB GIBSON

 FriesenPress

Suite 300 - 990 Fort St
Victoria, BC, V8V 3K2
Canada

www.friesenpress.com

ISBN
978-1-5255-7810-6 (Hardcover)
978-1-5255-7811-3 (Paperback)
978-1-5255-7812-0 (eBook)

1. FICTION, MYSTERY & DETECTIVE, INTERNATIONAL MYSTERY & CRIME

Distributed to the trade by The Ingram Book Company

2019

PROLOGUE

THE BIRTH OF A WITCH - 14 MARCH 1987

In the village of Munyati, Zimbabwe, a young mother was giving birth to her first child under the supervision of an older woman and her helper. The moon was rising through the clear sky, gently nudging the stars from its path. Odd shadows were appearing amongst the neighbouring acacia trees. Nearby, a lone striped hyæna was cackling its eerie laugh-like song. It was time for Prosper's baby to arrive. Babies are not delivered by a Marabou stork in Munyati, but not all arrive in the normal way.

Mama Prudence, a hefty but very attractive and nimble woman was wearing a large red scarf wrapped around her head. She was the eldest and most experienced midwife. The second was Veronica Mashaya, who had been introduced late in life to the sisterhood of witchcraft by her friend, Mama. Her decision to accept Mama's invitation came after she had with-stood years of abuse and beatings at the hands of her husband. Veronica eagerly absorbed Mama Prudence's teachings, for Mama was renowned for her knowledge of all aspects of witchcraft. Veronica was a tall, gaunt, severe-looking woman whose expression was frozen in time, in memories of great unhappiness. Prosper had selected Mama Prudence and Veronica as soon as she had become aware that she had been possessed by a *shavior*, acquired through some medicine given to her by an unknown *nángaor*. Prosper knew that her child would have problems coming into the world, and she was counting on Veronica, also a *nángaor*, for her particular ability to reverse the spell that had been cast upon her baby. They were the only women Prosper could trust with the course of her child's life.

Before Prosper had even begun her contractions the women knew that something was different with this baby. Mama Prudence was massaging Prosper's tummy with a lubricant made from the internal fat of a leopard blended with a number of other secret ingredients taken from local plants. She then sprinkled her with a mixture of ground roots, salt, and the dried, crushed, yellow-green flowers of the young Mopani tree. While Mama Prudence knelt, chanting quiet incantations and sprinkling the powdered mixture, Veronica continued to massage Prosper's lower pelvis up toward the ribs.

Prosper felt the pain. The woven mat on the floor of the rondavel offered no relief. She chewed a form of *ganja* to help deaden the ever-increasing, pulsating pain. Inside Prosper's small pelvis, a little girl had become disoriented and rather than being prepared to meet the world headfirst, she had decided to sit on the floor of the pelvic cradle; in effect, she had chosen to stay where she was — regardless.

The mother was likely going to die but they must save this baby. Veronica had managed to massage the baby into a position where it might enter the world feet first, the sign of a *varoyi*, a powerful witch. The current problems of presentation and arrival would be insignificant compared to those the child would face later in life. She was to be born a witch. She would have powers that must be kept so secret that only the two older women bringing her into the world would know who and what she was. They would be assigned the responsibility of raising and training the girl in the aspects of the occult. Mama Prudence and Veronica had long ago sworn their vows and practiced their skills secretly, without accusation from the community. Mama Prudence often reminded the younger sisters of an old admonition taught by the sisters of the east: "Never share your secrets with anybody. It will destroy you."

In *Shona* communities it was often suspected that some women were witches. The adherents to witchcraft were usually the women endowed with either excessive beauty or exceptional ugliness. Those most often suspected were usually the widowed, those who were lonely and who often were identifiable by tooth decay, which was thought to be caused by eating human flesh. Mama Prudence must have been very beautiful as a young girl. She retained a great deal of her youthful advantage in her later years.

Veronica gently fed Prosper a cup of warm tea brewed from a concoction of ground roots and certain animal fluids. The laugh of a striped hyæna cackled again through the chilled night air. The time was closer now. Prosper heaved her body and then suddenly went completely limp, her sweaty arms falling to her side as she fell into a cold silence. Her soul had departed, leaving only the hope of her child.

Mama Prudence knew exactly what must be done to save the baby. Using a sharp shell of a razor clam, a tool which had been in her family for generations, she immediately sliced Prosper from side to side across the belly, just above the pelvic bone. The first cut was through the layer of skin. She then cut through the layer of fatty tissue to reach the fascia, which covered the pelvic muscles. She had placed a small gourd in position to collect the blood. Once Mama Prudence punctured the amniotic sac, there was a flush of fluid. She continued to cut then to stretch the sac to reveal the baby. She grabbed hold of the baby by its midsection and lifted while Veronica reached below and guided the head out of the womb, using a long straw to suck the fluid from the nose of the new baby girl. By tickling inside the baby's nose with the straw, Veronica encouraged her to breathe her first breath. Mama Prudence twice wrapped the umbilical cord with some fibres from a tendon of a young impala and then cut the cord between the knots. They quickly and efficiently cleaned and wrapped the baby securely in a red sheet of linen. The entire episode was over in less than ten minutes. After another short incantation by the two elders, Mama Prudence departed with the baby.

Veronica was left to wash and to stitch Prosper and to allow her to lie in repose on the mat. The baby's father would be told that the baby was born deformed and the wife had died peacefully. He might choose to visit the corpse of his wife but there would be no funeral, for everyone feared contamination from what was obviously a bad omen. He had been a violent husband and had wanted his wife to get rid of the baby early on. After midnight, Mama and Veronica skidded Prosper on the mat to the edge of the nearby river and presented her as an offering to the crocodile. Crocodiles were familiars of the witches. Prosper would then be struck from the memories of the villagers, as would the non-existent daughter.

JIM - OKANAGAN - 18 APRIL 2014

I stared at the odd rug lying off to the side in the den near the hearth of the fireplace. It was not the first time I had sat in this chair, and it was not the first time I had been distracted by the unusual animal that stared directly at me with a contemplative gaze. The animal was a brown hyæna, my host had explained the first time I had enquired. It wore a long, shaggy coat of dark brown fur. A ruff of creamy colour around its neck accented the vertical mane that ran from the top of the neck and down the back to its short tail. *Hyaena brunnea,* my host had added, as he had noticed me seemingly transfixed by the eyes, glass eyes, looking directly at me from its broad muscular head. There was a resemblance to a Staffordshire terrier I had seen before, a biting machine.

I shivered.

"Sorry," I said, "I was just thinking...."

My thoughts drifted off again.

I met Jim two years after I first heard that he lived in our community, just outside town. The townspeople had no clear knowledge of his history, referring to legend and conjecture, thinking they knew something true about him, when in fact, nobody knew who Jim really was. I had visited with him on one occasion thus far and was no more informed than the others. The fact that I had actually met him set me apart as an expert among those who felt uncontrollable curiosity. Unfortunately, there was little I could add to their speculations and even less that I felt free to share, since Jim had asked me politely, but firmly, over our first shared Glencairn of delicate but peaty Laphroaig Scotch, to respect his privacy.

Our community was a cluster of modest towns in a valley that had been carved by the rushing torrents that came out of the last ice age. The great melting glaciers drained from the surrounding mountains, filling the intersections of valleys with hundreds of feet of stones, sand, and silt, ultimately forming ideal sites for complex human habitation. For thousands of years the *Syilx* Nation had enjoyed this land. When the *Suyapix* decided to overstay their welcome in the 1800s, the *Syilx* had been encouraged to share these lands.

Many of us have retired to this community because of the mild winters, the proliferation of golf courses and the convenient availability of inexpensive but pleasant recreational wines. Not much of substance has happened here. Occasionally a car has been driven too fast in the winter and has slid into one of the lakes. From time to time the Mounties have captured a drug user or a car thief. Teachers have gone on strike, schools have been shut down, and the relevance of other news to an older retired immigrant has declined from there. All in all, there has been very little earth-shattering local news. This has left us with few subjects of any depth for our Saturday morning discussions at the local coffee shop. One of us expounds upon ISIL or Mr. Putin or Mr. Obama or the prospect of Donald Trump becoming President of our southern neighbour. Someone repeats a story that has recently appeared in the press. Gossip has become its own art form.

The stranger, Jim, lived back in the hills on a road that went nowhere. Most could not bring themselves to ignore the 'No Trespassing' signs to see what was there. This alone perpetuated relentless gossip: he was a drug dealer with one of the international gangs; he flew drugs in and out of the country in his helicopter. If that was challenged, he was a retired operative from Canada's Security Intelligence Agency, surreptitiously coming and going without being noticed. Perhaps he needed to keep his head down because of some action he had succeeded in carrying out that allowed him to qualify for his own personal *Fatwa*. Some locals knew other stories, none of which was particularly comfortable—none was accurate.

My introduction to Jim occurred by sheer accident. I was driving up a graveled road on a Sunday afternoon with no particular destination in mind, other than ending up in the vicinity of home prior to dinner. The noticeable tug of the steering wheel toward the ditch indicated the possibility of a flat tire. I pulled over to the edge of the road, climbed out, walked around, and noticed that the shoulder of the road was quite muddy. My diagnosis had been correct. I went to the trunk to retrieve a jacket and the car jack. It had been so long since I had had the need to change a tire that I could not remember where the jack was supposed to be stowed. The trunk full of golf clubs and other summer paraphernalia impeded my access, naturally, so I began to deposit them into the mud. As the pile on the muddy shoulder grew, I felt certain I was getting closer to the mother lode - a jack and a spare tire. As I removed the last rain jacket and umbrella, I found the handle that allowed entry to the special compartment containing my objective. I lifted the cover, reached in and felt a very soggy spare tire; it was flat! Worse than that, the jack was not where it ought to have been. I set the cover back in, wondering whether I should unload the spare tire or refill the trunk and repeat the process after being towed to town. I pulled out my cell phone to call the tow service - no reception. Not one grey rectangle of hope on the screen of my iPhone 5.

The wind blew hard from the south and along with dampness, it carried the last of the winter's cold. I climbed back into the driver's seat and turned on the caution lights. As I sat there, I tried to determine whether I would walk up the hill until I could get reception or down the hill to reach town. Just as I chose the downhill option, a vehicle pulled past and drew to the shoulder of the road in front of me. The door opened and a man descended from the cab. He approached my car slowly. I rolled down my window. He greeted me politely and asked if I needed some assistance. I replied in the affirmative and explained my situation - the lack of a jack and the flat spare tire.

"Let's get your gear locked up in the trunk, then hop in with me," he suggested, as if there were no alternative. I followed his suggestion, and in a few minutes, all was stowed. Whatever we couldn't fit back inside the trunk we stashed in the rear seat. The stranger strode toward the driver's side of his older model, mud-covered Ford 250. As he opened his door, he glanced over his shoulder to see how far behind I was. Was he leaving without me? I put my feet in gear and jogged up to the pickup. By the time I was seated, the motor was running, and the pickup was ready to go. As soon as he heard the buckle click, the stranger pulled out and headed up the road.

"We'll go up to my place and call a tow truck. We'll then have something to warm you up. I'll wheel you into town as soon as the tow truck has your car. How's that?"

"Sounds fine," I answered, with nothing else to say.

We bumped and banged our way up the gravel road, crossing ripples that made the whole vehicle chatter. Soon we reached a rather large log house, hidden behind hills and timber, and revealed to us as we turned the last corner. He hopped down from the truck and strode to the door, unlocked it and swung it open - again waiting for me. I stepped in and started to remove my muddy shoes.

"Just scrape them off on the rug and come on in," he instructed.

He led me into the first room off the entry and pointed to a chair. He walked briskly over to the landline phone, called a tow truck company and provided instructions without any reference to my credit card or me. As he hung up the phone he looked over and said, "What will warm you up—a scotch, a beer or a coffee?" He then added quickly, "I'm having scotch," and disappeared around the corner into the adjacent room. I could hear the sound of a bottle clanking against glass and heard him shout, "Decide yet?"

"I'll have one too, then," I called back to him.

He called me into the next room and motioned to a comfortable leather club chair. He walked across the room with a couple of crystal glasses in one hand, a decanter in the other and a small water pitcher hanging from his little finger. He set them down in well-practiced fashion and handed a scotch to me. He picked up the pitcher and dispensed a few drops into the Glencairn and then repeated the process in his own glass. Before he sat down, he held his glass in a toast.

"Well, *slangevar*," he said and put the glass to his lips before waiting for my non-existent response.

"My name is Jim. Tell me about yourself." he quickly followed with, "where are you from?"

"Saskatchewan," I answered.

"Long way from home. Why would you be so far from home without checking your spare?" he asked.

"Well, I meant I was born and raised in Saskatchewan. I live up the valley in Lake Country now, retired," feeling that I had clarified things. "How about you?" I challenged.

"Here for now," satisfied him, "who knows where next?"

"Retired?" I asked, more from his situation than his age. He appeared to be in his mid-fifties, very fit and very mobile.

"Usually," came his unusual response.

"What do you do?" I asked boldly, since I was already sitting there drinking his scotch and couldn't think of anything else to say at that moment.

"Let's just say I am a hunter," he replied, "I like hunting."

It was quite obvious by the trophies mounted on the walls that he hunted many species from many countries. As I looked around at the variety, I noticed a few Cape buffalo.

"They are pretty dangerous, eh?" I asked, pointing up at one of the skulls.

"Yup, not too bad. They do tend to surprise a lot of people, though, and they often win," he observed, "Some things are a bit more dangerous."

"What do you think is the most dangerous?" I asked, thinking I had been invited to do so.

"Humans," he answered, without further thought.

He quickly added, "Don't think that I hunt them for sport, though."

I was saved from asking the next question when the phone on the kitchen counter sounded a techno ring. He left the room and I could hear him grab the receiver, speak tersely, then hang up. He returned, looked over at me and said, "We'd better go. The tow truck driver has radioed the shop. They have your car loaded and are on the way to town. We should be able to get there at about the same time as the truck. Good with you?"

I took the last few sips of my scotch in one swallow and headed out behind him.

He drove quickly but expertly over the gravel until we reached the hardtop. He headed toward town and pulled up to the tire shop without saying another word. I was concerned that I had offended him, but he showed no sign that I had. He just looked over at me and said, "Good luck, we'll see you around some day," and as soon as I was solidly on the ground, he was off. I entered the shop and sorted out the simple details with the older man at the counter, settled the tow bill by credit card and thanked the driver, then sat down to wait for the tire repairs to be done.

I looked up at the guy behind the counter who appeared to have nothing more to do than I did at the moment and I asked, "Do you know that guy, the one who drove me here?"

"Yup," he replied, as he looked at me vacantly.

"Know what he does?" I asked.

"Nope!" Again, his reply was curt. "Do you?"

"Nope, not really," giving the only reply I could.

I looked about silently while he returned to staring blankly at the counter, until someone announced that my tire was repaired, and my spare replaced. I settled the bill and finally was on my way home.

My first encounter with Jim had been interesting, but unfulfilling. I had learned enough to know that I was far more uninformed than I had previously thought regarding this stranger. I had learned his rather innocuous first name, if indeed it was his name. By the time I was to stumble upon Jim next, winter had come and gone. I happened to be in the local grocery store shopping to refill the larder when a huge voice called out behind me.

"Got a new spare yet?"

I turned and there was Jim, standing before me with a broad grin and an armload of groceries.

"How are you, Jim?" I replied gingerly, "I see you made it through the winter."

"Yep, but not much of it here," he replied, again closing off that potential line of questions.

"Come on up for a visit tomorrow, after lunch," he said, more as an instruction than an invitation.

"Sure," was my meek reply, and he joined the express line, leaving me in the crowd lined up for cashier number five.

That evening I sat contemplating what Jim had said the first time I was at his place. What had he meant when he said that he hunted people? Did he really say that or was that my extrapolation? He had mentioned spending time working in Namibia. He had mentioned a few other places, too. When I asked, he said he wasn't in the army, but that could be true or not. If a guy worked in the covert world, he would deny it if anyone implied that he did, and agree if anyone said he didn't. I guess it was all part of the mystery of that small but very large world. What did he mean by saying that he had not spent much of his winter here? As I continued my ruminations, I had to ask myself why I felt so suspicious of Jim. Why would it even occur to me that a man living in the small community in which we lived, who just happened to keep to himself mostly, would be a mysterious operative of some sort? I had to chuckle when I realized that I had listened to all the gossip about Jim and had taken it as gospel. He was indeed mysterious, but I would soon discover - unintentionally - just how deep the mystery went.

The next day was Friday. After spending a relaxing morning reading and eating a filling lunch at Tim Hortons, I left town and drove in the direction of my flat tire event. Once there I continued up the gravel road, struggling to remember the turnoff. The road headed northward, and I followed it until I noticed the side road. I turned left, fairly certain that I was on the right track. Minutes later, after passing some old 'No Trespassing' signs back in the bush, I found the driveway. After a few more corners, I spotted the house through the trees. I was right! His Ford pickup was sitting in front of the shop. I parked in front of the house, climbed out and approached the door. An old black lab laid sprawled on the ground beside his pickup. He paid no attention to my arrival. I pressed the doorbell and waited. I was about to press it again when a heavy hand landed on my shoulder from behind. I spun about and there was Jim, smiling broadly.

"Come on in," he invited.

How had he walked clear from the shop across the gravel to where I was standing without making a sound? I stepped up and in through the open door, asking myself, "how?"

"Just scrape 'em off," he said loudly, already in another room, "come on in."

I followed him to the room where we had had our first scotch.

I saw him standing at a credenza, pouring scotch. He offered me a glass and pointed to a leather chair by the hearth, right in front of that very ugly hairy animal rug. He started talking, more rapidly than before, spilling out hunting stories one after another. After a few stories he would stand and refill his glass, offering me some. I had taken hardly a sip yet. I was riveted. How often his life had seemed to be in serious danger—yet how unconcerned he appeared as he relayed to me his adventures. He made no attempt to create a sense of tension or excitement; they just seemed to pour out, almost nervously at times.

"Which animal was the most exciting to you?" I asked during a pause.

"Do you mean the most frightening?" he asked slowly. as he stared steadily into my eyes. "Or, do you mean the most deadly? The closest I came to being killed?" He added.

"Sure," I said, "whichever you prefer."

He began to tell me a fascinating story about when he had gone on a hunt with an old friend who was making his first trip to South Africa, looking for plains game primarily.

"I was going along as more of an observer," Jim started, "there were few species I didn't already have."

SAFARI STORY

"On the last day of our ten-day safari near Vryburg, the Texas of South Africa, I received a call on my satellite phone. It was one of my long-time friends, a Professional Hunter. He asked me if I wanted to join him in Zimbabwe after our hunt in South Africa to help track and eliminate an old lioness that had been killing cattle in the North Country. I told him that I was hunting with a friend. The PH said he was welcome to join the party, but that he would stay in the truck or in camp, not having enough experience for the task. I asked my pal and he accepted the conditions happily, excited to extend his experience, since he, like many others, had fallen in love with Africa. When we got back to camp that night, we faxed our papers, along with our rifle serial numbers, to the PH. Then I sent a message to my travel agent to change our flights.

"Once we finished in South Africa, we packed, tipped the staff, bid our adieus and then began the five-hour drive to the O.R. Tambo Airport in Johannesburg to catch the 10:40 South African Air flight to Bulawayo. Once there, we were met by my PH friend, who had all our permits. We retrieved our rifles, went through the registration process, grabbed our bags, then cleared Customs and Immigration. The driver and his helper grabbed our gear and they dropped us off for the night at Cecil Rhode's old haunt, "the Bulawayo Club" We were going north right after breakfast.

"What is the Bulawayo Club like?" I interrupted.

"I love it," Jim replied, "The old Bulawayo Club is a comfortable and fascinating piece of history. It began life at the end of the nineteenth century, as a classic old gentlemen's club. We stayed in the three-story white building that was built in 1935. I always enjoy staying there whenever I find myself in Bulawayo. They say it is frequented by ghosts: the ghosts of hunters like Frederick Selous and James Sutherland, and mining promoters, the Hamburg Diamond King, Alfred Beit and his partner Cecil Rhodes."

"We had a wonderful dinner," he continued, "a few drinks and a good night's sleep, waking the next morning to a wholesome breakfast of eggs, sausage, toast and coffee. We were eager to head out when my friend, the PH, strode in from the lobby to find us. His workers had hauled out our gear and loaded it into the Toyota Land Cruiser. We were ready to head north. Our destination was a farm east of the Hwange area and southeast of Mbizi, a village that sat along the Zambezi River. We headed up the A8 and in about three hours we turned east toward Manjolo.

"Soon we were on gravel and dirt, much different than the paved road to Vic Falls. As we reached the village of Tinde we stopped to relieve ourselves and fill up with gasoline, and then we headed farther east across the high savannah. Fortunately, it was winter there and the temperature was mild at 28°C. After two hours we arrived at a farmstead. It was one of those classic, old Boer homesteads with a whitewashed house, a deep verandah, whitewashed outbuildings, all interspersed with blue gum trees and backed by acacias and blackthorns. The lawn was cut short to reveal the snakes that passed through occasionally during the summer. As we were driving into the property, we looked out over the plains of acacia and buffalo grass. There were kopjes - you know, rock hills. They are home to lots of wildlife. Some of the fields were cultivated, some were grazing paddocks.

"We pulled up to the house and were greeted by the owners, Jacobus and his wife, Marina. Two Ridgebacks stood quietly until we were out of the vehicle, and then they proceeded to inspect us before deciding we passed muster and going to lie down in the shade of the verandah. One of the girls came out and offered us cool glasses of water with lemon, and little towels to wipe the accumulated grime from our hands and faces – a very welcomed gesture. Jacobus led us into the house. The bags disappeared to our bedrooms and our guns to the safe room.

"We walked into the kitchen and sat down at the long table. Strong coffee appeared before us almost as quickly as sandwiches and cake slices.

After the pleasantries were over, Jacobus began to explain what had been happening. He had started losing the odd calf every few weeks. That wasn't so unusual as there were leopards, caracals, and lions, and there always had been. This time, though, it was different. The calves were killed and only their hearts and livers eaten before the carcasses were abandoned to the scavengers of the savannah. They had reached only two of the carcasses quickly enough to notice this. In one instance the head was missing. Usually there was little left once the vultures were done; they had destroyed any remaining evidence of the killer. From calves, the deaths progressed to healthy cows and finally to two of Jacobus's farm workers.

"The locals believe in *Zaka*, a form of witchcraft. They believe spirits can travel on the backs of animals. Sometimes they travel on the backs of owls, sometimes the backs of *bere*, or hyænas. The witch travels by night, naked and in secret. When the two workers did not show up at home for the evening meal, fellow workers searched and found them late in the night. Each was missing his heart, his liver and his head. The workers refused to touch the bodies because if the witches were still there, they could then hop onto them and infect them, in effect turning them into witches. The head man noticed that one of the dead workers was missing two copper bangles that he had worn for most of his life. From then on, no workers would go out alone and none would go out in the dark. Jacobus and his son scoured the area for tracks but all they found were the tracks of the hyænas, and, unless one believed in *Zaka*, one could not think that they could possibly have been the culprits. Jacobus had perpetuated the story of the rogue lion so that he could convince someone to come to find the culprit. Very few had any interest in hunting a spirit.

"'Well,' my PH said, 'We must mek a plan.'"

"We spent the rest of lunchtime debating the best approach. We decided to try the traditional method of staking a goat near a machan and waiting. Jacobus dispatched some workers to gather materials and tools while we set about checking our rifle sights. I would have a scope and my PH would have open sights. My friend would stay at the farm with Jacobus. Darkness descended by about 19:00, so we had to hurry to be set up for that evening. Most of the kills had taken place in one particular area. Jacobus believed the killer was spending the days in the heavy jess near the stream that ran north of the paddock or the great kopje nearby.

"Once completed, the machan stood nearly twenty feet high and supported a small platform about four feet by eight feet. There was no ladder built into the machan so at 17:30 my PH and I scurried up an aluminum ladder the workers had brought, and pulled up our gear, coats and the rifles, by rope. The bleating goat was tethered twenty yards north of us and some old intestines and blood were scattered about, and then the truck and the workers left us to wait.

"When the sounds of the departing truck finally faded in the distance, all that remained was the cooing of doves, the bark of nearby baboons, and the trickling of water from the stream in the distance. As night fell there was a quick crescendo of vervets, baboons and birds and then, at once, the world was black and silent - dead silent - and there we waited as quietly as possible. We could soon see the heavy jess by the stream and eventually, under the limited light of the stars and of the waxing crescent moon, it was possible for us to see the outline of the nearby kopje. We could see the tethered goat, which foolishly had begun bleating as the moon rose. Wait, stay awake, sip coffee from the thermos, and above all, listen. We waited all night. We could feel the deepening chill before the sun pushed the pink and violet layers of sky from the horizon to make room for its own grand entry to the day. The bush came to life. We could hear the truck returning to pick us up. Soon we heard the banging of doors, the clunking of the ladder, and other sounds from the workers. We could still see nothing in the jess or on the kopje, so we cleared the chambers of our rifles, climbed down, and solemnly trudged to the nearby truck. The workers had caught the goat and loaded it into the box with the other workers. Then we drove off to the farm for a hot breakfast.

I heard my PH tell Jacobus that we had heard nothing, not a sound. Not a single animal moved. He suggested that we should have some sleep and head out earlier that evening, walking in the last few hundred yards and shinnying up the machan; it would be less noisy and possibly prevent sending out a warning of our presence.

"Sounds lek a plan, maan," Jacobus said, as he poured us another round of strong black coffee. He told me that he was going to take my friend for a drive around to see if they could spot some spoor.

"We enjoyed our breakfast of *pap* with butter, *boerewors*, eggs and gravy, and then headed down the hall to our rooms. I tried to induce my body into some much-needed sleep, and finally I fell into the deep sleep of a dead man. When I woke up, I wandered in to join the others in the kitchen for a late lunch.

"Soon enough our driver appeared at the door. We grabbed the thermoses filled with hot coffee, climbed into the truck and headed out to the machan. When we got close by, the PH and I walked in the last three hundred yards to the base of the machan. I worked my way up the pole first and had the PH pass the gear and the rifles up to me. He then dexterously climbed up himself. A tracker had led the goat in, with a bandana stuffed in its mouth, and tied it to the tether rope. When ready, he removed the bandana and left to join the others in the truck. The remainder of the afternoon passed slowly. The heat and the flies were a continuing nuisance. As night approached, we decided that we could only snooze one at a time because of the lack of any guardrails. My PH took the first shift - I started mine at 18:00. By nightfall we were both awake and alert. Each of us watched two quadrants, divided by a white rock near the centre of the growth of jess bush. I watched to the right and my PH to the left.

"What you do," Jim explained to me as if we were there, "is slowly focus close…then far…then back…then a slight turn, repeating this again, again and again.

"When it got close to 01:30, we both heard the sound of a pebble being turned. The goat stopped its bleating. Our nerves were now fine-tuned, and we were wide-awake. We listened for the next sound, trying to confirm the direction and the cause. Nothing, nothing. My heartbeats gradually slowed. Then it was there, the sound of another pebble. Something was coming down the bed of the stream two or three hundred yards away. Not close enough to see, even in the moonlight, even if there had been no jess bush.

"Perhaps it was a leopard but again there was no telltale sound of the soft repeated purring sound, like that of a chainsaw that wouldn't start. It was a solo animal, so not likely lions. Wait and listen. My PH tapped me on the wrist with his index finger then pointed in the direction of a white rock. I turned my head slowly, just in time to catch a slight movement at one hundred twenty yards. It faded in and out of sight like a ghost, like a kudu in the acacia trees at dusk. Slowly I lifted my binoculars to my eyes. There, I recognized instantly the strange, almost shy, sideways walk of the hyæna. Still, there was no noise. It was very, very unusual for hyæna to approach so silently. But it was equally unusual for them to be killers; they were designed for it but for generations they had tended to scavenge. The goat let out a few mournful bleats, then pulled back to the end of its rope, head down. The PH tapped my wrist twice, indicating that I should bring my rifle up for a shot. I slowly and quietly rolled to one side in order to bring my rifle around, then, as I quietly disengaged the safety, I rolled onto my belly. I was ready. My PH was also ready. The hyæna was now visible clearly through my Schmidt & Bender scope. I waited for the next tap that would be my signal to shoot. My finger was on the trigger. The hyæna stopped its movement, its ears tilted to the front, then it turned its head up to look at the machan. As it did so, I felt the tap. I squeezed the trigger. My rifle roared, sending the 300-grain bullet through a flash of fire over that short distance at a speed of 2650 feet per second into the upper shoulder of the Hyæna. I could imagine the trajectory as it passed through the bone, down through the lung, the upper heart, through a rib, then out the abdomen wall. A shot rang from my PH's .458 Lott pushing a 500-grain soft point into the same target, nearly deafening me at the same time. The hyæna leapt into the air in an arc, snapping at its belly as it rose then running as it landed, heading back towards the bush.

"There was nothing more that we could do until morning light. We reloaded and put our rifles on safety. We agreed that one of us would keep watch while the other slept. The goat also decided to sleep, allowing the remainder of the night to pass quietly. I couldn't get to sleep.

"The truck arrived at sunrise, with Jacobus and my buddy, along with the PH's tracker and a few workers. The tracker located the blood spoor near where the hyæna had been hit and followed it toward the jess. My PH had all hands remain in the truck while he and I followed the tracker, both rifles with scopes now off, both slings removed, both with cartridges in the chamber and safeties off. One step, then look, then listen, then another step; rifles shouldered. Slowly we made our way toward the jess. The tracker was unarmed except for his stick. Occasionally he would pause to test the winds with a quick puff from his bag of Mopani ashes. It took us over an hour before we reached the passage into the jess. My PH whispered to me to remain silent and about twenty feet back while they went in. I was to watch, to see if anything came out. If it was the wounded hyæna, I was to shoot it. The tracker and my PH were now on their hands and knees, gradually disappearing into the warrens of the jess.

"I stood there, my rifle at the ready, for what seemed like an hour before I noticed the first sign that they were returning. The tracker appeared first, soon followed by my PH who was dragging something behind him. As he cleared the last of the bush he stood up with a big grin on his face and held up what looked like a big hairy wolf with the head of a pit bull.

""This is it," he shouted for anyone who wished to hear, "hard to find in there."

"Once they had seen what it was, the workers backed away from the beast, none wishing to touch it or to be touched by it. Jacobus was also reluctant to touch it. Not that he believed in superstitious nonsense, but why take the risk? As the PH rolled the animal over onto its other side, I noticed something immediately. There were two copper bangles wrapped around the right front leg. As soon as the workers saw this they began to run and wail. With a puzzled look Jacobus looked first at the PH and then at me.

"Perhaps these were the bangles of one of the dead workers," my PH observed.

"They gutted the animal carefully, checking for clues. My PH found a piece of half-digested denim and a green plastic calf tag inside the guts.

"Looks like we may have the culprit," my PH said calmly to Jacobus then turned to me and said, "Jim, do you want a trophy?"

"Of course," I replied, "a rug with full head mount."

The PH spoke to his tracker and then we loaded the truck, tying the beast to the hood of the vehicle for the ride home. The tracker had to do the skinning, as none of the locals would come near.

"My PH and I had our showers as Jacobus and my pal started drinking Castle beer and sharing stories. Soon after I returned to the sitting room, my PH appeared, looking refreshed. Jacobus ordered a few more beers and we all sat for a visit.

"Just before dinner the tracker came to the door and said a few words to the PH. The PH walked over and sat down and began to make a small speech about the quality of my hunting prowess and straight shooting, after which he presented me with the two copper bangles, all cleaned and polished.

"You might as well be wearing these, since no one around here will even touch them, Jim," he stated, as he handed me the two trophies.

"We'll get a permit for the hyæna so you can have it exported. I'll look after the taxidermist," he added.

"After lunch, we laid down for a few hours nap, got up, and dressed for dinner. The table was full of food as we were treated to a typical Afrikaans *braai*. There was *biltong* and *droëwors* for appetizers, followed by *potjie*, *boerewors* and zebra filets and the ever-present *pap*. We all ate too much and imbibed far too much beer and some good South African wine. The main course was followed by helpings of *koeksisters* and *skuimpies,* then brandy and coffee. Although this wasn't the best way to get to sleep, it was a delicious way to end the evening.

"The next morning, we loaded all our gear and the tracker into the Land Cruiser to return to Bulawayo. My PH got my friend and me to the airport in time to catch a flight to Johannesburg, which would allow us to connect to Frankfurt, on to Vancouver, and then home. I'll tell you for nothing, we were tired puppies by the time we arrived in Kelowna – we were nearly forty hours on the road."

Jim sat back as if had just relieved himself of an overwhelming burden. I took a sip of my scotch. As I looked up, I noticed that he was wearing the two copper bracelets on his left wrist. Obviously, he was not worried about the witch. I looked again down at the animal on the floor and observed that the rug was tacked solidly to the floor. I looked up to the wall and noticed a heavy skull hanging on a shield of teak, beside a variety of other skulls. I looked at Jim and asked, "Is that his?" pointing up to where the skull was hanging.

Jim sipped his whiskey again before answering. He looked at me with the gaunt look of a Robert Service protagonist. In the space of telling his story, he seemed to have aged twenty years and he had paled noticeably.

"Yes," he replied.

Jim seemed to have lost his focus. He started to stand up but sat back down, rubbed his temples and closed his eyes, as if he were struck by a sudden migraine. He stood again, got his balance and put his left hand across his sternum then rubbed his lower back as a man might after driving for too many hours. He sat down again for a bit longer and he looked at me once again with that far off look and said, "Well we should wrap it up. It's getting late and I still have a few things to get done."

I swallowed my last bit of whiskey, stood up and set my glass on the tray next to the scotch bottle. He rose slowly from his chair and glanced over at the rug of the beast, then up at its skull. He followed me through the kitchen to the door. I noticed that he kept rolling the bracelets back and forth around his wrist as if they were itching or burning him.

"Have a great night, Jim," I said, "I really enjoyed the afternoon and especially the stories. I've never been to Africa but would love to go sometime."

"Have a good night." Jim replied.

I headed out the door and climbed into my car, buckled up, fired up and hurried off to town.

"Boy, that felt weird," I said to myself as I drove toward town. I wondered what it was that was so powerful to those workers in Africa that it scared them to the core. Was the mind that powerful or was it real to them? What had bothered Jim?

I continued on home, parked my car and went into the house. By now, I was beginning to feel haunted. Jeez, what a joke! I made a sandwich and popped a Budweiser then watched a bit of TV. Suddenly, I felt very tired. I got up, shut off the TV, undressed and climbed into bed. I didn't wake until nine the next morning, after an unusually deep sleep, two hours later than normal. Although I was wide-awake and quite relaxed, I felt strange. I climbed out of bed, had a shower, got dressed, and then went to the kitchen. I made myself a steaming hot cappuccino, poured some Corn Flakes into a bowl, added a bit of milk and then sat to enjoy my breakfast.

I tried to work on the crossword puzzle from last Sunday's paper but wasn't progressing too well. I couldn't concentrate. My mind kept going back to Jim and his story.

The silence and my thoughts were broken by the sound of the doorbell. Ah, the Jehovah's Witnesses again or was it the Mormons this time? I walked slowly toward the door, thinking about what smart-ass response I would have for them when they asked if, 'I had been called by the Lord yet'. I opened the door and there were two Mounties standing there - definitely not what I was expecting.

"Come in," I said, curiosity getting the better of me.

The older of the two looked at me and said, "Please put your shoes on, you're coming with us."

REMAND CENTRE - KELOWNA - 19 APRIL 2014

started putting on my shoes without daring to ask why. I reached around to grab my jacket and then turned back to him and asked, "Why? Didn't I pay a parking ticket or something?"

"Just come with us, please. You are not under arrest...yet." That last word really caught my attention.

They led me to the patrol car and the young Mountie opened the back door, motioning me to get in, which I did promptly. The older Mountie continued to talk, telling me that they wanted me to provide a statement about what I knew about Jim and what had happened. What had happened? What *had* happened? Was Jim okay? I wanted to ask, but my thoughts were jumbled, and I was suddenly nervous, filled with foreboding. We were driving toward the centre of town...no doubt to the police station. We pulled into the parking lot and the young Mountie opened my door. I climbed out slowly, waiting for his instructions.

"Follow me," he said, leading me into the building and into an interrogation room. Then, to my surprise, they offered me the opportunity to call a lawyer.

"Whoa!" I thought, then promptly answered, "Yes please, I would like to call a friend who is a lawyer," hoping he would be home on a Saturday morning. I used my speed dial. I heaved a sigh of relief when he answered the phone.

"My friend, I might need a little help if you have time. I am at the Mountie office. They want to ask me questions about something that happened last night and suggested that I might want my lawyer present. I don't know who else to call on a Saturday."

The words fell out of my mouth like I had practiced the script. Too much television, I imagine.

"I'm not a criminal lawyer, but I can probably help you out this morning," he suggested, "I'll be there in about twenty minutes."

He had already hung up.

The young Mountie offered me a coffee.

"Black, please. Thanks." I replied.

Soon he returned with a cup of coffee and then he took a chair on the opposite side of the table, leaving the door open. He led the chatter. We talked about the weather, the news and the challenges of policing the valley. Before too long my lawyer was shown into the room by the older Mountie and they joined us at the table.

"What's this all about?" my lawyer asked.

The older Mountie explained that they were investigating a homicide that had occurred during the evening or early hours of the last night.

"We think your client is a potential witness, if not a suspect."

"My God! How can you say I am involved in a murder? What did I witness?"

I was really curious, but more than that, my stomach was tightening in deep concern. Was I being mistaken for someone else? Had someone seen someone who resembled me? I am not sure whether I was thinking the words or speaking them.

The older Mountie turned toward me and asked, "Where were you between one and four yesterday afternoon?"

"I was at Jim's place," I answered confidently, suddenly relieved that I had an alibi for whatever had occurred.

"Jim who?" the older Mountie asked.

"Just a friend," I replied.

"What was his last name?" he asked again.

"I don't know," I realized, "I just met him about last summer."

My lawyer interrupted, "Don't answer questions unless they are asked."

"How did you meet him?"

"I had a flat tire on a side road, and he stopped to help. My spare was no good and we couldn't find the jack, so Jim drove me up to his place and phoned a tow truck," I answered promptly.

"What does this have to do with Jim?" I asked.

"He is dead," the older Mountie revealed.

I was shocked and so was my lawyer.

"When did this happen?" I asked, unable to absorb the information.

The older Mountie ignored my question.

"What did you do after you left his place?"

"I went home."

"Then what?"

"Then I made a sandwich and watched television until I went to bed," I answered.

"What time did you go to bed?" he asked.

"Around eight or nine," I paused.

"A bit early, isn't it?" the young Mountie asked.

"I was just really tired, that's all," I answered.

"Who can confirm that?" The older Mountie spoke.

"I don't know," I said, "I live alone."

Suddenly being alone felt like a bad thing.

"Was there anyone else there when you were there?"

"Where?"

"Jim's," replied the older Mountie.

"No, no-one that I know of," I answered, "no-one that I saw."

"How did he seem to you when you left?"

"I think he was fine," I thought, then added, "he was a little pensive, but nothing unusual."

"What were you doing while you were there?"

"We had a scotch, he told stories about hunting in Africa and that was about it."

The older Mountie turned to my lawyer and asked, "Do you have time to come out to the deceased's house?"

My lawyer replied in the affirmative. The older Mountie turned to me and asked if I would mind accompanying them.

"I am OK with that. How did he die?" I thought it was a simple question.

"We don't know."

"Why do you think it is murder then, if you don't know how he died?" I asked.

I noticed that my lawyer was now writing notes in his booklet.

"Let's go, then," the older Mountie said, ignoring my question, "the sooner we get there the sooner we'll get back."

As we drove toward Jim's place, I sat in the back of the patrol car, worried about what I would see. My lawyer was quiet. He had told me we would debrief after the interrogation. The ride seemed to take forever. Finally, we arrived. The older Mountie led us into the house. It was surrounded by yellow tape. As we walked into the kitchen, I noticed nothing that was different. The older Mountie asked me to tell him how we moved through the house. I led him, describing the way we went into the other room, sat down, how he served me a scotch, and then how we sat, me listening to his stories until I left. I went and sat in the chair where I had been the day before. As I reflected on the afternoon, my eyes were drawn to the teak shield on which the hyæna's skull had hung. It was empty. I looked at the beast on the floor. It was there but it was no longer tacked to the floor. I started to feel very sick.

"What's wrong?" the older Mountie asked when he noticed my change of state.

"Nothing," I replied. "Nothing. I am just thinking of my friend. Are we done here?"

"We can go," the older Mountie said, and then turned to my lawyer.

"We will need to keep him in custody. We may lay charges tomorrow morning. You can have a bail hearing on Monday morning."

"Aren't you going to show me where he was killed?" I asked.

"No, we'll show you some photographs later."

We climbed back into the car and returned to the Mounties' offices. By now I was feeling very ill.

"How did he die?" I asked of no-one in particular. Why won't they tell me? I wondered to myself.

There was no response other than a look from my lawyer cautioning me to be quiet. It was only minutes later that we arrived at the detachment offices and were led back into the interrogation room.

"Would you be prepared to look at some photos?" the older Mountie asked.

"I don't think so right now. I just want to talk to my lawyer for a bit, please."

The older Mountie left us together in the interrogation room. "Use this. Ring the buzzer when you're finished."

My friend the lawyer sat across from me and asked, "What happened?"

"Nothing happened. The guy is dead, but I had nothing to do with it," I insisted.

"They can place you at the scene of the murder. They told me that, according to the security cameras, you were the last one to enter the house. The Mountie shared that with me before he brought me in to see you. They don't know your motive. I don't know your motive...if you have one. There is no one else who had access to the victim after you were there yesterday afternoon. Do you have any idea how we can explain this?" my friend then sat waiting for my answer.

"Who phoned the Mounties?" I asked, "How did they know he was dead? Was it the cleaning lady?" I added, instantly regretting it.

"Why did you say that?" my lawyer perked up, "Who told you it was the cleaning lady?"

"Nobody told me. I just guessed. I don't know. I don't know why he is dead. I don't know." I didn't know what else I could say.

My lawyer looked at me and said, "You know that you will be booked and spend a day or two in remand until we can get you out on bail."

"I guess I know," I sulkily responded.

"I'll be going now," said the lawyer, "I'll be over to see you tomorrow." He stood, rang the buzzer, and left when the door was released.

A constable I hadn't seen before came in and led me to the booking room. The process began and within half an hour I was in a cell by myself, for the time being.

I sat in the corner on the cot and started to think. As much as I felt like going to sleep it was only four in the afternoon. No shoes, no belt, no pen, no paper, nothing. I stood and paced the cell for ten or fifteen minutes. Ideas flooded through my mind. None made sense. How could he have been murdered if no one was there? Was he poisoned? Was he shot? How? And then by whom? Who would want him dead? I was just going in circles and only confusing myself.

I laid down and tried to close my eyes. The lights in the cell were bright, parking lot bright. I pulled my left arm over my eyes, trying to block out the light and fell asleep. I awoke to voices and clanging doors. I sat up, feeling slightly dizzy. Three men were approaching the cell, followed by a young Mountie. He reached past them, unlocked the door to the cell and let them in. He looked at me and smiled.

"Your roommates for the night," and then he retreated down the corridor.

I laid back down, not feeling particularly sociable.

"What are you in for?" asked a muscular guy with tattooed arms and a mustache.

"Nothing." I answered.

"One for murder, one for fighting and one just very drunk." Tattoo man announced, and then laughed loudly.

"Sleep good!" he added.

I closed my eyes and covered them again. I could hear the frame of the bunk bed strain as he pulled himself into the top bunk. I started to worry that it might not hold; just then he rolled over. I held my breath, ready to roll out if it started to collapse. I peeked out from under my arm to see a smaller, dirty, bearded guy sitting on the edge of the bunk across from me staring at me with a slight, spaced-out grin. A very drunk man had somehow made it to the top bunk opposite and was already snoring loudly. It was going to be a long night.

I had just fallen asleep when I heard another commotion and more clanking doors. The big tattooed guy leapt from his bunk to the floor in a practiced, athletic move, landing by my bunk, silent as a cat.

"Fucking near time you guys were feeding us," he hollered down the hall. He turned to me and smiled.

"Dinner time, sweetie," he laughed. He stood by the door of the cell, waiting.

I looked around the small cell again, trying to figure out how this was going to work. I noticed the small, bearded guy still sitting on the edge of his bunk staring at me. The upper far side guy was now sitting up with his legs dangling down a few inches from the bearded guy's face. An older woman pushing a dinner trolley rolled up to the cell and handed small plastic trays through the slot to Tattoo guy, who turned and handed them to the other residents, me being first. As soon as she was finished, the young Mountie with her encouraged her forward. There must be someone I had not noticed in a cell further down the corridor.

Tattoo motioned for me to slide over and then he sat beside me. Meticulously he took the plastic wrap from what looked something like a TV dinner and folded it before stuffing it into his shirt pocket. The small tray barely bridged the gap between his knees, as he slowly opened the small package containing utensils. Again, he folded the plastic neatly and stowed it. I tried in my unpracticed way to duplicate what he was doing. Once he was finished opening everything, he straightened his utensils properly along the tray, leaned forward and quietly said a grace. Politely and without conviction, I joined him for the Amen. Tattoo turned toward me and gave me a shy smile.

I couldn't help but wonder how he had ended up here. But probably he couldn't understand why I was here. The main difference I suppose was that I was innocent. I began to eat, not that I was hungry, but I didn't know what was coming next in this unexpected turn of events. Dirty Beard was eating voraciously, still staring, not at me, but at some point in a space beyond the wall of the cell. Upper was sitting, head down, glowering at his food, picking the odd morsel with his fingers, and then eating it slowly.

Tattoo finished before I did. He took the napkin, which he had placed between the tray and his right thigh, wiped his plastic utensils, wiped the composite plate, set the plastic cutlery neatly between the plate and the tray, then set his napkin on his plate. He stood, took the tray over to the door of the cell, and then slid it carefully under the door and to the right, out of the way. He returned and sat by me, quietly consumed by his own thoughts, while I finished my meal.

Dirty Beard was finished long before I was and had set his tray on the floor at the end of his cot. Upper was still picking his way through his food. I guessed that it must be about seven in the evening. Absentmindedly, I tried to mimic Tattoo's after-dinner ritual. No sooner had I set the utensils on top of the napkin, than he stood reaching for my tray. I was surprised but offered it to him. He walked over and set it neatly by his tray and shoved both of them further to the right.

"Thank you very much," I couldn't help saying to him as I wondered, why?

"It's OK," he responded, as he sprang up into his bunk above me and laid down.

Before I laid back down, I again observed Upper and Dirty Beard. They were sitting just as before, but Dirty Beard's plate was empty.

I began to mull. This is not a place I should be. This is not a place I have ever been or ever expected to find myself. Why had I acquiesced so easily to the Mounties locking me up here? Why had my friend, my lawyer, allowed them to put me in here? There wasn't any solid evidence that I was guilty; only, as they say in the detective movies, circumstantial evidence. How did Jim die? I wondered again. I had to organize my thoughts; I couldn't keep rolling over the same unanswerable questions. I started a discipline—who, what, where, when and why? These were the core questions I remembered from some class at school. *Who*? I don't know, but it wasn't me. *What*? I had no idea how Jim was killed. *Where*? It was at his house. Wait a minute. I don't even know that. I am assuming that because the Mounties said that I was the last person at his house, at least according to the security tapes, that it was there that he was killed or, at least, found. No, my lawyer had asked me how I knew that the cleaning lady had found him. She must have been there, and likely in a room we didn't visit this morning. *When*? It had to have happened sometime between four yesterday afternoon and eight this morning—between the time I had left Jim's and the time the cleaning lady had arrived. Good! Now, I had a few anchors. *Why*? Was it someone from his past? Was it a jealous girlfriend? Was it something to do with where he had worked or been over the winter? And what did the hyæna rug have to do with it? Why was the skull gone? Come to think of it, why was Jim behaving in such an unusual way at the end of his story-telling yesterday? What were the 'other things' that he had to attend to?

"STOP!" I told myself, "You are not the detective. You can't solve this. What are you going to do about yourself? You're not part of Jim's family. You don't even know his last name. Just have something prepared to convince your lawyer to fight for you and get you out of here on Monday morning. The rest will take care of itself. In the end you will have a good Saturday morning story."

I really didn't know much. I knew it was their job to find enough evidence to convince the magistrate to keep me locked up, at least that is what I had heard.

"What evidence could they have? They know I had been to Jim's place a few times, including yesterday. They know I was there from two until four yesterday. They know I drank a glass of scotch with Jim. They know Jim told me hunting stories from Africa. They know Jim was dead. What else they know, I don't know and won't even begin to know until tomorrow or, more likely, Monday. I need to have a look at the photos. No, I don't need to look at the photos as long as I am a suspect. How do they have anything to do with me?"

I was getting flustered and upset with my situation. I needed to calm down and wait. What difference did it make where I slept for one night or two, as long as I could sleep? I will pull the blanket over my ears, go to sleep, then have a tray of breakfast in the morning, after which my lawyer might even get me out of here. He should if he is on my side.

HARARE - 8 APRIL 2014

The Zambezi River separated Southern Rhodesia (now called Zimbabwe) from Northern Rhodesia (now called Zambia) and then flowed into Portuguese East Africa (now called Mozambique). The first two countries had been created out of the empire of Lobengula, the famous northern N'debele Chieftain, who had been hoodwinked, along with the foreign department of the British Empire, by Cecil Rhodes, a notoriously successful mining entrepreneur or, as some would say, a scoundrel. The exploration license had surreptitiously evolved from 1890 –'permission to look for minerals on N'debele lands during the life of Lobengula' - into a fifteen year charter, first with the assistance of a 'missionary' translator, and then with the help of the Governor of Cape Colony, into a British Charter to the British South Africa Company. This provided the basis for aggressive exploration, but more intrusively, for the settlement of hundreds of farmers and ranchers who were 'deemed necessary' for the production of food and necessities for the exploration activity and future mining. It eventually grew to be a great portion of arable southern Africa. In 1923, when the charter to Rhodes expired, the British Government simply declared it a colony. Many things began to happen in the Rhodesias.

One of the most significant was the awakening of Black Nationalism. The first African National Congress was founded in 1934 under the leadership of Aaron Jacha. Its objective was simply to participate in the negotiations with the Rhodesian government. It was not a nationalist or a revolutionary organization. The Second World War distracted Britain and the Commonwealth Nations from any 'superfluous' activities while the focus was on war. After the war the ANC was revitalized and once again it attempted to participate in negotiations to obtain parliamentary representation for black Rhodesians in the colonial parliament. The great general strike of 1948 was inconsistent with the aims of the ANC who preferred rational discussion and open negotiations. It achieved no success and disappeared in the early 'Fifties. The Central African Federation (comprised of Northern and Southern Rhodesia and Nyasaland (now called Malawi) took up the challenge in 1952 and later, in the days when it was still believed that all Rhodesians could live together in peace and strive for the prosperity of Rhodesia, the Southern Rhodesian National Congress, a relatively moderate and non-racial organization stepped in. By the mid 'Fifties the Southern Rhodesian National Congress was placed within the Central African Federation in order for the British to use Southern Rhodesia's wealth, coal and accumulated managerial resources, along with Nyasaland's labour assets, to develop Northern Rhodesia's mineral riches. The Empire was loath to let go of colonies as long as they were financially beneficial to the British.

The Central African Federation was dissolved in 1963 after Nyasaland (now Malawi) and Northern Rhodesia (now Zambia) became independent, and Southern Rhodesia became Rhodesia. This led to the rise of the black nationalists, who had observed the increased repression of moderate organizations by the Rhodesian Government. By 1964 the struggles over what would be the new Rhodesia intensified. The Unilateral Declaration of Independence in 1965 introduced another round of pressures and counter pressures. The 1972 Pearce Commission represented the intense negotiations between the white government of Rhodesia and the white Empire of Britain. The voice of the black Rhodesians began to be heard only through the nationalist guerilla movement and an increase in guerilla activity. This led to the negotiations that resulted in the famous Lancaster House Agreement in December, 1979, and which continued until April 1980, when Rhodesia became the Republic of Zimbabwe, and school-teacher-become-revolutionary, Robert Mugabe, became Prime Minister.

White Zimbabweans, some of whose ancestors had arrived in Southern Rhodesia as early as 1890, found themselves defending their farms, so devotedly developed over generations, from the 'soldiers of the nation'.

Bloodshed was not uncommon, even though the moderates tried to maintain a peaceful coexistence.

Robert Mugabe was aging. Like an old lion, the younger ones who wanted possession of the pride, were challenging him. He fought each incursion as if it would be his last, with all the violence necessary to quell the threat. Even his young wife attempted from time to time to take a piece of his authority, and of his wealth. To protect himself, he had tried to create a wealthy middle class, some of whom were called the 'Barons' and who had vested interests in sustaining him. He had selected them to carry out the indigenization of business in Zimbabwe. It was they who held fifty one percent of the Mercedes dealerships, or fifty one percent of the road construction enterprise. They were accumulating wealth for themselves and power in Mugabe's nation. They were constrained only by the recognized need to have a market for all their activities. The Barons needed one another, but there were others who were not in favour, and whose objective was the disintegration of the existing regime, which would then allow them to become dominant. The apparent leader of the new movement was Morgan Richard Tsvangirai, a former labour leader, and Prime Minister from 2008 until 2013. Aside from the inner power struggles, though, there was another threat, one far more dangerous to Mr. Mugabe and to Mr. Tsvangirai and to the Barons of Zimbabwe. It was a threat that, unbeknownst to them, had kept them from destroying one another.

THE EXPLORERS CLUB – HARARE – 8 APRIL 2014

On Tuesday, the eighth of April 2014 a meeting between two men occurred in the Explorer's Club Bar off the lobby of the Meikles Hotel in downtown Harare. The teak trimmed decor accented the hunting trophies over the bar. The wicker chairs and the paintings by Thomas Baines, who had travelled across southern Africa with his companion, James Chapman, in 1892, created a soothing and comfortable retreat.

The first man was tall, erect, impeccably dressed in a dark blue suit over a crisp, fine sea island cotton, Turnbull and Asser shirt, set off by a royal blue and white spotted silk tie. He stood in his oxfords, shiny and black, purchased from Crockett & Jones on Jermyn Street in London. He was fit. His dark skin set off his intelligent eyes as he casually scanned the room.

The tall man selected a seat in the far corner of the room near the kitchen entrance and far from the front entrance. He sat facing the entrance. The second man was not tall but not short either. He had grey-brown hair, which was obviously being prevented from becoming totally grey by the application of some concoction or other making it all appear rather dull and mousey, with a dark brown crown. His grey suit hung on him like a sack. It was cut badly, and it looked as though the man had worn it for weeks. The back sagged down, even though there was a roll across his back just below the collar. He did not appear fit. His shirt was a polyester-cotton blend that had been worn yesterday and possibly the day before. He wore his tie in a loose knot, with the collar button undone, likely due to the expansion of the wearer rather than to the shrinkage of the material. His sloped shoulders made the whole person look far older than his passport indicated.

The bar was a pleasant retreat from the heat and humidity outside on Unity Square; the prolific purple flowers of the Jacaranda trees had long been washed away by the rains of the past November. Now all that remained of summer was the heat and humidity. A black Mercedes S550 sedan sat conspicuously at the curb in the No Parking zone across the street from the main entrance of the hotel. The two front seats were occupied. The occupants were unknown.

The men sitting in the Club spoke in low voices, clearly not wanting to be overheard. Although the mousy man's lips were unreadable, the tall black man was very expressive in a conservative, well-mannered fashion. Judging from the observable part of the conversation, they were discussing money. Money was that magic eraser of colour. Its magnificence was that it was more liquid than water. There were no tsunamis of money—it flowed too freely. From appearances, it was flowing abundantly toward Mr. Tall. What seemed to be under discussion was magnitude rather than principle. Suddenly Mr. Tall frowned, leaned across the table, growled something, left his seat as he threw his hands toward the ceiling, and marched from the room, leaving the tab for mousy man, who seemed to have no interest at all in moving.

Discreetly observing the meeting was a striking, attractively dressed, perfectly fit young woman. She did not move when Mr. Tall left the club. As she sipped from her tall glass of sparkling water, she reflected upon the last twenty-seven years, and how she had been nurtured by an old lady, how she had begun to learn English at three years of age. She had been curried and cuddled by Mama Prudence and initiated into the secret arts of witchcraft, of making potions, of using juju. She was schooled in all aspects of poisons, and in relationships with familiars, in handling snakes and milking their venom, and in how and when to use them. She had learned how to make potions from common products to induce coma or death. At the age of eight she had been introduced to the deadly arts, the means of killing swiftly and quietly. She was as proficient with the short knife as a surgeon with her scalpel, and as silently deadly as a black mamba. She had been a brilliant student in all undertakings, ahead of her class in school, and as Mama Prudence described her, a most brilliant star. She had graduated at the top of her class in secondary school, and she had graduated Summa Cum Laude from Witwatersrand University in Johannesburg, South Africa. Now she was working, serving two masters. One master represented by Mama Prudence, the other by her current employer. She understood her power and she carried it calmly. Her life was full. She had no time for relationships outside her work, yet she remained peaceful and charming. Tonight, however, was a night of observation, not a night of action. Action would come soon enough.

REMAND CENTRE - KELOWNA - 20 APRIL 2014

Dreams come easy in a deep sleep. How I ever got into a deep sleep on that hard, rubber-coated cot, the bottom shelf of the bunk bed, I don't know. The soothing massage I was enjoying was interrupted by a crash. My heart jumped as fast as I did. I cracked my head on the frame of the bunk above me and the blood immediately started to trickle down my face. Dizzy and disoriented, I looked around the small cell trying to make sense in my brain of what my eyes were seeing. Tattoo was on his knees in front of me pounding with his fist at something. Upper was looking down with bleary eyes, legs hanging loosely from his cot. Where was Dirty Beard? I finally realized he was under Tattoo. I hesitantly tried to grab Tattoo's arm and stop him. Just then three Mounties burst into the cell and lifted him off, then noticing that he didn't resist, simply moved him to the corner of the cell by our bunk. Dirty Beard was squirming in a mess of his own blood, moaning but not speaking.

The first constable calmly asked Tattoo what the hell was going on. Tattoo was a little reluctant to responds, but turned toward them and spoke softly.

Then he turned to me and said, "Sorry," and added, "are you alright?"

I was puzzled, "I just woke up from a dream and you were pounding the piss out of that guy."

Tattoo looked at me and said, "Must have been a hell of a dream if you didn't feel that bastard's arm under your covers. I didn't trust him, so I kept one eye open. When he crawled over by you, I jumped him. You don't know what the son-of-a-bitch was up to."

I nearly felt sick to my stomach. I looked at the Mounties then looked back at Tattoo and said, "Thank you...really, thanks a lot."

Two of the Mounties were kneeling, attending to Dirty Beard, as I said to the other, "I hope there is not a problem for this guy over helping me out," then I asked, "can that guy get moved somewhere else for the night?"

"We'll likely have him in the hospital by the looks of things. Things should be OK."

Upper looked over at Tattoo and finally spoke, "Whoa, fuck! I ain't gonna piss you off, man," then flopped back down on his bunk.

The Mounties got Dirty Beard up onto his feet and led him down the corridor. Before Tattoo leapt back into his bunk, I looked at him and said again, "Thanks, I really mean it, and let me know if there is anything that I can ever do for you, Ok?"

He just looked at me with his kid-like grin and said, "It's Ok," and disappeared onto his bunk. I sat on the edge of mine and suddenly felt afraid. My legs started to feel soft and weak. My neck and back were sweating. My breathing was shallow and erratic, like a kid before he starts to cry. Another first, I thought. This is sure as hell not what I was expecting for today!

Bright lights and banging doors jolted me from sleep. I half sat up in the cot and looked around. I could see that Upper was awake, sitting with his legs dangling. It sounded like Tattoo was getting ready to jump down, so I stayed where I was for a minute.

Tattoo looked over the edge of the bunk and, accompanied by a big grin, greeted me, "Good morning, sweetie, how was your sleep?" He jumped down and laughed, and then stretched to welcome the day.

"That was a piss off!" he spoke to no one special, "hope the son-of-a-bitch stays in the hospital, or I'm likely to get charged for something." The food trays were being wheeled ponderously down the hall. I jumped up and said, "I'll get it," to which Tattoo responded politely, "Thanks." He sat down on my cot, leaving me room to get by.

I handed Tattoo the first tray off the trolley, then passed one up to Upper, who also thanked me. I took mine, sat and began the ritual. Again, Tattoo said a quiet grace, and again I joined in Amen. The day was beginning.

'I wonder what time my lawyer is coming?' I thought to myself, 'what the hell am I going to be able to tell him? Maybe we will get to see the photos first, and I'll get some ideas. Maybe I will just get released because they don't have enough to keep me in. I'd really rather not spend another night here.'

I turned to Tattoo and asked where he was from, just to make conversation and to get my mind off my problems.

"Northern Alberta," he answered in an unusually soft voice, "I grew up at Cold Lake.

My Dad was in the Air Force." He was almost apologetic.

"Why are you here?" I finally had screwed up the courage to ask.

"A guy died after I hit him," he replied easily, "I think they charged me with some kind of murder. I didn't mean for him to die, I just meant for him to stop wailin' on this other guy. He was nuts."

Tattoo had a 'gentle giant' demeanor about him. Although physically intimidating, he was kind.

"I've spent the last few years working on the rigs, made a few bucks and bought a small place out here, close to Oyama, out in the bush," he continued, "I commute. Things are going pretty well. I make a grand a day as a directional driller now, but who knows how long that will last? Make hay while the sun shines, eh?"

I had to agree. I folded my napkin and was ready to put the tray away, so I picked up his and offered to take Upper's, but he wasn't finished. I placed the trays down near the door and saw the constable coming. He walked to the door, pointed at me, and said, "Come with me, please."

I stood up, turned to Tattoo and said, "See you later. Good luck."

He answered, "Turner, Will Turner. In the book, if I can help you."

"Thanks," I said, without thinking to offer my own name, then I followed the constable down the corridor.

We walked past the washrooms and it dawned on me that I hadn't even had a piss since I got put in the cell.

"Do you mind if I get my face washed up and ease springs?" I asked.

"No problem." He opened the door for me and followed me in.

I finished my morning ablutions as best I could with someone watching and no toothbrush or comb. We headed back down the corridor, through the main door and into the area where I had been booked. As we turned the corner, I saw my lawyer standing with another fellow chatting to the older Mountie.

"Good Morning," my lawyer said, turning to look at me, "well maybe not so good for you, eh? Did you get some sleep?"

"Yes, I slept a bit," I didn't know why I was being curt with him, but I didn't feel like exchanging inane pleasantries with him in the outer hallway.

"I'd like to introduce you to a criminal lawyer from our firm," he stated matter-of-factly, "he will be looking after you from now on. This is all over my head."

The criminal lawyer shook my hand with the strength of a limp rag and, without even looking at me, turned to say goodbye to my lawyer as he headed out the door.

"Well, let's get at it."

He turned to the older Mountie and said, "Where can we meet for a few minutes?"

The older Mountie showed us to the same interrogation room I had been in the day before.

Once we were in, he instructed me, "Sit down."

He went to the other side of the table and pulled some papers from his briefcase. Still without looking at me directly, he said, "I assume my colleague – your friend – explained that we need an engagement letter signed and a retainer paid before we can do anything."

"No," I answered, wondering where the hell this was going. I liked this guy even less.

"Read this, then sign here," he ordered, and then continued, "I'll need a cheque for ten thousand dollars, as well. I suppose you can do that, right? Your friend says you're good for it."

"Is that for the bail?" I asked impudently, thinking that would make him lift his head. It didn't.

"No. We'll talk about that later," He shoved a pen over to the edge of the paper and returned to the contents of his briefcase, which was half hidden under the table.

I signed in the spot marked on page three on all three copies without really reading it. I didn't know any other lawyers and would have trusted my lawyer's advice anyway, even if I didn't like the guy he had chosen for me.

Once everything was signed, he finally looked at me.

"How are you going to deal with the ten thousand?" he asked.

"I'll have to write a cheque for some and get some from the bank when I get out of here," I replied. "Come to think of it, I have to get out of here to write a cheque. They're at home."

"Ok," my helpful new criminal lawyer said, once again reaching into his magic briefcase.

"Here is a promissory note you can sign in the meantime and we'll be able to get started." He filled in the numbers and the date, then slid it across the table with the pen.

"Let's start at the beginning and you can explain to me what happened."

He leaned back in his chair, looking at his knee, which served as a perch for his big pad of yellow paper.

"Just start with who Jim is, first," he added clumsily.

"Crap," I said to myself. Why start with the easy ones like that?

"Jim is a guy I met last summer..."

Before I could get any further, he jumped in, "What's his full name?"

"I don't know, I just know him as Jim," I answered honestly.

"What does Jim do for a living?

"I don't know," then added hopefully, "I think he's semi-retired."

"How long have you known him?" came the next easy one.

"Ahh, I met him sometime last summer," and then, "I have been up to his place a couple more times during the summer and the day before yesterday."

"And you still don't know his last name, or what he does, or what he did?" the jerky lawyer asked with a smarmy, sarcastic tone.

"No," I stated.

"This is going well." he commented while he thought of the next questions.

"Ok, then, why don't you tell me how he was murdered?" as if he already knew the answer and wanted my version.

"I don't know," again firmly.

"Why do you think you are here, then?" he asked incredulously, "By accident?"

"I don't know why I am here. All I know is that the Mounties showed up and told me to go with them. When we got here, they suggested I might want to call a lawyer, so I called my lawyer friend, the only lawyer I know. When he arrived, we went to Jim's house and the Mounties asked me a couple of questions. We came back here to the detachment and they put me in the cell overnight." I tried to be concise, "I slept, then had breakfast, then you showed up and here we are."

"Why do you think Jim was murdered?" again another unanswerable question. This guy was really going to find my alibi easy to swallow. If I even chose to tell him.

"No idea," I answered tersely.

"What did the Mounties tell you about his death?" he tried another approach.

"Nothing other than that he died between the time I was there and the time they received word from someone that he was dead, before eight yesterday morning."

"Have you not seen the photos?" he asked hopefully.

"No, I didn't feel up to looking at them yesterday," I said, feeling the compression building in my chest, "I guess I was maybe in shock. I don't know."

"Do you feel like looking at them now?" he asked, without much hope, "You might refresh your memory. I'll call in the Mounties and they will show us some of the photos. Just don't make any comments. Just answer questions if you know the facts and only answer what you are specifically asked," he lectured, "I'll interrupt if you get carried away."

"Wait," I almost pleaded, "when my lawyer left yesterday, he said we were going to have a bail hearing today or tomorrow, and that I would be out of here. What has happened to all that?"

"Well, it isn't quite that simple, you see," he replied, looking at his knee again, "you are in a strange situation right now. Apparently, they have your fingerprints on a glass that links you to the cause of death and you aren't being very cooperative in providing a credible alibi. I need you to explain things in a much more forthright way than you have so far. Maybe seeing a few pictures will help," he added doubtfully.

"OK," I answered despondently, "bring 'em on in."

The jerky lawyer got up and, just as he was headed out the door, looked over and said, "You wait here."

'What a prick!' I thought. I really did not like this guy. But...

The door opened and the older Mountie came in with the jerky lawyer and the young constable. He had a tape recorder, which he set in the middle of the table, and a folder, which he set on the table in front of himself. The young constable had a yellow pad just like the one my lawyer had slid in front of himself.

"This interrogation is taking place with your consent and in the presence of your lawyer. It is being recorded in order to retain an accurate record of what is said. Please speak clearly and to the microphone when you speak. The microphone doesn't record nods of the head or shrugs of the shoulder so please answer each question verbally. Do you understand what I have said?" he asked.

"Yes, I do"

"Do you consent to this interrogation given that you have not yet been charged with a crime?"

I looked at my lawyer, who seemed to be busy doodling on his yellow pad.

"Yes," I said again.

"I presume this is your lawyer. Could you please provide your name and address for the record?" said the young constable, practicing his school language.

"Please describe the man that yesterday you referred to as Jim," the older Mountie instructed.

"He was a tall man, about six foot three, lean, fit-looking, about 55 or so. Otherwise he was quite ordinary." I did my best.

The Mountie slid a black and white photo of a face across the table to me.

"Is this the man?" he asked politely, as if it were a photo of one of my own next of kin.

I looked at the picture for a while, puzzled by the peaceful look on Jim's face and I wondered how you could tell from the photo that he was dead. He looked as though he were having a wonderful sleep.

"Yes, that looks like him," I replied calmly. My jerky lawyer was scribbling furiously.

"Do you have any idea how he died?" asked the older Mountie.

"No, I don't. He looks like he just passed away. Like it was natural causes or something," I replied as honestly as I could.

He pulled out the next photo. It was another black and white. My jerky lawyer must have seen all of these before, since he didn't even bother to look. As I studied the photo, I saw a torso, covered by what was likely blood, with a clean gash from the lower pelvis up to the sternum, in a straight, unhesitant line. The edges were bowed outward and the hole had a shape that almost resembled a narrow football. The photo showed only the area from the bottom of his neck to his crotch. I felt woozy in the pit of my stomach but held it back. No one spoke, so I didn't either. I just stared.

I wanted to ask, "Were his liver and heart gone?" but I couldn't. I turned my eyes away and looked toward the door.

"What do you see?" the older Mountie asked, staring right at me.

I started breathing deeper and faster, my thoughts were racing ahead of what I could say, trying to figure out where the quicksand lay.

"I see a torso that looks like it has been sliced open," I answered finally.

"Is that all?" asked the older Mountie, as if I was holding back on some important clue.

"That's all," I said looking back at the door.

The next photo was of the whole room. "Do you recognize anything here?" asked the older Mountie.

There was much more in the photo. I could see Jim lying in bed. Two bedside tables, a chest of drawers, a woven rug from somewhere, maybe Afghanistan, and in the corner by the chest of drawers... I held the photo closer. Was that the skull of the hyæna? I turned away and paused. "I have never been in that room before," I said.

"What was it you saw in that photo that caught your eye?" he asked quietly.

"Nothing," I answered abruptly.

"Answer the questions honestly, please," my lawyer admonished. He must have noticed my pause when I saw the skull.

"I just noticed that skull by the chest of drawers. It looked out of place," I suggested.

"Where should it be?" asked the Mountie.

"I don't know for sure, but not in front of a dresser, I wouldn't think," I replied, feeling that I had provided a good explanation.

"I am going to show you one more photo today. Please tell me if there is anything that comes to your mind after you have seen it," the older Mountie asked politely.

He then selected another photo from his file and slid it across the table. It was like the photo of Jim's face but taken with a broader view. It appeared as if he had gone to sleep with his hands behind his head and feeling very relaxed. There were no bracelets. He had been wearing them during our visit. I didn't remember seeing them on the bedside table when I looked at the photo of the room. Should I tell them that? Will that bring up the whole witch story? 'Ohhh, crap!' I thought.

"Could I have another look at the room photo, please?" I asked.

He retrieved it and slid it across the table. No bracelets.

"He was wearing two copper bracelets on his left wrist when I saw him," I answered conclusively.

"Are you certain?" asked the older Mountie.

"I am positive," I replied.

The older Mountie looked at my jerky lawyer, and then reached into the file and brought out a thick plastic freezer bag. He held it in front of me so I could see the contents.

"Would they be like these?" he asked.

"Yes, that looks like them; at least very similar, if not them. Where did you find them?" I enquired, "They weren't in the photos".

"The older Mountie ignored my question, instead turning to my lawyer and asking, "Do you have any questions for now?"

"Nope, thank you, Sergeant," he answered, "I'll just spend a few minutes with my client, if you don't mind."

"Not a problem. You know the drill when you are done."

The Mounties departed the room and suddenly the atmosphere felt very, very heavy.

My jerky lawyer was still scribbling notes on his yellow pad. I sat nervously, wondering what the hell had happened. God, I wanted out of there!

HONG KONG - 13 APRIL 2014

Three Americans carrying their suit bags and briefcases, rushed toward meeting area "B" at the Hong Kong Airport Arrivals area in order to avoid missing their pick-up car. For some unknown reason, they had been held up for more than half an hour in Immigration and Customs. They hadn't been able to use their cell phones to call the hotel to advise them of the delay. The three Americans, all dressed almost identically in charcoal suits, white shirts, black leather Italian shoes, and likely matching belts, were now walking at full tilt toward the exit.

'All in a rush! They should know that being in a rush in Hong Kong just wastes energy and time,' thought the older man observing them. He removed photos from his front pocket, glanced at them and slipped them back. He dialed his cellphone. Very few words of spoken Mandarin and he disconnected, returning the phone to his jacket pocket. He wore a tan-coloured pea jacket and a pair of very roomy grey slacks and scruffy brown shoes. His almost totally grey hair was cut in a cross between a military cut and a prison cut, short hair on the sides sticking out like quills on a porcupine. His eyes appeared barely open and his walk looked like a shuffle to any observer willing to study it.

The Americans had arrived on a Cathay Pacific non-stop flight from New York City. Even in the First-Class compartment, sixteen hours was a long time. They had been served a nice breakfast after their frustrated attempts at sleeping. Their brains were now upside down. They had departed New York on flight 841 at 21:03 the night before last and it was now nearly 15:00 in Hong Kong. The tall, young American just wanted to get checked in and have a decent sleep. He had been awake or partially awake for two and a half days already, writing his brief for tomorrow's meeting. Of the other two Americans, one was chubby and somewhat out of shape. He was taking almost two steps for each step of the quiet one. His shirt was soaked with sweat and his forehead was covered with sweat, and he puffed as he pushed the cart holding his suit bag and briefcase. The quiet man strode through the airport as if he had just risen from a good night's sleep, showered, dressed and was now walking the eight blocks to his office. They all reached the curb at about the same time. The quiet one recognized the Brewster Green Rolls-Royce Silver Shadow from the Peninsula Hotel. As he walked toward it, the driver walked around the car and greeted him as he opened the boot and started setting in the limited luggage.

"Here only few days, sir, yes?" he spoke to the quiet man. "Good you come back," he smiled broadly, then rushed over to open the rear door for the chubby man. The tall young man had found his own way into the far side rear seat. The driver closed the door for the quiet one, rounded the front and quickly climbed in, looked over his shoulder and sped away.

The older man in the pea jacket watched surreptitiously, once again pulled out his cell, pressed a button and chatted briefly in Mandarin before hanging up. His day was over. He would now catch the bus to Nathan Street, walk up six flights of stairs, knock on a door and enter a room where he would find sexual pleasure for the next several hours. He had earned it!

The car arrived at the entrance to the Peninsula Hotel, where the American disembarked. A concierge met them at the door and handed them the keys to their rooms. The tall, young one had a room on the twentieth floor. The two older men would share the Marco Polo Suite on the twenty-sixth floor.

The quiet one said, "I've made a booking at Gaddi's for 8:00 this evening. We can review and refresh our presentation. See you there. By the way - ties, guys," he added, as the young man stepped from the elevator when the doors opened to his floor.

As the young American prepared for his nap, downtown, at the Captain's Bar in the Mandarin Oriental Hotel, a chic, well-groomed, Oriental-looking man of about thirty-five years was holding court. He sat at the end of a long table encompassed by a booth of red leather banquette. What he wanted required only a nod or a look. A couple of taps on the table with his finger would bring to his side a sparkly young man to whom Chic would whisper instructions, after which, Sparkly would run his errand. While his entourage was celebrating, challenging one another on their knowledge of scotch whiskey, Chic was reading an article on the third page of the *South China Morning Post*.

"HONG KONG —TWO MEN FROM ZIMBABWE ARRESTED, — Two men were arrested yesterday at Hong Kong International Airport carrying 40 kilograms of ivory in their luggage. The value of the seizure was estimated at HK$400,000..."

'Another $30 thou' gone. Lucky thing they only catch about one in twenty. Have to hand them one once in a while. Why the hell were two of them travelling together? They know they are never to travel on the same flight or on the same day and never on non-stop flights. The best routes are through Dubai or Johannesburg. 'Oh well, bigger fish to fry,' the chic man thought to himself, 'Maybe tomorrow will bring something worthwhile.'

Chic was born in Hong Kong and moved to Vancouver at the age of five to live with his aunt and uncle while he attended school. He did extremely well and graduated with honours and a clean record. The clean record did not imply innocence, but it did suggest a certain level of sophistication in his illegal activities. He tried to stay away from marginal activities, as he chose to call them, but the miniscule salary his father allowed him just didn't do it. He was careful and maintained distance from the activities. The thirty grand a month that selling ivory brought in allowed for a few mistakes and made life in Shanghai quite pleasant. It was more pleasant in Hong Kong.

Chic completed his business undergrad degree at the University of British Columbia. He performed very well and transferred to Harvard for his MBA. Many offers had come from the major banking houses, but he had promised to return to work with his family. That was ten years ago. He was equally comfortable in either world. He was fluent in Cantonese,

Mandarin, English, Spanish and Russian. He understood accounting and finance, and he knew where to find the best lawyers. His father was old school. He did have many friends in mainland China. He had gained his wealth by helping them to achieve their dreams and by helping them to move their money quietly and with integrity.

In 2003, some family friends in mainland China had requested the assistance of Chic's father in taking an independent review of investment opportunities in Africa. Although Chic was fresh out of Harvard, he knew that both Zambia and Zimbabwe were hungry for foreign investment. He knew that the leaders of China had not only hinted but had strongly suggested that they wanted to see Chinese investment in agriculture and resource extraction throughout Africa. He had suggested to his father that he might give consideration to starting in one of those countries and suggested as well that Zimbabwe might be first.

Tomorrow, Chic was to meet with a partner of Sullivan, Wachtel and Pope from New York. The firm had exceptional connections, and experience with foreign affairs issues, which was the nature of advice his father's clients needed now. The firm had an excellent reputation for discretion. A friend's firm, which Chic had helped to establish in the diamond business in Zimbabwe, had a few problems. A large amount of its money had been frozen, thanks to US interference, and there were indications that their partner in Zimbabwe would plead an inability to be of assistance, as the Indigenization rules were leading to nationalization. Normally the family would turn to the Zhang Lee Law firm in Hong Kong, but in this particular case there were various sensitivities that required sensitive maneuvers.

TATTOO - OKANAGAN - 21 APRIL 2014

Tattoo had finished his stay in the cell. By Monday morning, the Crown Prosecutor and his lawyer had met and agreed that Tattoo had no intent at any point in the conflict to kill the other guy. No charges were going to be laid.

Tattoo drove north toward his home, looking forward to a good sleep. A neighbour had been feeding his dog and checking on the house while he was away. He stopped at Sobeys to pick up a few groceries before heading on. As he drove down the driveway, he looked over his property, relieved to be home. The driveway from the gravel road down to the house was steep. The house was sturdy, made of pine logs finished in their natural colour. The landscaping looked professionally maintained. A walkway snaked from the driveway to the front entrance. From there it continued down toward a garden area.

As Tattoo drove down toward the house, the neighbour let the dog out to greet him. The dog ran across the yard and stopped, tail wagging happily as he saw Tattoo's pickup come to a stop. As Tattoo opened the door, the dog's nose poked up into the cab. His whole body was wagging in rhythm with his tail.

"Hey, Buddy, good to see you," Tattoo said, as he ruffled the head of his Alsatian. Tattoo preferred to refer to Zeus as an Alsatian even though it was simply an alternate name for the German shepherd breed that was chosen by the rightfully sensitive British during World War Two. To him, it sounded more sophisticated and more disciplined. He and Zeus had been close friends for seven years, ever since he had brought him home as a pup. Whenever Tattoo had gone up to work the rigs, Zeus had gone to training school.

His neighbour stood on the deck watching the reunion. She was about thirty, a tall and attractive brunette. Tattoo had no interest in the idea of marriage at this point in his life. It was not because he had any problem with women, or that he had any problem with commitment. It was simply that he had always made other commitments that inevitably were in conflict with an exclusive relationship with a woman. His neighbour was, however, one of his closest friends. Tattoo had asked the Mounties to call her to take care of the dog. Tattoo's pickup had been left at the shopping centre where he had tried to help a young man being beaten by three other men on the prior Saturday evening. The Mounties had never considered him to be a high risk and were very surprised to get a 911 call from him about the same time another 911 call on the same matter reached the office. He was known to a few of the members from previous times and they had maintained mutual respect.

When Tattoo got into the house, his neighbour offered to make lunch for him. He walked to the fridge and grabbed a cold beer, and then turned to ask her if she wanted to join him. She smiled and nodded.

"Well?" she said, leaving the question open.

"Well, what?" he replied.

"What the hell happened?" she pressed.

"I was in town on Saturday night, about to head home, and saw three guys kicking the shit out of another guy," he began. "I drove over, got out and walked over, asking them to quit," he continued, "one guy turned and told me to f... off, and the other two didn't listen, so I yelled again. The mouth came at me, so I put him down and grabbed the next guy by the arm and it accidentally broke. The third guy was about to take a kick at me but slipped and fell flat on his back," he explained, "I checked them out and called 911 cause the first guy had stopped breathing. I called one of the Mounties I know and told him what had happened."

He drew a long swig from his beer and looked over at her.

"And now, after a visit at the Crown hotel, I am here."

He smiled his innocent puppy-like smile, and winked, "All is Ok. I guess the guys had outstanding warrants and were causing a bit of trouble to the guys downtown. I'm sorry he died, but what could I do?"

After lunch his neighbour looked at Tattoo, "I think you need a good nap, man. I am heading out. Give me a call sometime and we'll go for a beer."

Tattoo smiled, "Thanks so much for looking after Zeus and my place, eh? We'll have more than a beer; I'll fatten you up and then we'll dance it off!"

She smiled wistfully, 'God I wish he were a little more available,' she thought to herself as she looked over her shoulder. She walked out the door and climbed into her red Honda Civic.

He walked back into the house and watched through the glass in the door as she drove away.

'In another world or another time,' he thought.

He walked into the kitchen, washed and dried the few dishes, then put them away in the cupboard. He went out to the back entrance and picked up Zeus's blue rubber bowl, and brought it back to the closet, where he filled it with Zeus's favourite food, 'Orijen Adult'. He filled the water bowl and left Zeus to his meal. He wandered further back into his house. In the master bedroom, he changed into some sweats and put his other gear in a laundry basket sitting just inside the closet. He opened the sliding door and stepped out onto the balcony.

He could see the lake through the pine trees that surrounded the house. Here he rolled out a small mat and sat down. He started breathing slowly. In - two - three - four, hold - two - three - four, exhale - two - three - four. His eyes slowly closed. His body began to relax. His mind began to clear. In - two - three - four, hold - two - three - four, exhale - two - three - four. The world began to disappear. The aches and pains of the years mellowed to insignificance. When a half hour had passed, Tattoo stood up and walked to the shower. He turned the taps and waited until the water was hot. He climbed in and let the sweat of the last four days flush down the drain. He scrubbed his hair and shaved with his old Gillette razor. He finished up with a bit of conditioner, rinsed, and then climbed out, dried himself and made his way to the bedroom. He flopped back on the bed and laid looking at the ceiling. Tomorrow he would be back to his regimen. He fell into a deep sleep.

It was 16:30 when he awoke, feeling fully refreshed.

Simplicity, Security, Repetition, Surprise, Speed, and Purpose—his daily affirmation once again passed through his mind.

MEETING LAWYERS FROM N.Y. IN HONG KONG - 14 APRIL 2014

Chic had finished his evening with his acquaintances and Sparkly a little before one in the morning. From the bar he had gone straight to his room, showered, meditated, and then tried to sleep. He knew that tomorrow would be a heavy day. He knew his father had left him to work out this problem in his own way. He had done some homework, but he also knew that his future rested to some extent upon the skills of others, a situation in which he did not like to find himself.

He asked himself once again, 'How did I get into this situation?' and 'Could I have avoided it?'

So far, he was not happy with the answers he found. This project had begun more than ten years ago when his father had asked Chic to consider going to some African countries to investigate the potential for investment by some of his acquaintances. Zambia and Zimbabwe were high on the list of potentials.

CHIC'S FIRST TRIP TO HARARE
- 11-12 NOVEMBER 2003

ordon Zhong made his first visit to Harare in November 2003, shortly after Robert Mugabe announced his desire for a new relationship with the East. He remembered how much energy it took for him to overcome his nervousness to project himself as being ready for 'the big deal' his father was suggesting. He carried inside himself concerns based not only upon his own ego, but more importantly, upon the risk of losing *diū liǎn* before his father and his father's friends. That loss of face would be a very inauspicious beginning to his career. He had boarded the flight in Shanghai, flown to Hong Kong, and from Hong Kong to Harare. There he had checked into a modest suite in the Meikles Hotel. He had the afternoon and night to enjoy a good meal and a luxuriously long sleep.

The following morning, he enjoyed a fifteen thousand Zimbabwe dollar, English-style breakfast at the Pavilion Bistro in the hotel. He had his small office in Shanghai set up a number of meetings, but he was also mature enough to know that only a small number would work out as expected, with the people expected or at the time expected. Well-rested, well-dressed and well-prepared with his questions he headed out to meet the day.

He started his day at the Government's Office of the Economy where he hoped to gain an understanding of the policies of the current government toward dealing with what was by then almost one hundred percent annual rate of inflation. The meeting was set for nine. He approached the receptionist, a short, cheerful and slightly plump civil servant with a big smile.

"I am here to meet the Minister," he spoke with confidence, "My name is Gordon Zhong. I made arrangements last week."

"Yes, of course, please take a seat," smiling again.

No other action, no other response. So, he sat and waited as the crowd grew. Soon all chairs in the room were filled and he felt obliged to stand to make way for an aged gentleman looking for a seat. It wasn't that he had been forgotten, no one else was being called either.

At a little past ten he walked up and quietly said to the smiling girl, "Do you have any idea when I will get in to see the Minister? I have a few other appointments today."

She looked up at him again and said, "Well, the Minister isn't here yet and everyone will take his turn."

Chic wasn't sure whether to take his leave in order to be on time for the next meeting with a lower level functionary or to wait for the Minister. As it approached eleven, his time to choose was limited.

"Do you have any idea when he will be in the office?" Chic quietly asked the smiling face.

"No," she replied, as if she had just answered the question a few minutes ago.

"May I reschedule for tomorrow morning?" he asked hopefully, "I do have to attend to my other meetings."

"Would the same time work for you?" she asked pleasantly.

"Yes, it would, if he plans to be here." Instantly he wished that he had left off the last part of the comment.

She looked at him with a slightly severe look, then laughed, "One never knows," then added, "It is worth a try if you do want to meet him."

Chic confirmed the time, turned and left the office.

The next stop was a functionary in the Mining Ministry. His title was descriptive: 'Chief of Administration of Recording for the District of Marange'. The building was at the corner of Leopold Takawira and Kwame Nkrumah Roads, less than a kilometre away, so he chose to walk. He entered the elevator and pressed the button for floor seven. The doors opened to a spacious reception area, much less crowded than the last one.

As he approached the receptionist she looked up and smiled, "You must be Mr. Zhong. Mr. Mbotozungi is expecting you. Please come this way."

"Thank you," was all he could think to express.

"Right through this door, please," she said, as she opened one door of a double mahogany entrance. Looking in past him, she said to a gentleman sitting at a large desk, "Here is Mr. Zhong," and then she departed, leaving a brief smile.

Mr. Mbotozungi stood up and gracefully carried his large frame around the desk with his hand extended. He said, "Thank you for being prompt, Mr. Zhong. We in Zimbabwe appreciate promptness, a carryover from the British, you see," as he shook Chic's hand while indicating a seat by a small table. "Would you have a cup of tea, or coffee?" he asked politely.

"I would appreciate a cup of tea, please," replied Chic.

The tall smiling girl from the reception desk appeared, as if on cue, with a teapot of super boiled water, two cups with saucers, teaspoons, cream and sugar on a silver tray. She turned and departed without comment.

"Shall we get down to business, Mr. Zhong?" asked the functionary, as he poured the first cup of tea and handed it over to Chic. Not waiting for a response, he continued, "You represent a firm which wishes to invest in Zimbabwe, is that correct? You have come to the right place."

Chic was a bit surprised at the power his host projected. With some surprise, Chic realized that Mr. Mbotozungi was definitely no lower level functionary.

"Yes, I am here on a research mission to determine the potential for some investors whom I represent."

"Or perhaps friends of your father, eh?" Chic heard, "well never mind, all the same. How can I help you?" the administrator inquired.

'He is obviously a step ahead of me' thought Chic. Chic did not like being on the lacking side of the knowledge balance. He paused before answering. The interviewee was now leading the interview.

"I would like to obtain information about your government policies and how legislation affects investment in minerals: gold, platinum and diamonds. I would also like to understand the nature of the protection of such investments from changes in government policies or government."

He hoped this line of inquiry might help him to gain authority in this meeting.

"That will be easy," the big man replied, laughing loudly.

"Young man," he began, "Life is very simple: you place your bets, you take your chances. Our leader has publicly stated that he wants better relationships with the East. Our legislation allows foreign ownership, subject to the requirement that some investment be made by local Zimbabwean investors. You should select your partners well, but that decision is up to you."

"You will take with you when you leave, a copy of the legislation, the 'Indigenization and Empowerment Act', but perhaps I should tell you that, because of our leader's generous encouragement and China's special place as a friend of Zimbabwe, we might grant exemptions to that legislation for large government enterprises. You might still find it comforting to avail yourself of some local investment and a number of local corporate directors. Copies of other legislation, such as the mining regulations, are available on the ground floor. I wish your group all the success in your investments. Have a good journey."

He then stood up and led Chic to the door, loudly instructing the girl at the desk to provide Chic with the necessary literature.

"Thank you very much," Chic responded as they shook hands.

He turned to pick up the package the tall smiling girl was presenting him.

"Where does one go for an evening in Harare?" he asked the receptionist.

"You are staying at the Meikles, correct?" she said, almost mischievously, "The Explorer's Club on the main floor. Six-thirty. Ta-Ta."

He had left feeling a little puzzled. As he entered the elevator, he contemplated the meeting. Definitely someone had been gathering information about him. That office seemed to be the repository. Chic returned to the hotel well after lunchtime. He needed some time to digest what he had seen and heard. He had planned his afternoon as a series of data gathering visits. He doubted that they would be as interesting as the last visit.

That evening, after refreshing himself, Chic wandered down to the Explorer's Club. He was a bit early for something, though he knew not what. He was neatly dressed without a tie, wearing black loafers, flannel slacks, a white Egyptian long strand cotton shirt and a blue linen blazer he had picked up at Brooks Brothers last time he was in New York. He found a table in the crowded room.

"Gin and tonic on ice, tall," he requested when the waiter approached. He glanced at the Patek Philippe Calatrava his father had given him on his twenty-first birthday. Five-fifty. He liked the watch, he thought to himself as he sat watching the second hand tick its way around the classic face. There are great opportunities here he felt, but great dangers as well. Two poles of a magnet, each pulling but not aligned. His aimless focus was disturbed by the appearance of the waiter, who set his drink on the table before him. "Would there be anything else at the moment, sir?"

HONG KONG – 15 APRIL 2014

The alarm radio sitting on the side table presented a chorus of classic Mandarin Opera, the volume much louder than he remembered when he set it much earlier that morning. It was five-thirty, but it felt much earlier. He climbed out of bed and headed for the shower with only four hours of sleep behind him. He was to meet the crew at eight for breakfast. Chic dressed to meet bankers even though he was meeting lawyers. White silk shirt with gold cufflinks, sky-blue silk tie from Emma Willis, a midnight-blue light wool suit set off by a pair of well-shined, double-stitched, black, capped oxfords from John Lobb on St. James Street.

Chic strode to the elevator and descended to the lobby where he was to meet his team at the Café Causette. Sparkly was already there looking as eager as a hunting dog on a Saturday morning. Chic wasn't sure why he had selected Sparkly to be his assistant. He was such a sycophant, but he was also exceptionally resourceful. Two others, one an associate from Hong Kong and one from Harare, joined them. They would serve as resources but would not attend the meeting with the lawyers. They ordered breakfast. Chic limited himself to tea. Sparkly indulged in a bowl of Nasi Goreng. The other two ordered organic salmon, hoping for some special experience.

Richard, from Harare, began the discussion with a description of the problems developing in Zimbabwe. He explained how the new Barons, as he referred to the nouveau riche, were attempting, quite successfully, to line their pockets at the expense of the state, but also at the expense and risk of the foreign investors. Richard had been a partner with a large accounting firm in London before returning to his homeland in Zimbabwe, where he and his father and his grandfather before him had been born. His great-grandfather had moved from Cape Colony into the hinterlands of Rhodesia in 1893 to grow food for the influx of mineral explorers and mining promoters who had followed Cecil Rhodes. His family had arrived soon after the Ndebele and he was proud to be Zimbabwean. His father, Michael, had stayed in Harare through the worst of the troubles and had participated in setting up the stock exchange as well as providing assistance to the schooling system.

At the present time, Robert Mugabe's stability as leader was relevant to both sides. Mr. Mugabe was aging but still functional. His wife was a bit of a wild card. The Baron class that he had created needed him as a legitimizing agent for their pressures to create more aggressive expropriation legislation. Not expropriation for the benefit of the state, but as a lever for them to acquire low-cost or no-cost entry into the controlling positions of the many enterprises in Zimbabwe. To these men land was still a sign of wealth, and so the accumulation of farmland under the guise of redistribution was useful so that they could recreate the feudal estates of their ancestors.

On the other side were the descendants of the original agitators who had sought more balanced rights for all citizens of Zimbabwe. This tight-knit group consisted almost equally of black and white. The number of whites was gradually decreasing as their children were moving away for education and, in fact, for safety and for a better life in England, Australia and Canada. Some were returning now, more mature and more comfortable in their capacity to help grow a better Zimbabwe. This group was more secretive than the Barons. Safety was still a priority, not safety from Mr. Mugabe, but from the aggressive leaders of the Barons and their columns of unemployable, janga-boosted followers.

In the beginning, the Committee For The Preservation Of Zimbabwe had heralded as a giant step forward the efforts made by the group represented by Chic's father. They appreciated the arrival of new capital and expertise in the mining sector. They recognized as a critical first step the importance of the capital that was being made available for the reconstruction of infrastructure. What was happening now, however, was pushing them in a difficult direction. It appeared that foreign governments, fearing success by Chinese investors, were funding agitation and providing support to the Barons in order to destroy public support for the 'Look East' policies. The Chinese investors were now being seen as colonizing Vikings, raping and pillaging, rather than as potential saviours of Zimbabwe, as had earlier been the case.

The United States, through the United Nations, had been able discreetly to force a policy allowing the seizure of funds arising from 'illegal extraction activities', equating all other foreign investors' product with 'blood' diamonds. New newspapers were appearing to tout the message to all Zimbabweans. Social media sites were filled with partially accurate news. The nature of the propaganda war shifted slowly from white to black.

George Wong, Chic's Hong Kong associate, was a wise and gentle man. He spoke softly, and most diplomatically, about the sense of the Chinese community in both Zimbabwe and Shanghai. He was, as most elderly Chinese were, ageless. He wore clothing of style and quality so subtle that he disappeared in a small group. He had shared life with Chic's father, from the days of Chairman Mao. To Mr. Wong, discretion was not only a courtesy, but also an essential for survival. Some of the investors were worried that activities were being conducted in secret by a member of Mr. Zhong's family. They were concerned that the selected directors in the mining concerns had either not been vetted adequately in advance or had not been managed adequately since then. They could see that behind the pressures being brought to bear on the companies by those directors was a desire to accelerate the growth of their personal wealth at the expense of the enterprises. Some were quietly joining with the Barons to push for political change that would allow them more power and more potential to present threats, always, however, in the third person.

Mr. Wong only disclosed as much as necessary to convey his message, but Chic could tell from his statements this morning and in previous meetings that he only presented the tip of his knowledge iceberg. The message appeared simple enough: solve the freezing of funds problem, disassociate himself from his ivory sideline, and neutralize the activities of his wayward directors where they were not in the interests of the enterprises.

With this knowledge and the aide-memoire prepared by Sparkly, he was prepared for the meeting with the cash vacuum of New York attorneys.

Only he and Sparkly would attend the meeting. The others agreed to meet at the hotel for a debriefing after the meeting.

Before Chic left, Mr. Wong quietly said to him, "Someone is watching you very closely. Be careful! I will try to find out who it is."

MEET THE LAWYERS - 15 APRIL 2014

A green Silver Shadow Rolls-Royce waited at the Connaught Street entrance of the Mandarin Oriental Hotel to pick up Mr. Zhong and Sparkly for their meeting across the harbour at the Peninsula Hotel. Chic thought it rather odd that the lawyers would send a car from their hotel over to the competition to pick them up. He supposed it was simply a New York attempt to impress him or to prepare him for the magnitude of the ultimate billing. The Driver opened the rear door for them to enter, making his presence very obvious to the doormen of the Mandarin. He pulled out into traffic, heading for the connector to the north side, which would place them at the entrance of the Peninsula Hotel on Salisbury Road. The Peninsula sat overlooking Victoria Harbor, Kowloon, Hong Kong. It was an old but still regal hotel, only four miles from the infamous Happy Valley Racecourse.

The Rolls progressed magnificently through the perpetual traffic jam. Chic paid no attention to anything but the warning from Mr. Wong. 'Who would be following me and why?'

As they pulled up to the entrance of the Peninsula, two doormen in dark livery and white gloves opened the rear doors of the Rolls. Chic and Sparkly slid out onto the stone esplanade and nodded in unison, and then headed up the stairs to greet the three Americans, with their store-bought smiles, who were waiting just inside the entrance. Chic introduced Sparkly only as, "this is my assistant," as he shook hands with the men, beginning with the taller of the two older men, guessing him to be the senior partner. He shook hands with the younger nervous fellow last, only adding to the poor man's lack of confidence. The chubby, out-of-shape man in the middle mumbled his greeting, obviously less than comfortable with the social aspects of foreign clients, especially those he expected to dislike. Sparkly followed behind, repeating the greeting process but adding a solicitous bow to each greeting. 'The perpetual suck,' thought Chic with amusement.

Alexander Pope, the taller of the two older men, was well-dressed in a sharp, modest suit, and he had the bearing of a man with a military background. He maintained his fit physique by playing squash several times a week and he kept his short, greying hair well-trimmed. Upon first meeting Pope, one was impressed immediately by his obvious intelligence and by the natural leadership quality that he exuded, rendering those around him willing to acquiesce. By the age of thirty-five he had made Junior Partner at Sullivan, Wachtel; by forty-two his name was on the firm's letterhead as a full partner. In1992, his name was added to the name of the firm: Sullivan, Wachtel and Pope. He suggested to Chic that they head up to the room and get started. They walked to the elevator reserved for the twenty-third floor, the former Presidential Suite, now called the Marco Polo Suite. Alexander Pope stood aside until all the others had entered and then instructed the elevator attendant to proceed. They soon arrived at the suite. The butler opened the doors, and with a sweep of his hand invited the guests to enter.

The view from the living- room was a grand panorama across Victoria Harbour to downtown Hong Kong. The brass telescope in the corner reminded everyone of the days of the Tai Pan, Compradors and clipper ships. The group was shepherded into the dining room, which would serve as the meeting room for the day. Alexander Pope assigned the seating and then seated himself at the head of the table.

His opening statement was short. He identified the founder of the firm as George Sullivan, a member of the OSS during World War Two, who founded the firm of Sullivan, Wachtel in 1947. Rather than continue with a conversion to the Central Intelligence Agency, he decided to establish a firm to provide services for companies involved in international trade and finance. Mr. Sullivan, at ninety years old, still came to the office. Mr. Pope joined the firm in 1982 and was a senior partner. The firm was still a boutique firm by New York standards and boasted ninety partners and two hundred associates. They now maintained an office in Washington supporting forty of the attorneys. Mr. Pope continued, stating that the firm prided itself on the high degree of personalized service they provided to their clients. He then offered the floor to Mr. Zhong.

Chic thanked Mr. Pope for attending from such a long distance on such short notice. He provided a quick summary of the issues they were facing and had Sparkly present copies of his report to the three money-gobbling 'pac-men'.

12 March 2014

I represent a group of investors which has made significant investments in Zimbabwe over the past ten years. Since the beginning there has been an increasing enthusiasm for action by NGOs, the UN, and the US Government to influence the outcome of those investments. We find ourselves now being unable to liberate funds that rightfully belong to our investors and the Zimbabwe Government, because they have been frozen in accounts due to accusations of improper activities. We need advice, but more importantly, political pressures brought to bear to obtain release of the funds and an end to the interference by the US government.

To summarize some of the activities by the investors I represent:

- In response to increased economic isolation by Western powers, Mugabe announced his 'Look East' policy in 2003. This policy swung Zimbabwe economically toward the Asia-Pacific region, with a resulting emphasis on closer trade relations with China.

- China's efforts to regenerate the Zimbabwean mining sector have followed a similar course. China's mining interests in Zimbabwe cover a broad range, beginning with US$ 300 million of investments in iron, chrome and platinum in 2003. This was followed by increasing investments in the commercialization of the diamond industry. The magnitude of these investments encouraged Robert Mugabe to make certain economic concessions to China.

- Some of our investors have invested in the small-scale businesses of providing "zhing-zhong" to street vendors in cities like Harare and Bulawayo. You know, telephone chargers, earbuds and so on, low cost- high demand. These investments are generally import-export activities and have been encompassed easily within Chapter 14:33 of the Indigenization and Empowerment Act.

- Since investing, we have been under increasing pressure from the Zimbabwe partners for accelerated distributions of dividends, and the payment of bonuses and gifts to keep the regulators out of our businesses. Our investments were being eclipsed by some very heavy investments by the Government of China, through regional industries.

- In 2009 China paid the Zimbabwe government about US$3 billion for exclusive access to Zimbabwe's platinum rights. The press being fed by opposition to China's activities indicated that the contract was worth US $40 billion, and that Zimbabweans were being ripped off. Another Chinese group agreed to a design/ build agreement for a new $US 100 million military college in Harare. Again, the press said that it was a rip-off of the diamond wealth from the Marange Diamond mines, when the trade of diamonds was the only means of payment.

- Many good things have been happening in Zimbabwe but many bad things as well. By 2010, trade volume increased to US$560 million in agriculture, tourism, and mining. China has also given development aid to Zimbabwe, in exchange for other products.

- There are really two groups at work in Zimbabwe. First, there are those who wish only to accumulate wealth for themselves as rapidly as possible and to hell with Zimbabwe. There is another group that is most interested in seeing Zimbabwe regain its relative position as the breadbasket of Africa, and as a stable, wealthy nation where blacks and whites can continue to live together in harmony. This group is comprised of a number of well-educated and well-meaning blacks, as well as some of the strong-hearted whites who have managed to survive and remain here through the difficulties.

"Mr. Zhong, I understand your frustration, but I fail to see what you expect us to do," stated the bored-sounding, short, fat lawyer, "perhaps you can try to reframe the issues for us."

Chic looked at the man, thinking, 'Is this what I get for a grand an hour?'

"Listen," he started again, "we are trying to conduct business in a straight-up manner, but because your government has a nit up its ass, our money is being frozen at the diamond auctions in Antwerp. The press is insinuating that we are pilfering those monies, and that crap is making it necessary for us to pay more and more 'regulators' just to stay in business. Totally contrary to your country's purported objectives! Is that easier for you to understand?"

Alexander Pope felt it was an appropriate time for a break - a decompression. He suggested reconvening at 14:00. Chic thought he would use the time to relax. He used the phone to call for a reservation for a massage, then suggested that Sparkly take the opportunity to enjoy High Tea at the Lobby Lounge Café while they were at the Peninsula Hotel. Chic knew that it was one of the most popular teatime spots in Hong Kong, well-known around the world. Besides the good quality classic-style scones and chocolate, the ambience was beyond the best in the world. The traditional British colonial legacy and live band performances transported guests on a journey back to the 'sixties. However, the scones didn't quite measure up to the uniquely delicious ones in the Clipper Lounge at the Mandarin Oriental.

Chic and Sparkly took their leave and headed down in the elevator. They agreed to meet back in the lobby at one-fifty to reconvene with Pope and his associates.

Naked under a warm sheet, Chic reflected while he rested. The masseuse began with his shoulders and neck. Chic's thoughts wandered back to his birthplace in Shanghai, Peoples' Republic of China in 1978. His father had been a senior member of the Communist Party apparatus. He was well-known among the now senior Party Members and was recognized as discreet, honest and honourable, not to mention exquisitely intelligent and worldly. Chic's father was nearing fifty when Chic was born. Being concerned about the well-being of their only son, Chic's parents worked to have him placed with his mother's brother and his family in Vancouver for his education. The Chen Family in Vancouver was honoured to assist, and once all the appropriate papers were completed, Chic was allowed to emigrate to Canada.

Chic attended private school from the time he arrived in Canada. During high school he attended Brentwood College School on Vancouver Island, where he achieved excellence in his grades. He won many scholarships and chose to attend UBC Sauder School of Business. His polite and charming personality, along with his brilliance and focused efforts, won him kudos from his professors and fellow students alike. He graduated with his BBA and proceeded directly into the MBA Programme. He completed his university education and convocated in 2003.

Chic also had an aptitude for languages. He had learned basic Cantonese and Mandarin while growing up in China. He perfected Cantonese while living with his uncle in Vancouver. He improved his Mandarin while an undergraduate at UBC. As a challenge, he studied both German and Russian as part of his MBA, expanding his time commitments by six months.

Chic then travelled to Shanghai to visit his family for an extended stay. His father was seventy-five years old and, over the years, had quietly built a business that served many members of the party, many retired and some still employed in senior positions. His father took the time to introduce his son to the available business opportunities, after having discreetly introduced him to many of his own clients prior to informing his son of their business relationships. His father encouraged him to remain in Shanghai to learn the business and gradually to take over. Honour-bound but also intrigued, Chic agreed. Though the salary was modest by what he could have earned from any of the investment banks that had approached him at UBC, it was sufficient to enable him to live a reasonable life in Shanghai. He was given an expense account for entertaining, and a large new condominium on Xin Zha Road in the Grand Summit Project to call home.

While in Shanghai, Chic learned of the interest by a few of his father's clients, in procuring a more direct line to African ivory. It was a business that his father chose not to pursue.

"Son," he explained, "very few people understand money well, but a great deal of money and effort around the world are expended to embarrass people in the ivory trade. People who are caught or implicated no longer have friends."

Chic remembered his father's words as he explained to Chic about the 'secret' ivory business. At the time, Chic had been meeting with his father and brother to discuss the problems of the Zimbabwe investments. His father had brought up the illegal importing business Chic thought he had been keeping secret. His father had informed Chic that there was a group in Zimbabwe which was unhappy with him for scooping some of the ivory business away from them. Some of those men were also partners in Anjin Mining and they had become suspicious that Chic had scooped some of their diamonds, as well. All at once Chic had realized that his life might be in serious danger. Worse than that, though, he knew that their business would be in danger if the Barons were to link Chic to the Chinese partners. Chic's partners/investors were not yet aware of the Zimbabwe First movement and so did not understand that some of what they saw as

Chic undercutting them was actually being done by those supporting their own country.

As the masseuse worked her way down his back, Chic's mind finally relaxed enough to allow him to fall into a deep sleep, but not before a vision of Akatendeka flashed into his memory. She had appeared at precisely six-thirty that first evening in the Explorer's Club in Zimbabwe, radiant, alive, and mischievous. It was a wonderful night.

REMAND - 21 APRIL 2014

As the day drew to a close, I realized that my jerky lawyer had not arranged for me to get out of the remand centre. I didn't even know if formal charges had been laid or why the hell I was still in jail. I did realize that I had better get my story together because it was beginning to look as though my only way out would be the witch story. I was already beginning to convince *myself* that it was real.

Jim is dead - verified. In my head I began to go over the facts point by point. The rug of the hyæna was no longer attached to the floor in the den - verified. The skull of the hyæna was no longer on the wall - verified. The bracelets were no longer on Jim's wrist - verified. Jim was cut open, just like he described the African workers, except Jim's head was still attached and there was no real sign of struggle. This was a slam-dunk case for the witch. If only I can convince my jerky lawyer about the reality of Zaka! I think that jerk now figures I am actually guilty. Mounties aren't sure and treat me very fairly.

I slept as best I could in my lonely, personal prison cell. Monday night was quieter than Saturday, and I was happy with the solitude. The cool walls coated mindlessly with monotonous paint inspired no thought. The steel cell enclosure constructed to hold a wild horse provided the only view, the only distraction, which was of another identical cell opposite the corridor, which was empty tonight. I outlined the witch story in my mind as I dozed off. 'Tomorrow when I meet my jerky lawyer I'll see if he is even more dismissive. It makes sense to me, but it may be a little difficult to convince a man who clearly had no imagination.'

I awoke after a dead sleep to the clanking in the corridor. My back ached as I tried to roll over. My head ached. As I turned to climb up from the bunk, I noticed how unpleasant I smelled. God, how I want to get out of here! I had always thought that a person was entitled to reasonable bail. Doesn't our Charter of Rights and Freedoms give us the right to reasonable bail, even for first-degree murder? Doesn't that jerky lawyer even know that? Or am I just dreaming of the laws I wish were there?

Breakfast arrived and I already knew better than to ask, so I accepted the tray and sat quietly. My blood started to circulate, and the aches eased. I began to eat. It looked recognizable as food, but it tasted like drywall paste, which I had inadvertently tasted before. The orange-coloured drink that I supposed might have been related to orange juice tasted like diluted battery acid. The texture of the toast was much like a few ink blotters glued together but the taste was not as good. I noticed that I was becoming slightly critical. I finished as much as I could without gagging, neatly placed the utensils on the tray, folded my paper napkin over the top and passed the tray back under the door. I found myself dreaming of a delicious Air Canada in-flight pizza.

At about ten in the morning, a constable came down the corridor and quietly asked me to get up. He opened the door and led me down the hall to the interrogation room. He pointed to the seat and I sat. Then I waited and waited. I tried to remember that last sane moment of life. I lived a quiet life. I worked, I married, I had children, they graduated, I divorced, then I lived by myself. Not exciting. Definitely not very confusing and in no fashion like the past two or three days, or was it four? When did I last change into clean clothes? When did I last shower? I think it was the night after I had been at Jim's. Maybe they have had Jim's funeral already. I had visions of his family standing around the grave, watching their father, brother, son, or whatever, being interred, universally sharing thoughts of gruesome punishment for me, the purported killer.

My drifting thoughts were interrupted by the sound of a door opening. It was my lawyer. His hands clutched at files that were slipping this way and that. He looked about as interested in being here as a six-year-old in the dentist's waiting room. He sat on the steel-framed, dull green leatherette chair and still didn't say a word or look me in the eye. He dropped his files onto the table, got up, left the room and then returned with a paper coffee cup, finally acknowledging my existence.

"We have a problem," he reported.

"I have a problem," I corrected, "what is your problem?" thinking that maybe he might share it so I could send him a big cheque.

At least I got his attention. He lifted his head and looked straight at my face for a minute.

Then he looked back down at his papers.

"They want to charge you with first degree murder," he almost grinned as he said it. It was probably the most excitement he'd had in his career in the backwater.

I nearly choked.

"What? What the hell do they have for evidence?" I burst out, "how do they think I did this thing?"

"They really don't have much yet, but everything they have so far points to you," then he continued, "the two copper bracelets found in your house on your night table appear to match those in a photo they found of him in his house: guilty. According to the security system you were the last person to be at his house: guilty. The expression you had on your face when you looked at the photos showing the skull: suspicious. In your favour, they have found the residue of a drug in his scotch glass and cannot tie it to you yet: tentative. So far, they cannot even identify the drug; it looks like some kind of a homemade concoction: witchcraft? Motive: they have no idea why you did it, but that is what we need to talk about. I need to know in order to frame a defense."

It was my turn to stare at him for a minute.

"You want to know why I killed him? You want me to tell you why I am guilty? What kind of bullshit is this?" I glared at him.

"I will tell you what happened! When Jim and his Professional Hunter were hunting that hyæna in Africa, all the locals were certain that they were hunting a witch of some kind. Whatever it was had already killed some cattle and two of the farmer's farmhands - slit them down the middle and took their hearts and livers, and then sliced off their heads. None of the locals would touch the hyæna after it was dead, but Jim said he wanted the hide for a rug. Jim's PH had his tracker skin the animal and then sent him the rug after a taxidermist had prepared it. Apparently, according to Jim, some witches ride hyænas at night and can make themselves invisible to whomever touches them or the hyæna. Since Jim had touched the hyæna and had possession of the rug, the witch probably came over with the rug or with Jim. That's likely why the rug had been tacked to the floor and the skull screwed to the wall apart from the rug,"

I was glad to get it out. The Jerk was scribbling as fast as he could. I waited for him to catch up.

When he was finished writing, he looked up at me with a strange look and asked in his condescending way,

"Are you feeling OK?" and added, "I might like to schedule an examination for you."

I lost it.

"Your job was to arrange bail and get me out of here. Let's talk about that before you send me to some nuthouse!"

I didn't regret what I said or how I said it, but perhaps I should have. I couldn't believe the blather of this idiot. Had he just given up before he even started? Did he actually believe I was guilty, even though the Mounties had only, at best, circumstantial evidence? Why couldn't he just get in front of a judge or whoever and get the bail set and get me out of here?

He looked at me again and said, "Perhaps I can come back later, if you would feel better about it."

"All I want is to find out how much the bail is to get me released," I snarled, "I have told you who murdered Jim and I can't prove it from a jail cell. I don't need to go to a nuthouse. I am not crazy. I know exactly what Jim told me."

As the lawyer got up to leave, I stood up. He spun around and said, "Sit!" like I was his pet dog—not likely! Fear was plastered on his face. He pressed the buzzer on the wall and two constables appeared almost instantly. I promptly sat down.

"I need to make a phone call," I said to the constable closest to me.

He smiled slightly, "Take it up with your counsel, sir," then he left the room.

TATTOO RUMINATES - KELOWNA
- 21 APRIL 2014 - EVENING

Tattoo walked into his library and selected his copy of *Arthashastra* from the shelf. He had found this to be a fascinating book. It had been written in India, long before Machiavelli, and Carl von Clausewitz. When he had the opportunity to sit, read and reflect, the book helped him to clarify his strategic thoughts. Often, he would spend his evenings like this. Usually he would pour himself a wee dram of Bruichladdich and add a dash of water. On very special days he might also light up a Romeo y Julieta Belicoso and allow his mind to travel through the ether. This part of his life was very private. He didn't share it even with his neighbour. As far as she knew him, he was simply a retired biker gone straight. Everyone else in town saw him the same way - a retired biker, a loner who had probably gone straight.

Tattoo couldn't help thinking about the death of his old mate, Jim. They weren't particularly close friends, since they were from very different branches of covert service, but once they both entered the freelance field, they did cross paths occasionally. Jim was born somewhere in Alberta or Saskatchewan, probably in the mid-fifties. As near as Tattoo could remember, Jim's father had been an assistant branch manager for one of the big Canadian chartered banks in some small town. They moved to Claresholm, then to Fort Macleod, where his father was promoted to branch manager. Jim completed high school, then attended the University of Calgary, where he completed a bachelor's degree in Accounting, after which he attained his CA designation. He worked for a large accounting firm doing audit work for five years before transferring to the forensic accounting group. In 1983, he joined the Canadian Security and Intelligence Service (CSIS) as an Intelligence Agent. It was a big pay cut, but Jim had become bored. He spent the remainder of his career with CSIS learning how to follow money trails. He resigned sometime around 2007 and began doing free-lance work for various clients around the world. It was on one of those jobs that Tattoo had met him. He had no idea who wanted Jim killed. Talking to the suspect might be a good place to start, he thought, and then he tried to figure out the best way to do it.

He would try to find out what was needed to get his former cellmate out on bail, if the lawyer hadn't already done it.

"First thing tomorrow morning," Tattoo thought, before going back to his book.

REMAND - KELOWNA - 22 APR 2014

The jerk finally got me out on bail. They reduced the charge to withholding evidence. I guess that let them keep a hook in me. Bail wasn't too onerous, but they kept my passport. That kind of anchored me. I did get home, which at the time was all I cared about. I climbed out of my grubby clothes and into a hot shower. I scrubbed until my skin was sore. I shaved, brushed my teeth twice and got dressed. I felt like a new man and was headed to the fridge for a cold beer when a thought crossed my mind. How did I convince myself so quickly that it was witchcraft that killed Jim? Had I touched that cursed thing? What was in the scotch glass? Was it the glass with my fingerprints on it? Damn!

As I reached the fridge the phone rang. I grabbed the receiver out of habit and answered, "Hello."

I heard a strange voice on the other end. Not strange so much as unknown to me, but still something strange about it. The man, who told me he was from Kelowna, wanted to speak to me privately. He was a lawyer, and that was all he would tell me. He provided me instructions for our rendezvous place and time. It all sounded very hush-hush and clandestine. I was a little disappointed that it was only the address of his law firm. He asked if I could be there at 4:00 p.m., since things would have quieted down in his office by that time.

I arrived at the address at about three-thirty and drove around, finding a space to park in front of an adjacent building. I walked into a little cafe situated in the opposite direction from the entrance to the lawyer's building. After sitting down, I ordered a coffee and a blueberry muffin, purely out of courtesy. I was not at all hungry. From my seat across from the entrance to the cafe, I could see anyone coming into the cafe and anyone crossing in front of the cafe looking to see where I had gone. I took a sip of the bitter, oily coffee and reached for a creamer. As I took another sip of coffee, I began to think that all the John le Carré and James Bond movies had really taught me to think in terms of conspiracies and covert operations. Somewhat to my disappointment, the only people I noticed passing the window was a very overweight couple who looked as though they were having one hell of an argument about something. They kept moving without even glancing at me. As the minute hand on the big, white, school clock on the wall dragged itself slowly toward the eleven, I got up, paid cash for my snack, and left a generous tip for the young waitress, in spite of her nearly perfected inattentiveness, then walked to the entrance of the strange lawyer's building.

As I pushed open the modern aluminum-trimmed entrance door, I stepped into the vestibule onto a corrugated rubber mat and then passed through the next set of doors. For some reason, I was expecting polished walnut or mahogany walls and Moneypenny. I found the door with the number matching the one I had been given. At least it was solid. There was no glass to be seen, just a solid door and a solid wall. I opened the door and walked in. The reception area was modest but nicely furnished. I noticed the carpet laid over hardwood did not come from Costco. The desk was made of wood and all edges were rounded, a sign of the days when things were made of real wood and made to last. I looked up when the receptionist asked if she could help. She was made top quality and made to last, too, I thought to myself, blushing slightly, I am sure.

"I am here to meet...," I had forgotten the lawyer's name - in fact, I couldn't remember if he had even given me his name.

"I have forgotten his name already," I said, blushing again.

"Wait one moment, please,' she said, granting me a smile to remember. She stepped gracefully down a corridor, returning in moments and asking me to follow her.

We arrived at another wooden door with no name on it. She ushered me inside and then closed the door behind me. The man at the desk stood, reached out his hand and said, "good to see you," then promptly sat down.

He was over six feet tall, obviously fit and well-tanned. The wall behind his desk was decorated with sailing photos and paintings. A number of real trophies sat on his credenza. These were trophies one would win at excellent schools or at European competitions, not the usual cast-plastic-dipped-in-coloured-gold-paint trophies that we are used to seeing. These were polished silver, made by a real silversmith. He looked around as if to see what I was looking at, then smiled, "one must have hobbies, and sailing was one of mine in my earlier years."

He looked up from his almost clear desk and introduced himself as Scottie MacIntyre, a senior partner of the Kelowna firm of Filson, MacIntyre and Pogue. He slid an agreement across to me and asked me to read it. It seemed simple enough: I promised to keep everything he told me confidential and vice versa, other than required by an order of the courts. I signed. He began by telling me that he had been Jim's lawyer for a few years, not hinting at a longer relationship. I thought that his slight accent might be a South African accent.

As he continued, he implied obliquely that he and Jim had shared some experiences several years ago. He said that Jim had left government service but had continued with his prior activities on a private basis. Jim had contacted him a few years ago and had asked if he would hold some papers in case anything ever happened to him. They were to be subject to solicitor-client privilege. Each time Jim made a visit to the office, the numbers of papers would increase, so that there were now several files. Late last summer, Jim provided my name and contacts to the lawyer and asked him to contact me if anything were to happen to Jim to take him out of the game. He was to make me a proposition for dealing with the papers. I politely informed him that I was about to go back into jail for killing Jim if I couldn't come up with a good alibi.

"Who's your lawyer?" he asked.

I told him the story of how I ended up with the jerky lawyer, that I had no interest in continuing with someone who actually thought I was guilty. I also informed him that the court had held my passport and had charged me with something like withholding evidence. Scottie grinned as if to say, "You don't have to brag about that - it's not much of a deal - yet."

He asked if I wanted him to represent me, and I didn't miss a beat before saying yes. He suggested that I would have to sign a letter in due course, but that he would get in touch with my lawyer and obtain all my files. We would meet after that.

I returned to MacIntyre's law office the following morning. He had already prepared a letter for me to sign, wherein I requested my jerky lawyer to transfer my file to MacIntyre. I signed.

"I spoke to your lawyer this morning and he is aware that the letter is on its way, so if you still want our help, then let's get started."

He slipped the letter into the file and then asked me to follow him. He took me to a small windowless conference room at the end of the hall. He called someone to bring the Sonneblom files. I accepted his offer of coffee from the fresh pot on the credenza and he poured one for himself. We sat and he began to chat.

"All my life I have been a tea drinker," he told me, "but since I arrived in this country, I have forced myself to learn to drink this stuff," he smiled. "If certain types of beans are used, and it is freshly brewed, I can find it tolerable."

"I guess I grew up the other way: coffee and, very occasionally, tea," I replied.

"Our coffee was boiled in a pot on the stove and every time it was filled up with water another handful of ground coffee was thrown in. When the pot became too full of grounds, they were thrown onto the flowerbed outside and the whole process started over. When the coffee started tasting too bitter, Mom would throw some eggshells in the pot," I reminisced.

Just then a trolley was pushed through the door by a huffing young man who looked as though he had slept on the couch in the office and had lost his comb.

"This is Albert," MacIntyre informed me, "and he is my associate."

He turned and gave me a quick wink as he grinned pleasantly.

"You may call on him for help anytime you are in the office here. This room is yours for the time being. Do not, and I mean *do not*, leave these files in this room unattended. If you are going out, even to the 'john', call Albert. If you are going to lunch, Albert will return with the trolleys and take the files away for safe storage until your return."

He turned to Albert and smiled and then said softly, "Thank you Albert, you may go now."

"Oh, thank you Mr. MacIntyre," he responded in a childlike way, "I will be ready, I promise."

He shuffled out of the room, forgetting to close the door.

After ensuring that I was comfortable but offering no explanation of why Jim had chosen me to oversee his files, MacIntyre spoke to me of the nature of compensation I would receive and outlined how my expenses would be reimbursed. He explained that, for legal reasons and for the safety of everyone involved, his firm needed to maintain a degree of separation from what I would be doing and from what was happening in Africa, a sort of Chinese Wall.

"For example," he explained, "you will pay for your own airfare, and then you will phone me and give me the cost of the flight."

A trust apparently related to one of my ancestors would deposit the amount into my account at the bank or would make a payment on a credit card, if I chose. My retainer would be deposited from different sources in varied amounts but would always be cumulatively greater than the monthly commitment.

I was beginning to figure out that Jim had been involved with some type of spying or tracking of illegal activities in Africa. I concluded that, for the quality of his work, he had been paid substantially more than I was offered, so I could well see how he had put away quite a pile. From what MacIntyre explained, it seemed the client in Africa was prepared to pay me for competent work in analyzing Jim's papers. I would need to visit the lawyers in Johannesburg soon if I decided I was interested. I told MacIntyre that I would need a few days before giving them an answer. He nodded, smiled, got up and left me to myself.

If I agreed to take on Jim's work, this small room would be where I would spend my time, in isolation, looking at the material he had left, and trying to figure it out. I opened a couple of files and took a quick look. Every person named in the files, with the exception of what I assumed were the "bad guys" was identified only in code. The material included a very explicit diary as well as a number of reports that looked very official. At first glance the cover letters indicated that the Filson, MacIntyre firm was sending them to Someone, Someone and Sonneblom law firm in Johannesburg.

After I spent an hour perusing files, I said my goodbyes and headed out across the parking lot to my car. As I drove toward my house, I wondered what I was getting into. Maybe sitting in prison would be easy in comparison. But at least I would be busy, and I knew enough about forensics to be able to decipher Jim's work, which at least would give me the skills to be of some help. As soon as I got home, I pulled out a tattered phone book from the left-hand drawer under the kitchen cabinet. My eyes scrolled down the columns for Turner, Will Turner. As soon as I found it, I called Tattoo. He sounded as though he didn't want to talk to me; I guessed that he was in a rush. We agreed that we would meet for lunch the next day at the Eldorado Hotel in Kelowna. In the meantime, there was a lot for me to organize.

A TUTORIAL IN COVERT
OPERATIONS – 23 APRIL 2014

When I arrived at the hotel, I wandered in past the front desk and glanced up at the beautiful old rowing scull hanging from the ceiling. 'Nice 'old school' touch,' I thought.

I spotted Tattoo sitting alone in a back corner, foregoing any view of the marina or of the lake, in favour of privacy. I walked over to join him and sat opposite, staring at the blank wall behind him. Before he even said hello, he lifted his briefcase onto the tabletop, opened it and indicated that I should shut off my phone and place it in the case. Once I had complied, he closed the case and set it between his chair and the wall, and then greeted me like a long-lost friend.

"We have a problem," he opened.

"How's that?" I asked him. I hadn't even discussed my meeting with the lawyer in Kelowna or my relationship with Jim. How could he know there was a problem? That "we" had a problem?

"It appears that something you have done has stimulated a lot of discussion in a dark recess of the internet," he replied. "Some very powerful people think someone is nosing into their business."

"I haven't done anything!" I responded, emphasizing my frustration, "I have been accused of something that I had no involvement in."

"Usually these people do not chase ghosts," Tattoo replied, "I don't suppose you know the guy you murdered, do you?"

"I didn't murder anyone! I knew the guy they accused me of killing only slightly and I don't know much about him," I answered in a firm but low voice.

"Look," said Tattoo, "I am sure you didn't kill him. I've known Jim for some years—we even worked on something together once, way back. He could have killed you with one hand before you would even know what happened. The question is why it looks so much like you are guilty. But before we continue, there are a few rules I need you to understand and agree to," Tattoo stated.

"First, we are never, and I mean, *never*, going to talk about this situation on the phone, or by email, or in any other way than in person. From now on, Jim will be referred to as your youngest sister. Cell phones will be left at home or locked in the trunk of your vehicle anywhere within ten miles of wherever we meet. I will provide you with a list of meeting places and their code names. Other than in discussions with me, never discuss the places on that list. Understand?" he concluded, looking at me sternly in the eye.

"I understand, but why all the secrecy?" I enquired.

"There are people looking for you and something you apparently have in your possession. They are far more interested in obtaining 'the package' than in seeing you or anyone around you left alive," Tattoo explained.

I looked at Tattoo in awe.

"Where the hell do you come from?" I asked, "How do you know all this shit and why didn't you try to tell me this in the slammer?"

"Easy, please," he replied calmly. "We couldn't talk in there and I sure as hell couldn't tell everyone that I knew Jim. Doesn't that make some sense to you?"

He stared at me for a minute and I shrank.

"Since it seems we will be together for a while, and you won't have enough time to determine whether or not you like, or at least trust me, I will quickly catch you up on my life," Tattoo said. "I think I told you I was from Cold Lake and that my dad was a jet jockey for the RCAF. My mother was a homemaker, to use an old-fashioned term, who cooked for dad, my brother and me. My little brother died of a drug overdose after having chosen the wrong path and getting into methamphetamines.

Mom took to drinking to drown her grief. Father lost heart. I was at the University of Alberta studying Civil Engineering. Uh - that was in 1993. My brother was younger by about four years. Dad had joined the Air Force in 1950 and became eligible for maximum retirement benefits two years after I went to university. A few months after my brother died, my Dad sent in his retirement papers. He had found a quarter section of land west of Grand Prairie and thought he could become a purebred Angus breeder. He was about to turn 67. Mom was a couple of years younger. One year after he bought the farm, Dad was diagnosed with terminal cancer. Mom's alcohol intake just kept increasing. They had fifty head of Angus cattle by then. Father was getting weaker by the day but wouldn't quit. With my brother gone, and my father dying, Mom got through the days by drinking. I skipped the first semester of my third year to go home and take care of the calving and to plant some barley for the summer feed. We also had forty acres of oats. Not much, but when it was baled green, it provided some of the winter feed. Dad continued to decline but refused to give up on the farm. No matter what I did, Mom always managed to buy and hide a bottle. That bottle and Dad were all that kept her alive. I stayed through the summer of 1996 and Dad died in September.

My dream of finishing University was gone, for a while anyway. A year later, 1997, in October, I got home from town to find Mom slumped over the kitchen table. Some kind of shock to her system, the Doctor said. I was now a farmer. I sure as hell didn't plan on being a farmer and I was pissed.

I thought about joining the RCMP but decided to give the Army a shot. I leased the farm to a neighbour and sold the herd. In 1998, I was accepted and sent to basic training. Once I completed my infantry basic training by mid-2000, I was assigned to the Princess Patricia's Canadian Light Infantry in Edmonton. The Army was looking for volunteers for Joint Task Force 2. The Army had taken over the Anti-terrorist Rapid Deployment Force from the RCMP in 1993. I had some engineering skills and I was fit, 6'3", 200 pounds of solid muscle and an excellent cardio package, so I was accepted. I then began another few years of training before I was ready for deployment.

In 2002, I was accepted as one of forty Canadians for a tour in Afghanistan. Task Force K-Bar, the first one for me, began just before I joined it. We travelled to neat places like Helmand and Uruzgan Provinces in South Afghanistan. We worked with elite forces from quite a few countries: Special Air Service (SAS) from Britain, US Delta Forces and the Norwegian *Forsvarets Spesialkommando* (FSK). Over a year our outfit was tasked more than forty recce and surveillance missions, as well as what some called "direct action" operations. We were part of commando wet-operations that took out at least 115 Taliban and al-Qaeda fighters and captured more than a hundred Taliban leaders over a six-month period. From then on it was one non-existent operation after another, usually with other allied troops, often wet, and always totally 'black'.

I made some tight friends while I was there. Guys from around the world. In 2011, I was invited to join a few friends who were working for a group out of London. I was about at the end of JTF2, since, as I got older, the opportunities got fewer. The next thing that was going to happen was that I would become a paper pusher! That, plus the appeal of a dramatic increase in pay for part time work made my decision for me. I went to work for Furiæ. Furiæ Services SA was registered in the Dutch Antilles, but operationally it was based in Dubai. They provide some high-level security services to companies and, occasionally, to countries.

"You know what the word 'Furiæ' means?" he asked, as if to give me time to catch up. I admit that I was feeling a little overwhelmed; I felt as though I were listening to the telling of a Tom Clancy thriller.

"It is the name of a Greek god from the olden days, whose duty it was to wreak vengeance against people who had committed a serious crime in 'our world'. Nemesis was their boss god and they would pursue criminals as long as they were still alive, not giving them rest or respite."

"Anyway, Furiæ Services was founded in 1990 by some retired British Army officers. In 1997, by putting together a couple of outfits involved in 'risk assessment and management', they created a new organization: Furiæ Services South Africa. They bid for a US military contract in Iraq in 2003 and 'poof' off they went! Rapid growth! I was a specialist at infiltration, security, and exfiltration. As activity wound down in the mid 2000's, I took up working on the oil-rigs to fill in time. My engineering background and leadership experience allowed me to make it as a directional driller. I moved to the Okanagan Valley and took on the persona of a retired biker.

One of my old JTF2 buddies was a Sergeant in the Kelowna detachment of the RCMP. I always keep clean and my buddy knows it. No hassles. From here, I could fly in and out of Kelowna to anywhere in the world via Vancouver or Calgary without raising any suspicions. I could be a biker or a driller—not much difference sometimes," he laughed.

"Now let me tell you a few more things," he reverted from a reflective retiree to a serious Sergeant Major.

"We do not meet at my place or yours. We go hunting or we go fishing. We discuss nothing about our activities while we are in the vehicle. We will remove the batteries from our cell phones, or you may just leave your phone in the metal box in the back of my pickup, but it's probably best just to leave it at home.

"If you want me involved, we can meet somewhere tomorrow and you can let me know what has happened so far," he suggested.

"I would really appreciate your involvement. This whole thing is way beyond my experience and I still have to get out of the murder charge. It all feels just a little unreal to me."

I could hear myself coming close to pleading. From that point, our discussion became general. I asked him how often he had to go drilling and how much time he could spend in the Okanagan. He filled me in a bit on his situation. He had done quite well. He was the only heir of his parent's estate; he had saved as much as he could during his previous career, which still remained somewhat opaque to me. He put away a lot from his current job, (even more opaque) and he had invested well. He worked by choice rather than by necessity.

Tattoo thought of things that would never have crossed my mind. I needed to trust him totally. He had saved my life in remand: verifiable. I was forever grateful: verifiable. Unless the lawyer or I broke the silence, the link between the lawyer and me would remain unknown, the link between Tattoo and Jim unknown. Good for the health of all three of us.

"Tomorrow morning at six-thirty, I will phone you on your home land-line and ask you if you would like to go fishing. You will say yes, and I will give you the address for our meeting please. It will be bullshit. I will pick you up at Tim Hortons on 22nd and Harvey in Kelowna at eight, regardless of the time I say on the phone call. Park your car at the shopping centre and walk to Timmy's. I would like to go over everything you have discussed with your new lawyer and we will "mek a plan."

He smiled, remembering something from the past.

"Remember, everything we say and everywhere we go can be recorded by someone, and probably is. The guys who are after you, or working for whoever is after you, are better than anyone. Our only hope is that they don't know where to start. I wish we had someone available to follow the followers."

MEETING OF THE CPZ IN BULAWAYO

The trip to Bulawayo would take most of Jacobus Van der Merwe's day. He filled his Toyota Land Cruiser with fuel from the large tank then returned to the house. He walked into the kitchen, picked up a bag of sandwiches and a thermos of coffee and milk from the kitchen table, his bag from the floor, then kissed his *frau* on the cheek and said, "*Tot siens, Ek sal more by die huis wees.*" At least Jacobus thought he would be home by the next evening. He whistled as he stepped onto the deck and his dogs came running.

"*Kom hier Brutus, spring!*" and the oldest of the dogs climbed into the passenger seat, very proud of his preferred status. Jacobus slipped his Gladstone bag behind his own seat and climbed in.

"What have I forgotten?" he asked himself, as he slid the keys into the ignition. Kembo, his favourite tracker was sitting quietly in the back seat with his cloth bag and his walking stick, observing everything. Jacobus turned the key and the engine started, just as it had every day for the last eighteen years. He turned his head and waved goodbye to his wife, and then drove down the alley of blue gum trees. "*Hey, Brutus, dit gaan 'n lang dag wees vandag, né,*" thinking of the length of the drive ahead. Jacobus loved his Ridgeback, Brutus and his tracker, Kembo and his life. He was very careful to take care of everyone, including the Ridgebacks.

Jacobus looked out over the opening vista of farmlands and thought of the proud history of his country. How his ancestors had come, first on foot and then by wagon train. Although they were Afrikaners, they had chosen not to fight the battle against the British, but they did help Oom Paul Kruger to create his new nation. Jacobus's ancestors had no part of mining and could care less who owned the rights to Nobel's dynamite distribution or who would administer the gold and diamond claims. His ancestors had first travelled this territory in 1532 and, ever since, had been travelling in and out as hunters and traders, competing with the Arab traders. The area of his current farm had been ranched and farmed by members of a Shona people until they were pushed out by Mzilikazi, founder of the Ndebele nation, who had in turn been pushed from the Transvaal by Shaka and also by the British who came north and west, devastating the region, forcing the Roswi out. Mzilikazi had prevailed, even though the Roswi had been known as great warriors and had used the 'horns of the bull' formation long before the great Zulu, Shaka.

Once the Ndebeles, led by Mzilikazi's son Lobengula, had been subdued by the British, Jacobus' great grandfather had settled on his current place and had returned the family to farming and to raising cattle. He took title to an area of 6200 *morgen* and proudly named it *Tweekudufontein*. The name came to them after he and his wife awoke in their wagon the first morning and saw two beautiful kudus drinking at the small river. They worked hard and died working. They had treated their black workers better than average and each had learned to respect the other. His family prided themselves on providing a school for the children of the workers long before the government thought to do so. They had a nurse come to visit all the workers and their children twice each year and anyone who needed more help was taken to a doctor in Victoria Falls. A few of the children had a desire to attend university, so the family made sure they could afford to go. It was like having an extended family, except when it came to marriage and that was more custom than rule.

Jacobus was travelling to Bulawayo for a meeting of the Progressive Farmers of Zimbabwe, being held in the boardroom of the old Bulawayo Club. The true purpose of the meeting, though, was to provide a covert opportunity for the Committee for the Preservation of Zimbabwe (CPZ), a small group of men, both black and white, whose families had lived together for generations in Zimbabwe, to get together. They had watched as the political turmoil of the postcolonial era allowed the economic wealth of the nation to spiral downhill to the point of near catastrophe. Now they watched as short-sighted and selfish opportunists sold off the nation's resources for short-term personal gain. They were all too aware that even well-intentioned politicians were helpless to prevent the coming disaster. The group had agreed to work together surreptitiously to bring members guilty of the abuse to the public eye, and to help to see the errant Barons brought to justice.

Johnny Moyo and Morgan Nkomo would also be there. Johnny Moyo was a descendant of one of the original founders of the Southern Rhodesian African National Congress (SRANC), the mixed group that had attempted, in the nineteen fifties, to reach a negotiated settlement with the British Government. Morgan was descended from one of the original members of the Capricorn Society, initiated in 1949 by David Stirling, with whom Morgan's father had served in the SAS during the Second Great War. Both fathers had avoided the worst of the guerilla war and had observed as the British Government had attempted to reach a deal with Ian Smith aboard HMS Tiger in 1966. Both had been distraught when, on the 4th of July 1964, the 'Crocodile Commando' had killed Petrus Oberhultzer, a white farmer, thereby kicking off the guerilla war. They had watched helplessly from the sidelines as Ian Smith's government, in an attempt to avoid the upcoming spectre of compulsory majority rule, made a Unilateral Declaration of Independence. Ian Smith and his cohorts knew they held the military strength to prevail against the guerillas. *Jong* Petrus Oberhultzer was a member of the CPZ. In spite of the fact that his grandfather had been killed by guerillas, *Jong* Petrus still clung to the belief that whites and blacks could live and prosper together in a beautiful country.

These men formed the executive committee of the CPZ. They had been able to employ resources from like-minded Zimbabweans who felt their right to be Zimbabwean was becoming more and more tenuous as the Barons committed more and more blatant acts of fiscal abuse. They had no wish to pursue violence unless it was required. If they did, it was to be focused at a particular individual whose abuse was so pervasive that no amount of negotiation or public shame would alter his actions. The group was inclined to use public disclosure and NGO pressure to engage foreign governments in a policy of condemnation and promoting processes that could trap monies gained illegally. They also tried to defend those who had been helpful. They were not especially focused on achieving vigilante revenge.

Jacobus arrived in Bulawayo in time to check in and have dinner. His dog went to the home of his tracker, Kembo. Jacobus went up to his room, showered, changed and came downstairs, where he met a few of his friends for dinner. At eight he excused himself and went upstairs to the boardroom to wait for the others. Peter and Johnny were already seated, and Morgan walked in right after Jacobus settled in his usual chair. After checking the hallway, Morgan closed the door.

"Well, good evening everyone," started Johnny, "Jacobus, I hope your drive down wasn't too exhausting. We have a bit of work to cover tonight and as we have all agreed, we will keep our meeting as short as possible."

Johnny had been educated in South Africa, Moscow and London. His accent was indefinable. His intelligence was not at all in doubt.

"Let's begin with a report on the abuses of the diamond mining. Morgan how about you go ahead?"

"Thanks, Johnny, and good evening, Petrus and Jacobus," he looked around.

"As near as I can determine, the untraceable funds are leaving our country at the rate of over four hundred million dollars per month."

This was a staggering amount for a nation with the economy of Zimbabwe. Morgan had studied in Zimbabwe until he was granted a government scholarship to continue his studies at the London School of Economics. In his graduating year he was selected as one of the top five students. He completed a Master of Arts Degree, after which he attained his Doctorate Degree in Economics at Harvard University in the United States.

"There are the normal culprits, but more and more of the legitimate funds earned that would have accrued to government revenues from legitimate enterprise, are being skimmed offshore. Since diamonds are now being sold at the diamond auction in Antwerp, the prices are better, but, due to the government, a noticeable portion of the funds is being diverted by 'assignment of funds', apparently signed by a Deputy Minister on behalf of a Minister, who denies any involvement. This presents us with two problems: the corruption within our own government is growing, in spite of assurances otherwise from Mr. Mugabe, and funds due to legitimate operators are being stolen, and they are being accused of doing the stealing. I have been able to track one person who appears to be the actual recipient of the funds. Another problem is that the forensic accountant who has been helping us for the past few years has suddenly stopped reporting. I am awaiting word from our legal counsel in Johannesburg as to what happened. I suggest that once we obtain the outstanding report from the accountant, we can have someone pay a visit to the party or parties to attempt to have them mend their ways. That's all I have today," he laid his folder back on the table.

"Any questions for Morgan?" Johnny asked.

"Morgan," began Petrus, "do you suspect a serious problem or just delayed delivery?"

"Hard to tell, Petrus," answered Morgan, "I will be in Johannesburg next week on other business and will meet our contact. I should know more then."

"Since we will not be meeting for a while, Johnny," Jacobus said slowly, "would it be a good idea to authorize Morgan to proceed with a replacement accountant if necessary, so that we can minimize downtime?" He looked at the others. "What do you fellows think?"

They all nodded in the affirmative, and then Johnny looked at Petrus.

"How have you made out, Petrus?"

Petrus would have skimmed his notes, if he had had any, but instead he looked around.

"Our person in Harare, through the accountant in Canada, has been kept busy gathering and interpreting financial material for us. Our person in Harare has kept us informed of a meeting in Hong Kong, where one of our targets, Mr. Gordon Zhong, was meeting with some American lawyers. We expect a more detailed report on this meeting within the next few weeks, once our contact can arrange for some discussion. She is also keeping an eye on a few of the Barons. Based upon her progress, we have added two more people to our target list, a Major-General and a Brigadier-General. They seem to be operating independently of each other and are rather clumsy, I think. Morgan, I think you are already following up on them, would that be correct?"

Morgan nodded in the affirmative.

"I hope to have some account details in the next ten to fourteen days. It may be only general information at this stage. The Major-General was in Antwerp at the time of the last showing and sale. Perhaps our agent can get a little closer to him, Jacobus, if that can be arranged."

Johnny looked at the other members, and then asked, "Jacobus, what's new in your area?"

"I still have a problem," Jacobus replied, looking around.

"Another one of my security guys was executed. We didn't find him for about three days. He was in pretty rough shape by then, and all we had to tie it to the others was the fact that his head was missing. We have not found it yet. I know it's an escalation of warning from someone: first, the calves, then the cows, then a few workers. I just don't want the workers to see it as anything other than someone running afoul of someone else and a witch coming to resolve it. I have hired another fellow, whom I hope will replace him. He is not local so it will take a while to see if he fits in. He has a great military background and seems quiet. By the looks of him he should be able to handle himself. I don't know who is behind it, but for some reason I don't think it is those Barons in Harare, even though they certainly seem to be getting more confident by the day. We also see that the public is more aware of whose money it is that the Barons are borrowing to enrich themselves. I will be dropping a few more stories to cast some light on the previous guys we discussed.

"We had good coverage on the Israel pilot story in March two years ago, and a few reporters are still following the leads from that. I don't know if you gentlemen remember the story. It was a meager 8500 carats, a small fraction of the take, but it was all they would print then. Now we have stories coming out referring to secrecy in negotiations and calling for more transparency. The press has hinted that Cidwa Diamond Mining Corporation and the Algor Investment Corporation deals are a bit iffy.

"We have a number of small successes, like the four workers in Cidwa who were arrested by the police for stealing some diamonds from the Marange Resources Diamond Mine. One of our Asian residents, Assim Khan, owner of Amica Investments, a diamond cutting and polishing company, and part owner of Amikadim Wholesalers, was accused of conspiring with some employees of Tankana Diamonds (Private) Limited, a JV of the Zimbabwe Mining Development Corporation (ZMDC), and the Infata Dawn Group of South Africa, to steal three million dollars' worth of diamonds. Once again, a small amount, but keeps it in the press and in front of the people. I don't think he was on our list, but he and his contacts will be now.

"I hope that in the next few years we will have enough pressure on the Barons and the government to clean up the diamond business before we run out of diamonds. I have arranged for our representative to get more NGO pressure and it looks like we've got a senior-level visitor coming from the Kimberly Protocol Office."

Once their business was complete, a few draft agendas for the Progressive Farmers of Zimbabwe, neatly typed and sloppily edited, were crumpled and tossed into the garbage can. Johnny provided each of the members with a typed set of minutes from a previous meeting, along with various relevant agricultural reading materials. The Committee for the Preservation of Zimbabwe kept no minutes, no notes and no records of any kind in Zimbabwe. Whenever Jacobus or Johnny travelled to Pretoria, they went to the office of Mr. S. at Wilberson, Jonas & Sonneblom and dictated a summary of the activities of the group. That journal of activity would provide sufficient detail to allow someone else to pick up their work if they were ever discovered and disappeared. It would be edited appropriately in order to avoid direct incriminations should it ever be found or successfully subpoenaed. The reports on the work conducted in Canada would be covered by solicitor-client privilege and were filed in a completely separate set of records. Using a Canadian forensic investigator was intended to eliminate any link to the CPZ.

GREAT ZIMBABWE

n the Mopane-covered hills of southeastern Zimbabwe, near the shores of Lake Mutirikwe stands the 'house of stone', the source of the name of the new nation. The twenty thousand plus residents of the nearby town of Masvingo remember it as the home of the Queen of Sheba. That 'house of stone' was the capital of the Kingdom of Zimbabwe from the time of the Late Iron Age. It was a city built of stone, covering over sixty acres, by the time England's Barons were trying to rein in the power of their King John on the plains of Runnymede. The Shona speakers were a Bantu people who settled there as early as 400 C.E. Originally settled by simple farmers and cattlemen, the Shona had built a powerful hierarchy. By the end of the first millennium, it was a King who was supported by an elite who held their wealth in cattle and ensured that the peasants carried out the work.

The King and the Barons had magnificent stone houses built by the peasants. Cut by highly skilled tradesmen from granite, the stones were formed into structures requiring no mortar or cement. The largest structure was the outer wall, at over 250 metres long and almost ten metres high, which enclosed the tall, cone-shaped tower. The elite accessed their porcelain from the orient, their engraved glass from the Middle East and their finely crafted gold and copper ornaments from West Africa. Certain men in Zimbabwe believed that it would be "The Great Zimbabwe" again. These men called themselves the Barons of Great Zimbabwe.

MEETING OF THE BARONS IN HARARE

The night air was cool and the moonless sky over Harare was like a black velvet cloth sprinkled with tiny diamonds. The first car arrived at the portico of the giant white house that was the home of Mr. Walter Nkosi. Mr. Nkosi was one of the more fortunate business successes in the new Zimbabwe. Although a relative of the President, he had begun his career at the bottom rung of the business ladder: alongside his mother he had bought and resold vegetables. From those humble beginnings he developed commercial skills and eventually was able to acquire a piece of property, which he successfully subdivided into lots. The profits from that project formed the foundation of his wealth. Mr. Nkosi had even deviated into politics for a time, which he still regretted because of the relentless intrusion into his personal life. He was proud of his success. Sheer determination, constant hard work and intellectual brilliance were crowned by his physical ability to intimidate. The Indigenization Act allowed him the opportunity to acquire more and to build his business empire. Some detractors believed it was more success by intimidation than by skill, but he achieved what most others could only dream of.

Mr. Nkosi was pleased that this evening's meeting of select movers and shakers of Harare would be convened in his home. The men arriving now were referred to by some as the New Barons. They were the men who would accumulate capital to fund the rebuilding of the nation of Zimbabwe, their nation. In attendance would be two government ministers, a Major-General, a Brigadier-General, a Detective-Sergeant, and a few other prominent businessmen. They would discuss and determine how business in their city would progress over the coming months. They would also attempt to resolve the political issues facing their country, not the least of which was their aging leader. They had another problem that required discussion this evening: someone was snooping into their business activities and releasing the information to the press, attracting some attention from other Ministries. The situation was more of a nuisance than a real threat, but still, they needed to nip it in the bud before it had the potential to become serious.

A tall man in military uniform appeared from the rear seat of a Mercedes. He wore the rank of Brigadier-General, an ambiguous rank, since it was a crossover between military field operations and general staff. Walter Nkosi walked forward to greet him.

"Good evening Brigadier Khuphe. I hope you have had a pleasant day," Mr. Nkosi stated expansively, fully aware of the slight glint of envy in the eyes of Brigadier Pius Khuphe as he took in the scale of the home.

"Yes, indeed and it has many more hours to run," answered the Brigadier.

Just then, two other cars pulled in behind the departing Mercedes.

"I will show you inside in a moment Pius. Let us first greet our new arrivals," suggested Nkosi.

The second car carried two ministers, Dr. Brighton Chidarara, Minister of Mines, and Mr. Goodwill Mashonga, Minister of the Treasury. As they were climbing out of their cars, Major General Isaac Nkala was exiting his black S63 AMG Mercedes.

"Good evening, Walter," the Major-General said, as he held out his hand in greeting, "Are we all here?"

"All but Detective-Sergeant Sibangilizwe, and he is often tied up. Fortune Makamba telephoned to send his regrets; he is out of the country at the moment. I think we can go in and the Detective will join us when he arrives," said Mr. Nkosi, courteously.

Mr. Walter Nkosi, son of a vegetable merchant, with the internal preening of a peacock, led this important entourage through the entrance of his huge mansion and down the hall of Venetian marble to a large meeting room, decorated in modern European fashion, and bounded by large leather chairs. As soon as they were seated, Timothy, a tall, elegantly dressed butler arrived to take orders for drinks. The lively chatter that accompanies a gathering of colleagues eager to be together filled the room until Timothy returned with the drinks and served them, whereupon Dr. Chidarara called the meeting to order.

"Gentlemen, we have much to discuss and little time available, so with your permission, let us proceed," the Minister began. "As you all know, the press in Harare has become very vocal about the mineral industries. They have been making wild accusations of theft and bribery, and all sorts of corruption. Recently, though, they have been writing articles that are too close to accurate. This has made it very difficult for our President to deflect them as nonsense without damaging his own reputation. He has been forced to take action against many whom we know. I believe that we have located the source of much of the problem of leaked information.

"A forensic accountant from North America has been conducting extensive research into the flow of funds relating to the auctions of diamonds in Abu Dhabi and Antwerp. As a result, some of the funds have been frozen by American action, theoretically under the auspices of the Kimberly Process. They have no right to do this. However, they do have the power to do it and they have done it. This has brought some of the Chinese investors into the problem because their funds are being frozen, as well. The options we have available to defend our actions would unfortunately bring our actions into the public limelight and to the clear focus of the press. Inaction on our part will bring increasing pressure from the Chinese investors, some of whom are backed by the Chinese Government, and hence, have substantial ability to pressure our government into disclosing who is responsible and what is actually happening. As you can guess, neither is a suitable option.

"I am not happy to have to report that two deaths have occurred. They are thought by some to be related to us. In the first death, action was taken to neutralize the Canadian forensic accountant, whom we suspected of working for a group in Zimbabwe. The other was the death of a security person working for another group here. The methods used in each death were slightly different, but both were consistent with the work of a witch. I am assuming that none of you present had any advanced knowledge of these events.

"A representative of one group of Chinese investors, not tied directly to their government, has been doing research into the reason behind the freezing of proceeds from the two diamond auctions. We do not know how much information he has accrued, but we do know that he has recently hired a firm of attorneys in New York City. They are reputedly very well-connected to the senior bureaucrats and committees within the United States Government. Currently, we are deploying resources to determine whether his research will be favourable to our cause or will turn out to be a problem for us. Our objective is to obtain some of the written documentation. If he is able to cause the U.S. to alter their position regarding the proceeds of the auctions, it may be favourable to all of us. If all that happens is that his work falls into the hands of the media, then it will be a major problem, too late to resolve.

"I would like to open the meeting for discussion and suggestions."

Before any discussion could occur, Timothy appeared, holding in two hands, a magnificent polished wooden box.

"Cigars, anyone?" he asked, in the modulated tone of a professionally trained and experienced butler. Walter Nkosi was very proud of his butler, as he was of all of his possessions. Timothy had been trained in England and had served in Abu Dhabi at a large new hotel until he felt a touch of homesickness and returned to Zimbabwe. He was an exceptional addition to the decor of the mansion, thought Walter, not recognizing the absurdity of his pseudo-colonial perspective.

TATTOO AND I - KELOWNA - 23 APRIL 2014

That afternoon Tattoo and I talked about what we could do to bring Jim's killer to the fore. What did we know about the killer? We agreed that he had perceived someone else was involved with Jim, primarily because he had not found Jim's original papers. It might be that he had thought that I was the other guy and so he had planted the bracelets in my house. Tattoo believed that the killer had spent at least two nights, and maybe up to a week near Kelowna so that he could scope Jim's place and get a feel for his movements, after which he set things up to kill Jim without a trace, and to make a clean exit. Tattoo thought there was a strong possibility that he was still around. How Jim was killed was still a mystery, but Tattoo assured me that it had not been a witch and that, in spite of what I believed, we were going to be much more successful looking for a human. We now knew that Jim had been doing some work for someone in Zimbabwe. We surmised that the killer was likely involved with the other side of that campaign or at least had been hired by them. All in all, we didn't know a hell of a lot.

We agreed that once I got back to work on the files at McIntyre's office, we might learn a little more. That was going to be delayed until I had been vetted and interviewed and that wouldn't happen until I had my passport back. Even if I chose to get involved, I would need some help with all the physical stuff, 'the field work', so to speak; exactly the kinds of things at which Tattoo seemed to excel.

I remembered Jim telling me the story of how they had staked the goat in order to attract the killer hyæna. I passed on that tidbit to Tattoo.

"What do you think?" I asked, "I never have had an experience where my life was totally in another's hands."

Tattoo laughed, "Well it would make a great story, but it would be an extremely dangerous approach for you. You don't have any training, let alone field experience. Best that we keep you working on the bookkeeping stuff, my friend."

A MEETING IN SHANGHAI - 21 NOVEMBER 2003

ordon Zhong and his assistant Sparkly were sitting and waiting in a small room in a restaurant in the Dragon Phoenix on Nanjing Road, a three-block walk from the old Hong Kong and Shanghai Bank building at Number 12, Zhongshan Dong Yi Road. Chic loved the Bund. He loved Shanghai. It was a great city, one of five ports opened for trade, with British encouragement, as a result of the opium wars. Sitting at the mouth of the Yangtze on the Chinese coast, Shanghai has for decades been home to smugglers and diplomats, to administrators and merchants. After the Treaties of Nanking and Whampoa in the mid-eighteen-hundreds, Russians, Americans, French and British, were allowed to make their homes in the International Settlement, whereupon, they thrived and continued even into the present day to add spice to its culture. Other than the disruption between 1949 and 1990, Shanghai was the Chinese centre for business.

They had been waiting for about twenty minutes when the first of the older men arrived. Within minutes, three more arrived, followed shortly after by Chic's father. After the traditional round of bows and greetings, they sat. Tea was brought and the waiter poured quickly and then disappeared, closing the thick door firmly behind him.

"Father," began Gordon with all due obeisance, "gentlemen, I would most humbly present my findings on the potential opportunities in Zimbabwe."

Sparkly handed copies of the document to each man.

REPORT TO INVESTORS GROUP
31 November 2003

PURPOSE:

This analysis was undertaken at the request of a syndicate of potential investors, who will remain anonymous, in order to determine the feasibility of making investments in the nation of Zimbabwe, Africa.

FINDINGS:

In the last reported fiscal year, 2002, total trade between China and Zimbabwe was less than US$ 200 million. Based on the described policies of the current Zimbabwe Government, they desire liberalization of trade with China, and to see trade in excess of US$ 10 billion by 2012.

The population of Zimbabwe is generally very well-educated and skilled. Education has been high on the government's priorities for a long time, in spite of economic pressures placed on them by the west.

Western governments are concerned that Zimbabwe's desire for Chinese investment will result in a loss of their own leverage in Africa.

Zimbabwe government officials are of two types: those who wish to make as much for themselves and their families from more liberal trade with China, and those who truly want to see improvement in the economic condition of all Zimbabweans.

The personal wealth seekers in Zimbabwe hide their true intentions for the new policies behind the stated desire by western governments and NGOs for African nations to liberalize their laws so that the west will have access to increased direct investment.

The group, which wishes to attain personal wealth, is being countered by another group who fear the increase in Chinese enterprises in Zimbabwe. The pro-Zimbabwean group sees the evolving Chinese economic laws and policies as an opportunity not only for China to rape Zimbabwe, but for much of its wealth to be skimmed by certain members of the Zimbabwe government and regulators.

The pro-Zimbabwean group has also expressed concern that a rapid increase in Chinese investment will result in a delay in development within Africa. Members of this group may present a risk to businesses that do not operate legitimately.

Our nation's leadership obviously regards its African friends with generosity in response to their avoidance of the troubling diplomatic pressures for change in domestic policies.

Small-scale investors will be required to register their businesses, but once they are registered there will be little if any tracking of activities. These businesses should be able to enter more profitable activities without the oversight of regulatory authorities.

Opportunities for these small businesses will exist in various business centres, especially Harare and

Bulawayo, and there will be significant opportunities for the import of low-cost products for resale by street vendors.

RECOMMENDATIONS:

Investments should be made through specific vehicles that would be recognized as being part of large Chinese firms, preferably linked visibly to Government.

Investor vehicles that are branches of parent firms headquartered in China's provinces should be especially welcome.

There is likelihood that these large 'state-owned enterprises' will be exempted from the Indigenization and Empowerment Act. That will help us to maintain operational control.

It appears that all aspects of the mineral business will provide considerable opportunity to provide capital to the Zimbabwe government that will allow them to accelerate their social infrastructure, while providing long-term access to a lucrative market for the product in exchange.

Our first focus should be on platinum, followed by diamonds and, eventually on gold. Each of these requires upgrading of the infrastructure, improved access to markets and improved production techniques. All can be very profitable.

I suggest that in each enterprise we search out a limited number of small partners who possess a thorough awareness of and influence in the local political scene. I believe It will be advantageous to us to choose partners from the pro-Zimbabwean side, since they will reduce the risks caused by the public perception of corruption. Some members of the military and others close to government have indicated both the ability and the desire to participate and appear to meet these criteria.

Our success in Zimbabwe will depend, to a large degree, on success in developing enterprises for the benefit of both sides over the long term, rather than on the exploitation of opportunities with only short-term objectives.

The size of our investments should be sufficient to convince all that the investors have power and support. Individual large investments should be commitments in excess of US$ 1,0 million.

Zimbabweans should be selected for certain management positions and directorships in the large enterprises.

It would be wise for us to make a number of small investments in the reportable category.

Chic went on to say, "Zimbabwe is expected to produce only 45,000 carats of rough diamonds next year and may receive as much as US$200 per carat for their exports. I believe that with improved mining processes and security, recovery rates can improve dramatically. The engineers I spoke to suggest that the same volumes of earth can yield more than ten times the amount of marketable roughs."

Chic's report was met unanimously with doubt.

The elder Mr. Zhong asked, "How much money would be required to acquire ten percent of the production? The answer will need to include the costs of scaling up to the level you have described as possible."

"I would suggest that a commitment of US$100 million would be needed. The value of overall exports should increase from 45,000 carats to 450,000 carats. This is not to imply that the volume of production will increase that much but that the reported sales will increase. Depending on how things are managed, and when ownership of the diamonds actually changes, the reported value could drop as low as US$100 per carat. Our initial investment for ten percent would be less than US$ 10 million. We will likely have to structure a deal with a combination of preferred shares and various classes of shares of common shares in order to meet the local ownership requirements. We will have to accept some locals who are politically connected as well as some who are management oriented. There is another fellow who is active on the Stock Exchange, who also may be helpful as a representative on the management committee.

"We will need to establish links with cutters and polishers so that we can trade the stones in such a way as to remain competitive. There is a large gap between the per carat price of a rough stone and that of a polished stone. It is also important not to be over-taxed at any level until the final stones have been sold," Gordon continued.

"What I would like to achieve today, gentlemen, is your commitment to the funding of up to US$30 million, subject to my negotiating a suitable structure that will provide at least a thirty percent annual return. I expect the funds will be required over the following six months and they will be returned over the next five years," he concluded, looking around the table for signs of interest.

"I will commit to US$3 million, my son, and I will hold discussions with the others to determine their interest. Please proceed to negotiate an arrangement, prepare a structure, and have a report from the engineers on cost and timing. Also have our lawyers prepare contracts," the elder Mr. Zhong replied.

He looked at his son and said, "You and your assistant may leave now."

Chic bowed to his father and, feeling very small but somehow at the same time hopeful, he led Sparkly from the room.

JIM'S LAWYER - KELOWNA, APRIL 2014

In 2013, Jim had been approached by the law firm of Wilberson, Jonas & Sonneblom, located in Pretoria, South Africa, to conduct research into an unknown group operating out of Harare, Zimbabwe, that had been taking positions in various diamond mining opportunities arising from the indigenization legislation. Some had been creating joint ventures with Chinese-based firms, purporting to operate as representatives of the Government of China. Their firm's client was undisclosed. When asked why he was selected, Jim was told that their research showed that, over a number of years, he had done a great deal of trophy hunting in southern Africa. They expected that this would allow him to travel in and out of the countries relatively unnoticed. While they were not specifically aware of his CSIS background, they were aware that he had served with KPMG for a number of years, and then disappeared. A client of the firm in South America had commended his effectiveness in tracking "disappeared" funds. The combination made it worth the contact.

Jim had stayed fit in order to pursue his favourite sport - hunting. It was also a necessity in order to maintain the schedule of world travel he often encountered. He had married early in his career, but the marriage did not last. By the time he applied to CSIS, which was only a year after joining KPMG, the marriage was going downhill. It disintegrated one evening when his wife informed him that she was leaving. He never pursued another relationship. He dedicated his time to his hobby and to his profession.

PROSPER AND VERONICA -
HARARE - 21 APRIL 2014

"How is my baby doing?" Prosper asked, looking pleadingly at Veronica.

"All I want to know is if she is doing well and is happy."

Veronica looked at Prosper, feeling deeply sorry, but knowing that there was nothing she could say without risking everything.

"Prosper, you know the arrangement. That is why you came to us in the first place. You were convinced your husband was going to kill the baby once he had found it wasn't his. As I remember, you were also convinced he would kill you and that is why we had to do it. No one was willing to come for you once they knew you had been tainted by the witches. Just accept things and let's get back to business.

"What have you heard about the last diamond auction in Dubai?" Veronica asked.

"The sale went well, over US$25 million worth of diamonds were sold," Prosper started, "it appears that about ten percent of the stones were replaced before the auction and sold under the other company. That batch was bought back in a closed sale and shipped to Antwerp. They brought close to six hundred dollars per carat there, compared to the one hundred-eleven dollars at the Dubai auction. The skim would have brought the syndicate a net profit of ten million. Not bad for one auction."

"Do we know when they expect to try it again?" Veronica enquired earnestly.

"I think the next caper will occur with a shipment being waylaid in London. I am not sure how they plan to do it, but my boss met with an investment banker from London for about two hours one morning last week. I filed the notes from their meeting, but they were too cryptic to mean much to me. My sense is that a shipment of diamonds will be stored with the investment bank and used as security for a loan to the syndicate. This will allow the syndicate to increase the rate of their activities by buying stones from India and shipping those lesser stones to the auctions. This substantially increases the carats available to sell, allowing them to skim more carats of the finer stones for sale in Antwerp or Tel Aviv. They have excellent contacts in both places." Prosper reported.

"Excellent work, Prosper!" Veronica complimented, "You are a very fast learner. How is your relationship with your boss?"

"He tells me that I am the best girl he has ever had, then he asks me to come to his house when his wife is out of town, the bastard," she said with disdain.

"His day will come. How is the degree coming? I am so happy you are working on your MBA. How long until you are finished?"

"I should be finished next semester, Veronica, and I will be so glad to be finished. I am only sad that none of my family will watch me graduate."

"How is your new male friend?" Veronica asked with a smile.

"He is very sweet," she replied, "he is also very helpful and does not ask questions. Believe it or not, he also has a very good job." Prosper smiled.

"Well Prosper, you deserve to have a good life. Much better than you ever dreamed, and you do have friends. More than you know," Veronica assured.

"Here is your supplement, and thanks. We will meet here in four weeks, unless I contact you earlier."

"Thanks Veronica. Life is good. I am saving money and when we are all done, I shall buy my own house," she said enthusiastically, then added wistfully, "and perhaps even take a husband."

"*Bhai bhai, ona iwe manjemanje,*" Veronica bid her goodbye.

"*Bhai Bhai,*" replied Prosper as she left, silently thinking 'good luck on the husband part'.

MAMA PRUDENCE AND AKATENDEKA
- HARARE - APRIL 2014

"Mama, it is so good to see you again," the young lady smiled, throwing her arms around the ample Mama Prudence, "I have missed you so much, and I am so glad to be back in my own country."

"How did you like your visit to Hong Kong?" Mama asked.

"It was incredible! I have never seen so many people," Akatendeka crooned, "I even bought myself a ruby pendant. How do you like it?" she asked, lifting it out from under her blouse.

"Elegant, my little protégé, and what did you learn from my old friend there?" she enquired, switching to a new subject.

"Very little of particular current value, but I did receive some information that may have some value down the road," she offered proudly. "The young Chinaman was there meeting with some American lawyers. Apparently, his clients have become increasingly concerned about their investments in Zimbabwe. He is under some pressure to clean up his own business activities. I think we will be seeing him again very soon. I am sure when he comes to Harare, that he shall find me," and she broke out in an inadvertent smile.

"You be very, very cautious, young lady!" Mama scolded. "It is a very dangerous situation to find emotional attachment to someone who may be gone."

"Mama, he won't be gone. He will be bent until things are correct," she chuckled, with some uncertainty. "Then he will help our country to succeed fairly, with new investors. I know it, Mama. He really is a good man. Every time I have seen him, he has surprised me with kindness. It was everything I could do to avoid telling him that I was in Hong Kong." She smiled.

"Well Akatendeka, you must get ready to return to your real job and to pay attention to what your boss is doing. You must think about how you are going to describe your vacation to all of your friends, and your boss if he asks.

"Perhaps you can tell them that a crazy aunt insisted that you go shopping with her," Mama smiled.

"Are you still enjoying your job over there?" Mama asked with real concern.

"Yes," she responded, "I really enjoy it. I especially like the fact that my boss is honest and loves Zimbabwe as much as we do. I should get home and get ready for work tomorrow."

"Is your flat still suitable for you?" asked Mama Prudence, then added, "don't forget your supplement," as she slid a brown envelope discreetly across to Akatendeka, smiling with as much love as any proud mother could feel.

Akatendeka left feeling wanted and loved by her wonderful Mama. She was able to hail a taxi to take her to her home. She walked up two flights of stairs and then halfway down the hall to the entrance to her flat. She looked down the halls both ways before looking for a hair marker on the top of her door. She paused for a few more moments, and then quickly put the key in the lock. In one motion she entered the room and closed the door silently behind her. She secured the locks and quietly searched the remainder of the apartment, checking the windows for any disturbance, and then returned to the living room. Akatendeka listened to the phone for messages - there were none. She removed a small recorder from the back of the drawer under the phone and checked it for any sound-initiated recordings - none. She turned on the teakettle and then settled on the soft, enveloping couch.

Sitting comfortably in the quiet of the evening, Akatendeka reflected on her life. She had been working for the Ministry now for six years. She had begun when she was only twenty-one years old and totally inexperienced. She was now one of the three executive assistants to the 'Chief of

Administration of Recording for the District of Marange' and he appeared sincere in his appreciation of her efforts. She reflected upon the years of effort, the years of study, the difficulty of completing the last two years of her undergraduate degree while working full-time, the striving that had been required to complete the first year of her Master's Degree, in spite of having a sabbatical year from work. She had been able to complete the degree in one more year, working at it part-time.

Her work for Mama Prudence had been exquisitely exciting. It had all the attributes of espionage: intrigue, intellect, competition, and occasionally, thrill. She felt clear in her conscience, since she knew that the information she obtained and provided to Mama was being used in the fight to save her country, Zimbabwe. She had never yet been involved in deadly activity, but she was very well prepared, should the occasion arise. Akatendeka spent many hours each week concentrating on her fitness and maintaining her martial arts skills. She had achieved Roku Dan in Karate. She still went three evenings each week to her dojo on Rezende Street for an hour of training with her sensei.

Although in most of the world witches are perceived to be evil because of their known ability to wreak havoc or mayhem wherever they go, in Africa they are often viewed differently. Mama Prudence had told her early on that there were two separate components to her schooling.

The first part of her education entailed learning to affect or confuse those around her without permanent harm. That skill included the magic of witchcraft, which she needed to learn in order to remain invisible. Becoming invisible did not mean the same thing it did in children's stories, but rather it meant developing the ability to blend into any environment and to remain unnoticed. The means of achieving such invisibility was often very different during the day than it was at night. She learned the power of the story and how the combination of story and indicators can create reality. Historical narratives claimed that witches were able to use a hyæna to travel at night. It required only small seeds of evidence to allow perception to create a new reality. Some were said to possess snakes for evil use, again very powerful. Other witches could travel in baskets. They could enter people's dwellings without opening doors, as if they were the spirits of the dead. These well-known stories allowed for the acceptance of the reality of witches.

The second part of her training was better defined as learning the skills of an assassin. Akatendeka was taught to bring about death quickly and silently at close range. She had been taught to create potions from easy-to-find ingredients, preferably plants, insects, and occasionally, small animals. Sometimes common modern chemicals were used, but they were detected far too easily. It was preferable to use powders and poisons that could be effective but almost impossible to detect unless suspected. The concoctions could create the illusions she desired or, if required, make the mind of a target pliable more quickly. She learned how to use delayed potions or poisons to deliver acceptable symptoms such as heart attacks or severe asthmatic attacks. She also learned how to create false death - the convincing appearance of death, from which the victim could recover on his or her own or by use of another potion. In that case the person applying the potion would be believed to have brought the victim back to life. She learned other means of delivering poisons without touching her victim. She was now capable of using whichever methods best fit the attributes of the target and the nature of the mission.

She became an expert in the use of the short knife, the garrote and her own hands. Her constant study with Mama Prudence of the skills of witchcraft had allowed her to become proficient at deception and death - Akatendeka was now superhuman!

MR. MACINTYRE CONTACTS MR. SONNEBLOM - APRIL 21, 2014 - 22:00 PACIFIC TIME

It was a brisk morning in Pretoria. The sun was just rising as Mr. Sonneblom climbed into the rear seat of the car. Two powerful-looking men sat in the front seats. Another one had climbed out of the back to open the rear passenger door. He had known all three for a number of years. They were all happy to own homes, have wives and families, and they appreciated the respect that Mr. Sonneblom had always shown them. The young, shapely woman on the television set had informed him that the temperature in Pretoria was plus eleven Celsius, with clear skies. Now that he had left the house, he could confirm it with his own senses. The humidity had dropped from yesterday and it promised to warm to a balmy twenty degrees by the time of his scheduled golf game that afternoon. It was a pleasant drive west from the east end of Edward Street to connect to the M9 through the old streets and then onto the M11, travelling farther west until reaching the downtown and the base of the office tower at the corner of Pretorius Street and Van Der Walt Street. The wide streets were lined with Jacaranda trees, which were gathering strength to burst forth with purple blossoms in October.

That convenience was part of the reason Daniel Sonneblom had decided to buy in Waterkloof twenty-three years ago. It was a mature subdivision from the mid-1900s, with lots of Jacaranda trees and lovely homes. The most suitable Pretoria Country Club was located literally next-door. Most of the street names in the area were in recognition of British royalty. This gave the development a serious cachet inherited from the British Empire.

Although this was of no particular interest to Daniel, it did please his British clientele. From his house on the hilltop, Daniel had a gorgeous view of the city and a genuine sense of achievement.

Once the black Mercedes entered the parkade and arrived at its designated stall, the embarkation pattern reversed. The man in the front passenger seat jumped out and opened the door for Mr. Sonneblom. By the time his feet landed on the pavement the second man had come around the rear of the car to accompany the two to the elevator while the driver remained in the vehicle.

Mr. Sonneblom arrived on the sixth floor and the elevator opened to the expanse of the reception area. The tall, thin, muscular, blonde man at the reception desk stood when Mr. Sonneblom arrived.

"Good Morning, sir," he offered pleasantly, but with the air of a corporal who really wished to become a sergeant. "Is there anything I can do for you this morning?"

"Good Morning, Pieter," the polite and affable response came, "not at the present, thank you very much."

The two men from the Mercedes disappeared down the hallway to the right. Mr. Sonneblom went to the left. Before reaching his own assistant's desk, he passed by the desks of two intense women who were engrossed in their tasks.

"Good morning, Abigail," he asked, "anything urgent?"

"There was a message left early this morning from Canada. It sounded as though it requires immediate attention. Shall I get Scottie on the line?" she asked.

"Please, and make sure it is a secure line." Daniel walked into his office and closed the door.

Moments later, the phone rang. "Mr. Sonneblom, I have Mr. MacIntyre on the line," came the voice through the receiver.

"Thank you, Abigail," and he clicked the button, "Hello Scottie, what time is it there?"

"Hi, Daniel, it's 22:00 here. I have some important news for you, if you don't mind me getting right to the point," Scottie responded.

"Please proceed Scottie, we are on a secure line," responded Daniel.

"The accountant is dead. He was killed on Friday night. I didn't hear about it until Monday and called as soon as I thought you'd be in," said Scottie.

"How did it happen?" asked a shocked Daniel Sonneblom. "Was it to do with our activities?"

"I don't yet know if there is a connection, but I can tell you a few things," replied Scottie.

"They have a man in jail but not yet charged with murder. There were some strange things related to the body and the way he died, as well. They might mean something to you," he continued.

"Describe what you know Scott. I'll let you know if it fits with anything."

"He was gutted. Whoever did it slit him up the middle and extracted the liver and the heart. They have found no sign of anything else. There was no sign of struggle. The security system showed only one person coming and going. It was the fellow they are holding. The cleaning lady came in Saturday to do her regular cleaning, I suppose, and she found him dead in bed. There may be more but that is all I have been able to find out so far," Scottie concluded, wondering what the hell had really happened.

"Sounds awful Scott! Was there anything else? Was he holding any of our papers? When was his last report filed with you? Did he ever tell you he was being shadowed or anything unusual?" Daniel enquired.

"Nothing at present. The guy in jail has a lawyer already. If you think it appropriate, I will try to slip in and get him under our care. That should help me learn more about him and his involvement with the accountant, if any."

"Scottie, do what you can do. Keep me informed. I'll ask some questions around here. I have another contact I will ask to do some checking on the guy in jail. Be in touch, stay secure. Ok." Daniel hung up the phone and stepped into the corridor.

Could you see if you can track down Mama Prudence for me, please, Abigail?"

MAMA GOES TO PRETORIA TO MEET WITH MR. SONNEBLOM

Just before noon on the 18th of April, a young barefoot boy arrived at the door of Mama Prudence's thatch-roofed, ochre-painted rondavel on the outskirts of Harare. He was smiling, even though he was out of breath. Mama was always generous with the food. He scratched on the wall beside the closed door. The door opened and Mama Prudence planted her feet at the entrance.

"What can I do for you today my little, underfed, young boy?" she smiled and laughed at the same time, then handed him a piece of cake. Come on in and have some special tea," she laughed again, her happy, there-are-no-problems laugh.

The young boy stepped in and wondered whether it was as important to get some tea and another piece of cake as it was to deliver the urgent message. The tea and cake won out. He sat down quickly and looked up at Mama with his big smiling, pleading eyes. She reciprocated with another big piece of cake and a glass of chilled tea. He gradually recovered his breath and remembered the purpose of the run.

"Mama Prudence," he gasped, then took another gulp of tea, "Mama Prudence, the man at the gas station," he took another gulp of tea, "he said a man called and you must go to Petory and fast now." He caught his breath then continued, "Mr. S. he sayed."

"Why thank you. Would you like a ride back to the gas station with me?" she asked him, "perhaps there is time for one more piece of cake while I get ready, then you go down the street and find a driver, Ok?"

"Yes ma'am, one more piece," he replied, staring at the unfinished cake.

Mama Prudence went to work packing a small travel bag, her passport and her wallet. She changed her dress and shoes before rewrapping her hair in a new red turban. As soon as the car arrived, Mama reappeared on the stoop. She laughed her boisterous laugh and climbed into the passenger seat of the little Toyota. The boy climbed into the back seat. She gave the instructions and then turned to the boy with a handful of change, which she poured into his hand. The boy's eyes got bigger as the weight of the coins grew. He could tell that they were Euro cents. He was stunned, once again, by the munificence of this lady. She must be some kind of princess or something, he thought to himself.

Mama Prudence hoped to catch the British Airways flight from Harare to Johannesburg at 2:35. She thought to herself, 'This will put me into OR Tambo by 4:15. I'll clear Immigration and Customs and get up to the second floor by the KFC in time to catch the Gauteng High Speed to Marlboro Station. I'll get there by 5:00 and then catch the northbound to arrive in downtown Pretoria by 5:40. I'll phone from the airport to let Danny know I comin' and he'll send the car to get me. Goodness, Danny would send a limo to bring me from Joburg, that foolish boy. Why waste money?'

Her plan was a success and she climbed into the black Mercedes at precisely 5:50 and headed toward the offices of Wilberson, Jonas & Sonneblom in downtown Pretoria.

On the way into town, Mama placed two telephone calls. The first call was to Veronica at her office.

"Good afternoon, is there anything you can tell me? I am travelling today," Mama asked curtly.

"No ma'am," Veronica answered, "call later."

That meant that Victoria had something to share and that Mama should call her at her special cell phone number at eight in the evening for a report.

Mama dialed Prosper's number.

"Hello," answered Prosper, "how may I help you?"

"Anything?" Mama asked.

"Nothing at all, I'll talk to you at eight," she said, "bye for now."

Prosper would be available for a phone call at nine o'clock. All was arranged.

Although the workday was officially over, the office was busy when she arrived. She swung off the elevator, dressed brightly, boldly drawing attention to her size and making it beautiful. The bounce in her step, the smiling eyes and the appealing voice made her a friend of all. She marched boldly into the waiting room. The receptionist greeted her with great joy, his weariness totally erased by Mama's vivaciousness. It was only a moment until Mr. Sonneblom appeared, smiled and invited her into his office. Abigail asked Mama and Mr. Sonneblom if they wished tea or coffee.

"Some strong tea for me," laughed Mama, then looked at her watch and said, "a stiff scotch for Danny."

Mr. Sonneblom chuckled as he led her to a conference room at the end of the hallway. They spent a short time on the pleasantries. No matter how urgent the discussion was going to be, Daniel had learned not to press Mama. The drinks arrived and she began regaling Daniel with stories of her journey, about the poor condition of the car that drove her to the airport in Harare, how efficient she thought British Airways staff was to get her on the flight at the last minute, how pretty the blue seats were on the new train and how fast it was. She also couldn't resist adding how much less expensive it was than the limo, but she made certain to thank Danny for sending his car to pick her up. It appeared that Mama was going to stop to take a breath, but before Daniel could begin, she stared at him and asked,

"Daniel, what is this all about?"

"Mama, we have a problem," he started, "the accountant was killed on Friday night." Daniel waited for a response. Mama just looked up with a resolute expression and closed her eyes.

"I am very sorry for you, Daniel. I know he was a friend," she reached for Daniel's hand and sat silently for a minute. "Daniel, tell me what you know."

He repeated the story as he had heard it from Scottie.

"What really puzzles me is how they tracked him down," he added.

"Daniel, tell me again how they found the body," Mama requested.

"From the bit I got from Scottie," he responded, "someone sliced him open and took his liver and his heart. There was no sign of struggle,"

"Daniel, it was done by a witch," Mama stated, "an African witch."

How indeed, she wondered. How would they have found out who the accountant was? Who might have gone to do it? Mama Prudence was mulling the same questions that bewildered Daniel.

"OK, Daniel, what should we be doing about it? What can we do from here?" Mama questioned.

"Do we have someone who can replace the accountant?" Mama asked.

"Not yet, but I have a few ideas," he replied, as if something else was on his mind. "You said a witch. What do you mean?"

"There are some witches in our country who have learned the technique of killing like that. There are some reasons for it. Unfortunately, there are also reasons that other people try to copy the technique. Murder by witch-craft elicits minimum investigation here in Africa. It would also be very distracting there in Canada. Remember a few years ago *Oom* Jacobus lost some cattle and two of his security men in a similar way? We have been waiting ever since to see if it was a single event or the start of something. It seems as if they somehow have linked into the accountant's activities. Let's hope they have not linked him to us," she said thoughtfully, "we had better be prepared to deal with it this time."

"Mama, we do not retaliate. This will all be accomplished without violence," Daniel emphasized.

"I understand the rules, Daniel. I am not talking about aggression or retaliation, I am talking about defending our ability to continue," explained Mama, "we need to know who is giving the orders. Did Filson, MacIntyre and Pogue get the last report from the accountant?" Mama asked.

"According to Scott, he delivered his latest report the day before he was killed," Daniel answered, "I wonder if they thought the fellow who was picked up by the police was a courier? Scottie thinks one of the guys in the cell with the accused killer might have been there to follow and retrieve."

"If that's the case Daniel, we must get someone over there and do it quickly. I will do what I can from my end to see if anyone knows who travelled such a long distance. Are you going to talk to Oom Jacobus?" Mama suggested.

"Mama, do you want to stay up at the house tonight?" Daniel asked.

"No, Daniel," she replied, "too many friends to visit here and too little time. Most of them live quite a way from your house," she replied with a smile.

"I will be here in the morning. See you then." She stood up and left the room, saying her goodbyes to the remaining souls as she let herself out of the office.

Mama Prudence left through the parkade and emerged into an alley, shapeshifting as she did. She walked hunched over. Her walk shrank from the strong upright stride, full of enthusiasm, into a bit of a shuffle, her body rolling a bit as if swinging her weight from side to side allowed her to move her feet forward more easily. She evaporated into the crowd, looking like a tired cleaning lady shuffling on her way to catch a bus to take her as close to home as possible. Mama was now invisible, even to those who knew her well.

It had always impressed Mama how much information Daniel could acquire from places he had never been. She had watched him grow up. Daniel's mother died when he was a child and his father had engaged Mama Prudence as an *au pair*. The family had lived in Rhodesia at the time. When Daniel left home for university, Mama left the employ of his father and, with his kind gift, she was able to build the home she had always dreamed of on the outskirts of Harare. She knew that Daniel had been born in Cape Town and moved to Salisbury with his father before the city had changed its name back to Harare. Daniel had gone on to complete his law degree at Witwatersrand. After completing his education, he joined the military for his compulsory service in South Africa, then spent six years living in England. Those were times he never spoke of. When he returned to South Africa, he joined the law firm of Wilberson & Jonas. His clients were primarily international. While he was still a junior partner of the law firm, and with the full consent of the partnership, Daniel had started Springbok Security S.A. As far as Mama remembered the company hired men who had no names and who travelled a great deal.

Daniel had explained to her how he was approached by a few Brits he had met and they asked if he would be prepared to merge his firm, Springbok Security S.A., with theirs and become a partner, and oh, by the way, move back to Harare and run the operations based there. That had occurred in 1997 and the merged firm became Furiæ Services South Africa. He made an arrangement with his partners in the law firm to establish and manage a branch of the firm in Harare and he ran both companies from the same floor of offices downtown. Daniel Sonneblom was deadly, but more importantly, he knew enough deadly men to start his own army, and in fact he had started a few. Furiæ Services was very busy during the Iraq invasion and even busier after. Daniel still retained his home in Pretoria, South Africa. He was well aware of how fast the winds can change on the African continent.

Mama was now more than a mile from downtown and she stood at a bus stop near an expensive neighbourhood, waiting. She blended well with the crowd and soon boarded a bus that would take her to her destination for the night. All she carried was her small bag and her walking stick.

Daniel left the office about thirty minutes after Mama Prudence. His driver and assistants always changed shifts at midday in an effort to ensure that they were always sharp and alert. As he sat in the back seat of the Mercedes sedan, he relaxed his shoulders and sank into the comfort and security. He let his eyelids close and reflected on the news. He thought about Mama. Daniel had always kept in touch with Mama. He had worked invisibly to ensure she had a decent income. She was too proud to take charity. Then there was the day that Mama came to his office with some news. He was being targeted. It was then that she had informed him that she was a witch. She offered to stop the hit from happening. He was puzzled at first, but she was very convincing. He was going to have all his own security in place in any event, so he saw no additional risk. He would also have sent his own men on the hunt starting the next morning.

"Mama," he had said, "I don't want you to put yourself at risk. I will look after it."

"Daniel," she had responded quickly, "you are so clever for a young man, but until I told you tonight, you didn't even know you were being targeted.

"I shall deal with it my way, Daniel. I will then tell you what happened," she concluded, as she had turned and left his office.

He remembered it like it had been only yesterday. She had arrived at his office the following day, just before lunch. She had worn a somber look on her face and had been wearing a very dull outfit. She lacked her normal smile; it had been replaced by a look of firm resolve.

"Sit, Daniel," she had said, as if he was still six, "your problems are not over."

She continued, "Your life is still at risk. The current problem is neutralized. The perpetrator passed away during the night of a heart attack, consistent with his family history of cardio disease. This morning another man, a friend of the dead man and a known hitman, succumbed to his injuries from a serious automobile accident. He ran into a tree after he left the road travelling at high speed. The senior man was on the wrong side of an operation you had conducted in northern Zimbabwe about one year ago." She added, "Even you, Daniel, need to have a way of watching your blind spot."

It was then that Daniel had recognized the abilities of his former nanny. Over lunch they had come to an agreement that would last a lifetime. He was never sorry for arranging that relationship—it was not only deniable but also unbelievable.

Coming back to the present situation, Daniel realized that it was time to assign some assets to neutralize the killers, if practical. Killing for any reason had been expressly prohibited by the client. He would have to speak to Uncle Jacobus. Daniel shared that with Mama. She had said if he needed her help, it would be there.

MR. SONNENBLOM CONTACTS MR. JACOBUS

Daniel was planning to be in Victoria Falls on Wednesday to meet with one of the firm's clients. He had a message delivered to *Oom* Jacobus by the secretary of the manager of the Victoria Falls Hotel letting him know that his reservation for Wednesday night was now confirmed. Uncle Jacobus received the message and the rest was understood. He placed a call to the receptionist thanking her and she in turn called the offices of Wilberson, Jonas & Sonneblom to confirm Mr. Daniel Sonneblom's reservation for the same night, as well as his dinner reservation at Livingstone's.

Daniel disembarked the Chinese built Air Zimbabwe MA60 aircraft at the Victoria Falls Airport, after a brief stopover at Lake Kariba. He hailed a cab for the hotel and arrived feeling refreshed and in time for a late lunch. He had once wondered about flying on an aircraft that even Robert Mugabe refused to fly on but decided that since the engines were the Pratt and Whitney 127J Turboprops made in Canada, he could afford the risk.

After a light lunch on the hotel terrace, looking out over the mist of the falls and watching the warthogs snuffling along the lawn with their babies trailing behind, tails held high, Daniel went to the registration desk and collected his key. He went to his room to prepare his thoughts for the meeting with Jacobus, which would occur later in the afternoon, as soon as Jacobus arrived. Daniel laid back on the bed and fell into a light sleep.

He was awakened suddenly by the faint sound of a footstep. Someone was trying the door to his room. He was on his feet and silently moved to the back of the door. There was no sound for a few seconds, then came a light knock, as if to test the presence of someone in the room. He waited.

This knock was followed by a series of loud knocks and the unmistakable voice of *Oom* Jacobus.

"*Daniel, maak asseblief die deur oop,*" followed by another pause, then, "Open the damned door!"

Daniel opened the door, laughing.

"Jacobus, sorry I couldn't understand your knock in Afrikaans," Daniel chided. "Good to see you friend, *hoe gaan dit met jou?*" He gave Jacobus a big bear hug and with the swing of an arm beckoned him to sit.

"Have you checked in yet?" he asked.

"Ya, I'm checked in and fed and ready to go," the strong-handed farmer said, as he sat down.

"Jacobus, we have lost the accountant in Canada. He was murdered." Daniel let the message sink into Jacobus' mind.

"Was it related to our work?" Jacobus asked solemnly.

"We believe it was," Daniel replied, "he died like those security men of yours did a few years ago, eviscerated."

"*O my God*, remind me Daniel, did he have a family, any children?" whispered Jacobus.

"His family broke up many years ago, Jacobus, and he had no children that we are aware of," explained Daniel.

"Very bad," commented Jacobus.

Oom Jacobus sank back into his chair and closed his eyes. He was a man who knew how to fight, and he had fought physically, close-up and personal, during the Rhodesian Bush War. He had served with the Rhodesian Special Air Force in what he thought was an effort to save the country he loved. Once confederation had disintegrated in 1963, The Special Air Force had difficulty recruiting. In 1974, Jacobus joined ZANLA, the military arm of Robert Mugabe's ZANU, and trained to fight against the insurgents. He had fought alongside the SAS and the RLI at various times including Operation Dingo. The Chimoio Massacre of November 1977, also called Op Dingo, was considered a bloody success by the government. Jacobus did not agree with that assessment. More than 3,000 ZANLA fighters were killed and 5,000 were wounded. It was shortly after that, that Jacobus submitted his request for release, which was finally granted in 1979; about the time of the move to the new Kabrit barracks. It was the excessive bloodshed and violence that convinced Jacobus to end his career as a soldier and to participate as an amateur diplomat in the search for peace and the preservation of his nation.

"Jacobus," continued Daniel, "we must do something to neutralize the person who killed the accountant. We may have to go wet."

"No, No," Jacobus stated, "we may track down who it was, but then we must turn him over to the Canadian authorities." Then, after some consideration he added, "You might prepare to go wet if necessary."

Daniel admired Jacobus's commitment to avoid killing unless absolutely necessary.

"Jacobus," began Daniel, "I know a fellow in Canada, who lives in the same area as the accountant. We could see if he is interested in trying to find the killer. We could also follow up with the suspect in custody to ascertain if he would like to carry on the accountant's work. Scottie's initial appraisal was that he is not the killer and that he is certainly capable of taking over. Scottie would need to read him in and bring him up to date. What are your thoughts?"

"Let us try to avoid having anyone killed, Daniel," Jacobus replied sadly, "we have both seen too many dead. At some point we must have a country based upon respect and common effort and not on not our neighbour's blood. Tell me a bit about the first man and how you see him helping."

Daniel began, "He is Canadian, served in the JTF2. After that he worked for a security group for a while. It appears he was acquainted with our accountant. They worked together on a few situations in the past. This man still does occasional jobs between stints in the oil patch. He is a directional driller, so he is called out for jobs around the world, which provides a great cover. Without being too specific, I spoke to him to see what his interest would be. He was quite open."

"He sounds like the kind we like to use - far enough from home to make tracking very difficult and to diminish any sense of threat that someone local stimulates," said Jacobus, sounding somewhat resigned.

"Will you and your committee want to interview him before we make him an offer?" asked Daniel.

Jacobus replied, "Do you think we could count on Scottie's assessment? We could meet him when he comes over. I think we need to move with dispatch to find who is behind this. It appears that whoever it is may stand out more in Canada, if they are still there. It may be better for our man to remain there to find them than to bring him over here to try to find them."

"I'll get ahold of Scottie and see what he thinks. If he wants to go with the guy, I assume I can tell him standard rates apply. He may also need an assistant for some of the forensic work, but we will come back with a plan as soon as possible. Would you accept Scottie doing the background check on the guy in jail, if needed?" Daniel suggested. Daniel updated Jacobus on the plans for the next diamond auction and the activities of the investment bank in London, and then informed him of the theft from the last sale.

"Thank you," Jacobus said, "How about you do the back check and get Scottie to check out his forensic accounting credentials?"

TATTOO PHONES ME – 24 APRIL 2014

The phone began its grating, grinding ring at the same time I woke groggily on Tuesday morning.

"Hullo," I answered, as I swung my body into a sitting position, "who is it?"

The answer came without a name. "We'll meet in two hours at the coffee shop in the Orchard Park Mall."

I gave my brain a moment to process this command. That was the code for us to meet at a campsite south of Kelowna. Two hours meant nine in the morning.

"OK," I responded automatically.

I had to get a move on. I dressed and grabbed a banana as I passed through the kitchen. There was no time to shower or shave. I climbed into my car and headed north. As I approached the exit for the campground, I signaled, slowed and pulled off the highway. I drove down the winding road toward Okanagan Lake until I found campsite forty-one. There was no one there. I was six minutes early, so I waited. After fifteen minutes, I climbed out of my car and scanned the whole area, but saw nothing. I climbed back in and waited some more, wondering if I had screwed up the codes. After almost forty minutes, I heard a tap on the window of my car. I was startled when I turned and recognized Tattoo. I unlocked the door.

"Where the hell did you come from? I have been watching the two roads since I arrived and never saw any traffic."

"Don't worry about that for now," Tattoo was more abrupt than usual, "I have heard that the charges against you are about to be reinstated and upgraded to murder."

"How can they do that?" I asked, "Where is the evidence against me?"

"I don't know if you remember what you did with your scotch glass when you left Jim's, but it seems that the one sitting on his bedside table had your fingerprints, as well as Jim's, on it," replied Tattoo matter-of-factly.

"Not only did it have your fingerprints, but it contained the residue of a chemical that can induce an instant deep sleep - sometimes the ultimate deep sleep. The autopsy has indicated that this poison likely caused paralysis, which allowed the surgical extraction to occur without much resistance. The carving occurred after Jim consumed the poison," Tattoo explained.

"What kind of poison was it?" I asked foolishly.

"I gather the coroner thinks it was *Conium maculatum,* along with some other plant materials. You've probably heard it called Poison Hemlock," he explained, "killed Socrates."

"I'll never get my damn passport back," I replied.

"What is that going to mean to my bail?"

"You'll have to wait until your lawyer is given the word, then you can have that discussion with him," he answered, "but you have bigger fish to fry! Someone believes you received some papers from Jim before he was killed. Whoever it is, they want the papers and now, apparently, they are authorized to take you out to get them. They won't do it until they have tried everything to get the information from you. If they are convinced that you don't have anything, they are likely to dispose of you."

"Crap! What do you suggest I do?" I asked earnestly. "I have never been a target before," I added. I was beginning to understand the magnitude of my predicament.

"We are far from having you prepared. Nobody can protect you all the time. It would take a forty-man team just to watch you twenty-four-seven. The choices are: get you out of town, put you back in jail, or remove the hunter. Those are the three options we are going to talk about this morning."

It suddenly dawned on me. Tattoo was not paying all this attention to my welfare as a hobby. I was hardly the best friend in his life. I wasn't the godfather of his kid. Why was he doing this, I wondered? Was it possible that he is the hunter? He ended up in jail with me; that could have been coincidence. He seems to have taken over leading my life -kindness or coincidence? He seems to know an awful lot about what is happening – just circumstance or...? I've got to think this through.

It was about ten-forty-five when Tattoo and I finished our discussion. Actually, it was Tattoo talking while I was thinking, listening and wondering...then he was gone. I was to wait fifteen minutes and drive into another camp spot, sit for five minutes and then leave, taking an indirect route to my home. Tattoo had given me certain maneuvers to use as I drove so that I might be able to spot a tail. If I spotted anything suspicious, I was to drive straight back to the Kelowna RCMP detachment.

As I drove toward the second camping spot, I spotted a pale blue SUV through the trees. It appeared to be sitting with the engine idling. Cold shivers went through me. I continued to the spot and backed my car in in such a way as to keep sight on the SUV as much as possible. Only ten seconds to go according to my watch. I looked in the rear-view mirror. The SUV was gone. I looked around and couldn't see it anywhere. I waited five minutes more, but still no sight of the SUV. I started to drive from the camp spot, my heart racing. My eyes darted from side to side. The back of my shirt was soaked with perspiration. I stopped at the entrance to the highway and looked again. I could not see any sign of the SUV, so I accelerated my car, joined the traffic and began the circuitous route to my home. As I drove, I thought, 'Should I be going home? Is it a trap?'

I VISIT SCOTT MACINTYRE'S OFFICE – 24 APRIL 2014

t was lunchtime by the time I reached home. I was afraid to enter my own house. Tattoo's warning still rang in my ears, "If they are convinced that you have nothing, they are likely to dispose of you."

How could I have known that all of this mystery could have been the outcome of a few interesting stories and a few glasses of great scotch? How had this world found me? I took hold of the door handle with trepidation, and carefully attempted to open it. It was still locked. As quietly as I could I inserted the key and turned it, pressing gently while turning the handle, as I had seen done in some movie. The door opened. Cautiously, I walked through the remnants of my previous marriage, peering everywhere for signs of anything out of the ordinary, listening with sharpened ears.

"I should have given her the damned house!" I thought.

I guess there are lots of things I should have done differently, and perhaps now I wouldn't be in this surreal situation, fearing for my life. I sat on my favorite chair, or perhaps I collapsed into it. I could have kept this chair, even if I had given her the house. My mind was full of strange feelings and stranger thoughts. It had been an exhausting morning and I hadn't expended a calorie.

'Who is on my side?' I wondered. 'Tattoo? MacIntyre? Who is after me? Whom have I seen who wants me dead? Do they actually mean dead or just moved out of the way or sent somewhere? No, I think they mean dead, unless they get the papers they want. How could I get them some papers? I could take some from Scott's office, maybe, and thicken them up with some of my own. How would they take them from me? Would they kill me anyway? Leave no trail, leave no evidence, and leave no witness. What good would all that do if I couldn't prove my innocence and I spent the rest of my life in jail for not killing Jim? I would have my best allies against me. Not a great idea! There must be some way to find the killer and get me cleared. It must be soon. I must talk to Scott MacIntyre.'

"Filson, MacIntyre and Pogue, good afternoon" the Miss Moneypenny voice answered in her kind motherly way.

It seemed like I was tongue-tied, "Scott MacIntyre, please."

"May I say who is calling?" she asked.

"Just tell him it is the friend of..." I couldn't remember Tattoo's name. I felt foolish.

"I am a friend of Will Turner," I finally remembered.

"One moment please." She put me on hold and a moment later Scott MacIntyre's voice greeted me.

"Where are you?" I was shocked by the urgency in his voice.

"Why?" I asked.

"I need to speak to you," he replied, "can you come to my office? Now?"

"I'll be there within an hour. See you then." I confirmed, not feeling particularly at ease. I went to my bedroom and changed into my 'visiting the lawyer' clothes, and then headed to his office, trying to remember all of Tattoo's instructions. As I pulled out onto my quiet residential street, I noticed a blue SUV parked in front of a house four doors west. Was it the same car? I paused and tried to remember. There didn't appear to be anyone in the vehicle, and it wasn't running.

"What kind of car does this neighbour have?" I asked myself, feeling somewhat stupid. What kind of cars do any of my neighbours have? I drove onto the street and headed for Highway 27A. There were blue SUVs, grey SUVs, and white SUVs everywhere. Was I right about the colour? Suddenly there was a car stopped right in front of me. It was a dark blue Mercedes GL 350. I jammed on my brakes, screeching to a stop just in time to avoid colliding with it.

"Stay focused!" I warned myself, "many klicks to go today."

I felt the presence of danger all around me. I could smell the odour of impending disaster. The route I had planned to take involved a circular maneuver. I turned right as soon as I was in Westbank and pulled into the gas station. I paused, looked around and left, going west. I stopped by the side of the road and watched. Nothing. I drove off again as if heading south, turned left, then turned left again to put myself back on the highway. Still nothing. I drove carefully at the speed limit until I was past the entrance to the shopping centre where Scott's office tower was located. I found a parking stall along the street and pulled in. I got out of my car and put a Toonie in the meter. Again, I looked around. People watching me must have thought they were watching a paranoid patient trying to find his psychiatrist's office. I moved in the direction of the tower, stopping to look in the window of a store, as if I was shopping. That was one thing I remembered. I stepped back then noticed I was shopping in the window of a Chinese Restaurant. I continued on until reaching the entrance to the building. I walked a few steps past it and quickly returned to enter. I was sweating abnormally. I walked quickly to the elevator, stepped in and was about to take a deep breath when I noticed another man standing there looking at me. I just stared back at him.

"Are you going to pick a floor or are you riding to the top with me?" He asked with a polite smile.

As I exited the elevator cab at Scott's floor, an overwhelming sense of safety came over me. I had made it! I stepped up to the receptionist and was acknowledged by a nod of her head and the one-finger signal that implied that she would be finished her call momentarily. Wandering toward the seating area, I wondered if I was losing it. Was I becoming paranoid? My reverie was broken by the voice of Scott MacIntyre.

"Come with me, please," spoken as if I were a homeless person he wished to remove from the sight of his more sophisticated clients. I followed him to the meeting room in the back.

He motioned to a seat, which I promptly took.

"We have a problem," he began, and then continued with barely a pause, "you are going to be charged formally for murder in the first degree under section 231, sub 2 of the Criminal Code of Canada."

I was always amazed at how lawyers started with 'we have a problem'. I have a problem; they have more income tax to pay; that is their problem. My problem is that I go to jail for life! No income tax problem.

He stopped and looked at me as if to gauge my reaction. I had none. I didn't know what to say. I sat looking back at him with what must have been the look of someone incapable of comprehending something of such magnitude, which I was. Thoughts raced through my head but none sensible enough to be spoken. I had been expecting this but really never expecting it.

"The prosecutor has asked me if you are willing to attend at his office this afternoon at three," he spoke to unhearing ears, "or he could send a car to pick you up. Your choice."

"I suppose I should go," I almost asked Scott, "then what?"

"I will attend with you and if we are fortunate, we will be able to establish bail requirements before the day is over. You will need to spend another evening in the remand cells while the details of the bail are finalized. Are you OK with that?" he asked, as if to relieve me of some concern.

"Do I have a choice?" I asked foolishly.

"Only which car you ride in," Scottie answered. "We can drop your car off at your home and we will go together to the prosecutor or you can drive yourself and I can meet you there."

"Let me go home and change, then I will go with you, if that's Ok." I spoke as if from a dream state.

"Fine," Scottie replied looking up at me, "are you ready to go or do you have other questions before we leave?"

"No, fine, let's go. Do you know where I live?

"Yes," he replied, "but I'll follow you."

Before we left the office of Filson, MacIntyre and Pogue, Scott and I discussed the route home. He suggested that if I was being followed by a car or if I saw him blinking his lights, I should pull into the next gas station and wait until he approached my car before getting out. Once I reached my house and could see him park down the street, I would park my car in the garage, go in, change clothes, pack my toothbrush and then walk out toward the street. Once I left the house, he would begin driving up the street and I would immediately climb into his SUV. He asked if I understood.

"What kind of car do you drive?" I remembered to ask.

"A white Lexus SUV, although it's pretty dirty today," he replied, "You just drive directly to Highway 97 and turn right. When I have you in sight I will blink once. I will do it a couple of times, then you should accelerate into the middle lane. Drive normally and carefully. I'll see you at your house."

I walked out to my car feeling like I was living in a different dimension, a fictional dimension that I had seen only in movies or on television. I climbed into my car and wormed my way around to 97 and turned right, as instructed. As soon as I was settled in the HOV lane I saw the flash of the headlights, so I accelerated into the next lane. The white SUV followed.

'All's well,' I thought to myself.

The drive was uneventful. I pulled into the driveway, then into the garage. Everything seemed to be as normal as it usually was. I headed into my room and changed. I then pulled a couple of shirts, shorts and socks from the dresser, dashed into the bathroom to grab my shaving kit, and tossed it all into an old briefcase and headed for the front door, leaving behind a mess.

I saw the white SUV parked six cars down on the opposite side of the street. I walked absentmindedly toward the street. I reached the sidewalk and as I turned to look for Scott's car, I heard the roar of a powerful engine and the chirping of tires as a blue vehicle screamed around the corner and headed straight toward me. Everything faded to black.

"Can you hear me?" a faint voice asked. I tried to open my eyes to see who it was. All my eyes could sense was the sterile glare of intense light flashing over me.

Where was I? I tried to move but couldn't. I tried to see but nothing made sense. I tried to remember but only a windshield and the colour blue came into my mind's eye.

SCOTTIE VISITS TATTOO – 24 APRIL 2014

Will Turner was sitting on his deck when he glanced up to view the beautiful view of the lake, contemplating whether Machiavelli was right in saying "Men are driven by two principal impulses, either by love or by fear." He had been enjoying "Discourses on Livy" when he thought he heard the sound of a vehicle. Rising quickly, he stepped back inside through the sliding door, and pulled the drapes closed. No one had been invited up today and no one had said they were coming. He needed to determine who it was. He stepped back into the room and tapped the front of a small stand. A shelf dropped and he lifted a 1911 Colt .45, which he tucked into his belt at the small of his back. He returned to the window. The vehicle was proceeding up his driveway. He closed the living room door, locked it, and then went to the front door and watched. A dirty white Lexus pulled up in front. It looked like Scottie. Tattoo slipped a sport jacket over his strong shoulders and then stepped out to greet him. Following Tattoo, fully alert but quiet, was his large Alsatian, Zeus. The dog was well-trained and required no command other than "take him."

"Scottie! What brings you up here without a phone call?"

"Let's go to your den and have a scotch," Scottie replied without hesitation, but in a quiet voice. He looked down at Zeus and thought, 'wouldn't want to piss him off.'

Tattoo led him into the house and through the door of the library, then through another door and into the den. Zeus took his position at the front of the door into the den and laid down on his blanket. Once the door was closed, Tattoo walked to the table and with the remote turned on the monitors.

"What happened?" he asked as he poured two glasses of Cardhu, offering one to Scottie.

"Someone took a run at your friend," Scottie started, "He was hit. He is in the Kelowna hospital now. We were on our way to the remand centre. I was picking him up at home after he dropped off his car. I was just pulling out when a blue Denali came screaming around the corner and nailed him just as he got to the sidewalk. It looked like two men, but when they saw me coming, they took off. It looked as though they might have intended to pick up his briefcase. Turns out all he had in it was a shirt, underwear and a shaving kit. He wanted to be clean in jail, I guess. I couldn't get the license plate. It was caked with mud, like mine."

"How is your client?" Tattoo asked, sincerely.

"Pretty beat up. He was unconscious but breathing all right. I didn't want to move him. The ambulance arrived about five or ten minutes after my call. In fact, 911 had already received a call, likely from a neighbour, even though nobody came out to help. My guess is that he has some broken ribs at the least, a concussion, and perhaps a break in his arm or leg. I'm going to head over to the hospital later or call, at least. I did call the prosecutor and tell him the story. I asked him if they would put a policeman on the door of his room at the hospital. He agreed."

"Do you think it was tied to our African friend's project?" Tattoo asked.

"A good probability, I think. I will get a message off to Daniel as soon as I find out what is happening at the hospital. By the way, I threw his briefcase into the back of my SUV," Scottie added. "I am going to head back to the office now. I think Daniel is going to ask us to go active—are you okay with that?"

"Yep, I might want some help. Mainly some eyes and ears," Tattoo replied. "Are you sure there will be some Mounties watching out for him while he is in the hospital? It might be wise to have some of our own watching out for him."

"I am sure that will be fine with the clients. Line up what you need and if necessary, I'll get confirmation tonight when I talk to Daniel. And yes, I'll confirm with the prosecutor that there will be extra security."

TATTOO VISITS THE HOSPITAL TO SEE ME - KELOWNA - 24 APRIL 2014

Tattoo jogged from the parking lot to the Emergency Entrance, not because he was in such a hurry, but because he felt the need to push himself a bit. His workout would come later in the day. As he strode through the entrance, he recognized the reception clerk, a quiet girl he had met in a bar with some friends, long ago. He walked toward her with a generous smile. Tattoo was still ten metres away when she noticed him coming toward her. She instantly began blushing as she wriggled in her seat.

"Hi Kathy, how are you?"

"I am fine," she answered shyly, as if everyone in the hospital were listening.

"Kathy, there was a man brought in about three hours ago, pretty scrunched up—a hit and run. Do you know where I might find him?" Tattoo asked, hopefully.

"Just a minute," she replied as she typed rapidly at the keys of her computer. "He will be on the third floor of the South Wing, Room 336. He is still in the operating room, though. I think there is a policeman up there, too."

"Kathy, thank you," he smiled smoothly, as he looked into her eyes, "we should do dinner one night."

"I'd...I think...I'd like that," she answered hesitantly, looking up almost pleadingly.

Will left Kathy to her work and strode down the corridor, around the corner and down another corridor until he reached the elevator bank for the South Wing. He pressed the Up button and waited. Soon he was part of a small scrum waiting to get onto the next car. He made it and soon stepped off on the third floor, then headed for the room assigned. It was neither guarded nor was it a single bed. Four beds, divided by hanging fabric walls, and one bed was empty. The one chair available was stacked with fresh linens. Will walked back into the hallway and wandered through the corridors looking for anything unusual. Soon enough, an orderly appeared pushing a gurney, accompanied by a nurse and a tall Mountie. Under the covers a shape was discernible. The head and one shoulder were wrapped in white dressing and tape.

'It must be my man,' Tattoo concluded.

He approached the gurney but was instantly blocked by the Mountie.

"Sorry, sir, protective custody," said the Mountie, looking at Tattoo knowingly.

"How is he doing?" Tattoo asked.

"Broken arm," the Mountie answered curtly.

"Beat up pretty bad," the nurse corrected, "Hairline fracture on the left humerus, total fracture of the left radius and ulna, dislocated right shoulder, moderate concussion, possibly some internal bleeding. They are just waiting for the CT scan results," she added gratuitously, to impress the Mountie.

"Thank you. When will he be able to talk?" Tattoo asked the nurse.

"Perhaps tomorrow morning," suggested the nurse.

"Are you here all night?" Tattoo asked the Mountie. "Do you need any help?"

"No thanks," replied the Mountie, "I have a replacement coming at midnight and we will have one man on twenty-four-seven."

"I'll see you in the morning then. Have a good night," answered Tattoo politely.

Tattoo turned and departed, retracing his steps through the hospital until he reached the exit. He jogged to his car, climbed in and headed home. He needed a meal, a shower, a workout, and a good sleep. Tomorrow was going to be a busy day.

IN A MOTEL IN KELOWNA - THE KILLERS

A lean man with ink black hair sat on the edge of his bed thinking. The light snoring of the man in the opposite bed was annoying but was not loud enough to be aggravating. Soon light would creep into the room from around the heavy drapery. It wasn't actually drapery, but some kind of rubbery stuff glued inside a much lighter fabric. It worked well enough; after all, the objective of a motel was to provide a place to sleep, not to luxuriate. They had succeeded in their first task. It was one that required stealth, but beyond that, it was easy. The tools were simple and transportable. *Veldtschoens*, moleskin pants, black merino icebreaker and vest, a small but very sharp folding knife, and a few capsules of mislabeled medication in a small conventional plastic medication vial with a legitimate prescription label. Each of the two carried separate medications in differently sized vials bearing prescriptions by different doctors, issued on different dates. The rest of the luggage was consistent with attendance at the wedding of a friend, the legitimate purpose for their trip across the continent. The wedding had been fun. They had not seen their buddy for at least five years, when they had all served together in Bravo Troop, 3rd Squadron, known as "The Destroyers", of the 61st Cavalry Regiment. They were flown out after the disastrous battle of Kamdesh in the Korengal Valley of northern Afghanistan. The battle saw a flood of Purple Hearts awarded. After leaving the military, their career paths had diverged dramatically. The groom had fallen in love and moved to the Okanagan Valley in Canada to work for his father-in-law's company. The two guests, on the other hand, had entered a dark world, far from the joys of weddings and love, where their public lives consisted of university and jobs. One had become a salesman for an obscure equipment manufacturer, and one was in management at an obscure restaurant chain. They were simple but sophisticated cover stories.

Their orders had been clear. Eliminate the target, acquire the papers in his possession and return home via Denver International Airport. At Denver they would be met by an individual at the baggage carousel, and to that individual identify a backpack that would contain a briefcase with the papers. They would then re-ticket and fly to their separate destinations.

They had located their target quite quickly based upon information they had been given of his previous work. Acquiring transportation had been relatively easy; a vehicle identified by a recent parking receipt and a week's duration was located, the plates were swapped with a similar vehicle, and away they went. At the completion of their task, the car would be returned to the parking area, in a similar location, and the owner could figure out the license plates upon his return. Hacking Jim's computer through his Wi-Fi connection, via the smart television, was an easy task. Access to the camera on the television had allowed them to observe Jim's movements and to access the AXIS security camera system controls. This allowed them to neutralize the beeper, which indicated movement outside the house. It also allowed them to freeze the video recording for an hour. Accessing the house was also easy once the alarm system was neutralized. The computerized locks on the front and rear doors could be opened at their will. Since the target usually took a drink to bed, either scotch or water, the means of delivering the medication simply required access to the room. This meant getting the target to the front door of the house for a few minutes, during which one of the killers would access the room via the upper window which the trees concealed from public view. Their plan required that one of them release something behind the garage that would attract the dogs and hence, the target's attention long enough for a team member to enter, add the medication to the drink and then hide. Once the target had succumbed to the drink, a click on one of the throw-away Motorola T100 Talkabout radios would signal the other teammate to return to the rear window where he would be unseen.

Then the disgusting part of the order would be executed. Over a few days the killers had acquired sponges, toweling and large garbage bags at the local convenience store, paying only cash. The second killer now passed the materials up to the window. They left the body to lie still for thirty minutes before the incision. They used the time to locate any files. There was to be no indication of ransacking or robbery, other than the removal of the copper bracelets, and the adjustment and relocation of the hyæna. That might be useful in confusing the police.

Methodically, the killers lifted the tacks from the hyæna rug and moved it slightly. They moved the skull to the bedroom pursuant to additional suggestions appended to the order; removing the target's head was on the order but was just not going to happen; some things were too gruesome and unnecessary. The operation was conducted quickly. The liver and heart were identified and carefully removed to avoid spilling any blood, and then placed into small garbage bags and passed out the window. The following bag contained the sponges, and the last bag contained the towels soaked with blood. The garbage bags were all placed into a large backpack for removal from the property. After a quick verification of the premises, the active team member exited through the rear door and both members headed down the hill. The security system would be reinitiated before morning but after they had returned to the motel.

They planned the hike back to their car carefully so they would avoid travelling near any houses or awakening any dogs. Once they were back at the rental car, they put on shirts and jackets, combed their hair, loaded the backpack into the trunk and began the drive back to Kelowna. They pulled into a Tim Hortons to join the crowd for breakfast. One partner pulled out his laptop and proceeded to connect in succession through three scattered URLs to the security system at the target's residence and edited a few of the files to eliminate any sign that the system had been hacked. They enjoyed their breakfast wraps with hot black coffee, and then departed, as any travelling men would do.

They drove to the lakeside lookout to a point where the shoreline was inaccessible to all but the most determined foot traffic. They added sufficient rocks to the punctured garbage bags to ensure their contents would sink and that water would infiltrate them. As one team member, appearing to be photographing the scenery, kept watch through his camera, the other tossed the weighted bags into the water. They returned to the motel with the remnants of their Tim Hortons coffee and disposed of their cups in the garbage.

What they hadn't anticipated was the guest who had arrived in the afternoon and had left just before dark. This had been a bonus for them. They had been able to obtain the license plate of the guest's vehicle and, without much difficulty, had traced it to his home address. They had gone to the home after returning to the motel, arriving just in time to see him being led away by the RCMP. Slipping through the rear door had been quick and easy. They deposited the bracelets and departed. Now, to track down the papers. They had two days remaining before catching their return flight, finished or not.

I AWAKE IN HOSPITAL - KELOWNA - 25 APRIL 2014

The big round white-faced clock on the wall stared at me. The long hand lurched from one black dot to the next, each move emitting a soft tick sound. The ceiling was bare, but there were lights hung at even intervals. I was partially surrounded by a hospital green curtain hanging from a stainless-steel tube. From looking at the ceiling, I observed that there should be four beds in the room. Beside my bed, on the other side of the one-legged table sat one lone chair. It was stacked with what appeared to be recently folded linens. It was taking some time for all of this new information to register in my head.

There I was, half lying, half sitting in my quarter of the room at the Kelowna General Hospital, watching the second hand on the big white-faced hospital clock tick, no, rather roll away the seconds. It has just passed 09:22:20. As I watched the clock, I heard the clatter of breakfast service and the scrunchy squeak of the nurses' designer running shoes as they rushed down the vinyl-floored corridor.

"We are going to check your vital signs now. Did you eat your yoghurt? Would you like something else with your cream of wheat? Some ginger-ale or toast?"

It all sounded so trite.

"Your blood pressure is very good; 110 over 68."

Good! The clock was telling me it 09:45:50. Only 24 hours and 15 minutes until theoretical departure.

The drugs were making it difficult for me to focus on anything useful. After reading only one paragraph, I dozed off. I felt no real pain. Maybe a bit of pain would perk me up a bit. It seemed like Grand Central Station in my room: pain management people, nurses, nurse's assistants, cleaning ladies, assistants and trainees of all types. I will admit that I had a positive bias toward the middle-aged nurses who have learned it all and yet have continued to demonstrate real compassion and concern. I gazed again at the big white clock face; it was 09:52:54. So far, the day was crawling by, in spite of all the activity. My oblique view from the window told me that the sky to the west was a dull grey. I think that yesterday, when I didn't have much desire to get up, was beautiful, but then, I don't think I was actually here yesterday.

Tick, whirr - tick, whirr – the Baxter was feeding me Ringer's Lactate at a steady 75cc per hour. Seemed like a small amount of fluid compared to what I could drink by myself. It kept me tethered to the clumsy contraption, which required that I drag it with me everywhere. It also meant I'd have to get back to bed every hour or so to get close enough to the one plug in the room to recharge the batteries.

The Doctor came to visit.

"There is good news and bad news."

Now all of those silly jokes suddenly became important!

"Good morning, how are you feeling?" he spoke as he felt my one arm and pulled back the covers to have a look at the rest of my body.

"You had a bad incident," he continued, "we were able to reset the broken bones in your arms, but the cast will likely remain for the next six weeks. Your upper arm has a stress fracture and the bandages will prevent you from moving it while it sets. You have some internal bruising but from what we can tell, no perforations or permanent damage. You have suffered a concussion, which will make you vulnerable to occasional dizzy spells and headaches. We will give you medication to control the headaches. I want you to take them just as I have prescribed. Don't be a hero and wait until the pain begins. The rest is just bruising, and it will clear up over the next few weeks," he added.

"You forgot the good news," I said, trying to be a bit humourous.

The doctor smiled, even though he likely heard something just as silly, three times a day.

"You should be out of here by tomorrow or the next day, provided there is no internal bleeding. You will have to limit your activity for the next six to eight weeks. As you likely know, you have one of the nation's finest sitting outside to ensure your safety. If you would like to meet him, I can let him know. You may have visitors, but their access will be controlled by the Mountie. I will be back to see you tomorrow morning, Bye for now," and he moved on. A nurse promptly arrived and opened the curtain half-way.

Six to eight weeks of this easy life? This I can't believe. I am officially on day two, I think, and I am already going nuts! I know so many people who are happy to live their lives from a nice soft couch, but not me. Living may not be an adequate word. Passion, fear, excitement, and the feel of a challenge are all the stimulants I needed for living. Avoiding death is a poor excuse for living!

The sound of a familiar voice woke me from the depths of my drug-assisted sleep, coming from somewhere not too far away. I allowed myself a few moments to come fully awake and to get my bearings before I opened my eyes in acknowledgement. It was Tattoo. I actually wanted to reach up and hug him.

"Well, hello, friend," he said, looking at me with partially concealed pity. In Tattoo's past life, my day would have been just a bad day at work, not a life crisis, as it seemed to me.

"How are you feeling?" he asked.

"My legs seem to work, and my jaw isn't broken," I tried to smile, "do you know what happened?"

"Scottie is going to be over in a half hour and he'll tell you," he replied. "He was the guy who watched it happen and saved your bacon. It looks like I might be involved in this mixed up relationship with risk that you seem to enjoy so much. Can we talk about a few things?"

"As long as they are not complicated. The way my brain is working, I don't think I could pass the entrance exams for a good kindergarten."

Tattoo tried to chuckle at my attempt at being funny, but he failed.

"Do you remember if you saw a dog when you were at Jim's last?" he asked, looking straight at me.

"Can't remember," I replied, "seems to me that one of the times there was one, a big one."

"Good. Do you remember where you saw him?" he continued.

"No, I just remember he was suddenly in front of me," I answered, "I'm not sure where he came from."

"Do you remember if the patio door was open when you left last time?" the interrogation continued. I thought the police did these things.

"No, not that I remember." I answered.

"Was there anything you remember as odd?" That seemed like a good final question. I thought for a minute.

"Well there was..." I started, "nothing I can remember," I concluded.

"What was it? Just stop and think a minute," he asked, watching me for signs or signals.

I struggled, trying to recollect what blurry memory had inspired the sentence. What was it that I knew and then forgot? It was something that struck me, but I couldn't.... I awoke to Tattoo's voice.

"Hey buddy, are you with me?" he was asking, as if I had passed on to another world. I noticed another person in the little cloth bedroom. I tried to look around and then I heard Scott MacIntyre's voice.

"Hey Scott, I didn't think you were going to be here for another half hour," I smiled.

Tattoo replied, "That was about half an hour ago, man. You went out like a bad light bulb and just woke up now." He chuckled.

"Hey Scott," I tried again, "Tattoo tells me that you saved my life. Will you tell me what happened? Please."

"You and I were picking up some clothes at your place before going to the remand centre. I was about to drive up to pick you up when you came out of the house and a blue Denali came around the corner and met you about the time you met the sidewalk. You and your black case went flying. Just as one guy seemed to be getting out of his truck, he saw me coming and took off," he described. "I recaptured your case and called an ambulance, then the prosecutor's office to explain our tardiness. The ambulance arrived and here you are."

"Was that yesterday?" I asked.

"Late yesterday morning," he replied. "You spent a while in the O.R. after you arrived, and you've been just sleeping away here ever since, like it's some kind of vacation," he grinned.

"I have brought your stuff. I would suggest that you keep what you want from this and let me have the briefcase. It may be the target of the men who hit you. I will discuss it with Will here, and it might be a good idea to let them find some relevant paperwork that will allow them to accomplish what seems to be their objective - stealing the files. As Will has said, that was their objective, and disposing of you was only secondary. They, whoever they are, want to stop the investigation Jim was conducting. For some reason they believe that you have taken over from Jim and have his documents," Scott explained. "What do you think, Will?"

In a quiet voice Will replied, "I will make a show of taking the case and concealing it somewhere. Do we have something we can put into it to give it a bit of authenticity? Something that, with a few magazines, would make them think they've found what they're after? They are looking for files, so if we can provide some that will convince them they've attained their goal, then it might give the Mounties the trail they need to find out who actually killed Jim. I will be meeting with the RCMP later today. We have to get the killers off your trail before it's too late. You Ok with that?"

"I am fine with that," I said, "Just leave a change of clothes and my shaving kit."

"How long do you expect to be stuck in here?" Scottie asked, "I'll have a chat with the prosecutor and see what we have to do. We may be able to deal with all the bail issues while you are still in the hospital."

"The doctor said another day or two, as long as there is no internal bleeding," I replied, "I feel pretty good inside. It's mainly the arm and shoulder that annoy me. As long as they keep me on whatever drug I'm on, I should be fine." I laughed feebly at my own joke.

LAST ATTEMPT TO GET PAPERS - 25 APRIL 2014

The killers had returned the blue Denali to the airport parking lot and the black-haired man had then gone into the Budget Rent-a-Car kiosk in the terminal to rent another car for a few days. After circling the short-term parking area once he picked up his teammate in front of the terminal. There was still one day and a half to locate the materials before they had to leave. They agreed to drive to the hospital to see if they could find their target. As luck would have it, Kathy was at the front desk when the black-haired man approached. He smiled and caught her attention.

"A fellow I met at a wedding the other day ended up here, I understand. He seems to have stumbled in front of a car. I hear he broke some bones. I am driving to Vancouver tomorrow and I wonder if I could get in to see him tonight."

The name was fresh in Kathy's mind, anchored there by Tattoo's connection. She looked up and said, "Room 336. Take the elevators over there and then go down the long hall. You will find his room easily," she said, "it's the one with the Mountie sitting in front of the door." She smiled at her cleverness.

"Is there a George Wilson on the same floor, by any chance?" he asked in a speculative tone.

"Let's see," she scanned the screen as he looked on obliquely.

Once he saw the name he was looking for on the screen, he said, "Aw, never mind, thank you. I forgot that you aren't supposed to tell me who is there anyway. Have a good morning."

He strode off toward the elevator bank. He slipped into a washroom and entered a stall. He opened the slim briefcase and when he exited the stall, he looked thinner, had curly black hair, and was wearing jeans and a tee shirt. He washed his hands and headed out the door.

As he turned down the hallway, he saw a Mountie standing in the corridor chatting with a pretty nurse. She didn't seem to be in any hurry to leave him. The tall curly-headed man walked up the corridor and around the nurse to enter the room.

"Whoa," the Mountie held out his arm. "Who are you here to see?" he asked.

"Oh, sorry, is Miss Johnston in this room?" he answered innocently, having quickly glanced at the four nametags on the wall outside the door.

"Let's check the door here," the Mountie said, as he swung the door away from the wall. "Yes, seems so, go ahead," he said.

The man walked in and looked around carefully. He saw his target in a bed near the window. Two visitors were with him, speaking in low voices. Another bed contained an old man, who was having great trouble breathing; across from the target was a middle-aged woman, sound asleep, and in the fourth bed, a teenage girl reading a book. Against the wall beside one of the men visiting the target was a black Samsonite briefcase that looked like the one the target had carried out of the house. He turned and stepped out.

He turned toward the Mountie and in a soft voice said, "She's sleeping. I'll be back later."

He walked back to the washroom to remove his disguise. As he approached the desk, he looked at Kathy and waved, while he mouthed her a thank you. She smiled again. Once outside the hospital, he walked past the car his teammate was sitting in. He continued walking toward the parking exit. After the car passed through the exit gate he climbed in and they drove off. Once they were clear of the hospital, the driver pulled the rent-a-car to the side of the road.

"The case is in there," the black-haired man said, "one RCMP officer at the front door, four people total in the room, two visitors at present. Option one is to wait for the case to come out of the hospital with one of the visitors; option two is to watch for the visitors to depart and then go in and swap the case. In either case we will have to be finished with this job this evening so that we will be on the flight in the morning.

"Let's start by getting a replacement briefcase, in case that's the option," he continued, "you take the car and go over to Staples to pick up a black four-inch standard Samsonite and I'll stay here to see if the target's case is brought out with one of the visitors. If it is, I will attempt to make a safe snatch here. You should be back in less than an hour. I'll meet you in the waiting lounge just inside the hospital."

The black-haired man got out and walked toward the front door of the hospital and his partner drove away. Black Hair stood just outside the entrance watching closely for potential trouble.

ALEXANDER POPE HAS A CONVERSATION WITH A SURPRISE PLAYER

In the offices of Sullivan, Wachtel and Pope, on the 42 Floor of a tower on the Avenue of the Americas in New York City, Alexander Pope was at his polished cherry wood desk reading a document. A soft buzzing sound preceded the voice of his long-time assistant, Marla Wilson.

"Mr. Pope, I have Senator Riley on the line Do you have a minute to speak to him?" she asked politely.

"Certainly Marla, put him on." Senator Riley had been a close friend of Mr. Sullivan. The Senator's relationship with the firm began long before Alexander Pope joined the firm. The Senator had been 'retired' for nearly fifteen years but was still very active.

"Hello Alex, how are you today?" the clear voice came through the line. Alex could picture the tall, thin gentleman with his perfect suit and his wavy silver hair.

"I am doing quite well thank you, and you and your wife?" replied Alex.

"Just fine. Some things get tougher when you get older, but many things become more beautiful, just fine. I would like to talk to you for a bit on the subject introduced by a young fellow who was down visiting my old firm earlier this week. Would you have some time?" the Senator asked diplomatically. "I think I know what you guys are after, but perhaps we could meet in person," he suggested, in a way that implied some urgency. "When are you here next?"

"I plan to be in Washington tomorrow. Do you have time for dinner?" Alexander Pope asked, then suggested dinner at the '116 Club' at 234 Third St. NE, knowing that it was a favourite of the Senator.

"Dinner's fine Alex, but let's do Charlie Palmer's. It's good and I feel like a steak; when my carnivore instincts kick in, I need a steak," he chuckled. "If that's OK with you, I'll have my girl make reservations for six-thirty. That should give us some time to talk before dinner."

Choosing where to meet for dinner in Washington was almost as important as selecting the company with whom one would be seen. The '116 Club' wasn't as famous as the Capitol Hill Club or some other restaurants, but it still appealed to some members of Congress and to some lobbyists because of its discreet membership. It had evolved from LBJ's friend, Baker's old Quorum Club. Charlie Palmer's was just a place to go for a great steak and a good choice of wines.

TATTOO TAKES HIS LEAVE – 25 APRIL 2014

Tattoo left the room and managed to catch an elevator cab full of nurse's aides off for their early lunch. He purchased a few magazines at the kiosk in the lobby before going to say good-bye to Kathy. He sometimes felt bad teasing her. She was cute but held no appeal for him. She needed a stable, loving farm boy to marry her and fulfill her life. He stopped anyway.

"Hi Kathy, I am heading out now. Don't forget that dinner, Ok?"

This caused her to blush and look down shyly again. She looked up and asked, "Did that guy find your friend? He seemed very nice," she stated.

"Who was that?" Tattoo replied, now on edge.

"He didn't give me his name, I don't think, but he was tall like you but thinner and had black hair. He also asked if Mr. Wilson or someone was on the same floor, but he wasn't," she added. It was the only name she could remember.

Tattoo's nerves went on full alert.

"Thanks very much, Kathy. Kathy, if he comes back could you please call me on my cell?"

"I'm not supposed to...oaky, I will. Anytime?" to which Tattoo smiled and answered, "Yes."

Tattoo left the counter and phoned Scottie's cell.

After a few rings Scottie answered, "Yup."

"Scott, someone was here looking for our friend. Alert the Mountie and get yourself safely home or to your office. I'll call the RCMP office and see if I can get the patient moved to a solo room with better security."

A number of phone calls later Tattoo had the plan in motion. The patient would be removed to a private room. There would be one Mountie in plain clothes posted inside the room, rather than a uniformed one outside the door. Tattoo was going to walk out to his car with the briefcase and then return a few hours later. Scott left immediately, heading to his office.

The blonde-haired man had been gone for about twenty minutes when his partner noticed Tattoo make his way toward the hospital entrance, carrying the black briefcase. Black Hair backed up behind a tree so that he would not be noticed. Since Blonde Hair had the car, all the other man could do was to note the vehicle and an unreadable muddy license plate as it left the hospital. He must wait. He walked back into the hospital and took a seat.

As he sat, he thought about the vial concealed neatly in the folds of a handkerchief. If they were unable to obtain the briefcase, they could execute the final plan, but it would have to occur at night. He hoped for the target's sake that the case was available.

The blonde-haired man returned to the hospital and parked the rental car in the short-term parking lot. He entered the hospital carrying a new black briefcase. Kathy saw him enter and move toward another man, who turned out to be the black-haired man, who looked up as the blonde approached. He caught Kathy's eye but he offered no recognition or acknowledgement, turning his gaze back to his companion. How much more insulting can a man be, thought Kathy. The two men began talking. Kathy took her cell phone out of her purse and dialed Tattoo.

"Hello, Kathy," Tattoo answered.

"How did you know it was me?" she asked, "That man is back."

"I had a feeling it was you," he replied, and she blushed to herself again. He was thinking of her, she thought.

"Is he alone?" he asked.

"No," she replied, "he is talking with another man in the waiting area. The other man is carrying a black briefcase."

"Kathy can you describe them to me, starting with the man with the briefcase please?"

Kathy gave as accurate a description as her experience allowed.

"The first man is tall, with black hair and a blue jacket, and the other guy is blonde, but he's sitting down, so I can't tell just how tall he is. He is wearing a brown leather jacket, and he is rather ordinary looking."

"Thank you, Kathy. Call me if you see them leave, please," he asked, "That's if you have time," he added.

"Of course, if I see them," she answered, responding to his polite and respectful tone.

He dialed Scottie. Not in the office. He dialed his cell, no answer. He left a message, "Scott, call me. Two guys have shown up. One has a black case, just like the one that belongs to our friend. I'm heading back over there now"

It was 18:10 when Tattoo arrived at the hospital for the second time that day. He went immediately to the third floor to see if anything had occurred. He noticed the Mountie walking down the corridor toward the room. He appeared more alert now. He must have received the notice of a change in security level. Tattoo approached him and asked if he could see the victim, but he was informed that there would be no visitors tonight. Tattoo went back to the entrance reception desk to thank Kathy. She said that she was going off shift soon and couldn't do much more for him.

AT THE HOSPITAL - 25 APRIL 2014

The blonde-haired man handed the briefcase and the keys of the rental car to his teammate. The black-haired teammate handed him back what looked like a handkerchief. The blonde then walked out of the lobby. He noticed on the large clock that the time was now 17:50. Their flights were scheduled to leave early the next morning. If they could not make the switch this time for any reason, they would return to their motel and try again later that night. For the time being, all they would be able to do would be to watch for the SUV with the other case in it.

The black-haired man wanted to confirm that the target was still in the room. He would simply show up at the room and appear interested in Miss Johnston. He needed to see if there was still a Mountie inside the room or at the entrance.

He stopped at the small kiosk before going up and purchased a small bouquet of flowers and a magazine. He made his way up to the third floor and down the corridor to room 336. There was no Mountie sitting at the door. He approached the entrance and tried to glance into the room. He could see that Miss Johnston's bed was empty, but the target's bed was occupied, and the occupant appeared to be asleep. He headed toward the nursing station, expressing concern that Miss Johnston was gone. The young nurse was diligently typing entries into the computer. She paused and looked up.

"Can I help you?" she asked.

"Where is Miss Johnston from 336?" he asked.

"One moment," she turned to the computer and typed her question. It answered her with an indication that she had checked out earlier in the afternoon.

"She is no longer in the hospital, sir," she informed him.

"Ah, damn! I was supposed to pick her up, but I guess I am a little late. Sorry," he apologized to the nurse for some reason. She smiled. It seemed that women always liked to see a man humbled and apologetic for his errors. It was an indication that in that gender empathy may actually exist.

"Well," he said, "these are no good anymore. May I give them to you?" he smiled in a serious way,

"Who was in jail there?" he asked, conspiratorially.

"Can't say," she replied.

"Just wondering if she was in any danger," he added.

"Oh, I don't think so," she commented, "I don't think he is in any shape to hurt anyone at the present."

She then returned to her work and he walked back down the corridor.

Black Hair needed a disguise for his later return to the hospital. He left the floor by the stairs and passed by the reception desk. The already flustered man at the desk was too busy to notice him. He wandered down the hall looking for an opportunity to pick up some scrubs from a cart or a closet. He passed a door labelled JANITOR ROOM. Pausing and hearing no sound he entered and took a grey smock with a nametag. He donned it and found a few likely tools to put in his pocket, and then headed for the exit. He reached the lobby, walked out the front door and into the rental car, just as Tattoo was entering the hospital.

"Drive into the short-term parking area!" the black-haired man instructed his team- mate.

"That's the guy who took off with the briefcase. Let's see if we can find his car."

The driver turned into the short-term parking and began to drive up the aisles looking for the SUV with the dirty license plates. In the fourth row they spotted it and continued past it. Six stalls down there was an empty space. The driver entered and drove to sit in the easy exit position on the next row. The black-haired man scanned the area through the mirrors first and then stepped out quickly, pretending that something had dropped on his lap. He brushed at his pants and turned. Seeing no one and identifying the angle of the security cameras, he waved to the driver as if he was thanking him for dropping him off, and he started walking down the aisle. When he reached the correct stall, he stopped, looked at his cell phone, looked around again and continued to walk between the cars as if he had been looking in the wrong place. He saw the briefcase in the back seat. He stopped again and let the slim-jim slide down his sleeve into his hand. In a rapid and disguised motion, he slid it down the side of the window and popped the locks open. He stepped back and opened the rear door, slipping the new briefcase into the space as he retrieved the one Tattoo had left. To anyone watching on the camera, it would look like the normal act of someone putting something into his car. He stood, set the lock and closed the door. The rental car pulled up at the same time that the black-haired man reached the next aisle, and he climbed in.

"Let's pick up something to eat and go back to the motel," the black-haired man suggested, smiling.

They drove north from the hospital until they connected to Highway 97 and then they turned east. Soon they were at the entrance to the motel. The blonde-haired man continued driving past, turning right and right again at the gas station, all the while watching to see if they were being tailed. Finally, he pulled out and turned right again to come into the motel lot from behind, where he parked in an inconspicuous spot.

They got out of the car and, before proceeding to the entrance of their unit, again checked to see if there was any tail. The black-haired man opened the door quickly and they both stepped through. The black-haired man tossed the black briefcase onto the bed nearest the window. He then reached into his pocket, brought out the handkerchief with the tincture and set it on the table. He walked into the kitchenette and took a knife from the drawer before walking back to the briefcase. First, he tried to open the lock with finger pressure. That failed so he tried a few simple combinations, the kind lazy people use, like 111. The lock opened. He gradually set the contents in piles onto the bed, magazines, newspapers, a file folder and finally a full brown envelope.

He opened the file folder. It was full of computer printouts: data upon data but no information. This would take some time to digest and they didn't have time at the moment. He set them in his hand luggage. He then reached for the brown envelope and carefully opened it using the knife. What he brought out looked like a report; nicely typed, printed and bound. He started to read. It was a summary of Zimbabwe's history. He flipped through some more pages. It seemed on target about Zimbabwe but did not contain anything confidential. Damn! It could not be the real report. They would have to neutralize the man in the hospital. Clearly, he had *some* information, but if he continued to dig, eventually he would have too much. More than enough to embarrass or imprison their employer. Once these guys start, they rarely know when to quit.

To the black-haired man's way of thinking, it was going to be necessary to return to the hospital to neutralize the target, if they could do it safely and without taking the lives of any civilians. They made a plan. They would drive to the hospital and select a parking spot along the curb in the fifteen-minute zone. The man with black hair would enter and proceed directly to the vicinity of room 336. His partner would drive the car around, regularly passing through the emergency entrance area.

Because of the risk, they would simply place the capsule into a drink headed for the target. They would not execute the gruesome part of the order at that point. Instead, they would carry out that step shortly before they had to head to the airport in the morning, when they could be certain that everything at the hospital was settled, that their target was dead. The black-haired man would simply wear his janitor's smock, look busy, and he would be able to enter the room without alerting the staff or the target. He simply had to enter the room, complete his task and exit without being stopped.

"Things look good for tonight," he smiled at his teammate, "it seems they pulled the Mountie. We will go back around 24:00. We should be packed and ready to go and have our bags in the car. We may not be able to come back here. Meanwhile, let's eat!"

TATTOO DECIDES TO RETURN - 25 APRIL 2014

Tattoo decided that his best option was to return home and get some sleep, and then go back to the hospital later in the night when the killers might make another foray. He climbed into his SUV and checked to see if they had taken the bait. The Samsonite was still there. He decided to call Scottie's cell again. The phone rang until the answering recording came on. He left a brief update.

"Hi Scott, still have the case. All seems Ok at the Hospital. Get ahold of me on my cell as soon as possible."

He then dialed the office. The receptionist answered and he asked for Scottie. He was still tied up in a meeting, but she would slip him a message. Tattoo needed to know if the Mounties were going to increase the security.

Tattoo headed up the road to his house. He entered cautiously and went to his den. Everything appeared secure. He went to his bedroom, pulled off his shoes and flopped onto the bed. He rolled over and set the alarm for 23:00; that should get him back to the hospital by Midnight. That done, he allowed his body to relax and his mind to respond to his meditative exercises. Soon he was in an oblivious sleep.

The distant and persistent sound woke Tattoo. It was the sound of the phone on his bedside table playing a blues riff. He grabbed it and answered.

"Will, sorry, I didn't get your message earlier. What's happening?" Scottie asked, sounding harried.

"Scott, what is the story on the security at the hospital? I was just there and there were no changes. I just missed one of the killers, who left just before I got there. I think something is going to happen to our guy."

Tattoo continued, "I still have the case. If our information is correct, they are likely to go back to the hospital to deal with him."

"Hold the line a minute. I am going to call the shop and see if they can tell me what is happening. Hold on." Scottie put Tattoo on hold.

"Will, they say that he is being moved as we speak to a solo room on a different floor. His watcher will be inside the room in plain clothes, no identification on the room, no visitors, including you. As his lawyer, I should be able to visit but they recommend against it unless urgent, no desire to attract anything."

"Scott, I plan to get back over there about midnight and have a look around. Kathy saw two guys this afternoon and was able to give me a simple description. One was asking about someone who fit the description of your client. I want to see if they are around. Keep your cell phone by your side, buddy. I may need to get ahold of you quickly. Talk later."

Tattoo hung up. He returned to his sleep position, but it didn't work. He climbed from the bed, put on a pair of comfortable slippers and headed into the den. From the small fridge in the credenza, he took a bottle of San Pellegrino and sat in his reading chair. He picked up one of the books and started to read. The book was the interpretation of Sun Tsu's Art of War by Ralph Sawyer; a much more thorough job than the first translation he had read by James Clavell. It was the one that piqued his interest in all things worldly and it was the one he often returned to for refreshment.

It was 23:32 when the rental car with two occupants returned to the hospital. The black-haired janitor entered the lobby, climbed the stairs to the third floor and wandered the corridors, looking busy. He checked the washrooms, he tested doorknobs, and he wiped windowsills until he became virtually invisible, a part of the furniture. The third floor was very quiet. One nurse was hard at work at the station and did not even respond to his "good evening". He didn't need to speak. The staff were used to new-comers to the country filling these roles while they learned English. The black-haired man had just enough tan to his skin to be from anywhere but here. He simply carried on with his work, responding with a simple smile if challenged. Once he had to point to the nametag on the smock, throw his chest out and smile broadly, indicating his impressive achievement. It was time to check the other floors and the exit routes, to determine which would be most efficient for a hasty escape.

Once he had completed his reconnaissance mission he returned to the lobby and checked to see if his teammate was still there. He was standing near the door with some smokers. As soon as he spotted the black-haired janitor, he moved to join him just outside the doors.

"I was getting too much attention from the security guard," he said, "I have parked the car in short term parking." He pointed to where it sat.

"Have the car in front in twenty minutes. We have to leave whether I am successful or not. Is the car fueled up? We may just need to sit it out in a coffee shop until we head to the airport," the black-haired janitor instructed.

He headed back into the hospital and casually worked his way to the third floor.

Tattoo succeeded in napping in his chair until 23:00. He set his book aside, went to his bedroom and put on his shoes. He stepped into the bathroom and splashed some water on his face, rubbed his eyes, and decided to brush his teeth. He brushed his hair and was ready to go. As he headed for the front door, he picked up a comfortable sweater from the shelf in the entrance vestibule. He climbed into his SUV and then suddenly remembered the briefcase in the back seat. He reached around, grabbed it and set it on the passenger seat next to him. The lights in the cab came on and he entered the combination. The lock would not open. He paused, wondering if somehow the killers had already made a switch. He turned the combination back to 000 and tried again. It popped open. He looked inside and, Yes! The switch had been made. The question now was whether the material in the other case was sufficiently convincing to keep them away from his friend.

He put his SUV into Drive and drove to the hospital as fast as he dared, arriving at 00:10. He parked in the short-term parking area, entered the main lobby of the building, and headed directly to the bank of elevators.

TALK AND THEN EAT - WASHINGTON - 25 APRIL 2014

Alexander Pope climbed from the Yellow Checker taxi half a block down from the United Brotherhood of Carpenters building, paid his driver and began to walk toward Charlie Palmer's Restaurant. He was wondering what the Senator might have to say. It was seldom that he required a face-to-face meeting to discuss anything. More seldom was it about the business of his old law firm. It was a lovely evening for a walk. The air was fresh and clean, washed by the recent rain. The scent of blossoms and trees helped one to walk a little taller. All at once he realized that he was at the entrance. He approached the maître d' and gave the Senator's name.

"I am sorry sir," the maître d' replied, "he hasn't yet arrived, but if you like I will escort you to the table."

"Thank you, and yes, please," answered Alex.

Again, he began to wonder what might be coming. He took his seat and again thanked the maître d'. It was still about five minutes until the actual time of the reservation. As he waited, his thoughts moved on to the diamond business. Something was fishy about the way certain and various governments were dealing with it. It should not be of much concern to any of the countries that appeared to be devoting a lot of time and effort to lobby on the subject.

The Senator had served in the OSS with Mr. Sullivan from late in World War Two until after it was converted to the CIA. Later he attended Yale University, and then entered the practice of law. After getting himself established, he ran for the senate and succeeded. After his first term in the Senate he joined the firm of Maxwell and Walker. In 1964, he joined the Board of Directors of investment bank, The Abrin Financial Group, and has remained there since. Alex was recalling some of the stories the Senator had told him, when the tall, graceful man walked to the table, with the stride of a much younger man. Alex stood and shook his hand.

The waiter approached and asked if they would like a drink. Both men selected vodka martinis, one with olives and one with onion.

"How is your time, Mr. Senator?" Alex asked in deference.

"I do have one more meeting tonight, so perhaps we can chat while we wait for our dinner. Have you had a chance to look at the menu?" replied the Senator.

"I know I can't handle the 'Cowboy Steak'," Alex replied, "but I have decided on something a bit more my size."

The Senator waved the waiter over.

"I will have the pepper crusted culotte steak, medium rare, with seared Hudson Valley foie gras on the side," he turned to Alex and asked, "What would you like?"

"I'll start with the house salad, then your European cut filet mignon, six ounce, medium rare with some blue crab as a side. I love the Angus steaks!"

Alex asked, "Senator, would you like some wine?"

"Perhaps we could share a bottle of Kosta Browne Pinot Noir Gap's Crown? Do you have a 2009?" the Senator suggested to the waiter, before he could signal the sommelier.

"I'll check," said the waiter and headed off.

"That was the last year before they were bought by Vincraft. It is still a lovely, flexible wine in my mind," the Senator observed.

"What's on your mind Senator?" Alex leapt in.

"Your young associate presented my old firm with a delicate request relating to the freezing of funds from diamonds originating in Zimbabwe. The firm agreed to make some representations in Washington. It came to my attention and I was required to inform them that they were stepping into a conflict of interest with some activities of Abrin Financial Group. I am not able to tell you how the conflict arises, you understand. May I ask what the objective of your client is, rather than waste time talking about things we can't talk about? Do you mind?" the Senator asked bluntly, albeit courteously.

"We can do that, but on the basis that nothing that I disclose will be used in any way to prejudice my client." Alex replied.

"That's fine," the Senator agreed.

"We were approached by a client from Shanghai and met with their representatives in Hong Kong. They have had some relatively long-term investments in some diamond operations in Zimbabwe. Recently, the proceeds of the sales in Abu Dhabi diamond auctions have been declining. According to the operating partners in the mine, the proceeds have been frozen as a result of American pressure on the Kimberley Process Committee," described Alex.

"Fundamentally, all they wish us to do is to determine the nature of the problem and to recommend a viable solution that will allow them access to their funds. Our research so far has not found any official trail to follow to end pressure being brought to bear on the Abu Dhabi Diamond Auction, but funds are not being released. Something is going on and so far, we have been unable to identify it. We have only been on it for a few weeks."

"Well Alex, your client is partly correct. The funds are being frozen. I can only confirm that, but I can't tell you precisely how or why," the Senator said, "how much money is being held back?"

"I don't have an accurate number, but my impression is that it is in excess of one hundred and five million as of the last sale," Alex replied. "We can likely get some more current and accurate numbers when they become relevant."

The waiter approached with the salads.

"Would you like fresh-ground pepper?" he asked, brandishing a large pepper mill. Both replied in the negative, waiting for a minute before resuming their conversation. No sooner had they begun again than the sommelier arrived with the wine and two glasses. The Senator nodded as he was presented the bottle and the sommelier began the show of opening the bottle, pouring a taste into the Senator's glass and waiting for his approval before pouring full glasses.

"Thank you," the Senator said, looking at the sommelier before turning to Alex and continuing.

"This involves some things which are far more complex than your client's problems. Our nation has policies from time to time, which are slightly difficult to pursue under the glare of the media cameras. You understand?" the Senator asked rhetorically. "They often engage entities to execute portions of the policy responses in order to maintain deniability. Your client may have been caught in one such situation. Compensation for the firms conducting such efforts is often indirect and occasionally questionable from a domestic law perspective." He paused.

"Your client must stop his investigation and accept that there is a conventional legal process which he must follow. Although it is tedious, it is their only safe alternative, if you understand me. How do you like the wine?" the Senator asked.

"It's nice. Not too heavy, lots of dark cherry and spice, a nice finish," Alex observed, "What do you think?"

"To me, it's about blackberry, tangerine and a touch of coffee, the tannins are very soft and smooth. Yes, very nice!" he replied, as he swirled the light garnet liquid in his glass.

"Let's have dinner, unless there is anything more that I can tell you."

"Senator, I cannot leave my client hanging with nothing to show for it, you understand that," Alex stated, "If you wish him to back off, then surely there is something of value that you can tell me that might encourage him. If he is the target, then at least let me know."

"Alex, he is not the main target. If he keeps digging, he may become a nuisance and put himself at risk. The target is more likely to be a nation's policies rather than an individual or an enterprise; they tend to be collateral to the objective," the Senator explained. "I'll check with a few people as to what might be done. You get him to back off before an accident occurs."

The waiter arrived with the steaks. As with any good steak, these released an indescribable aroma that stimulates the appetite of any true carnivore. The meal was as delicious as it was filling. Alex finished dinner reflecting on the essence of true power and how the retired Senator and his acquaintances were able to exercise it.

"Give my regards to Mike and Nadine," the Senator said to the maître d' as they left.

"Of course," he replied, "thank you for coming."

TATTOO AND BLACK HAIR AT HOSPITAL
- KELOWNA - 25 APRIL 2017

As Tattoo was walking toward the entrance of the hospital, he noticed a car pulling away from the entrance. The driver fit the broad description given him by Kathy, but it wasn't enough to act on. It did however make him alert. Could the other man be in the hospital already? He moved a little quicker toward the elevator. The elevator car opened on the third floor, and he started down the corridor. The first thing he noticed was that there was no Mountie in the hallway. He picked up his pace until he reached room 336. He nodded to the nurse at the central station as he walked past. She seemed quite uninterested in him. He looked around carefully and walked into the room, then stopped and let his eyes adjust to the thin light. He heard no sounds of anyone awake. He made his way to the bed. The occupant was lying on his side snoring. The covers were pulled over his head, preventing Tattoo from seeing who it was. Tattoo carefully walked around to the other side of the bed, avoiding the curtain that formed the wall. Quietly he lifted the sheet to have a view of the man's face. Wrong man! He retraced his steps slowly until he was back in the hallway. He walked back to the nursing station and asked where the previous occupant had gone. She looked up with a confused look and asked, "Who is gone?"

"There was a fellow in 336 this afternoon, who is a friend of mine and now he is gone. Do you know where?" he asked politely, not really expecting a useful answer.

"I am sorry, sir, but there has been no change in that room since I came on duty at six. Funny thing though, about fifteen minutes ago one of our janitors was asking where he went and I had to tell him the same thing," she responded.

"You might check at the front desk. There doesn't seem to be any record on my computer about anybody being moved. Sorry."

"Thank you very much for your help," he said, started to leave, and then, as an afterthought, turned and asked, " What did the janitor look like?"

"He was about your height, thinner, moderately dark complexion and pure black hair."

"Thanks again," Tattoo said with a smile as he left. He headed for the elevator bank hoping that he might see the janitor on the main floor if he waited a bit. He also dialed Scottie.

Scott answered his cell with a tired hello.

"Hey Scottie, what did they do with our man?" he asked.

"They moved him to a private room with a Mountie inside and a female plainclothes Mountie at the nursing station, 'visiting' the nurse on duty."

"Good!" Tattoo responded with relief.

"Can you call your contact and let them know that I think the guy might be in the hospital dressed like a janitor. He has black hair, dark complexion and is about six feet tall. I am heading to the lobby to see if I can spot him when he comes out. Talk to you in a bit."

The elevator door opened to the lobby just in time for Tattoo to see a man dash out the front entrance and jump into the car that had pulled away when he arrived. Tattoo ran. By the time he went through the doors, the car was long gone. He went back inside and sat in one of the lobby chairs in case he was mistaken. He called Scottie and updated him. Scott informed him that the Mounties had had no contact from anyone and that their charge was still safe.

"I'm going to sit here for fifteen or twenty minutes. If nothing shows, I'll head home. They have the briefcase and the papers in it. That may satisfy them for now," he added, before saying good night.

CHIC RETURNS TO HARARE - 26 APRIL 2017

Chic arrived in Harare after a long flight from Shanghai, through Dubai, on Emirates Air. It had been a long haul, but he had been able to sleep most of the way from New York to Dubai, thanks to the cot-like beds in business class. On his arrival in Harare, and after appreciating the efficiency of Immigration and Customs Special Services, he had gone straight to the hotel. Sparkly had already checked them in, had sent the bags to the rooms, and then had joined Chic for a light meal.

Chic was able to spend the afternoon visiting with some of the ministries to discuss the problems his investors were experiencing with the frozen assets at the Antwerp and Dubai Diamond Auctions. He disclosed that his firm had engaged a law firm from New York to get to the bottom of the seizures of money. He explained that his partners in Zimbabwe had told him the problems were caused by the actions initiated by the U.S. Government under the Kimberley Process. He also told the men he visited that he believed that the problem was likely far deeper than investor money being frozen. To a few of those with whom he shared that message, it indicated that Chic might have stumbled onto some information that was extremely confidential. It sounded as though Chic's knowledge and his investigative efforts might be the very investigations they had become concerned about; the information that absolutely must not be released to the press.

Among certain parties in positions of power and responsibility in Harare, word was spreading fast that an accountant had accumulated some very revealing information. That information, if released before a cover could be created, could put a number of senior politicians in jail, or even worse. It was clear that the United States was after the money and had provided some information to the Kimberley Process investigators - complete with names and amounts, but it appeared that there might be something more, something not yet obvious. The more often the money was frozen in Dubai, Antwerp or Tel Aviv, the more likely the cutters and middlemen in India were to get nervous. Some of the Indians had been trying to balance their books in order to save themselves, and that was disrupting the relatively free flow of duty-free diamonds. Those problems were leading one London-based English investment bank to reduce their exposure and, with the help of their government and under the guise of Kimberley Process compliance, they liened funds at Antwerp Auction that were due for Zimbabwe. The heat was on for the Barons to find the report and to extinguish it at any costs. There was however another group who wished to maintain control over the volatility of the diamond business and the fate of Zimbabwe, as well.

If the Barons believed that *they* had concerns, they could worry and fret, and the other group could act to protect the Barons' investments. This was the group that had identified Jim and who knew about Jim's visitor. Now the group was aware of Chic's involvement with a New York law firm, which had begun to make very high-level inquires. This group also chose to exploit the wording in the Zimbabwe Mines and Minerals Act that granted "dominium ... right of searching and mining for and disposing of all minerals to be vested in the President." It also used the benefits of the Kimberley Process, which had, since 2003, controlled and certified 99.8 percent of the world's diamonds. The group utilized whichever served their needs at any given time. They were absolutely capable of implementing their own remedies to problems.

SCOTT MACINTYRE TELEPHONES DANIEL SONNENBLOM – 26 APRIL 2014

Scott MacIntyre was sitting in his office in Kelowna reading through papers related to his conventional law practice. He glanced at his watch and then dialed a special number he had been given so he could reach Daniel. The answer was curt, "Leave your message. It will be retrieved within one hour." He left a message describing the recent activities, including Tattoo's limited description of the two men he believed were involved in Jim's murder. Scottie went on to explain the switch of the briefcases and the involvement of the RCMP in protecting their prisoner. He added one more piece of information: Jim was treated to poison Hemlock before he died. He rang off, stating that Daniel should call if he required more. Scott would have a secure line at the office.

KILLER TEAM TO DENVER AND BEYOND - 26 APRIL 2014

To the black-haired man, it seemed like weeks ago that he had picked up the rental car at the Kelowna airport. As he drove cautiously toward the airport, he was surprised by how much heavier the traffic had been than he had anticipated. It was 07:30 when he finally parked the car at the Budget Rental area in the parking lot. His teammate had taken a cab to the airport. The four-year-old Prius taxi had felt as though it had been driven a dozen times around the world and it pretty much looked like it. The driver sank deep in the compressed seat springs and peered over the dash. He continually chattered into the Bluetooth cell phone headset in a language not remotely familiar to the blond- haired man. Occasionally, the driver would peek at his rear-view mirror to see if he still had a passenger. Continuing his conversation once they pulled up to the airport entrance, the driver shoved the credit card slip, clipped to a map book, which appeared the same age as the cab, over the seat back. Once the blonde-haired man signed it, the driver flipped a switch and the trunk popped open. He continued talking into his Bluetooth and, with a flick of his hand, indicated to the passenger to get out and grab his luggage. The blonde man restrained himself from saying something rude about the customer service, simply climbed out of the cab, grabbed his bags and walked away, leaving the trunk lid flapping in the morning breeze.

Before packing, both men had ensured that their luggage was clean, that any unnecessary materials had been disposed of and any labels removed. The cell numbers had been cleared and their computer caches had been wiped. The man with the black hair picked up his boarding pass at the kiosk in the concourse in front of the Air Canada booth and then checked his luggage. The blonde-haired man stood in line until his turn came along and he proceeded to the counter.

"Where are you going this morning?" asked the attractive redhead.

"Calgary on 8406, then Denver," he replied with a soft smile.

"Do you want me to book your luggage through to Houston sir?" she asked.

"No, thank you, just book me as far as Denver. I may want to change my flight there. Thanks," he replied.

"Will do. May I see your passport, please?" came the habitual request. He handed her his passport and waited.

"What brought you to Canada? You haven't been here very long," she observed, making conversation.

"A buddy's wedding," came the quick answer, "had a good time though."

"Great," she replied mindlessly, "I have you in seat 7C. Please proceed to security, down to your right, please. Next." she said, dismissing him without another thought.

The black-haired man stuck his luggage receipt to the back of his passport and then headed for the security gates. He had a trusted traveler card but simply chose to use his passport for identification as the short, chunky South Asian lady stopped him with a hearty, "Bonjour, hello, passport or government identification with a photo, please," then she added, "May I see your boarding pass, please?" scribbling something on the front and returning it to him, as she turned to the next in line.

He continued in the line, removing his belt, pulling his laptop from his carry-on bag, placing his wallet and coins into his jacket pocket in preparation for the ivory plastic trays. One for the jacket, one for the computer—removed from its protective case, one for his shoes and belt, and one for his bag. Then toes on the red painted line while he waited for the person in front to be scanned. The tall man in the handsome blue turban waved him forward, thanked him and waved forward the next person. Soon his ivory trays began to spill down the incline from the X-Ray machine. He reversed the process and headed for the waiting area by his gate. He found a seat that gave him a good view of the security area and watched for his teammate to clear. He knew they would proceed through U.S. Customs and Immigration in Calgary before boarding the United 5344 flight for Denver. They should be in good shape, since it wouldn't depart until 15:40. They should arrive in Denver at 18:10, have their bags by 18:40 and meet their contact shortly thereafter. It would be a relaxing evening in Denver or on another flight to somewhere. He picked up a used newspaper from the empty seat beside him and pretended to read.

The one-hour flight to Calgary passed quickly and easily. The teammates were seated far apart and didn't communicate on the flight. They had to pick up their bags in Calgary to clear for the trip to the United States and they had plenty of time. Soon they were in the US Homeland Security line-up. A few curt questions and some thorough looks and they were on their way to the security line. This was slower but progressed at an adequate pace. Once through, they headed for the boarding gate to wait for the two-and-a-half-hour flight to Denver, the Mile-High City. So far everything was uneventful.

The aircraft landed in Denver at 18:06 and they had retrieved their bags by 18:41. They met outside the baggage carousel area. They were to look for a limo driver holding a sign for Frederick. They would follow him to the limousine and obtain their instructions. It took a few minutes to identify him. The 'driver' was short, Latino-looking, with grey-tinged hair. He was wearing a charcoal suit and a matching chauffeur's hat. The teammates approached, carrying their bags. He nodded in recognition and they followed him out the exit of the airport to a Lincoln Towne Car, and climbed in. The black-haired man sat in the front passenger seat. The driver started without delay.

"You are being dispatched to Harare, Zimbabwe," the driver instructed. "You," pointing to the man in the back seat, "will fly to London and connect to South African Airlines for a flight to Johannesburg. The flight through London is simple. Land, clear Immigration and Customs, and then connect to the South African Airlines flight. From there you will travel to Harare International. Your cover story will be that two hunters, unknown to each other, are going to enjoy a Safari with a well-known outfitter. One of you was able to get a bargain due to a last-minute can-celation; the other had planned ahead. The expediter will meet you at the

Johannesburg Airport and will have all the permits and the back-story. He understands you to be totally normal clients.

He turned to the black-haired man, "You will take the flight through Atlanta. You will have a .375 H&H rifle with sixty rounds of ammunition to check. You have all your permits to exit the United States and you will be met in Johannesburg by an agent, who will take you through the process of registration in South Africa. The rifle and the ammo will be checked in for the next flight to Harare. You will both be checked in to the Meikles hotel there. There you will do all your own registrations. You will have about two hours between flights, which is just enough. Rooms have been registered for you at the hotel and you will be on separate floors. I have one bag and one carry-on in the trunk for each of you. Make certain you take the correct bags. Your carry-on bags contain some of your documentation, some Euros and US Dollar currency, a change of clothes, sports shoes, binoculars and cameras. One contains a first aid kit. Within that kit is a prescription made out to you as Malarone, a malaria prophylactic. In the other is an actual prescription for Malarone with sufficient tablets for both of you. There is also a prescription for Rosuvastatin. Not to be confused with the real thing. It will have the terminal effect you require.

Your target is an Asian by the name of Gordon Zhong. He should arrive about the same time you do. He travels with an executive assistant who sleeps in a separate room. They often take their meals together. He maintains a relationship with a woman who works at one of the government ministries. She is not to be hurt. Your contact, in case of emergency, is a Detective-Sergeant Sibangilizwe, at a cell number on a business card that appears to be that of a travel agent in Harare. Upon completion of the task, you will report first to him so that he will be able to become the investigating officer. Maximum call length twenty seconds, no names required. Number One is Gordon Zhong. Number Two is his assistant, if necessary. Collect papers from their briefcases. Deposit the papers in the hotel safe and leave the check receipt with the bell captain. The Detective will approach him and collect the papers once you have gone hunting. After that, you will just live the normal lives of tourists who are on their way to a hunt. You will have two days to complete your mission. You will then be picked up by a P.H. and flown by Cessna 206 from Charles Prince

Airport to the Riga area in the Zambezi Valley for a two-week safari. This should allow enough time for everything to be cleaned up before you get back to Harare. Any questions?" he finished the briefing. He drove the limousine to the Departures Gate for the flight to London.

The man in the rear exited the limousine and went to the trunk. The driver handed his bags to him.

"Please double-check your papers once you are inside. Call me immediately if there is a problem. I will return after dropping your teammate at his flight."

The driver returned to the driver's seat and left for the Departures Gate for the Atlanta flight.

"Please double check all of your papers when you get inside the airport and if you have a problem call me on the number on my receipt. You will need a cart because you are carrying the rifle. Are you familiar with the process for travelling with a rifle on the airlines here?"

"Yes, I have done some hunting, thanks."

They walked to the trunk and unloaded the bags. The black-haired man slung his carry-on bag over his shoulder and stepped off to bring back a cart. The aluminum covered Americase rifle case was loaded onto the cart and held in place by his Red Oxx travel bag. He accepted the receipt from the driver and calmly continued through the doors to the check-in kiosk. Once the agent confirmed that the bolt was out of the rifle and the serial number recorded, she was able to place a seal on the case and attach a baggage tag. He opened the bag that contained the ammunition. He removed the case from the travel bag, so that it could be weighed and sealed and then he replaced it. The bag was then sealed and tagged. He received his boarding passes and was on his way to the security gates.

Twenty-one hours later, after changing aircraft in Atlanta, he arrived at the O.R Tambo International Airport near Johannesburg where, after the formalities and rifle registrations, he was able to enjoy a cold Castle beer and a small breakfast. Three hours later he was on the flight to Harare and three-and-one-half-hours later he exited the aircraft into the shiny new terminal. The Immigration and Customs check was normal, the ammunition was counted, and a receipt provided, a record of the rifle with the serial number, the owner's name and passport number were placed into the rifle case and he was good to go. Taxis waited at the front of Airport Customs and the first one picked up his luggage, loaded it and welcomed him to Zimbabwe, happy to see another big-tipping American hunter. The driver chatted for the entire ride to the hotel. As he pulled up to the entrance portico, they were met by a bellboy who opened the door while the black-haired man paid the driver in American dollars.

"Good day, sir, welcome to Meikles," he began, "you are here for a safari?" he asked, and not waiting for an answer asked, "Would you like your rifle stored in the hotel gun safe, sir?" He moved ahead with the luggage on a cart, pointing the black-haired man in the direction of the main entrance, while he took the cart through the service door.

Check-in was efficient. His room was on the fifth floor.

"Your luggage will be brought to your room shortly," the clerk informed him politely and, "here is a receipt for your firearm, which will be locked in the hotel gun safe until you are ready to depart. Enjoy your stay with us."

The black-haired man turned to find another smiling man, holding his room key.

"Follow me sir, please. Welcome to Zimbabwe. Is it your first trip?" he asked, as he led the man to the elevator banks.

"First time, looking forward to the hunt," he replied, economically. Moments later they were on the fifth floor and moving toward his room. The bellman opened the door, reached in and turned on the light, then stood aside, motioning the black-haired man to enter. "I hope this is satisfactory, sir."

"Very nice, thank you," and the man reached into his pocket for a five to tip. The bellman smiled, thanked him profusely and left. The door closed softly, and the man put down his carry-on. He laid down on the bed at the same instant that he heard a knock on the door.

"Your luggage, sir!"

He arose and opened the door, allowing the bellman to push the cart into the room and fling the bag onto the luggage rack. He reached for another five and the bellman left smiling, thinking, 'rich Americans!'

The black- haired man prepared for a few hours' well-earned rest. Before doing so, he decided to see what he could learn about the location of Gordon Zhong. The front desk was prepared to put his call through but would not provide a room number. He finished sorting out his clothing and decided that the lobby might provide more opportunities. The elevator returned him to the main floor where he recognized the bellman who had taken him to his room. He approached him with a twenty in his hand.

"I have a couple of acquaintances who may be staying at the hotel: young Chinese fellows arriving from New York. I'll be in the Explorers Club and if you see them would you let me know? It's to be a surprise," he winked knowingly at the bellman as he handed him the twenty. The black-haired man knew this would stimulate some extra investigation in anticipation of an even bigger tip. He proceeded to the Explorers for a cold beer. His nap could wait. He dialed his teammate, who had arrived on an earlier flight, and let him know where he was, inviting him down to the lounge for a drink.

PROSPER IN HOTEL LOUNGE - HARARE - 27 APRIL 2014

Prosper was sitting at a table in the corner of the Explorers Club with one of her younger workmates for an end-of-work-day treat. It had not been a long day, but it had been a hard day. A new customer walked into the lounge, something in his demeanor catching her attention. She continued the conversation with her co-worker but kept an interested eye on the black-haired man. He was handsome, dressed casually, obviously American. He wasn't dressed well enough to be an investment banker. He was too comfortable with himself to be a salesman and too relaxed to be a diplomat. He must be a hunter, here for a safari or something. The look in his eye and something about his conduct made Prosper think that he was hunting for prey in the lounge.

Prosper's co-worker noticed Prosper's eye wandering to the man and whispered to her, "Hey woman, what are you thinking?" and then turned to glance at the man, "Ohhhhh, he's cute, but too young for you, and just right for me."

She smiled at Prosper.

Prosper looked at her and said; "Young lady, I am not that old, and he is not that young, but if you turn slowly you can see what's coming," she smiled conspiratorially at the girl. The blonde man was walking slowly across the lounge toward the black-haired man.

The young worker turned enough to see, "Oohwee, mama, one each! He is mine, and you can have the older one all to yourself!"

She laughed much louder than she spoke.

Prosper strained to hear the conversation and by combining what she could hear with what she could glean from reading lips, she was convinced that they were hunters, but something else as well. She would tuck the information away and report it to Mama Prudence during their next visit. She appreciated and admired how much detail Mama could absorb and retain. It was like she was doing jigsaw puzzles in her head while she wore a serene smile on her face.

Later that evening, a young Asian came to the bar and had a drink with a very attractive young local girl. No sooner had they left the lounge, apparently on their way to dinner, than another young Asian appeared. This one was definitely a bit different, from the way he walked, to the way he was dressed, to the proud way he held his jaw and his lips.

'This should be interesting,' Prosper thought to herself.

The black-haired man stood and walked to the bar. He wanted to look at the bar chit belonging to the man who had just left, so that he could ascertain his identity and his room number. He slid a hundred to the bartender, who 'carelessly' let the chit sit on the counter.

The exhilarating feeling of great good luck came over the black-haired man, and grinning, he returned to his table.

"The guy who just left has to be the assistant to the target, but I've got his room number. The other guy must be the target, so maybe you can find out more or track him by camera. Likely they are on the same floor," he spoke quietly to his blonde teammate.

"I am going to follow the assistant to see what he is up to, and then head up to the room for a nap. It is likely going to be a late night. I'll buzz you about eleven and we'll get together. Will you be able to deal with the hotel CCTV cameras somehow? Give us a window of midnight until one for the third to fifth floors," he requested.

"Will do," said the blonde, "I think I'll stay for another beer and a sandwich before I head up. I might even have a chat with the target," he said, smiling.

The black-haired man left the lounge and the blonde looked over at the crowd that now nearly filled the tables. He spotted Prosper and her young friend at a moment when they were both looking at him. He smiled and observed the others in the room. He spotted the new rich and he spotted the Mercedes salesman. He identified the long-married couple in the midst of a conversation of indifference. Reading people had been something he had been taught and something he had liked to learn. He was very good at it. Relating to and befriending those people was another challenge for which he required the skills of a chameleon. His eyes went back to the target.

Sparkly had no need of a girlfriend. He sat smiling to himself, as he sat at his table looking out at the crowded room. He also was enjoying the people-watching. He noticed the way the blonde athletic body walked into the room. He noticed how well-groomed he was. The blue blazer fit his body smoothly and the cream-coloured slacks followed his muscular legs to a pair of strong leather sandals. The knotted paisley scarf accented the lean lines of his neck. Blue eyes glanced from the rigid but welcoming face. Did the diamond stud in his right ear signify anything or was it a modern neutral decoration? He dropped his eyes then and went back to enjoying his drink.

Once the black-haired man left, the blonde guy signaled the waiter and ordered a light sandwich, the house salad and a vodka tonic.

Sparkly wriggled in his chair just a little. He loved men like this. He made eye contact and received a slight smile in return. Prosper casually watched this courtship develop until the blonde man received his meal and, with a subtle signal, invited the Asian man to join him.

'They had better be careful,' she thought to herself, 'Zimbabwe is not that liberal. Witches are OK but homosexuals are not.' She laughed out loud at her unheard joke.

SPARKLY IS KILLED - HARARE - 27 APRIL 2014

Late that afternoon while between meetings, Chic had phoned Akatendeka at her office and had arranged to meet her later in the evening at the Explorer's Club at the Meikles Hotel. At the end of the afternoon, Chic returned to his suite, wondering if he had made any progress in the meetings. He wondered if powers far beyond his abilities and experience were in play. He wondered if he would disappoint his father and his father's investors. He set his briefcase on the credenza and carefully hung his jacket in the closet. He kicked off his loafers and flopped back onto the bed in the darkened room. He felt the cumulative fatigue of travelling through time zones and of sitting for hours on airplanes. He thought about setting the alarm and having a short sleep but decided against it. He began to think about the upcoming evening and smiled to himself. She is really a lovely, spritely woman.

Chic realized that he knew nothing about Akatendeka's past. She was obviously well-educated. She was naturally athletic, both in build and in nature. Her complexion was flawless. Her teeth were a perfect ivory, well-formed and spaced without the brittle white look of fine American teeth. Her eyes held a life of their own, so vivacious, so engaging, so close to her soul! He closed his eyes and he could smell her fragrance and almost feel the heat from her closeness. Chic found himself drifting off and jumped up from the bed. He decided a shower would wake him and remove him from the state of never-never-land.

At six, Chic closed the door to his suite and walked down the hall toward the elevator. He selected the down button and waited. He couldn't be falling in love, of that he was certain. He had decided that the commitments of love would wait until he was well established on his own. Enjoying the pleasures of love, however, he was willing to practice until then. The gong rang, the door opened, and he stepped into the elevator, riding it to the lobby. He walked across the marble floor, down a few stairs and across to the entrance to the Explorer's Club. It was busy. He realized as soon as he sat down that, in Zimbabwe, things had changed. The lounge was full of well-dressed, well-groomed people engaged with great enthusiasm in lively conversations. He sensed a strong aura of confidence. Much of the new wealth in the room had resulted from what would be considered either illegal, unethical or other 'unfair' actions of the government. Several of the people in the lounge were accumulating wealth by acquiring interests in previously foreign-owned companies, in order to allow those companies to comply with the Indigenization Act. Some interests were acquired by strictly illegal extortion, others by sheer effort and good management skills. They were all represented here.

Chic sensed her arrival before he could even see her. Standing up, he looked around, but she was not there. As soon as he sat, she appeared beside him, smiling. Before he could rise to greet her, she leaned over to accept a kiss on her cheek. Akatendeka took a seat beside Chic.

"Good evening, Mr. Zhong. Welcome to Zimbabwe," she purred, "I hope your day was productive."

"Hello to you too, Akatendeka," he replied, sounding a bit like a schoolboy talking to a teacher on whom he holds a crush, "relatively productive, but I am happy to be here - now. Would you like something to drink?"

"Sure," she smiled, "as long as you don't use it to take advantage of me. I'd like a Castle beer please, in a glass."

Akatendeka knew that Zimbabwean women had a reputation for being binge drinkers. She had never imbibed in the beautiful cocktails and exciting champagnes that seemed common among the women in this lounge, but she did enjoy a refreshing Castle or Zambezi beer from time to time. This was one of those times.

The waiter arrived and politely asked, "May I get you some drinks?" as he wiped the imaginary spill from the table.

Chic replied, "The lady would like a cold Castle in a frosted glass, and I would like a Springbank 18-year, if you have it."

The waiter smiled and excused himself without a word, soon to return with the drinks, which he set in front of the guests. He once again excused himself and disappeared.

"So, tell me," Akatendeka said, with eyes sparkling and a smile that would melt any ordinary male, "what is going on, Mr. Zhong, or should I call you Gordon?"

As she watched him blush, she remembered Mama Prudence telling her, "The world's greatest power is the youth and beauty of a woman."

Chic still felt like a school kid not sure of where to go. "Ahh, not really very much," he looked up at her, knowing that she knew that not to be true.

"I am having some problems sorting out what is actually happening in the diamond business here, and who is really who, and who is legitimately working for the country and who is working for themselves and pretending to work for the country."

He would have gone on, but the number of potential conflicts was quite staggering. He looked at Akatendeka with almost pleading eyes and asked, "Do you know?"

"It is very difficult or very simple, depending upon how you frame the question," she answered looking straight into his eyes. She stopped. How much should I discuss with him? Mama's warning flashed back into her mind. She smiled at him and asked, "How much do you think you know?"

Chic took a sip of his scotch. He loved the taste of a good single malt, so complex yet so simple—like Zimbabwe.

"I know that since we first invested here in 2004, things have changed a great deal. I know that, when I first arrived, it was not too difficult to judge an honest man from a corrupt man. I know that the whole economics of the diamond business have changed domestically, and it has taken a large cut from the income of our investors, vastly disproportionate to the rest of the world's diamond business. How is that for a start?" he almost challenged.

"Those questions require complex answers," she replied bluntly. "Have you thought about the problem from the simple point of view? Maybe the people of Zimbabwe just want to keep more of what, historically, is theirs?"

Chic realized that he had rubbed a nerve. He paused to reflect while he took another sip from his glass. To continue would likely offend

Akatendeka. He grasped that he must really take the time to reflect before answering. He could tell she was waiting to see which direction he would take with his answer.

"Let's drink up and go for some dinner," he suggested, "I've made a reservation upstairs at La Fontaine. It's really quite nice."

"I've been there before, Gordon," she replied, with a touch of ice in her voice, "I live here, remember? This is my home."

Chic was a bit puzzled by the tone. He realized again how little he really understood women. Again, he tried thinking before speaking, an idea that had once been suggested to him by a female friend. "Yes, sorry," was the best he could come up with at the moment. He hoped it would be sufficiently neutral to avoid escalation. Akatendeka smiled knowingly. 'Men,' she thought to herself, 'they are so predictable when they start thinking about the wrong thing.'

Chic signaled the waiter, who laid the check in front of Chic and waited for a credit card.

"I'll just sign it to my room, thank you." and the waiter departed.

Chic rose and reached for the back of Akatendeka's chair. She looked at him with that look of independence and he paused. She stood and slid her chair back and turned in front of him to leave. Chic followed as she led him to the dining room.

"We have a reservation under the name of Zhong," Akatendeka spoke first to the maître d', receiving a special smile in return.

"My name is Stuart," the Maître d' said, "please follow me," and they both followed to the table, where Stuart slid a chair out and Akatendeka gracefully slid onto the seat.

"Thank you, Stuart," she said with a polite smile, as he swept the napkin across her lap.

Gordon seated himself. Stuart walked around the table and politely dropped the napkin onto his lap, turning to Akatendeka and asking, "Would the madam like something to drink, perhaps?"

"Perrier, please Stuart, on ice."

"Twelve- year-old Springbank please," added Chic.

"Yes, thank you. I'll be right back with the drinks," Stuart methodically replied as he turned to leave the table.

"Well," Akatendeka opened, "have you thought about which perspective you would like to consider?"

Chic was confused. He could not figure out this woman and it was disturbing him. He wasn't trying to offend her, nor was he trying to elicit information. He was trying to answer her question candidly and to develop their relationship a bit. She seemed encouraging then dismissive, pleasant then cold. He wasn't sure which tack to take, which would be the most advantageous. When she smiled, he couldn't help but feel strongly emotional towards her. When she was curt, he felt hurt. Where could he take the conversation from here?

"What did you mean about Zimbabweans just taking what was already theirs, or did I understand correctly?" he tried.

'I have him,' she thought, 'now I must feed him and find out where he is really coming from.'

"Gordon," she began, "I simply mean, did you ask the questions from the perspective of a native Zimbabwean? Or did you ask the question as a frustrated foreign investor who does not understand our country?"

"I asked the question from the point of view of a foreign investor who has empathy for your country and who has invested millions of dollars in developing the country and now finds the systems in the country working against him, and I don't understand why." He tried his best to be firm and accurate.

Akatendeka saw her chance, "That is why you and that Indian are smuggling ivory to China illegally, I suppose?

Gordon Zhong flinched. His answer was not going to fit. He had not told her about his small investment in the ivory business. Maybe she didn't really know. He knew he could not confess. His silence was condemning in itself.

"Here are your drinks," said Stuart, as he slowly set the frosted glass in front of Akatendeka, then slowly poured the Perrier with one hand while holding aloft his silver tray with the other. He then walked around the table and set the scotch down in front of Chic and placed a small pitcher of water beside it.

"Have you had time to look at the menu?" he asked.

"I have a question for you, Stuart," she spoke first, giving Chic a little more time to think. "What is the special tonight?"

As if reading from a previously rehearsed script, Stuart continued the dialogue, "Sweetbreads ma'am, with risotto, and a selection of fresh vegetables."

"Thank you, Stuart, that would be just wonderful for me," she answered, "and could I have a small garden salad to start?"

"And you, sir?" Stuart watched Chic as he struggled to read from the menu. Attempting a French accent, he said, "I'll start with an aperitif: Gourgeres with confit duck, then I'll have the poached and roasted fillet of veal with braised snails and carrot puree;" he paused, thinking it was necessary to let Stuart catch up, "and we will have a bottle of Cave de Ribeauville, 2010 Riesling, please."

He looked up at Stuart, feeling proud, thinking that he would cater to her menu choices. He then looked over at Akatendeka to see her reaction. There was none. Her thoughts were obviously somewhere else. He wondered to himself what gourgeres might be. He was running out of time to answer the question she had asked. Chic looked up at Akatendeka once Stuart had left the table.

She smiled back at him and said, "I hope you don't mind, but I don't drink wine. Thank you for offering, though." And thanks very much for asking, she thought—unspoken, but heard clearly by Chic.

There was a long pause while Chic sipped his scotch as if it were the first time that he had ever tasted it.

"Shall we change the subject?" Akatendeka asked, offering to let him off the hook. "At least until after we have finished dinner?"

Chic breathed a silent sigh of relief before speaking, "That's a good idea. Why don't you tell me about yourself? Where were you born? I'd like to know you better."

"You will," she smiled and sat silently, adding to his confusion. The meal came and went, and they said very little. The wine was excellent but tasted bitter to Chic since he was drinking it alone. Gourgeres turned out to be delicious fluffy little cheese pastries. The snails were uninspiring. By the time the meal was finished, Chic had gathered the courage, and the courtesy, to ask, "Would you like dessert?"

"Yes please. What are you going to have?" Akatendeka replied.

"I was thinking about the chocolate fondant with white chocolate mousse and honeycomb, and a cup of cappuccino. How does that sound to you?"

"It sounds lovely," she replied with a bright smile, staring into his eyes with a tinge of curiosity.

They sat looking at each other as they drank their cappuccinos and tasted the chocolate fondant. The waiter brought the ticket and once again Chic signed it to his room. He then realized that it was the Maître d' who had taken their orders and who had served them. 'Akatendeka must be more than she appears to me,' he thought to himself, as he stood to leave the table. He was turning to leave when he realized that she was still sitting, with a whimsical smile on her lips. He wondered...then walked over to slide the chair back so she could stand.

"Thank you, Gordon," she said politely, as she rose from the table.

She walked out ahead of him and, once outside the restaurant, she turned slightly, waiting and then took his hand into hers and gave him a slight squeeze and a smile. As they reached the elevator, Chic politely reached for the Lobby button. Akatendeka slid her hand over his indicating that he should select his own room. He was becoming more uncertain. Was he accompanying an extremist or a potential lover? There was no question that she was leading him, but to what? He felt mesmerized, helpless, putty in the hands of this woman. What power did she have over him? He followed quietly, even though he walked in front. He opened the door and held it open for her. She slipped lithely between him and the doorjamb and into the living room. She slipped out of her shoes, kicking them to one side of the sofa.

Chic offered her a drink from the bar fridge. With a slight shake of her head Akatendeka declined. Chic took out a small bottle of scotch, a mediocre brand, and poured it into the glass on the counter, and then took a long sip. He walked over and set the glass on the table beside the bed. Akatendeka had excused herself and was in the bathroom. Chic was nervous with excitement. He took another sip, then removed his tie and kicked off his loafers. Thinking better of it, he picked up his loafers and set them by the old wooden valet where he had hung his jacket.

Akatendeka emerged from the bathroom wearing a fluffy white hotel robe and she set her clothes neatly on the chair on the far side of the bed. Chic drank in her incredible, beauty as she lay on the bed. He excused himself and took his turn in the bathroom, quickly splashing his face with cold water and then washing his hands carefully before rubbing both dry with the towel. By the time he was back in the bedroom she was lying under the covers of the bed. He walked over to her side of the bed, leaned over and kissed her cheek. She smiled lightly. He walked around to the other side and completed the process of undressing and properly hanging his clothes. Naked, he stood and glimpsed himself in the tall mirror. He felt good about what he saw. Chic lifted the covers and climbed carefully into the bed beside Akatendeka. He slid closer to her and wrapped his arms around her, pulling her closer to him, his right arm resting gently on her breast. As their bodies touched, he kissed her again, a long deep and exploratory kiss. She responded by taking his hand. He hugged her close, as though she would leave him in an instant, as though, if he held her close enough, she could not go.

"I love you," he whispered into her ear. She responded by holding his arm tighter and closer. The mild scent of her hair was glorious as he breathed it deeply into his lungs, feeling his passion rise with each breath.

Sometime later..."You were wonderful," she said.

Chic rolled flat on his back. He was not tired or physically exhausted, but simply mellow. His muscles were soft and without feeling. He was completely conscious and alert but seemed unable to move, yet he felt filled with joy.

"Chic, you are in danger!" She was leaning toward him from a half sitting position, her eyes glistening with tears. He wanted to reach out and hold her, but he couldn't. Akatendeka felt the strength of the conflict between her obligations to her boss and her feelings for her friend. She turned and hurriedly climbed out of bed. She walked slowly to the bathroom and returned minutes later dressed and still crying softly. She was ready to walk out the door but paused.

Chic summoned his strength and half shouted, "When will I see you again?"

She turned and walked slowly to where he was lying, all the while looking at the floor.

"We must say good-bye Gordon," she sobbed, "there is no way for our relationship to continue. I am so sorry. Just be careful."

She left the room. As she entered the lobby the bell captain waved to the doorman, who in turn waved for a car. The Mercedes quickly appeared at the front door and Akatendeka climbed in, settling in the rear seat. She had barely begun to clarify her thoughts when the driver eased the car to the curb in front of her building.

Once in her flat Akatendeka boiled water for a soothing cup of her special tea and reflected on the years she spent in the sisterhood, learning and training for the life she was now living. She sat in a quiet spot on the floor, legs crossed, back erect and slowly sipped from her porcelain cup. When she finished her tea, she undressed and climbed into her very soft western-style bed and fell into a deep, but unique sleep.

At six in the morning her alarm began to play Leonard Zhakata's "Musadaroba". Akatendeka rolled over and pulled the covers over her head, trying to forget the remnants of her dreams. She had flown, she had fought, she had felt terror and seen blood; she had fallen but had awakened before landing, saved by the voice of her favorite singer.

She climbed out of bed and headed for the shower. Perhaps hot water pouring over her would wash away her dark thoughts.

The shower did not help, so she dressed and went to the office. Upon her arrival, she was suddenly overwhelmed by nausea and she knew she would not be able to make it through the workday. Akatendeka went into the Minister's office and requested that she be excused for the day to recover from her nausea. Without hesitation, he shooed her away, admonishing her to rest and get well. As she walked slowly down the sidewalk toward her apartment building, she reflected on Gordon Zhong. Was he actually evil or did he simply not understand what was happening in Zimbabwe? Oh, well, it mattered little now, since her loyalties were to her country, to her boss and to Mama. That was sufficient.

ASIAN MAN FOUND DEAD - HARARE - 28 APRIL 2014

The monotonous flash of the camera filled the room with a strange strobe-like light. The body was in the bed, eyes fixed on the centre of the ceiling. The face was a powdery pale, greenish white. He had hung his jacket and trousers neatly over the wooden valet, with his cufflinks sitting in a small bowl on a shelf atop the valet. His freshly polished black shoes were waiting for the new day, and he had placed neatly folded black calf-length nylon stockings over the shoes. The dry cleaner's wrap had been removed from the white shirt, which hung in the closet to air through the night. An open briefcase sat on the desk under the window, empty, but unharmed. Everything else was in perfect order.

There was a strange, oppressive air in the room. Present were the minimum number of people required to measure, photograph and otherwise record the facts of the position of the body. Blood was visible on the top sheet, but surprisingly little. Those who had looked under the top sheet had quickly reached their conclusions, and no one else felt the desire to verify the outcome. The body had been sliced open with precision. There was no sign of a blood trail from the bed. To most of the investigators and police who had first arrived at the scene, the answer was as clear as it was undesirable. No one would touch the body. Instead, they must wait for a *n'anga*. Madzibaba Jonathan, respected as a traditional healer, was also appreciated as a member of the homicide squad because of his powers to neutralize any witch's curse. No one risked touching a suspicious body until Madzibaba gave his permission. Once he arrived and reviewed the body, he solemnly chanted a few incantations and then sprinkled a secret concoction of ground herbs on the wound and into the nostrils of the dead man. He put his ear to the mouth of the dead man for nearly a minute. Satisfied, he stood upright and, with his latex-gloved hand, reached inside the cavity. Two of the man's organs had been removed cleanly and neatly, and there was no sign of them anywhere in the room. He asserted the strong possibility that the ritual murder had been committed by a witch. The others nodded in agreement, but without enthusiasm.

Detective-Sergeant Sibangilizwe stood at the foot of the bed waiting for the ident crew to finish measuring and photographing the scene. He noticed a small glass of amber liquid sitting under the lamp on the table at the side of the bed. He kept his eye on it until the team finished. He walked slowly toward the head of the bed and deftly grabbed the glass through an inverted baggie, as if he was collecting a dog dropping in the park. He zipped the baggie closed and slipped it surreptitiously into his pocket.

He waved over a young constable who had just entered the room. Constable Khumbulani rushed over and humbly greeted the Sergeant.

"*Livuke njani?*" he greeted, and then asked, "*Ufunani?*"

Discreetly, the Sergeant handed the young man the bag containing the glass.

"Take this and dispose of it where it will never be found! Do it now!" barked the Detective-Sergeant in a tone that brooked no dissent. Both men were Ndebele and from the same tribe. Constable Khumbulani had achieved his dream job directly as a result of the intercession of Detective-Sergeant Sibangilizwe. In his young mind, there was no question of a hierarchy of loyalty. He disappeared from the room.

The investigators had learned that the dead man had checked into the hotel with an associate. They knew the name of the associate. They did not know the location of the associate. Detective-Sergeant Sibangilizwe knew that they would find him, but that he was not yet of urgent concern.

SPARKLY MISSES BREAKFAST - 28 APRIL 2014

hic woke early, still a bit tired from his night of tossing and turning. What had happened? His bedding was soaked with sweat. He struggled from the bed and shuffled to the shower. He turned the water on hot and let it run until steam filled the bathroom, and then turned it back to a tolerable temperature. Standing there in the cascade of scalding water, Chic felt his blood pulse through his veins. Finally, he turned the water to cold. The shock of the icy water pounding his body woke him thoroughly. He shaved, dried himself, and then dressed for the day.

Minutes later, Chic was on his way to La Pavillion, on the first floor, to have his breakfast and coffee. He was ahead of schedule and it would be, another twenty minutes before Sparkly would join him. He ordered orange juice and coffee and picked up a copy of the Herald, which the eager young waiter had kindly set on the table beside him. Without delay, the waiter brought the fresh coffee and poured a glass of orange juice from a large silver pitcher. Chic added some sugar and a touch of cream to the cup and began to stir his coffee in an absent-minded way. What had she meant?

As it approached nine, he thought of checking to see if Sparkly had gone to the Tanganda Tea Lounge instead. He would wait until five after to check. He folded the newspaper open to read the headlines:

GOVERNMENT REVOKES
DIAMOND MINING LICENSE
Zimbabwe News, 28 April 2014, Bradford Mpfuno

In a move to consolidate its control over the production of diamonds, the Ministry of Mines announced the withdrawal of the mining license of Kwame Mining, due to non- performance, it was announced yesterday.

The Minister scolded the mining company for its practice of concealing the true value of production. Continuation of these practices by any other company, he said, would result in further actions by the Ministry.

Although the investor in Kwame Mining was from Ghana, the Zimbabwe partner was the Zimbabwe Mining Development Corporation, recently plagued by bribery scandals.

The article was disconcerting. It was consistent with what Chic was hearing in his meetings, but now it was beginning to hit close to home. He stopped and asked himself again where Sparkly might be. As the waiter passed by, Chic told him that he was going to run over to the Tanganda Lounge to see if his breakfast partner was there. It took only a few moments to confirm that he was not there, so Chic lifted the receiver of the house phone on the desk and asked the hotel operator to put him through to Sparkly's room. There was no answer. He called Sparkly's cell phone, again receiving no answer. He went back to his breakfast table, trying to convince himself that Sparkly was still in the shower. Chic placed his order with the passing waiter and re-read the article. Once that was done, he got up and walked to the bell desk and asked if the bell captain would have someone check Sparkly's room. The bell captain confirmed that they would check once the cleaning staff was available. Chic returned to his table. While he sat there waiting, he had an uncomfortable foreboding that something had gone drastically wrong. Once again, he called Sparkly's cell phone, to no avail. His concern grew.

Chic signed his tab to his room and then left the hotel, heading for the Office of the 'Chief of Administration of Recording for the District of Marange', where Akatendeka worked.

"She will not be back to the office today," a young woman at the front desk informed him, and then returned promptly to her paperwork, as if to preempt further questions. As Chic left the office, he called the hotel and asked the front desk to put him through to Sparkly's room. It was not like Sparkly to be late or to avoid returning a call. A voice answered the phone. It did not belong to Sparkly.

"Mister Zhong, you must return to the hotel as soon as possible," the voice instructed.

He did not recognize the voice as any member of the hotel staff with whom he had conversed. Chic's concern grew exponentially to dread. He disconnected the call, and then promptly called the next Ministry he was scheduled to visit and postponed his meeting. They agreed to delay until the next morning. He decided to call his local partner in the ivory business, but then thought it might be risky to use his cell phone. Reaching into his pocket, he found he had no change for a pay phone. Chic walked down the street a few blocks toward a young man wearing a lime green T-shirt emblazoned with the slogan, 'Indigenize, Empower, Develop, Employ,' who was sitting on an inverted plastic bucket, smiling enthusiastically. In front of him was a blanket covered with used phones and chargers. Chic purchased an older cell phone and the matching charger.

"Is it fully charged?" Chic asked before he paid the boy.

"Ye, ye, you think I am foolish to sell what doesn't work?" the boy grinned up at him with his hand held out for the money. As Chic walked away, he noticed that the back of the boy's T-shirt had the word 'Revive'. He remembered that he had seen those slogans many times in Harare.

He searched for an 'Econet' shop and bought a SIM card containing five hours of time. Immediately he used the new/old phone to call the hotel again, informing them that he was on his way, and asked what had happened. The desk clerk acknowledged his call, calling him by name, and in the background, he could hear someone ask gruffly when he planned to arrive. The clerk parroted the same question into the phone. Without answering, Chic disconnected. Still on his new cell phone, he tried to call Mithoo, but got no response. Since he couldn't travel to the mine without creating a very real risk to the business, he was reluctant to visit Mithoo there.

He continued to walk, unconsciously making his way back toward the hotel, while wondering what to do. He stopped three blocks away, shrinking to the inside edge of the street when he heard a siren shrieking. Several more official vehicles were assembling at the entrance to the hotel. Behind Chic, unnoticed by him, stood a small-framed, inconspicuous older man. His drab jacket and wrinkled charcoal trousers were those of a poor placer miner dressed for his monthly visit to town. His hair was unkempt, and his shoes were a tired pair of Li-Ning Samurai III's. Those superficial attributes distracted from a pair of dark, clear and focused eyes, the types of eyes that indicate superior intelligence. When Chic moved, the man moved, a shadow totally invisible to Chic, whose focus was laser sharp on the hotel. What is going on? Why wouldn't anyone tell him anything? Why didn't Sparkly answer his cell or his room phone? What could explain...why did Akatendeka say 'beware'? Each time his thoughts, unbidden, turned to her, he asked himself what power it was that she seemed to hold over him. He believed he loved her, but was what he felt really only a severe case of infatuation or did she have something sinister on her mind? Gordon Zhong was unaware of the source of his misgivings, but it was like a thick cloud around him. All at once, he found it difficult to breathe.

MAMA AND DANIEL MEET - PRETORIA
- MORNING - 28 APRIL 2014

A ragged-looking woman, her back hunched from years of carrying excessive loads, shuffled along the walkway. Her tattered dress dragged sadly in the dust as her sandals seemed to ski across the dirt. She carried a stick carved from a piece of forest teak and darkened and polished by years of use. Her head, wrapped in what appeared to be a large dirty white bandage, only added to the appearance of a life spent in hopeless futility. Mama Prudence had only one more stop to make before going to the offices of Wilberson, Jonas & Sonneblom.

The door to the Flower Home for the Aged was always open to Mama Prudence. She entered and was greeted at the reception desk as though she were a member of royalty. Over the years, she had given to the Flower Home much of the surplus money that Daniel gifted her. It was used to take care of friends, family and the less fortunate at the facility. She requested the use of a room for half-an-hour and was promptly led to a vacant unit.

"Mama, your old Oriental friend has come home," the lady managing the enterprise said, "he would like to talk to you when you are free."

"Thank you," Mama smiled softly and said, "please let him know I shall contact him this evening."

Mama emerged fifteen minutes later, looking thirty years younger. She wore a floral dress and her bright red turban. On her feet she wore functional, but stylish, shoes and she had somehow magically converted her carry bag into a designer tote bag. She now carried her stick as an accessory to be used for the theatrics that accented her bold personality. As she departed the Flower Home, she smiled broadly, looking four inches taller and fifty pounds lighter. She continued to walk the remaining four kilometers to Daniel's office, arriving forty minutes later. She marched into the building and took the elevator up to Daniel's offices. She strolled into the reception area with generous greetings for everyone, and everyone present returned her greetings with enthusiasm. She looked toward the corridor to Daniel's office, and then back to the man sitting at the reception desk. He granted her a smile and a nod, and off she went.

"Good Morning, Abigail," she said with a broad smile, "is he free?"

"Good Morning, Mama. Please give me a moment to check if he is on the phone," she replied.

In a moment, she returned and guided Mama through the door. Daniel was focused on a document on his desk and reaching up blindly with his left hand to encourage her to sit. Moments later her looked up and slid the paper onto a growing pile.

"Good Morning, Mama, pardon my rudeness," Daniel said with a sincere voice. "How was your evening?"

"Daniel, it was, shall we say, somewhat productive," she replied, "may I have a cup of tea, please?"

Daniel buzzed Abigail and, within minutes, she appeared, carrying a tray that held a large pot of tea and two cups with saucers. Abigail didn't actually need to wait for instructions from Daniel. They had worked together for so long that she could anticipate his wishes before he stated them.

"Daniel," Mama started, "there is something happening. A body will be found this morning in a hotel in Harare. It will appear to be a witch's act but is not. I may have been wrong when I told you that the death of the Canadian was death by witchcraft. We shall soon know whether or not there are similarities between the murder in Canada and the murder in Harare.

As we have always suspected, there are some powerful people working together. I now know that this group includes a senior policeman and some other highly-placed individuals, perhaps one or two government ministers, as well as some businessmen, who are achieving great success in this economy."

"Mama, how do you know there was a murder in Harare?" asked Daniel.

"Where did it happen? Were any of your friends involved? Tell me truthfully, Mama."

"Daniel," she retorted, "I do not lie to you, but sometimes I receive information that could cause problems for you if I were to share it with you. For that reason, I need to keep it to myself, at least until I know that it will not affect you."

"Mama, please answer my question," he looked straight at her.

"Daniel, accept that I know, or not, as you wish." Mama was slightly annoyed.

Daniel lifted the receiver and dialed Abigail.

"Abigail, please check with the police and find out if there were any unusual murders in Harare overnight. Call me as soon as you learn anything, even if you suspect prevarication."

"Now, Mama, please, what has happened?" pleaded Daniel, impatiently.

"There was a briefcase with materials relating to the diamond business, which was of interest to the group I spoke of. It may have been taken. In any event, the owner has moved his soul to a different plane. His heart and liver have gone missing, as well. From what my friends could tell me last night..."

"Mr. Sonneblom," Abigail interrupted, "I have some information for you. May I come in?"

"Come right in," Daniel encouraged, then turning back to Mama, "we may learn something."

"We may learn that we already know what is important," replied Mama in a huff.

"Mr. Sonneblom," Abigail, her face ashen, reported nervously, "there was a man killed by witches at the Meikles Hotel last night. He was cut open," she proceeded fearfully.

"Apparently, he had been asking many questions related to the diamond business. Oh," she said before she left, "they think he may have been Asian."

"Thanks very much, Abigail."

Daniel sat contemplating the information and asking himself how Mama had gained that knowledge before the media had. He looked up at Mama and asked, "Who?"

"I think it was one of the Chinamen," she speculated.

Daniel came back with a question, "How did you know how he was killed?"

"Daniel, I have friends," she tried to calm him. "There are eyes and ears everywhere, Daniel. They are seldom wrong on the fundamentals.

"Do you want to know what else I learned last night?" Mama asked, waiting for an affirmative reply.

"Yes, Mama, please go ahead," he said, apologetically.

"I believe I have identified two of the members of the group," Mama stated.

"Would you like their names?"

"Go ahead, Mama," Daniel replied already feeling exhausted, though it was not yet mid-morning.

"Brigadier Khuphe and Major-General Nkala were seen driving together last night, to the house of an esteemed businessman, where a meeting was held," Mama stated.

"What is so unusual about two military officers travelling together?" Daniel asked, "Whose house did they meet at?" he added.

"I must do more investigation before I can tell you that," Mama Prudence said softly, as if distracted.

"The sources of my information have told me that the death of a person may have been discussed, but that it happened a week ago in a 'far-away' place. The participants affirmed to one another that no one of their group had anything to do with it. They spoke of other deaths in Zimbabwe that were not their doing, either. My source is reluctant to say too much as it may give away his identity and then he might be terminated."

"We already know one other member of the group and suspect another. Both are Ministers and close to the President," continued Daniel. "Do you have any idea why they are playing such a dangerous game, Mama? Why would they involve themselves with the military? Are they trying to get a business advantage or are they actually planning a coup d'état?

"Mama, pardon me for asking a question, which you had me promise not to ask," Daniel asked uneasily. "Are you speaking directly to the source or is this hearsay?"

"Daniel, you know why I told you never to ask," she replied.

"It is a very close friend of the man with whom I speak. She is a sister. Now stop those kinds of questions and just trust me to sort out the truth."

"You mentioned someone being killed far away from here. Can you determine if that may, by chance, have been our accountant?" Daniel requested, hopefully.

"The timing seems to fit and perhaps the motivation. Do you still believe that his murder was only made to look like the work of a witch?"

"Daniel," she scolded, "you sound almost like you are beginning to believe in witchcraft! No, it was not done by a witch and the man in Harare was not killed by a witch."

Then she added, "And the person who killed the accountant is not from here but is from there."

Daniel almost asked how she knew that but caught himself before he was too late.

"What do you propose we do next, Mama? Do you think you can get more information for us on this visit or do you need to go back to Harare?"

"I can always get more information, Daniel. It is only a matter of time,"

She smiled at him as a mother might smile at a child who had just spelled his first complicated word. "It might be more efficient if I return to Harare."

Daniel reached into his top drawer and drew out some envelopes. He handed them to Mama Prudence.

"This is for the next month, Mama Thank you for everything and please, thank your sisters."

"Daniel, you are so foolish with your money," she scolded him again, "someday you might end up old and poor, and then what? I'll be gone by then and who will help you?" she smiled indulgently and rose to leave.

"I will call you tomorrow morning if I have anything to report to you. Ta ta," and she left the room. When she was travelling, she never left a way for Daniel to reach her, but she always seemed to show up when he needed to speak to her.

Daniel knew that he must find out if the man who died had any link to the activities of the Barons. He knew that, by tomorrow, Mama would have more information, but he needed some now and he also had to contact Jacobus.

CHIC CALLS HIS HOME OFFICE - 28 APRIL 2014

Chic looked at his watch, and then thought for a minute. He had extraction plans. If he was going to use them, then he had to decide quickly. He still didn't know what it was all about, but he was certain now that something had happened to his assistant. His decision was to give his office a heads-up so that they would have time to prepare. It was only ten-thirty-four in Harare...so sixteen thirty-four in Shanghai. He pulled his new used cell phone from his pocket and dialed.

"*Xiàwǔ hǎo*," a soft feminine voice answered.

"*Hóngsè de tiānkōng*, Harare," Chic replied and hung up the phone. The office knew from the code word that it was Gordon Zhong calling. "Red Sky" was his code word to prepare for extraction from Harare. They would phone him back at this number in one hour. If, for some reason, they did not call him, he must call the office. If neither happened, someone would be dispatched automatically, and the insurance team would be contacted.

Gordon Zhong knew that he would need another cell phone and another SIM card. He also needed to find a place to wait where he was not so exposed. There was a shaded concrete bench sitting in an alcove by a stone fence. He moved toward that bench, thinking that it was out of the way enough for him to seek refuge and to rest for a few minutes. He needed to think things through. Although he had no specific reason, he intuitively had no desire to be inside a jail in Zimbabwe, waiting for a lawyer to get him out. His eyes were drawn toward the plaza across from the hotel and the police cars and ambulance in the front of the hotel. He was confused and concerned, in equal measure. He slid his own cell phone from his pocket and dialed Sparkly's mobile, not knowing what he would say if someone else answered. Someone else did answer, and the voice was that of the man he had heard earlier.

"When will you be here Mr. Zhong?" the voice demanded, in a tone that was almost an instruction, rather than a question.

"Earlier you were going to be here shortly. It is important that you come now!" The phone went silent.

Chic slid the phone back into his pocket and stared at a cloud floating above, trying to calm his thoughts. Suddenly, he sensed something. He turned quickly, only to find an elderly man sitting at the other end of the bench, head down, looking almost asleep. He did not move, and he showed no sign of recognition. He appeared simply to be an old derelict sitting peacefully at the other end of the bench. Chic wondered what the world would be like if he could feel like that old man, with his nondescript clothes, his old hat pulled down, his wrinkled hands lying across his lap, and... his running shoes. The only fashionable thing the man wore: China's best running shoes! How did they get here? He wondered.

Time to act! Chic realized that he needed to make a decision immediately. Would he go back to the hotel and risk a setup of some kind? He knew that something certainly was very wrong, and that, for some reason unknown to him, it involved him and Sparkly. Would he exercise the "Red Sky" and leave a trail of suspicion? Or could he find a way of staying low until he could glean more information? He had forty-seven minutes to prepare for the call. If he decided upon an extraction, he would likely have to be at the Charles Prince, 18 km northwest on the A1, or at Harare International.

The phone call would be very simple: the third and fourth letter of the ICAO code, sent in Morse code repeated behind a brief statement, which would end with the time of departure minus two hours: _ . _ . . _ . for Charles Prince or: _ . _ . . _ for Harare International. The time would be the last three digits of the twenty-four-hour clock, minus two hours, so 17:10 would simply be 15:10. There would be no confirmation. He would just have to be there at a predetermined door at precisely the time given. A person would meet him there with an appropriate passport and visa waiting, and a flight out of the country. Luckily all Chinese look the same to others! The running shoes, he thought, turning to look again at the man. The man was gone.

TATTOO CALLS DANIEL – KELOWNA – 28 APRIL 2014

Tattoo looked out over the Okanagan Valley. He was concerned. What did the motive for the death of Jim have in common with the motive to kill the man accused of killing Jim? Who was after Jim? Why was Jim dead? Why was this other man nearly killed? What might have been in the files that Jim had prepared that had someone so spooked? What gave them reason to believe that those particular files might have been in the briefcase? Lots of questions but little in the way of solid answers. Only speculation!

Jim had been travelling to Zimbabwe and the Republic of South Africa, to Belgium and to Saudi Arabia: gold, Chinese, diamonds, Indians, platinum, South Africans, rhinoceros horns, and Saudis? Jim wasn't an expert in any of those trades. Or was he? Something in this mess links to something else and, together, they link to Jim and to the man in the hospital. The strange buzzing sound in the living room indicated a phone call. Tattoo climbed out of his cedar Adirondack chair and walked into the den to take the call. It was early afternoon.

"Hello," he spoke softly, and then waited for a response.

"Hello, is this Will Turner?" a soft-spoken woman with a slight, unplaceable accent asked.

"Who is calling?" Tattoo replied.

"I am telephoning you at the request of a man you know as Lion," she responded. "Are you secure and do you have instructions?"

"I have his line. I will call him in a few minutes on a secure line," replied Tattoo.

'Lion,' he thought to himself, 'I haven't spoken to him for a number of years. A conversation with him might help me to answer some of my questions. He sat at the desk in his inner den and dialed the fifteen digits, and then waited the obligatory eight-tenths of a second for the signal to be routed across the land, to a satellite, and to another in geosynchronous orbit over Botswana, to the land line, and back to Pretoria. He heard the strange, modified-European ring, followed by a brusque," Hello?"

"Daniel, how the hell are you, old boy?" Tattoo responded, happy to hear his old friend.

"Haven't seen you for four or five years now. How is everything? Business still brisk?"

"Doing well for an old man, Will," Daniel mumbled, sounding a bit preoccupied, "Will, I wonder if you might be able to give me a hand? I have something complex and confidential and, as it turns out, there is someone over in your neck of the woods who is trying to eliminate the help. They have already taken down one of our consultants and might make a try on another. Interested?"

"I am unemployed. Let's talk," Tattoo answered, recognizing a sense of urgency in Daniel's voice.

"I have been engaged by a group of unnamed people in Zimbabwe to use a foreign consultant to assist them in researching and analyzing certain activities in the diamond business. I'll get into the details of that in a minute. The man we engaged was killed recently, and we suspect that it was on orders from one or more of the persons he was investigating, or who, at least, was involved with one of the groups being investigated. We have two requirements to help us to get to the bottom of it. First, we need to determine who killed our man in Canada and stop them legally, which means to identify them and turn them over to the local police for processing. Second, we need help looking out for a man with whom we have connected, who actually is located very near to where you are. He has indicated some willingness to assist us with the analysis, but we understand he has been charged with the murder of our consultant there.

We are using a local lawyer as a cutout. He has done some work for me in the past; you might even know him. He has suggested sending the candidate to Pretoria for vetting. Still interested?" Daniel asked.

"Yes, I am still good to go, but I think I may be involved already. This isn't a very big city and murders don't happen here all that often," Tattoo continued. "I shared an evening with a fellow who had been brought into the Queen's Hotel when I was locked up for a bit of a nuisance. He was pretty rattled, and I actually introduced him to a lawyer whom I know, Scott McIntyre, who is now looking out for him. I worked with Scottie some time ago. Is he your man? By the way, Scottie asked me to check in on this guy, who was on the wrong end of a hit and run that has him in the hospital at the moment, getting patched up for some broken bones and a concussion."

"Sounds like the same story," Daniel said, sounding surprised. "Are you alright working through Scottie? We need to move quickly and quietly, if possible. It might be necessary to use the man as bait, if you have some spare eyes available."

"I should be able to get some on board, and I have a few friends in the legal system," Tattoo was starting to sound enthusiastic.

"What can you tell me about the way your man, Jim was his name, yes? What can you tell me about how Jim was killed?"

"All I can tell you at the moment is that it sounded very much like a couple of killings that occurred here and that are slightly related. They appear to have been carried out by witches," Daniel answered, to Will's surprise.

"You do understand the power of witchcraft over here don't you, Will?"

"Yes, I do," Tattoo replied, "the funny thing is, that is the story the suspect in Jim's death concocted when he was trying to get out of the slammer. This guy told the cops that Jim was killed by a witch that he had brought back with him. It had something to do with a hyæna Jim had shot. I have heard about the witches but have never had to deal with one myself. Why would they try to spook anyone here in that way?" Tattoo asked.

"Don't know, but you likely will figure it out as you find more information. I'd better get back to things here Will. When you contact Scottie to work everything out, he will see that you are paid in the same way as before. Might even see you over here at some point. Are you still doing some hunting?"

"Less now that I am getting older," replied Will. "See you one day, Daniel. Take care."

ACTION - TELEPHONE CALLS - HARARE - 29 APRIL 2014

Detective-Sergeant Sibangilizwe reached the conclusion that the dead man's associate was not going to attend at the hotel any time soon, if ever. He slipped his private cell phone from his pocket and speed-dialed a number.

A voice answered, "Name?"

"*Sawubona 317*," he replied.

"One moment." the voice answered, and then another delayed voice came on the line. "Hello? Do you have a report?"

"We have the files from number two and the bags from number one. He is likely headed to the airport. I'll send one of our men to redirect him. The files are on the way to you."

He clicked off and restowed the phone. The Detective-Sergeant stepped into the hallway, pulled the phone out again and dialed another number.

"I need a man picked up and returned to me. Unofficially. His photo and ID will be left at the front desk of Meikles within twenty minutes. Ask for a brown legal envelope addressed to Wilson. Scheduled flight manifests are being scanned now. Respond on this line within an hour."

With that done, Detective-Sergeant Sibangilizwe went down to the lobby. He handed the front desk clerk the package addressed to George Wilson and told her it would be picked up soon. He asked if there was a package for him. She stepped into the back room and returned with a large envelope. He handed her a business card with a name and address in New York and asked her to re-address the package, to mark it Personal and Extremely Confidential and to send it by the fastest means possible. He then handed her his card and asked her to bring the bill for the shipping to him in the café. He went directly to the Tanganda, found a small table, and ordered a bowl of *pap* and a cup of straight coffee.

THE BARONS MEET - HARARE - 29 APRIL 2014

I t was twelve minutes past nine o'clock on the evening of April nineteenth and Walter Nkosi was sitting in his thick, comfortable, leather chair looking out the window of one of the many sitting rooms in his recently constructed palace. It was only on occasions like this when he would feel comfortable calling it a palace, but he liked the feel of it as it allowed him to think from the perspective of a lawgiver rather than one controlled by the law. He could think of his country and what was necessary for his country.

Walter Nkosi had paid more than one million United States dollars for his plot, seven point three acres of a fifty-five-thousand-acre farm that had once been granted to three British military officers for their services against the residents of what is now Zimbabwe. The irony was not lost on Walter. The cost of the palace was not yet completely tallied. To reach the area one drives up the appropriately named Enterprise Road. Spectacular scenery and broad vistas are enjoyed by a generation of nouveau riche. It is the land of the new Barons, located in the exclusive Borrowdale estate in north-eastern Harare. The well-groomed lawns of the Nkosi estate sprawled to the Msasa-treed ravines that meandered gently, eventually connecting to the Umwindsi River, interrupted only by a three point two-metre stone wall. The palms, pines and eucalyptus trees were absent but the jacaranda, one of the other remaining symbols of British colonialism, was planted generously to provide a cushion against the hardstone boundary of the Nkosi estate. Walter was not the only man who felt it necessary to build such a monument to his own success nor was he the only one to shroud his monument with fences and guarded gates to conceal it from the less fortunate people. A magnificent palace cuddled in a cocoon of privacy. There was something else important that he had learned on a visit to Russia a number of years ago, "It is not how powerful people believe you to be, but rather how much power they believe your friends can bring down upon them."

Timothy refreshed Walter's Glencairn wide-bowl crystal glass with an ounce of Macallan twenty-five and then applied a tiny dash of pure water. He returned the decanter and pitcher to the walnut trolley then offered the polished humidor from which Walter selected a Partagas Series E number two. This was his favorite cigar; six and one eighth inches long and fifty-two ring gauge. He very gently took the cigar and rolled it in his fingers, moistened it then took the cutter and clipped the end neatly. His cigars had already aged three years at his tobacconist. The cigar was named after Don Jaime Partagas who started making cigars in 1827 from the best tobacco grown on the best plantations of the Vuelta Abajo, in the Pinar del Rio province in the far west part of Cuba. When Walter was ready, Timothy presented a de-sulfured match for the light. Once the cigar was properly primed, he put it to his lips and took his first drag. Walter had learned to appreciate the creamy, leather taste and the smooth draw of this cigar and simply claimed it as his favorite. Timothy disappeared and Walter leaned back in his chair, savouring the exquisite life of a 'right proper gentleman'.

He was now part of a group of powerful men who were well placed and capable of affecting the recovery of their country. Some were Shona; some were Ndebele. All had a love for their country. As Walter contemplated the world, he realized that if Zimbabwe was to be successful it required certain things; it required men of power to get things done, an educated management class and motivated workforce combined with capital. He saw the problem as being one of returning certain capital to its rightful owners, the people of Zimbabwe. Because of their nature and genealogy, the people controlling the capital appeared to be the remnants of the colonizers; the construction equipment, the car dealerships, the breweries, the banks. These were all owned. The farms had been 'owned' by the white farmers who had been granted lands under the British Charter. In spite of Ian Smith's claims, they had never been granted in freehold. The British in

Hong Kong at least had the grace to return the island of Hong Kong to China. President Mugabe had tried to negotiate a reasonable arrangement to have lands turned over by compensating farmers on a willing seller - willing buyer basis under the terms of the Lancaster House Agreement. However, when the British, followed by the Americans, retracted their funding commitment, there was not any money to pay. This led to breached promises and the need to repossess lands in order to compensate the warriors who had fought for the freedom of the land. Still, in 2002, 4500 white farmers owned seventy percent of the richest farmland in the country. After William the Conqueror's land grab in England, he retained a quarter, the Church retained a quarter of the land, and William distributed the remaining half to a dozen Tenants-in-Chief and 8,000 barons.

Occasionally Walter Nkosi compared himself and his friends to the barons at Runnymede in 1215 and Robert Mugabe to King John of England. They all wanted to be rich and they all wanted power. They were well down the road to having a great nation, but the powerful barons were still required to ensure progress. Now it was time for the Barons of Great Zimbabwe to continue the process and to acquire the control of the various elements of the economy and to take the capital necessary, however they could acquire it.

Foreigners accused them of corruption and theft. This may seem true by modern western liberal standards, but what was the reality? Did not the Normans take the lands of the English in 1066 and give it to the warriors who helped to capture it? Is not one third of England still owned by 1,200 Aristocrats? Did not the Robber Barons of the United States use means to acquire control of businesses that annoyed the British investors? Did the English not finagle lands from the Native Indians in Canada by false or at least misunderstood promises in return for granting tiny reservations? Did the Aboriginals of Australia not have their lands taken and are only now gaining some of it back? How silly Ian Smith and his cohorts were to fight the reasonable requests for representation in the governance of the country, and how stupid they were to preempt the granting of representation by decreeing the Unilateral Declaration of Independence on the eleventh of November 1965.

And why, Walter asked himself, after all these years did he let that aggravate him? He had overcome the constraints for himself, but he needed to help others do the same. He had learned from reading about the New York bankers who had come to his country to help. He had learned from the Chinese who had come to help. He felt no guilt for his actions. Some people were crushed in the move forward. It was, as George Bush once put it, 'collateral damage' when an innocent suffered for the better good of his state.

Did President Mugabe not use extreme measures to achieve his policy objectives—to maintain control of government? Did not Mugabe deploy the North Korean trained Fifth Brigade—*Gukurahundi*— *'the early rain, which washes away the chaff before the spring rains'*— under the command of Colonel Shiri—to wreak havoc in the predominantly N'debele region of Matabeleland, against the supporters of Joshua Nkomo? Was it not under the orders of Robert Mugabe that the slaughter at Cewale River on the fifth of March 1983 took place and nearly sixty men and women died? Did not terror, incited by the Red Berets, get locals to sing Shona songs in praise of ZANU after being beaten and marched to the centre of town? He did what he thought was necessary to stay in power.

Who was to blame Walter Nkosi and his friends for their minor intrusions into the state's monopoly on the application of violence? The judicious application of death after all, was a way of getting people to respect intimidation, or at least to respond more quickly to it. Intimidation is sometimes necessary to encourage transactions, which are necessary for the progress of the state. Haven't rulers used that argument over the centuries? Why not Walter Nkosi?

The American or was it a Canadian, who had been getting into too much detail on certain business transactions and stimulating the media in the wrong direction, needed to be discouraged. It was not yet the time for transparency. It certainly was not the time to be feeding information to foreign NGOs who had no other purpose in their existence than to disrupt the orderly restructuring of the wealth of his nation. It would be very destructive if it was provided to most of the western press to be printed in their self-righteous euro-centric perspective. How could a nation where everyone seemed to get a fee for everything they did, refer to it as a brokerage fee, an agency fee, a finder's fee, a management fee or a legal fee, but when a black man did the same, he was corrupt? Was it the quality of his business card that made the difference?

"One concern that all the members of our group have in common," thought Walter Nkosi, "is how to restore Zimbabwe to its position as the economic power centre of Africa that it once was." This was not going to be achieved by riots by subsistence farmers or by protests by mining unions or by 'social workers posing as political action groups'. It required powerful men, well-capitalized men, men who were comfortable taking control of government and fixing it. It required men who had the ability to correct the terrible injustices wreaked upon Zimbabwe's economy by apparently well-meaning American and British consultants working for the World Bank, or by the mass of NGOs sent to help their nation. All the Barons desired was to make Zimbabwe great again! They had the brains and the power and soon would have the capital to do just that! There were other very powerful people from far away who simply wanted to strip Zimbabwe of its wealth and keep it for themselves, to hell with Zimbabwe!

MAMA PRUDENCE ARRIVES IN HARARE - 29 APRIL 2014

Mama had a premonition of trouble as she arrived in Harare. She went directly to the phone booth in the train station.

"Akatendeka, good evening. May I come to see you?" Mama asked.

"Of course, Mama! You don't know how badly I need to talk to you. How soon will you be here?" was Akatendeka's response, "I have tried to contact you the old way but wasn't successful."

"I will see you within the hour." The phone went dead.

ALEXANDER POPE REQUESTS
A MEETING - 28 APRIL 2014

On his way to the airport, Alex Pope called Gordon Zhong's office in Shanghai. Gordon was not in, but the office would try to pass along the message for him to return the call as soon as possible. Alex headed for Dulles Airport to catch a late United flight back to New York City.

It was ten-ten in Harare. Chic had four more minutes before the decision would be made for him. His company cell dinged a message. He slid it from his pocket.

CALL ALEX IN AM NYC TIME.

He returned it to his pocket and waited. The call came through exactly as expected.

"Sixteen-forty—dah-dit-dah-dit dit-dah-dah-dit," the female voice stated, after which a tone signal followed. Gordon interpreted this correctly as 14:40 at the Charles Prince Airport, two-forty in the afternoon, three hours and seventeen minutes from now. He would leave his bags and have his office notify the hotel once he was out of the country. In any event, the police would be searching through them. He began walking away from the hotel, and once he felt safely distant, he flagged a taxi, even though it would mean that he would arrive too early at the Charles Prince Airport.

The taxi headed up Sam Nujoma Street through the tangled traffic. Accelerate and brake; accelerate and brake. Chic felt a little unsafe and certainly uncomfortable in the back seat of the older Toyota Corolla. As they crossed Princess Drive, Chic noticed that the driver in the adjacent car was staring at him. The car moved closer and its driver shouted loudly to the cab driver. An argument ensued between the two and grew in intensity. The two cars bumped. The driver of his cab was swearing loudly but jammed on the brakes and pulled over to the sidewalk. The other car cut in front. Its driver leapt from the car and ran back toward the cab. Suddenly, a pedestrian jumped from the street, engaging the man as he approached Chic's cab. Within moments the driver from the other car was lying on the sidewalk, immobile. The pedestrian jumped into the passenger side front seat and told Chic's driver to proceed, apparently with instructions to get away from the scene as quickly as possible.

Chic was in shock. He had just observed some kind of action about which he knew nothing. Did it have something to do with him? Was he in danger? Was he being kidnapped? The cab driver continued quickly, but not so fast as to attract attention. He maneuvered efficiently through the traffic, making progress up the street as it widened into the A-1 heading for Charles Prince Airport. The driver and the new passenger ceased speaking until the cab approached the field. By hand gestures the passenger directed the cab to the flight centre on the east side of the terminal. The taxi stopped. The passenger partly turned and threw an old raincoat over the seat.

"Put this on," he said to Chic, and then he paid the driver and climbed from the car. He stepped to the back and opened Chic's door.

"Follow me!" he commanded.

Chic followed blindly and without question, since they were headed to the same place. As soon as they walked through the door of the FBO, two men approached Chic and led him to a small meeting room. They introduced themselves as his security team from Furiæ Security SSA. They explained that they had been engaged by Chic's office on the recommendation of his insurers.

"Please have a chair and make yourself comfortable for a while. We have a takeoff slot booked for five past three and will have to wait until two thirty-five for the Immigration guy to come over. We have a clean wardrobe for you, if you require it. We have a Canadian passport made in your Chinese name. It contains a number of appropriate entrance and exit stamps with visas. There are three credit cards, each with a different expiry date. The pin code is the same for each until you reset them. 8888. There is paper confirmation of your hotel reservation and it matches the one on your replacement cell phone. The SIM card on your new phone has enough activity to suggest you have had it for a month and that you have been dealing with the office of a company in China, as well as various offices in Harare. We would like you to review this information, so you might answer any questions accurately, if you are asked by Immigration or the police. This is a precaution, just in case they arrive and mistake you for who you are.

"The man outside this room is your expediter, Clive Fotheringham. You will identify him as your Executive Assistant. He will be with us until you have cleared Immigration and Customs in Dubai. He is an expert in ensuring that such clearances go smoothly. He will also carry your brief-case and passport."

Chic was impressed by the proficiency of this new team, but their seriousness made him even more concerned for his well-being. They continued with his security briefing, letting him know where he had been in Harare, for whom he worked in China and what his position was, at which hotel he had stayed in Harare, and a variety of other details. He wouldn't remember it all, they acknowledged, but the E.A. would be able to jump in at any time to correct little details. If the interrogation became too intense, they had a plan 'B'.

"Do you know what happened back there, when I was on the way here? That old guy, whoever he was, got into a fight with another driver, who was arguing with my cabbie. He knocked him down, jumped into my cab and rode out here." Chic was still feeling bewildered.

"Yes, we are aware," spoke the older of the two, "the objective of the man who bumped into your cab was to stop you and to keep you from leaving until another person arrived. You were fortunate that your cabbie had a temper."

"Who was the old guy? What did he have to do with things?" asked Chic.

"We don't know," answered the same gentleman, "the information we received was by phone passed through our office in Pretoria. You weren't hurt, were you?"

"No, just stunned!"

After that, there was not much to do or to talk about for the forty-minutes remaining until it was time to load up. They sat in the meeting room. Chic listened half-heartedly to pilot stories and about the places they had been and the women they had met. The hostess joined the banter until she received word that the provisioning was aboard. The E.A., Clive, joined her outside and walked to the plane with her, returning about five minutes later and suggesting to the pilots that they were to commence their pre-flight inspections and then board. He and Chic would await the arrival of the Immigration Officer, likely in ten minutes. He hoped that the Officer would be content merely to look at the manifest and review the passports, rather than to interview the pilots and the hostess.

A few minutes later the door opened and a large man in a light blue uniform entered and stared at Chic.

"Are you the criminal everyone is looking for?" he asked, looking sternly at Chic.

Chic paused for a moment before answering.

"I don't think so. What is it I am supposed to have done?"

He was obviously nervous.

The big man looked over at the E.A. and burst out in a boisterous laugh.

"Your friend here looks nervous. Let's see the manifest, please."

Clive handed him the manifest and the stack of passports. The big man sat down, took out his official stamp and started flipping through the passports, stamping the exits. When he was finished, he stood up and shook hands with the E.A.

"You must teach your boss how to stay cool like you do or some new guy is going to think he has something to hide."

He roared again at his joke, slapped Chic on the back and bid them bon voyage.

Chic's legs had almost turned to rubber. He had to sit for a moment before he could walk to the aircraft. Clive smiled at him and said, "Let's get this show on the road. You will feel much better when we get out of their airspace."

The two Pratt and Whitney 308C engines of the Dassault Falcon 2000LX were idling when Chic was escorted onto the tarmac at Charles Prince Airport. On the way to the aircraft his E.A. explained that the flight to Dubai International Airport would be about seven-and-a-half hours, assuming winds were as projected. Two pilots would ride in the cockpit and a third would ride with the two-man security team and the hostess in the forward cabin area. Clive would ride in the aft compartment with Chic. They mounted the stairs and found their seats. Chic appreciated the delicious smell of the soft leather and admired the comfort as he settled in and found his seatbelt. He heard the engines rev and felt the aircraft begin to move on to the taxiway. The disembodied voice of one of the pilots came over the intercom and announced, "Good afternoon. We will be departing shortly for Al Maktoum airport in Dubai. Our departure runway is number thirty right. Once we are airborne you will be able to watch the flight map to see our progress today. We should arrive in Dubai at nine-forty this evening."

Chic had to place a few calls quickly. First, he would call his office in Shanghai to let them know he was airborne, which likely they already knew. Then he would call Alex in New York. He picked up the receiver of the telephone system and looked at the E.A.

"Is this secure?" he asked.

"See the little switch on the bottom?" asked Clive. "Once you have made contact, flick it to the right; that will put you on scramble mode. It will ask your office for a code. Once that is entered you will be secure. Otherwise, only your half of the conversation will be secure."

"Thanks," said Chic as he started to dial his office.

"*Xiàwǔ hǎo*," the soft feminine voice answered.

"*Xiàwǔ hǎo*," Chic replied, "I am airborne and the ETA is..."

She interrupted him, "I have the information. Call in when you are on a secure line or route the call through Furiæ. *Zàijiàn*."

She was gone. He had told her nothing. He needed to tell someone something. Experiences like he was having needed to be shared or they became something else, fantasy, maybe, or a wild imagination. Or craziness. Right then he was feeling like a ball being bounced around with no input from him. He was totally in the hands of others, of strangers. He would like nothing more right now than to lie next to Akatendeka, to tell her everything, to get it all off his chest, no matter how surreal it sounded. He couldn't have conversations like that with his father. His father would just stare at him with incredulity implying that he "grow up, boy, it is about time." He had no one to talk to honestly and openly. He dialed Alex's number in New York.

"Sullivan, Wachtel and Pope, how may I help you?" the voice spoke automatically.

"Alexander Pope please, it's Gordon Zhong returning his call," Chic replied equally automatically.

"One moment please. Please hold." Music clouded the phone line until the voice returned. "Mr. Zhong, he will be with you in a minute." The music resumed.

A moment later Alex was on the line.

"Where are you, Gordon?" he asked, "We need to talk."

"Dubai," responded Chic, "are you able to get to London, about halfway for each of us? I can likely be there tomorrow evening."

"London works for me. Where would you like to meet?" Alex asked.

"I like to stay at the Millennium Hotel just west of Gloucester Road. It's out of the way and quiet. We could meet in the lobby there and choose a place for dinner."

"Sounds good to me. See you at about seven tomorrow evening, unless I hear otherwise." He hung up the phone.

Chic sat back in his seat, took a deep breath and let it out in a long sigh. The hostess promptly asked if he would like something to drink.

"I would like a vodka martini with an olive, if possible," Chic said, sounding exasperated, then he lifted his head and smiled apologetically. He dialed his office again and asked to have his flights to London arranged. He waited impatiently until his drink arrived and was set on the writing table. He reached into his case, brought out a legal pad and began to write everything he could remember. Chic knew that the next morning he would have to retain a lawyer to sort out what was going on in Harare.

He decided that he would call Richard Hammersmith, his representative in the mine management company, to get some advice on a lawyer who understood criminal law and who could act very discreetly. Next, he needed to get Sparkly back to Shanghai so he could explain, face-to-face, to Chic's father what was going on. As he was thinking about what else he would need to do tomorrow, he dozed off and slept deeply.

Chic had always wondered what the appeal of Dubai was. He remembered from his school days that it was a dry, hot desert city with nothing but a bit of oil, many camels and a few nomadic Bedouin. Somehow, since his last visit, it had magically transformed into the Cinderella city of the desert. It was now an impressive, modern city. The answer, it seemed, was the collision of two factors: geographical location and a far-sighted sheik. Its location was reasonably central for people doing international business. Dubai was just southwest of Abu Dhabi in the United Arab Emirates, but from a more international perspective, Harare was only 2974 nautical miles, Shanghai 3474 nm, London 2957 nm, New York 5953 nm, and Moscow, only 1986nm. The longest flight to anywhere in the world was to New York, at fourteen-and-a-half hours.

It was about nine-thirty when the aircraft began its descent into the Dubai Airport. Chic had awakened only a few minutes earlier. The red desert sun had set long before. The hostess reminded everyone to secure their seatbelts and return their seats to their proper upright and locked positions. Chic began to pack the papers back into the briefcase and then passed it over to his E.A. The two security men sitting in the forward part of the cabin began to talk with an elevated urgency about the time.

The aircraft commenced its final approach and three-and-a-half minutes later the tires chirped onto the tarmac. They had arrived! As the Dassault taxied to the FBO, a white limousine appeared on the tarmac. The aircraft was brought to a stop, the access door was opened, and Clive stepped down to greet the official who had arrived simultaneously. Moments later he peered his head into the cabin and waved everyone forward. One of the security men stepped down before Chic, the other waved Chic forward and then followed. The Immigration Agent nodded and welcomed each to The Emirates. The leading security man opened the rear door of the limousine and ushered Chic inside, while the E.A.

entered the front passenger seat. The other man climbed into a less osten-
tatious GMC Tahoe, along with some others. Apparently, the pilots and
the hostess would make their own ways to their destination.

As the limousine departed the airport, the Clive explained the choice
of hotel. They had selected the Time Grand Plaza Hotel because of its
proximity to the airport, only four kilometres down Damascus Street. They
had chosen a limousine rather than a rental or a taxi for the drive to the
hotel in order to pre-empt questioning at the airport. Once at the hotel,
transportation would be more modest, but in keeping with a middle-man-
agement executive. He also stated that once they ensured he was checked
into the hotel their mission was officially completed. He would leave Chic
with a business card and a code word that he could use if something came
up that required their assistance.

"And by the way, the Brio restaurant in the hotel is quite good. Alfredo,
the Bell Captain, will reserve a good seat for you as we are checking you in,
if you wish," suggested the older security man.

They arrived at the hotel in what seemed like moments. Chic still felt
strangely as though everything was happening around him and he was just
there to accept the actions of the team and to follow his man. While the
senior man completed the check-in process, Clive led him over to meet
Alfredo. A bellman carrying Chic's bags, accompanied by the two other
security men, passed him on their way to the elevators, while the senior
man accepted a room key.

"Alfredo, good to see you again. Could you arrange for my friend to
have a good table for dinner at ...?" he looked at Chic for a time.

"Ah, I think it is much too late for dinner this evening," Chic blurted
realizing that everyone was watching, waiting for his response.

"Good, then breakfast at seven, it is. Thanks, Alfredo," said Clive, as
they turned and walked toward the elevators, together with the senior man.
They arrived on the fifth floor and found the room, which was situated
close to the elevator bank. The E.A. knocked twice, paused, then knocked
twice again and the door was opened.

"Everything is fine," the other security man said to Clive, as he moved
toward the elevator. The E.A. stopped and asked if there was anything that
Chic required of him before he departed. Chic shook his head no. Clive

shook Chic's hand and then the senior man shook his hand, reminding him of the business card. He and Clive left together, ensuring the door was closed securely behind them.

"Good night, and thanks," Chic said in an exhausted voice.

He turned and faced the bed. Instantly he felt a profound need to sleep. He undressed quickly, hung his clothes tidily, polished his shoes, and then headed to the bathroom, brushed his teeth and rinsed his mouth. Finally, he climbed into bed. He laid on his back looking at the ceiling. He closed his eyes, but he could not unwind. His mind was racing with bizarre images, but soon exhaustion took over and he fell into a deep sleep, though the images morphed into weird dreams. The reality of Sparkly's death had finally sunk in, along with it the further realization that perhaps he had been the actual target. He dreamed of Akatendeka and what she had said when she left the room.

"You are in danger," and she had also said "there is no way for our relationship to continue."

What had caused her to say those things? Had she been aware that something was about to happen? Was it possible that she was involved and that somehow, she had diverted the killer to Sparkly? No, impossible. Would the police consider her a likely suspect? She had been seen, after all, having dinner with an Asian man. She would have been observed leaving the hotel alone late that night. She had been on the same floor as Sparkly's room. Then, though he did not want to consider it, he wondered: was there any way she could have done it?

AKATENDEKA LEARNS THAT "CHIC" WAS MURDERED - HARARE - 29 APRIL 2014

katendeka strode into the office after her day off. She headed for the coffee room for her morning java. The coffee machine was surrounded by the usual morning 'coffee cluster' but today their chatter was particularly animated. Flora, one of the newer girls, called out to Akatendeka as she walked toward the machine.

"Did you hear what happened yesterday, while you were away?" the girl asked enthusiastically, anxious to spread the gossip while it was still valuable.

"No, what?" asked Akatendeka, showing appropriate curiosity.

"That cute little Chinaman who comes to the office was murdered," came the blunt response. "It was on the news this morning. They are looking for a woman who was seen leaving his floor and then the hotel. Apparently, they were able to get good photos from the CCTV cameras."

Akatendeka was horrified. All at once, she couldn't catch her breath. She felt the blood drain from her face.

"Did they give his name, by any chance?" She hoped against hope that it was a mistake.

"No name, yet," the girl replied, seeing that Akatendeka was stricken by the news.

"Tell me you didn't know that guy, I mean outside the office?" she looked straight into Akatendeka's eyes.

"Oh, my God! You dated him! Didn't you? Was it you? Were you the woman?"

Akatendeka had trouble keeping her cool. Calling upon the years of training and discipline she had undergone, she forced herself to be calm, and replied with a small smile, "I don't have time for dating, and if I did would it be that little foreigner?" she queried with a wink. "No, it wasn't me! Anyway, I was so sick I couldn't get out of bed."

She took her coffee and headed for her desk.

Her insides were churning, fear mixing with the remnants of breakfast to create nausea that she may not be able to control. She thought about the photos taken from the video of the CCTV cameras. She must contact Mama Prudence at once, before the photos could reach the newspapers or the television news.

DETECTIVE-SERGEANT NOTIFIES HIS BOSS – HARARE – 28 APRIL 2014

Detective=Sergeant Sibangilizwe needed to explain to his superior that he had decided to withhold the photos from the press for the time being, in order to reduce the possibility that one or more of the parties may flee. They had already lost the second Chinaman and the Detective-Sergeant was curious about that. 'Why would he tell me that he was returning to the hotel, and then run? What caused him to feel that he needed to get out of town? Was it guilt? Fear for his life? Perhaps he somehow suspected why his partner was killed. It wouldn't take long to identify the woman who had visited the floor. She wasn't a priority, since she had not visited the room of the deceased. He needed to arrest someone soon so that his superiors did not begin to question him about not solving a killing that should be easy to figure out. He could release the prisoner when he found an appropriate witch on whom to lay blame. Meanwhile, he still needed to report the death to his Zimbabwe superior, a man he did not like, a man he held in contempt, for he was one of the state's "valuable foreigners" who were helping themselves to the resources of Zimbabwe in order to glorify the President.'

All those thoughts swirled through his mind as he waited on hold to speak with his Inspector downtown.

"Inspector Butholezwe, who's on the line?" barked the Inspector.

"Sibangilizwe here. Just wanted to give you an update on the murder at Meikles Hotel. Body on the way to the morgue, looks like witchcraft, some organs missing, will be reviewing security tapes for unusual traffic. I want to minimize press beyond having let them know that someone was murdered. I don't want to incite the perpetrator to panic and run before we have some information to work with. Any questions, sir?"

"Not at the moment, Detective," the Inspector replied, "keep me informed."

"Will do," he replied, "I'll likely see you in the shop this afternoon. Have a good day."

"You too."

MAMA ARRIVES AT AKATENDEKA'S FLAT - 29 APRIL 2014

Mama was puffing slightly by the time she reached the top of the stairs and started down the corridor toward Akatendeka's flat. She approached silently and then lightly scratched at the door. There was a slight pause before the door was opened. Mama slipped through the door and into the flat's vestibule. Her arms flew open as she took Akatendeka into her embrace. Akatendeka was distraught, a very unusual state for her protégé.

"What's wrong, my dear?" she said, as she gently patted her back, "What has happened?

"I just found out that my friend was murdered at Meikles Hotel the night before last," she explained, "I had just had dinner with him. We went to his room for a while. I told him that I couldn't see him again and then I went home."

"Carry on," Mama encouraged, "what has happened since?"

"Well, I got up yesterday morning but felt so sick when I got to work, then I just came home and went to bed. When I went into the office this morning, they were all talking about the murder. I feel so bad, Mama."

"I understand," Mama said, "but you must sit and listen to me. It was not your friend who was killed. It was his assistant. Now listen. This is part of something very important and may involve your boss. We need to obtain some information. We have a second problem. The police are likely going to end up talking to you because they will know that you were on that floor on the night of the murder and that you had dinner with the victim's boss. They will want to know what has happened to the boss. Apparently, the police spoke to him and he said he would be at the hotel soon, but he never made it. Nobody has seen him since."

Mama continued, explaining what she had been told by her contacts.

"You must use your training to stay calm and mature. Only answer what you know for a fact. Only answer the questions you are asked," she advised firmly.

"I understand. What do you need to know from my boss?" asked Akatendeka, her composure almost restored.

"I will need you to get into a discussion about the problem you keep reading about - the issues regarding the money from the diamond sales in Dubai and Antwerp. Try to understand where his sympathies lie. See if you can get a sense of whom he believes is right and who is wrong, and on where he stands politically on the issue. He is in charge of the Morange District and there are many Chinese investors and many Zimbabwean partners in his district. See if you can ascertain who he thinks is responsible for the disappearing funds, and if he believes there may be other factors at play."

Mama continued, "Do you believe that your little Asian friend believes in Zimbabwe or do you think that it is simply a source of quick money for his investors? Do you really think he loves you or does he find you convenient while he is here? Think hard young lady! Lives may depend on the true answers. One's life may depend upon what one believes."

"I will do what I can Mama. It might involve dinner or something else for me to find out," answered Akatendeka.

"You have been well trained in many arts," spoke Mama, "now is the time to put your skills and all that you have learned to good use. I will be at the Mojo café at noon tomorrow, in case you have something for me. I shall come back here to your home late tomorrow night in any event, and with your permission, I shall let myself in if you are not here. Now I must go, and you must start thinking."

Mama rose from her chair and swept from the room without looking back.

DANIEL CALLS CLIVE FOTHERINGHAM
- 29 APRIL 2014

D aniel was beginning to create a picture in his mind. The attack on the Oriental fellow at Meikles had, from all indications, been related to Jim's death, and perhaps to the deaths on Jacobus' farm. He sensed that more were coming. The killers were back in Zimbabwe and obviously were active again there. The common factor of Jim's death and the Asian's seemed to have something to do with either the ivory trade or the diamond trade. Jim had been investigating all investment and trade but had focused primarily upon resources. Ivory received a great deal of attention because of the American funding of NGOs. From what Jim had learned, the Asian man was active in diamonds and, to a smaller extent, in ivory. Daniel thought that the attacks on Jacobus' farm were probably related to stopping Jim's investigations, but it was impossible to be sure just yet. He wondered how the three deaths could be related, since, so far, the existence of the CPZ was unknown in Zimbabwe. If there was another party outside the country who was sufficiently concerned about the results of Jim's investigation and the subsequent publicity, then there might be a motive for someone to order these killings. In the midst of all he did not know, Daniel did know one thing. He knew he needed help.

"Abigail," Daniel spoke into the intercom, "can you reach Clive for me, please?"

Her reply was prompt.

"I am sorry Mr. Sonneblom, Mr. Fotheringham is away on a job."

"When he checks in, make sure you put him through, please. It's rather important."

When he clicked off the intercom Daniel was already planning his next step. Clive and Daniel were very good friends. They had been together since the merger with Furiæ. Clive was advancing in years, as well, but anything he lacked in physical acuity he more than made up for with street smarts. He had earned his spurs with the SAS. He had lived on Benzedrine tablets, while standing for days in the swampy river of Sierra Leone as part of Operation Barras. While it was in 'enemy' hands, he had entered Abu Ghraib prison to recover a mate and an American. He was fearless, intelligent and an incredible judge of humans.

As Daniel was reflecting on the outstanding qualities of his friend, the intercom clicked on, "I have Richard Hammersmith on the line for you, Mr. Sonneblom. Do you wish to take the call?" Abigail's pleasant voice enquired.

"Yes, thank you," he responded, and Abigail connected him.

"Hello, Richard, how have you been?"

"Fine Danny, just fine. Dealing with the vicissitudes of life here, but all is well. Danny, I wonder if I can request your assistance in a bit of a bother we have here?" Richard opened.

"What seems to be the problem, Richard ... are we talking as lawyers or are you looking for security services?" Daniel asked.

"Perhaps it might be both, but for now it is a legal issue," Richard continued, "Would you like me to proceed?"

"Richard, should I be there, or can you come here? Or, shall we do this over a secure line?" asked Daniel.

"I'll call you back on a secure line. It will be a half hour." Richard hung up the phone.

Daniel wondered how the pieces of this puzzle would come together. He was receiving information from Scottie that indicated that Jim likely had been murdered by two men who used poison Hemlock as part of their M.O. Those men had then secured a briefcase containing what they thought were the target files. They might have come to Harare to deal with the Chinaman and to obtain his files. It was becoming increasingly clear that someone big was guiding this operation, someone who had money and tremendous backup capacity, and who would apparently stop at nothing to prevent information from becoming public. Early on, Scottie's friend, Will Turner, had found only a whiff of information on the web that might indicate that a private contractor was committing the murders. If it turned out that Richard's issue related to the same Chinaman who was wanted for questioning, then the man's life was in severe danger.

The intercom buzzed.

"It's Mr. Hammersmith on the secure line, Mr. Sonneblom."

Abigail clicked off.

"Richard, go ahead, what's happening that you need a lawyer?" Daniel began.

"A representative of one of the Chinese investors in a couple of our diamond mines up here has put himself in a bit of a pickle. He and his assistant were in the Meikles the other night and the assistant was murdered. I don't know if you heard about it or not, but my guy didn't hang around to visit the police. He just scooted. He called me from Dubai and told me his problem and asked if I could recommend a good criminal lawyer for him. I thought that, since he is safely out of the country, it might be foolish for him to come back until some things are resolved. I want to recommend you to him if it is Ok with you, even though I know criminal law is not your forte," Richard summarized.

"He most probably told you he was innocent and that he had no idea who the perpetrator was, right?" Daniel suggested, "Do you believe him?"

"I believe him, but I am not experienced in these things. He has always been quite straight in any dealings I have had with him, even to the point of naivete at times," Richard described, "I think he just has a fear of being jailed in a foreign country for the convenience of the local police, and of never finding a way back out. I will let him describe to you more fully what he it he is looking for, if you are prepared to take him on. If you wish to use counsel in Harare, I am sure he would be amenable to that."

"I would be willing to meet with the two of you, if we can work it. Is he still in Dubai?" Daniel asked

"Yes. I understand he will be going to London soon and after that, I know not where." Richard finished off.

"Well, contact him and get back to me on this line. We'll set something up right away. Bye for now. By the way, we should get together for some tennis if you are down this way."

"Great idea! Talk to you soon." Richard rang off.

The intercom buzzed again, "Mr. Fotheringham for you sir, on the secure line," Abigail clicked off.

"Clive, how are you? Where are you?" Daniel asked.

"I am once again enjoying the lovely desert of the Middle East, Dubai at the present. What can I do for you, boss?" Clive asked.

"I wonder if you can travel to Harare for me and do a touch of research. Some things are happening that are becoming a bit of a bother, and I would like to put a stop to it before it grows," Daniel replied.

"I expect to be there tomorrow. I thought I might treat myself to one night's sleep first if that is Ok." Daniel could hear the grin on his face.

"Call secure as soon as you get to the office." Daniel hung up the phone.

JACOBUS LEARNS DETAILS OF SPARKLY'S DEATH – 27 APRIL 2014

Daniel placed a call to the Victoria Falls Hotel and asked if the reservation for Jacobus had been confirmed, and then hung up without waiting for an answer. An hour later, the buzzer rang, and Abigail put Jacobus through on the secure line.

"Ja, Daniel, *Hoe gaan dit met jou*? Jacobus started.

"Fine, Jacobus. Look, I think we have an accelerating problem," Daniel stated.

"We have a person in Harare who met the same fate as the accountant. Too similar to be coincidental! The victim is not someone with whom we have dealt or whom we know. I am trying to get some information together. You and the guys must lie low for now. Stop doing or stimulating anything that might link back to you in any way. I have a feeling that something big is involved and that the target group is growing. I need a bit of time to sort it all out. I am sending one of my men back to Harare to work on it. We may have to meet soon. How much lead time will you need to bring your people together, say in Harare or Vic Falls?"

"I think we can meet in less than a day, if you don't care which of the two places it is." replied Jacobus.

"I will leave a message for either Meikles or Vic Falls to call you confirming the reservation time and the time for dinner, and that shall be your target. Sound Ok?"

"Ja, goed," Jacobus replied, "*tot siens*," then hung up the phone.

CHIC MEETING IN LONDON - 28 APRIL 2014

Chic departed on the two-twenty-five am flight from Dubai to London Heathrow. The six-hour and forty-five-minute non-stop flight was uneventful. He and cleared Immigration and Customs easily and quickly, exiting Heathrow just after eight in the morning and purchasing a ticket for the train to Paddington Station. In most cities, he would have taken a limousine but in London the train was much faster, and from Paddington, he had just a short and convenient taxi ride to the Millennium Hotel. It was a block down from the Bailey's Millennium and lacking the character, but it was better set up for the meeting he was about to have. He checked in with just a small bag and carried it himself to his room. He phoned the front desk to ask if Alexander Pope had checked in yet. He hadn't. Chic unpacked his few belongings and reviewed his agenda for the evening. They were to meet at the 'Bombay Brasserie' on Courtfield Road, just up the street from the hotel, for dinner. It was only noon and Chic decided that he had enough time to purchase a few clothes to replace those he had left in his room in Harare. He walked up the street and across to the tube station. He caught the blue line up to Green Park Station, walked across Piccadilly and then down St. James to Jermyn Street. He stopped into Pinks and picked up a few casual dress shirts, ties and some other light clothing. A few doors down the street he purchased a pair of comfortable oxfords from Crockett and Jones. He felt properly dressed again and would feel fine until he recovered his luggage from the hotel in Zimbabwe.

When he returned to the hotel, Chic checked the front desk and found that Alex had arrived. As soon as he got to his room, he phoned Alex.

They agreed to meet in the lobby at six-thirty and walk to the restaurant together. Chic climbed into bed and set his alarm for five-thirty, which would give him enough time to shower and change before dinner and arrive with a clear mind. He also knew that the few hours until they met would help Alex shed the jet lag of his flight across the Atlantic.

Feeling quite refreshed, Chic was sitting in an easy chair in the lobby when he spotted Alex emerging from the elevator. He stood and Alex walked to greet him. They shook hands and then left the hotel, turning up Courtfield toward the Brasserie. They were greeted at the door and soon found themselves seated, with a busboy pouring water and a waiter asking for drink orders. They both passed on the drinks and requested a minute to look at the menu. The waiter returned a minute later.

For his appetizer, Chic selected a glass of salted *lassi* with Prawn *kalimiri*, and for the main course, the *Gosht ki nihari*, a lamb cooked in delicious gravy. Alex chose the *Khada masala,* spiced scallops, for his appetizer and, for his main course, chargrilled chicken thighs with a tomato and cream sauce. They agreed to share some sautéed spinach, fried garlic, cucumbers with mint, and an order of *naan* bread. For dessert, they would have the *Pista phirnee* with carrot cake and some tea. During dinner they made small talk.

After dinner, Alex began his brief report. He explained the research they had completed and then the strange call he had received from Washington. He gave Chic some background on the Senator and on his powerful relationships. He told Chic how the Senator had gracefully suggested a course of action, which, translated, comprised a threat to stop digging around or be prepared to suffer the unpleasant consequences. Chic asked for Alex's advice.

Alex said matter-of-factly, "If you don't want to wake up with flowers growing from your chest, we must back away on the research."

Chic wondered what the hell was happening, and who was making a threat that seemed to be so serious that Alex was advising him to back off.

"Surely there must be more that we can do," Chic suggested.

"We can't be expected to walk away from that kind of money without knowing why!"

"We might be able to negotiate something through the Senator, maybe some kind of cash release, or something in return for stopping our investigations. It seems that someone else has been digging into things far more deeply than the Senator's associates appreciate, and they, whoever they are, have become excessively prickly about it," Alex suggested.

Chic told Alex about the death of Sparkly. He wondered aloud if it might have been intended for him, especially since whoever was behind it seemed deadly serious. The gravity of the game was beginning to sink in.

"I have no idea if it is related, Gordon," Alex said, "if it was, they must be very powerful and very committed."

Chic then told Alex about his plans to fly back to Harare the following evening and asked if he had any further suggestions.

"Be careful!" he pleaded, "Stay low-profile and avoid asking questions for a few days. When you get back, we will talk by phone. By the way, the Senator knew about our meeting in Hong Kong, which tells me that these people have a long reach! Hopefully, I will be able to have another chat with the Senator as soon as I get back, and I will have something to tell you."

They walked back to the hotel through a light drizzle. Chic got back his room feeling very nervous, and not reassured by what Alex had told him. The meal had been delicious, and Alex had been most gracious, but the message he conveyed was vicious! Just as he finished double locking his door, his phone began to ring; he answered immediately.

"Hello?"

"Richard speaking, Gordon. I talked to the lawyer in Harare. He is willing to work with you, but wants to meet in Pretoria. How soon can you be there to meet with him and me, assuming you want me to be there?"

"I can't catch a flight until tomorrow evening and will be in Johannesburg the next morning. If you think it is urgent, then I shall have to see if I can charter," Chic answered.

"I still wouldn't arrive until the middle of the day tomorrow, assuming an aircraft is available for departure later tonight. Actually, based upon my discussions here, I must get back there as soon as possible. I will try to charter."

Chic hung up, and then called the number on a card he carried in his wallet.

"Global Aviation, how can I help you?" a woman's voice answered, from someplace in the world a few milliseconds too far away.

"I need to fly tonight from London to Johannesburg," Chic stated as if it was an everyday request.

"May I have your account number, please?" Chic provided all the material she requested.

She then asked, "How soon would you be ready to leave your hotel?"

Chic replied carelessly, "Fifteen minutes."

"Make your preparations and I will call you on your cellular within five minutes. You may go ahead and check out of your room. We will send a car for you," she instructed firmly.

Chic packed the few things he had with him and left for the lobby to check out. He arrived at the desk and turned over his keys in exchange for a prompt receipt and a thoughtful, "Thank you for staying with us, Sir."

He was about to turn toward the door when his cell vibrated in his jacket pocket.

"Yes," he answered.

"The car will be there within five minutes, Mr. Zhong, assuming the traffic is not unduly slow. We should have you in Johannesburg by twelve-forty local time tomorrow. I hope that is satisfactory. Have a good flight."

She rang off without waiting for a response. He walked outside as a black Mercedes pulled up to the curb. As he opened the rear door, the driver confirmed Chic's name and took his luggage to the boot of the car. Presently, they were driving through the streets of London.

"Mr. Zhong, you will be flying from Biggen Hill airport on a Bombardier Global Express direct to Johannesburg. The airport is just southeast of London. You should be on board by ten-thirty and the flight time will be about eleven hours. Of course, you will have to add two hours for time zone changes, so you should arrive there about twelve-thirty-five tomorrow. You will be served breakfast and a light lunch aboard the aircraft. A car will be on the tarmac to meet you upon landing, and Immigration has been advised to minimize loss of time. I hope that is satisfactory to you."

Chic dialed Richard's number and transmitted the information through his answering service.

MAMA PRUDENCE HAS INFORMATION
- PRETORIA - 30 APRIL 2014

Daniel was at the airport to pick up Clive Fotheringham when he arrived from Dubai. When they got back to Pretoria, Mama Prudence would be there to meet with them. As much as Mama preferred not to meet at Daniel's house, he had prevailed on this particular night and had arranged to pick her up when he and Clive arrived in town. Clive appeared from the airport Arrivals Gate and came straight to the familiar car. They both sat in the back. They were accompanied only by the driver and one security guard, both of whom sat in the front seats.

"So, Daniel, what is happening?" asked Clive.

"We have a few issues and they may well be colliding," Daniel stated.

"The night before your extraction, an Asian man was murdered in Harare, and I wonder if there is any connection to the subject of your extraction. A week or so ago, a man in Canada was killed, using a similar M.O. An old friend, who works for a Chinese-controlled company in Zim, will be flying down in the morning to talk to us. His client is scheduled to arrive from London tomorrow mid-day, and we will meet with him at about 2:00 pm at the office," he summarized.

"This whole situation is very unusual. It seems too big. Are you okay with the meeting tomorrow afternoon?"

"Sure. I am at your beck and call, sir," Clive joked with him.

"Of course, you will stay at my place tonight, right?"

"Sure, I think it is big enough for both of us," he replied, smiling. He was ready for a good sleep. At her request, Daniel stopped for Mama on the street a block east of the Flower Home for the Aged. She could not face the prospect of being seen by her friends climbing into a limousine full of white faces. They arrived ten minutes later at Daniel's house in the hills. A light dinner was waiting for them and they attacked it with gusto.

They agreed to wait until morning to start the discussions that had brought them together. They would need their wits about them. The night was still early when they all retired.

The following morning in Pretoria was lovely. Both Daniel and Clive had risen early and with one of the security men in tow, had gone for a five-kilometre jog. They had been unable to persuade Mama Prudence of the wisdom of that, and although she was awake before either of them, she enjoyed sipping her morning cup of tea in the backyard. The joggers returned, showered, dressed, and then joined Mama for breakfast on the patio.

Daniel started by bringing Clive up to date on the CPZ group and the Barons, as he called them. He discussed his group's engagement of the accountant, Jim, and why they had involved someone in Canada. Without naming Jacobus, he described the deaths at Jacobus's farm, recounting the progression from calves to cows, and finally to the fieldworkers. He divulged that he now believed that the deaths were all escalating warnings to stop the research. Daniel further disclosed the attempts by the killers in Canada to obtain a briefcase from an innocent friend of Jim's, and that they ran him down with their SUV in order to do so. He told Clive that Will Turner had become involved in order to protect the man, who was recovering in hospital. Daniel revealed that another, almost identical death had been perpetrated in Harare and that the unfortunate victim was not the intended target. He, Daniel, had puzzled over the potential linkage among all of the deaths, and now that it was getting close to home, and required all hands on deck to figure it out before another death occurred.

As Daniel concluded, Mama spoke up.

"Daniel, I do not think the killers have left the country. I also don't believe that they are receiving their orders from anyone here. They seem to move rapidly from country to country, without any problem. They must be well-trained and, more importantly, well-supported. Somehow, we must find them and stop them. This is not the work of our Barons. It is far too sophisticated."

Clive Fotheringham decided it was time to discuss his trip to Dubai.

"We got an emergency evacuation call from one of our insurance clients to get a Chinese businessman out of Harare as quickly as possible. We were able to get a back- haul on a Dassault 2000, and were able to get him out and settled into a hotel in Dubai without incident. No, I shouldn't say without incident. On his way to the airport in a cab, some driver got into a shouting match with the driver of the cab and tried to bump them off the road. The cab driver pulled over and the other driver jumped out, and was coming back toward them. Some old guy on the street dealt with the aggressive driver, after which, he jumped into the front of the cab and told the driver to get our guy to the airport. The Chinaman thought the old guy was one of ours. He disappeared right after arriving at the FBO, so no one else saw him. Our client was quite shaken from that and from whatever prompted the evac. Sounds very much like our client could have been the partner of the guy who was killed."

"A couple of guys will be at the office at about two today. One is flying down from Harare and the other on a charter from London. We'll know for sure if there is a link when we meet with them. The guys coming down need some representation in Harare. If Mama is correct, which she usually is, there are two killers running around Harare. The only guy who has seen them is a guy from Canada. The killers are either after information or they are after the investigators. I am pretty sure that there is something they are aware of that has been 'found out' and they want to get it killed before someone uses it. It must be pretty valuable if they are going to these lengths to deal with it. What do you think?" Daniel asked Mama and Clive.

Clive responded, "It will be pretty hard to find the killers if we have nothing on them, right? Whatever they are after, they are going full out to get it. Someone else will be dead if they aren't stopped. If we can stop them, we will have a chance of finding out who employs them before another team goes active."

Mama stepped in, "How good is the description that your friend in Canada can provide?"

"It's not too detailed," Daniel began, "one is tall, has a swarthy complexion, is about two metres tall, and the other is blonde, about the same height. Both are fit."

"What cover would they likely use if they were coming to Zimbabwe? Hunters, yes? And where would they likely stay? Meikles. Why don't I see if one of my girls can keep an eye out for someone who resembles the description, and we will see what happens. If not, maybe your guy will have to come to Africa to help look for them," Mama suggested.

Clive offered, "I can check around. There are a few hotels besides Meikles. If they killed the other Chinaman, I doubt that they would hang around very long, unless they were after someone else. That someone else may be flying in here today."

"Let's eat lunch and then get over to the office. We can continue with our brainstorming. It might be best to hear from Richard and his investor before we concoct a solid plan to resolve this."

Daniel led them into the house, where the cook had laid out a light, cold lunch for them.

They reached Daniels' office just after one. Once they were in the office, Mama asked if she should call her girls and get them started, since that may actually save some time. They all agreed, and Mama dialed on Daniel's phone, the number of the Treasury Ministry.

Prosper answered the phone.

"Hello, my dear," started Mama, "a task for you. Do you have a minute to listen?"

"Yes, Mama, go ahead," she replied.

"There may be two North Americans somewhere in Harare, who only recently arrived. One has black hair and is tall and lean. The other is the same height, and blonde. They may or may not be together. Can you get ahold of Veronica, and maybe the two of you can see what you can come up with at some of the likely places, please? I will contact you the usual way," Mama instructed.

"Mama, I may have already seen them!" Prosper answered excitedly, "I was with a co-worker in the lounge at Meikles on the night Akatendeka went for dinner and whatever with her skinny friend. The other Chinaman came in looking all flashy. There was a dark-complexioned guy with black hair. He looked Latino or something, maybe Italian. He sat at a table by himself and a sweet blonde guy came to join him for drinks. The black-haired guy left, and the little Chinaman ended up joining the sweet blonde guy. Last I saw, they were flirting away like they had known each other forever. Mama that was the night of the murder. I will get the girls looking. Speak to you later tonight."

Mama relayed to Daniel and Clive what Prosper had told her.

"Sounds like it could be the guys we are looking for," Daniel surmised, "we need to find out who they are and if they are still there. Clive, subject to what comes up later this afternoon, can you look after that, first thing, when you get back to Harare?"

"Sure, boss," Clive smiled, "and then what?"

"Don't know yet," said Daniel.

The intercom buzzed and Abigail's voice came on, "Mr. Sonneblom, Mr. Hammersmith and another man are here, saying that you are expecting them. Shall I bring them in?"

"Please," Daniel responded. "It looks as though they have arrived. We will soon know if it's the same Chinaman."

Richard entered the office first.

"How are you Daniel?" He stepped aside and said, "I would like you to meet Gordon Zhong."

"Very pleased to meet you," Gordon bowed slightly, and then turned toward Clive, and with some surprise, smiled.

"I know you. I have your card. What are you doing here?"

"Just more work," Clive answered.

Daniel interrupted to introduce Mama Prudence. Gordon shook hands gently with her.

"Let's sit down and get to work, Daniel suggested, "Let's start with Mr. Zhong or Richard. What may we do for you?"

Richard started.

"I have known Mr. Zhong for some years now. He represents some of the investors in the diamond mines that I am involved in operating. Gordon called me the other day and explained how his executive assistant went missing and, fearing the worst, he did not want to fall into the hands of the police in a foreign country without understanding his options for exit. It was after that that I called you Daniel, to see if you felt comfortable representing him from outside Harare, albeit through appropriate local representation if and when required. Do you have anything you would like to add, Gordon?"

"Well, Clive got me out of Harare very efficiently. From Dubai, I flew to meet one of my lawyers from New York, whom I had engaged to find out why our funds are being frozen at the Dubai Auction and in Antwerp. They had done some work, had made some headway, when out of the blue, Alex, Alexander Pope, received a call from a former Senator, apparently a powerful man in Washington, requesting that Alex meet him in Washington. The Senator essentially told Alex to stop his investigation, letting him know only that a very powerful Washington group was active and did not want any disruption in their plans. Alex concluded by warning me that if I intended to continue, I would end up with flowers growing in my chest, or something to that effect," Gordon paused, and then continued, "my executive assistant was killed and I believe that I was the actual target. I think the killers made a mistake. Because he always took care of any financial transactions, I always signed everything to his room, so whoever killed him might have thought that I was in that room."

"Gordon, why do you think anyone might have been after you at the time? I know you found out later what the Senator said, but at the time?" Clive asked.

"Well, some old guy sitting beside me on a bench told me to be careful and a woman with whom I had dinner also told me to be careful, that I was in danger. I was confused, but after I discovered that my E.A. was dead, I began to put two and two together" Gordon replied.

"Mr. Zhong, what was the girl's name, if I might ask?" Mama interjected.

"Her name is Akatendeka," he replied, "she works in one of the ministries in Harare. We had dinner the night my E.A. was killed."

Mama looked across at Daniel and nodded slightly.

"Mr. Zhong, did you see two Americans sitting together in the lounge at Meikles that night?" Mama asked.

"No," he replied, "not that I noticed."

"I think that Clive and I will return to Harare with Mama and Richard. Unless you are planning to remain here, Richard. We will meet with the investigating detective and let him know what we know, or believe we know. Then we will meet with the prosecutor and let him know that Gordon is in safekeeping here. We can also let him know about the murder in Canada and our suspicions that they are connected and that the perpetrators are the same. If we get adequate assurances that they are not considering Gordon a person of interest, we will contact you, and you will be free to carry on. You might consider just staying here until we have sorted out who these guys are, because they may want to finish their job if they find where you are."

Daniel, Richard, Clive and Mama spent the time on the train discussing options.

DANIEL SPEAKS WITH DETECTIVE-SERGEANT - HARARE - 30 APRIL 2014 -

"Detective-Sergeant Sibangilizwe, good evening. My name is Daniel Sonneblom. I am with the law firm, Wilberson, Jonas & Sonneblom in Pretoria. I have been engaged to represent Gordon Zhong, the employer of the man killed at Meikles a few days ago. He was here but had to leave town on urgent business. I wonder if we might have a word?"

"About what?" the detective asked, rudely.

"About the investigation and about whether my client can be of any help," replied Daniel quite politely.

"Did he do it?" the detective asked.

"Of course not," Daniel replied.

"Then why does he need a lawyer?" the detective asked more directly.

Daniel realized he was getting nowhere, "Detective-Sergeant, is there anything you can tell me about the investigation? The man was almost family to my client." he tried again.

"The Chinaman was killed by a witch. We have a photograph of her from the CCTV camera in the lobby. No one in the hotel admits to knowing her, but I can tell that they are lying," answered the detective.

"Why would a witch wish to kill a visitor to our country?" Daniel asked in a different way.

"First of all, it isn't your country, it's my country. Second, I have answered the questions I'm going to answer from you. If you have more, go talk to the prosecutor," he replied in an angry tone.

Daniel knew it was time to put an end to this unhelpful encounter. He had been about to commence an argument about who had been in Zimbabwe the longest, his family or the detective's but...he hoped the prosecutor would be a bit more open-minded.

"Good morning, Sir," Daniel introduced himself to the prosecutor assigned to the murder case. It was one of forty-three open cases he was handling. Some of them involved important local people, implying a sense of priority.

"I would like to discuss a recent murder that occurred at the Meikles Hotel. I have already spoken to Detective-Sergeant Sibangilizwe about it briefly, as I was told he was the investigating officer. I represent Gordon Zhong, the employer of the deceased. Do you have some time to talk with me about the case?"

"Yes, please sit down," he invited, "What would you like to know?"

"For a start, I would like to know how he died and whether or not there is any suspected involvement by my client," Daniel stated.

"Well," the prosecutor said opening a file, "let's see what we have here."

He spent a few minutes flipping through the pages and the photographs.

"The summary here says that the fellow was found in bed, no sign of a struggle, his middle cut open and a few parts removed. Conclusion: witchcraft. Apparently, there was a woman caught on the CCTV camera in the lobby, as she was leaving the hotel. Very attractive lady, I would say. The detective thinks she might be a witch."

"Were there any photos taken from the CCTV cameras on the individual floors?" Daniel asked.

"Let's see… no, it seems the cameras were not operational on the third, fourth or fifth floors during that night. When the I.T. people came the next day to fix them they were working properly. Don't know what happened there," the prosecutor continued, "it seems that there were two men travelling together, and only one left town. That must be your client. Why would he do that without talking to the police? I wonder. Not much else. They are looking for the witch, no fingerprints or anything found beyond hotel staff and the deceased," he concluded, and looked at Daniel, "Do you have any further information?"

Daniel began, "We are aware of a murder in Canada about a week and a half ago which had an identical modus operandi. The victim was a contractor for a firm from here. He was investigating some funds lost from the diamond auctions."

"That might create a few enemies," the prosecutor added, "why do you think they are related?"

"Information we have from Canada indicates that two males were likely involved, and we have basic descriptions. Two males fitting the descriptions checked into Meikles the day of the killing. It may be mistaken identity or coincidence, but it also may be important. My client also has received serious warnings from U.S. sources to give up the investigations which he was conducting." said Daniel,

"My main task here, though, is to determine if my client is free to travel in Zimbabwe without fear of incarceration for no cause."

"And if I say no?" the prosecutor asked, his forehead wrinkled as his glasses rose on his nose.

"He will likely stay elsewhere," Daniel shrugged. "I will assure you that we will have access to him, should you require affidavits or something. You may also decide you will want to call him as a witness, in spite of the small amount of information to which he could testify.

"We shall see," the prosecutor said in a noncommittal way, "I have your business card and I shall know fairly soon if the police will arrest the witch."

Daniel added, "By the way, I did not disclose to the detective-sergeant the information I just gave you about the two men. He seemed to have his mind pretty well made up. Another thing which I did not mention to the detective was that you should have the blood tested for *Conium maculatum*, poison Hemlock."

"Ah, yes," he started, "there is so much work and so little time. We tend to appreciate easy cases. Witches make cases simple," he smiled and, offering his hand, "good-bye for now, Mr. Sonneblom. I will be in touch. Please feel free to call me if you discover anything that may be relevant."

"Thank you, I will. Have a good day," Daniel responded.

MAMA RECEIVES NEW INFORMATION
- HARARE - 29 APRIL 2014

Mama Prudence, Clive and Daniel met in the café in the lobby of Meikles. Daniel described the results of his meeting with the Detective-Sergeant and with Inspector Butholezwe.

"Gentlemen," Mama began, "I spoke to some of my sisters last night and have obtained some new information. You will remember that I told you that, on the night of the murder, the one Chinaman spent some time in the lounge at the hotel with a tall blonde-haired man. That man seemed to be American. The two appeared to become friendly, actually, *very* friendly, and they left the lounge together and got into an elevator. About two hours later the blonde man returned to the lobby alone and immediately left the hotel by a service exit, carrying something in a plastic bag. After about twenty minutes, the blonde man returned to the lobby and took the elevator to the floor of his room. About nine the next morning, the police began to arrive at the hotel. Detective-Sergeant Sibangilizwe arrived about nine-twenty and went up to the floor of the Asian man. About ten minutes after he arrived, one of the young constables came rushing from the elevator carrying a plastic bag, and he exited by the service entrance. Later in the morning, Detective-Sergeant Sibangilizwe returned to the lobby and, at the front desk, had a conversation with one of the managers, at the end of which, he handed the manager two brown envelopes. According to my sister, one package was a regular brown envelope addressed to a Mr. Wilson and labelled 'Hold for Pickup'. It was picked up shortly thereafter, but she didn't see by whom. The other was a larger package, like a full FEDEX package. The Sergeant left a business card and asked the manager to arrange to ship it to the address on that card by the fastest means available. That package was sent to an address in Washington D.C., to the Abrin Financial Group.

"By the way, a different group committed the earlier killings, up north. They were likely locals, and likely under the orders of our Detective-Sergeant. It was his way of warning Jacobus and his friends to back off investigating the Barons. The murders were planned to make it look as though they had been witches' deeds to ensure a minimum of investigation. Once Jacobus's group had sorted out their security, the Detective assumed that the group had understood the message and given up their activities. Also, those killers did not use any chemical poison. Those who killed the Asian man used a chemical poison. One of the staff, who is a sister, noticed the smell when she went in to clean the room after the body had been removed. There was one drinking glass missing. The police must have it. It was likely taken by the constable, on orders from the Detective-Sergeant."

CLIVE AND VERONICA VISIT
MR. NKOSI - HARARE - 2 MAY 2014

It was early evening and still light when Clive and Veronica were dropped off near the estate of Mr. Nkosi. As they approached the gatehouse, a man appeared from within. Veronica walked forward toward the gate and smiled. They chatted softly for a few minutes, and then Veronica's friend opened the gate and they were waved through.

All Veronica would tell Clive was, "This is my friend. He will get us into the house. The CCTV cameras are off until 19:00 when night security comes on duty."

They were led around to the edge of the house and entered through a pantry. The friend whispered to Veronica and pointed the way. She and Clive moved silently toward the smell of fresh cigar smoke. Clive crouched and entered the room, positioning himself to the rear of the target. Once he was in place, Veronica started walking slowly toward Mr. Nkosi, who spotted her before she was halfway across the room.

"What are you doing here?" he shouted before Clive clasped a hand over his mouth. He tried to spin to see who was attacking him. He could not move. He could not shout.

"Mr. Nkosi, we are here to talk with you and perhaps to save your life," Veronica spoke softly, as she continued toward him. Mr. Nkosi seemed to relax slightly.

"If you are prepared to speak with us, we will release you. If not, we will remove you to another place," she stated.

He nodded and Clive released his hand enough that Mr. Nkosi could answer properly.

"Yes, we can talk here," he answered, "what's all the stealth about? Why not phone me at my office? Why this?" he spoke in a strong voice.

"Mr. Nkosi," Clive began, "we know you have a group of friends who have done some bad things. We know that a member of your group is Detective-Sergeant Sibangilizwe. Do you understand what I am saying?"

"Go ahead," he stated, sullenly.

"There is evidence that your Detective-Sergeant Sibangilizwe has other bosses besides the Police Department," Clive continued, watching the expression on Nkosi's face.

"Go on, what has this to do with me?" he asked, uncertainly.

"You and your group have been building fortunes from the wealth of Zimbabwe. You believe you are responsible for driving Zimbabwe's progress. You have a great deal of power," Clive continued, "you tried to neutralize the bit of opposition you had by 'practicing witchcraft' against a man you thought was heading the investigations against you. Does that sound familiar?"

"What do you expect me to say?" Nkosi snarled.

"Nothing really," answered Clive, "if you don't care about living long."

"What is that supposed to mean? Do you plan to kill me if I don't answer?" he asked with alarm.

"No, but many lives within your group will be in danger soon if something doesn't change. The threat is not merely a threat, but a statement of fact. It will not come from the people you perceive as your enemies, but from others who are much more powerful and far more ruthless, and who have more desire for wealth than even you, but care nothing about Zimbabwe."

"Listen to me," said Walter Nkosi looking slightly desperate. "Our group killed no one. We talked about scaring the one person we suspected of feeding stories to the press. He stopped, so we left him alone."

"Are you aware of the Chinese fellow who was murdered at Meikles?" Clive asked.

"I heard about it," he replied, "but we had nothing at all to do with it."

Clive looked at Walter and said, "No, I know you did not, but the group that is also coming after *you* did. There are at least two assassins in Harare at the moment. I am sure they will have less problem getting to you than we did. We know that a member of your group was responsible for the deaths up north," he added.

"That's not possible," Walter replied.

Veronica took over the conversation.

"You will call Detective-Sergeant Sibangilizwe now, and you will tell him that you are being shown proof that he committed those murders. You can judge for yourself from his reaction. If he doesn't react then ask him what his relationship is with the Abrin Financial Group in Washington D.C. Do it now!"

Walter took his cell phone from his pocket and dialed.

" *Sawubona*, how are you Walter?" asked the Detective-Sergeant.

"*Yebo*, I have two questions," he was very blunt, "Did you kill those guys up north?"

There was a pause, "What are you talking about? Why are you accusing me? Who have you been talking to?" The swift flow of his questions began to sound desperate.

"I have been provided some evidence and I need to know the truth, now!" Walter attacked.

"You cowards would have given the country away to those foreigners. None of you had the courage to deal with the problems properly," he shouted back.

Walter responded quickly, "When did you start working for the Abrin Financial Group?"

The connection was cut. He had hung up the phone. Walter was startled by the impertinence.

"Did you hit a nerve?" Clive asked.

"He did it," Walter replied. "Who in hell is the Abrin Financial Group?"

"We know very little about them," Clive began, "they seem to be a very respectable investment bank, perhaps based out of Washington D.C. They have a reputation for being merciless in their dealings. They have investment positions around the world. Those appear to be only the tip of the iceberg. Do you remember the financial crisis in 2008? We believe that they not only came out unscathed, but tremendously profitable. They play governments and use government agencies when it suits them. They have no problems using contractors to achieve the elimination of nuisances."

"What do they have to do with us?" asked Walter.

"We believe that they are concerned about some information being leaked that can tie them to market manipulation activities relating to Zimbabwe. Those activities are extremely profitable for them and they will go to any length to protect their turf. The U.S. Government is aware of some of the activities and because those are consistent with the foreign policy of that nation, they turn a blind eye, and some even believe they provide some assistance through the CIA. Your government, your little group, and those who oppose you, form a convenient means for them to play one against the other and to create the volatility necessary to earn large profits. That is why they need to control which actions cause the volatility."

"What do we do about it?" Walter asked.

"There is no easy answer," Clive answered.

"We must begin by stopping the killings. That is the priority. Then we must attempt to persuade them to act in a more positive way toward Zimbabwe and its resources. They are far too large and dispersed for the U.S. Government to control effectively. They are damn sure too big for us to control. The best we can hope for is to reduce the negative impacts on Zimbabwe. Your group must find a way to work with the CPZ and the government, so that you provide a united front against them. It's possible that, if you can work together, you will succeed in eliminating their ability to encourage the disruption. Perhaps you will be able to agree to a plan that will satisfy all of you and that will give hope to the majority of your people, while allowing the government to transition smoothly when the time comes. Such a plan would eliminate any specific target they may find, and will, as a result, destroy much of their motivation. I know that Daniel has some ideas about that and will want to talk to you about it.

"You need to contact Inspector Butholezwe and have him place the Detective-Sergeant under watch. Provide the Inspector with a serious accusation. I am sure that if the Detective-Sergeant is interrogated well, he will provide some valuable information. Let the Inspector know that you understand that someone, perhaps a young constable, removed evidence from the crime scene in order to protect the killers, and that the Detective-Sergeant is aware of that."

Clive wrapped up his proposal, "It is the worst of colonialism, but *sub rosa*."

"Let me call the Inspector. After I speak with him, I will contact my colleagues to determine what they are prepared to do. How do I get in touch with you?" Walter asked.

Clive provided the information and then suggested, "Perhaps you would be prepared to let us leave by the front door and to arrange for a car to return us downtown? Thank you."

DANIEL MEETS WITH CPZ - HARARE - 2 MAY 2014

Jacobus left his farm early in the morning. This was his favourite part of the day. The sun was beginning its assent from behind the kopje that kept it hidden from his house until well after breakfast. He decided to leave his dog, Brutus, and his tracker behind today, since he was picking up Petrus Oberhultzer and Morgan Nkomo on the way to Harare. The plains spread before him and filled him with pride. He had been able to hold his land, in spite of the voluntary land reorganization of 1990 and the Fast Track Acquisitions of 1993, and he hoped to continue holding it. He drove down the highway feeling proud and happy.

He turned northeast onto the A5 and drove into Gweru, where he would pick up Morgan.

"*Goeie môre*, Morgan," Jacobus shouted out the window. as he watched Morgan lumbering toward the Land Cruiser. "Welcome aboard."

Morgan climbed slowly up into the cab and, with a handsome ivory smile greeted Jacobus,

"*Mangwanani* Jacobus, *makadini zvenyu?*"

Jacobus replied, "I'm doin' fine my *maan*. You lookin' forward to the trip to Harare?"

"I am looking forward to making some progress, Jacobus, but I have much patience left," replied Morgan. "They say the country isn't going anywhere, but the stuff from under the ground is moving out of here pretty fast. The gold and diamonds are going everywhere, and the money doesn't seem to come home. Maybe one day, eh?"

"According to Daniel, that is one of the things we will be speaking about in the morning, or maybe tonight, if we get in early enough," answered Jacobus.

They continued on the northward route of A5 toward KweKwe. Jacobus figured it would take about an hour or so. As they drove along the Great Zimbabwe Dyke, an intrusive formation striking in a SSW-NNE direction and extending for over 500 kilometres across their nation, they spoke of the great mineral deposits in Zimbabwe. The dyke is an elongated, narrow body of inward-dipping peridotites, displaying various intrusive elements aligned along the highway. Geologists have told them that it is a stratiform igneous complex and not a dyke at all, but whatever anyone called it, it was filled with wealth.

Zimbabwe sits on a core of Archean Basement known as the Zimbabwe Craton. The craton is composed principally of granitoids, schist and gneisses, and it incorporates greenstone belts with associated epiclastic sediments and iron formations. The craton is overlaid in the northwest and the east by Proterozoic and Phanerozoic sedimentary basins.

The wealth of mineral resources in the dyke includes coal, chromium and nickel ore, gold, platinum, lithium and, not to be forgotten, diamonds. This was wealth in precious metals second only to South Africa, yet Zimbabweans remained poor. How were they to ensure that the country received a fair share of the wealth retrieved from these massive deposits? So many of the current problems sprang from the perceived failure of the land equalization programs that people had lost sight of the wealth the minerals would provide.

"Someday, Morgan, we will have things sorted out," assured Jacobus, "there is certainly sufficient for everyone, if we can figure out how to work together."

They arrived in KweKwe, its wide boulevards planted with the occasional palm tree and its curbs painted in black and white stripes. The main street was comprised of two-story buildings, many needing a touch of fresh paint. The sidewalks were crowded, with smiling people rushing to get somewhere. As Jacobus drove toward the north edge of the city, he pulled off the highway onto Bessemer Road and stopped at a Petro Trade to fuel the Land Cruiser and to grab a few hands full of biltong. So far, it had been a smooth drive. In about ten minutes they would pick up Petrus just north of the roundabout near the KweKwe Mosque. The KweKwe Mosque, with its picturesque golden dome has the reputation of being the most beautiful mosque in Zimbabwe. The architecture is reminiscent of the Taj Mahal. Construction on the Mosque was begun in 1970 and finished in 1977. It is home to the Varemba people of the Midlands, who are considered to be 'a lost tribe of Islam'.

Fueled and fed, with Petrus in the back seat of the Land Cruiser, they continued northeast on the A5 toward Harare. They passed remnants of farms, the only signs of settlement that remained being Amarula, Acacia and Msasa Trees. Gum Trees and Jacaranda trees marked the old home-steads. Industrious women harvested the yellow thatching grasses that grew along the side of the road. Occasional rusted skeletons of cars lying in the shallow ditches were a reminder of the hazards of night journeys.

About two-and-a-half hours after they left KweKwe, they arrived at the outskirts of Harare. Jacobus maneuvered his Land Cruiser toward the centre of the city. They agreed that on their way to the meeting, they would check in to the Cresta Jameson Hotel, located right on the A5. It was only a half-a-dozen-block walk to the Meikles Hotel, where Daniel preferred to stay, but was much more appropriate for the budget-minded. Jacobus did not become a wealthy farmer by parting with his money foolishly, like his lawyer friend. It was early afternoon when they checked into the hotel. Jacobus parked the Land Cruiser in the secure parkade and headed to his room. They would meet in the lobby in half an hour. In the meantime, Jacobus would call Daniel and fix their meeting time. Agreeing to meet for dinner at Monos, just down Park Avenue from the hotel, at 18:00, gave the travelers time for a rest and a shower beforehand.

Daniel entered the restaurant promptly at 18:00 and spotted the three men sitting at a corner table in the back. He smiled at the receptionist and pointed to his friends. She insisted on leading him to the table. It was nice to watch her move. The three men were grinning as he reached out his large hand to greet each of them. As Daniel took his seat, the waiter approached, and they ordered their drinks. Jacobus chose a pint of Zambezi Beer, Petrus selected a glass of rye whiskey with Coke, Morgan chose a glass of juice, and Daniel asked for a glass of single malt scotch, water on the side.

"How was the drive up?" Daniel asked Jacobus, "Any accidents?"

"None. We made good time and I didn't lose either of these fellows," replied Jacobus, "no accidents, no problems, just a good drive."

The foursome enjoyed a bit of relaxing small talk as they reviewed the menus. Three decided on pepper steak with salad, while Jacobus insisted on a large rib-eye steak, rare. The waiter flinched as he wrote it on his pad.

"Let's get down to business, if you guys are ready," started Daniel, "and we'll see how far we can get before the place gets crowded."

They acquiesced genially, so Daniel began. "I can update you on what we have learned about the killings. I will start with the ones up at Jacobus's place. We suspect strongly that they were carried out under the direction of a Detective-Sergeant in Harare, who appears to be associated with the group we suspected, but who, in fact, was working with a large and secretive American group, as well. Inspector Butholezwe will be taking control of the investigation of that series of incidents. Mr. Walter Nkosi, about whom most of you know, will be applying strong pressure on Butholezwe to have the Detective-Sergeant secured and kept quiet for the time being. It appears that he may not have been instructed to conduct those killings but undertook them on his own.

"The killing in Harare at the Meikles appears to have been committed by two men from America. The M.O. seems to be the same as that of the Canadian accountant's - Jim's - killers. I understand that Jim was poisoned with hemlock prior to being eviscerated. The same seems to be the case with the Asian guy at Meikles. The link seems to be investigations into the movement of currency, the freezing of assets, and other activities around the diamond sales. The Asian fellow worked with a Gordon Zhong, with whom we have met. When Mr. Zhong had continuing problems with the assets of his investors being frozen at auctions in Abu Dhabi and Antwerp, he engaged a New York law firm to help him to get a large amount of money released from those auctions. It appeared that the funds were being held under pressure from the United States, using the Kimberly Process. It is likely that this was happening at the encouragement of the Abrin Financial Group, which I will talk about a little later.

"When Gordon Zhong met with his lawyer in London recently, the lawyer informed him that a well-placed gentleman in Washington had advised strongly that Mr. Zhong cease looking into the issue immediately. It was hardly a veiled threat.

"The Abrin Financial Group is a very large and quite secretive investment bank that operates around the world. From what I have been able to determine, it has a large and effective Board of Directors, a number of whom are retired world leaders. They seem to have access to state departments in many countries, as well as to intelligence services, of which they make very good use. They earn large amounts of money by speculating correctly on currencies and even on the outcomes of wars. They provide financing with favourable terms to borrowers who have difficulties obtaining funds from traditional sources. They take exorbitant security and are absolutely vicious in collecting their debts when they are due. They will take large assets from a country and exploit them in order to recover any unpaid monies. They do not pay taxes, nor do they allow themselves to be made subject to foreign laws. They simply do what they need to do to collect their principal and interest, and in the case of default, their exceptional fees. They do collect, without exception. Interference by politicians can occasionally be a deadly mistake. They place a high value on their secrecy, and they will do whatever is necessary to ensure that information about their inner workings is never made public.

"One of my colleagues, Clive Fotheringham, met with Mr. Nkosi of the local group last night. He impressed upon Mr. Nkosi the risk that he and his fellow-members faced if they provided to the Abrin Financial Group any information that implicated them in the release of secret information. Clive was the one who suggested that the Detective-Sergeant be put into protective custody while he was under investigation. It is my opinion that we are in a tremendous position to work out an arrangement among the three parties, if you gentlemen can agree on a course of action with the Barons. If that can be done in a way that is acceptable to the political hierarchy, it will remove much of the opportunity for the Abrin Financial Group to continue to capitalize on the present volatility in Zimbabwe. From my perspective, the Barons and the CPZ have similar objectives. The key, it seems to me, is to accept that many mistakes were made in the past and that many mistakes will be made in the future.

"A few thousand years ago, a wise old man named Chanakya advised his king that, 'we should not fret for what is past, nor should we be anxious about the future; men of discernment deal only with the present moment.'

"That, gentlemen, is what I think we need to focus on tonight. The window of opportunity is very small. Does this strategy hold any interest for you?"

Daniel wrapped up his presentation just as the waiter arrived with the steaks.

"Gentlemen, let's eat," said Jacobus, looking hungrily at his huge juicy steak, the end lapping over the edge of his plate. The others gaped, wondering how one man in one sitting could consume such a huge piece of meat.

"I wonder if we could focus on five core objectives," Daniel suggested.

"If we can agree on those, then we can meet at Meikles and have them typed up for a presentation to the Barons. Petrus, after we have finished eating, would you like to sketch out a draft of what we decide are the key issues? We'll brainstorm as you write."

Once they had a good start on their meals, Daniel brought up another issue.

"We have to find out where the two Americans are. Jacobus, based on the information from some of the hotel staff, they may have headed north on a safari, probably as part of their cover. Do you think you could contact some of your PH friends and see if anyone knows where they might be? About all we have for a description is that both are tall and fit, one has black hair and the other is blonde. The one carries his rifle in an aluminum Americase. Likely both are trained marksmen."

"Once we get our points worked out, I'll make some phone calls," Jacobus agreed.

"The most likely place to start will be with the charter pilots. Do you know what date they left Harare?" he asked.

"We believe they left the morning after the killing, which would have been the twenty-eighth or so," Daniel replied, "it would be good if we could let the Inspector know where they are, so they don't slip away. They will expect their vulnerability to peak when they return to board for their flight to the U.S."

Once Petrus finished the last of his exquisite steak and asked for a cup of coffee, he asked the waiter to remove his plate and to return with paper and a pen. They began to brainstorm, and Petrus extrapolated the salient points to include in their final presentation.

If they could iron out their presentation this evening, then Daniel could send a copy of it to Alexander Pope in New York, and then follow up in the morning with a phone call. That should allow Pope plenty of time to meet with his contact in Washington.

At the end of their discussions, they had their presentation just as they wanted it:

- Accept the men who have obtained great wealth in Zimbabwe, using whatever means they deemed necessary to allow them to invest in Zimbabwe and to build their fortunes, while also helping others to climb into the middle class.
- Accept, as you already have, that there have been major failures and abuses regarding land redistribution, but work to ensure that, into the future, it will progress in a better way.
- Work together to determine the allotments for small subsistence farmers. Have the state lease 10 or 20 Ha to each family, with an option to buy.
- Offer commercial-sized parcels to farmers, either black or white, who have demonstrated a knowledge farming successfully. Let them commit to assisting smaller farmers.
- Offer special financing for experienced farmers to work with the new commercial farmers.
- Commit to a fundamental acceptance of land ownership. Titles are sacred as long as the land is being used for grazing or farming in areas suitable for farming.
- No further expropriation of lands until the country can afford to pay from its own resources and has

appropriately compensated farmers for any freehold
acquired since independence.

"Ok," said Daniel, "sounds like we have enough to construct some good
negotiating points. Let's get a good sleep and meet at Meikles for breakfast to finalize our points. I will arrange for a room for 08:00 and a steno
for 09:00, and then I will set a meeting with Mr. Nkosi for lunchtime.
Have a good sleep, gentlemen. I am heading back to the hotel and I will
see you in the morning."

It was still reasonably early when Daniel walked toward his hotel. He
took out his phone to call Clive.

"Clive, how are you this evening?" Daniel asked, "Successful day?"

"Not bad, Daniel. How did you make out with your guys?" he responded.
"Were they onside?

"Yes, they are, thankfully. Are you at the hotel?" he asked.

"I'll be there in half an hour," Clive suggested, "how about a beer
at Explorers?"

"See you there." Daniel continued on, thinking about how he was
going to deal with Nkosi and, even more challenging, how he was going
to present an argument that Alex Pope could present that would cause
Abrin Financial to back down. He knew that, for them, it wasn't about
the diamond business only, nor the ivory trade. Nor was it about the
apparent corruption of the heavies in Zimbabwe. Maybe it had something
to do with the U.S. trying to block the growth of Chinese influence in
Zimbabwe. Neither the U.S. Government nor the CIA was sponsoring
the killings, though. Those definitely were being directed by another very
powerful group that did not seem to be bound by the niceties of international relations.

"They are global, they are supra-national, and they are efficient!" Daniel
felt that he recognized the pattern, and all at once he recognized who
might be behind it. Believing something and proving something are two
very different things. They were not going to win anything in a court
of law. They needed to win on the chessboard of reality. He would need
to come up with a position that would be acceptable to the Barons, the
CPZ, the Zimbabwe Government, and that also would encourage Abrin

Financial to accept that position and permit the release of the funds owed to the Chinese investors.

Daniel strode up the steps to the hotel entrance and nodded to the doorman, who had swung open the door with a smiling welcome. He walked on by the bellman and turned into the Explorer's Club. He recognized his favourite waiter and said, "the regular, please, Charles."

He continued to Clive's table.

"Hi, boss," Clive smiled, holding up his glass, "are we winning yet?"

"Don't have a clue," Daniel replied, "I think the guys will come up with a credible position. The question really is, can we come up with a package that will sway the people in Washington?"

"Well, let's start by getting the Barons on side while they still believe that they are up against a mortal enemy," Clive continued, "we need to get ahold of those two killers. They aren't going to talk, but their bosses won't know that."

"And if we can get the CPZ and the Barons on side without costing the government much, we should be able to get the Barons to convince the other government guys to go ahead. Maybe one of the keys is figuring out how to hold a sword over the head of government until they have made the changes needed," Daniel added.

"Let's get ahold of Nkosi and see if we can meet tomorrow. What would be a good time?" Clive suggested.

"I think noon, if it is possible. Let's make it somewhere where we can talk confidentially. That will give everyone a chance to get things off their chests before we get into any negotiations. What do you think?" Daniel asked, and then added, "Clive, do you think that you and a squad of our guys could quietly bring the two guys into custody before the local constabulary does and get them into South Africa?"

"I was beginning to think you'd never ask, boss." Clive replied, "I am going to check with Jacobus, Mama Prudence and a few other sources of my own tonight, to see if we can get a clear confirmation about where they are. I have a team coming off gas plant security in Nigeria tomorrow. They'll still be hot. Well, here's to a great day tomorrow!" Clive raised his glass as a toast to their success. Daniel responded with a grin.

"Let me get ahold of Nkosi now, if I can," Clive continued.

"Excuse me for a minute," Daniel asked, "I've got to ease springs. Back in a few minutes."

Clive dialed, "Mr. Nkosi, good evening, are you and the key members of your group able to meet at lunchtime tomorrow? We have some information that you need to have and you will want to be able to respond to it quickly."

"I'll call you back in thirty minutes," replied Walter, sounding somewhat concerned.

Daniel returned to the table. He and Clive chatted about the various approaches they could take with the Barons. "We'll meet at six tomorrow in my room, if that's Ok with you, Clive. Then I will meet with Jacobus and the guys before going to see the Barons. When the time is right, I'd like to be able to tell them we have the killers in our custody. I also don't want anyone else finding them until after Alexander Pope has negotiated with the people in Washington. A lot of things are going to have to move awfully fast to make this work. The downside should be capturing the killers and getting them out of action. The upside is that we get more than that, right?" Daniel smiled, and by the far-off look in his eyes, Clive knew that his brain had already moved onto something else.

Daniel returned to his room and called Jacobus.

"Jacobus, any news yet on the two hunters?" he asked.

"Nothing very firm, Daniel, but I do have a few leads," Jacobus replied, "I should get some calls back tonight or first thing in the morning. I think I have narrowed it down to three areas but have not been able to talk to the PHs at any of them yet. Last Tuesday, an old farmer friend turned charter pilot, flew two groups of two men into the strip at Dande. Two of the men fit the description, but they appeared not to know each other before boarding. Two others fitting the description were flown into Chifuti last Friday, along with two others. All four seemed to be friends. On Wednesday at mid-day, a couple of hunters and a couple of observers flew into Lake Victoria on a charter and then were flown by Jet Ranger out to a camp east of Hwange. I'll call you in the morning when I have some more news."

"Great! Talk to you then, man."

Daniel sat down and started writing his ideas on a legal pad. Unless he had a good agenda, he would have little time the following day to develop a consensus. He laid out his clothes for the next day and climbed into bed. Things seemed to be moving quickly, just as they needed to do.

At five-thirty-five, there was a knock on Daniel's door, accompanied by an insistent voice announcing, "Room Service".

Daniel climbed out of the shower and pulled on the fluffy hotel robe as he shouted back, "I'll be there in a minute, just hold on."

As he did so, he heard a key inserted into the lock of his door and the electrical mechanism turned. By the time the door was beginning to open, he was already across the room, standing with his back to the wall behind the opening door. As the tray rolled past the door, Daniel stepped behind the man and had his arms pinned before he could utter a sound. In the same motion he flipped the door closed and pushed the man to the floor.

"Who the hell are you?" Daniel demanded.

The scared, faint voice squeaked out, "Room service sir. I have two breakfasts for you." The small man was quivering with fear.

"Please don't kill me."

Daniel paused and quickly frisked the man before helping him to his feet.

"Sorry," he said, "I ordered breakfast for six a.m."

The old man looked at Daniel and stammered, "I-I-I j-just deliver them when I-I g-get them. It's so b-busy. S-s-sorry to intrude, b-but I did announce myself before c-c-coming in."

Daniel handed him a fifty rand note and signed the chit to the room.

"Thank you, and sorry if I roughed you up a bit. I hope this helps you forget."

"Yes sir, thank you," and the man departed quickly, leaving the tray unattended for Daniel to sort out.

Ten minutes later, Clive arrived, looking quite dapper.

"We have our team ready to go for this afternoon!" Clive said with considerable satisfaction.

"They seem to be excited about doing something a little more intriguing than wandering around steel decks all night and sleeping in hard bunks. Do you know where you want us to go yet?"

"Clive, you are not going. I need you here," Daniel responded firmly.

"We are pretty certain the killers are at one of the camps in the escarpment or on the Zambezi. My guess is that it will turn out to be the Rifa Camp. Jacobus will be here in an hour or so and we will see what he has learned. I would suggest you prepare your guys for an extraction using the Zambezi as your approach. Perhaps a large Zodiac, dropping in a few kilometres upstream, and then coasting east down the river. What do you think?"

"I think I am the only one of the team who is familiar with Rifa Camp, so I will have to lead the team, boss. I know it's not ideal to have me gone, but we will be able to collect them at around midnight and get them downstream toward Mozambique. We could get them into South Africa, but it might be easier to get into Mozambique and hold them there. We will need an eight-man squad to capture and extract, and then a twelve-man team, plus a leader to hold them in Mozambique. If we have to get them out of the camp, then we can transport them anywhere, once the authorities are involved. I'll keep searching and line up the gear, in case. We will definitely need a Huey and a Zodiac. There will be two loads, when you consider the crew. We need a five-ton to head up and do the pick-up if we decide to go that way. If we are going into Mozambique, we will need to select a camp that we can slip into from the Zambezi. Let's wait and see where they are before we make the final plan."

"Are you sure you don't have anyone else to lead this thing, Clive?" Daniel smiled, "I know you and how much you want to convince yourself that you never get older, buddy, but it has been a while, you know."

"We'll talk about it later," Clive shot back, "at least I haven't been sitting on my ass playing on a computer for the last five years!" Clive smiled and carried on, "if I don't go, I will use the best man I have to lead the team. Now, on to some other stuff. How do you plan to deal with Nkosi and his crowd?"

"Clive, we need to convince the Barons that we know where the two killers are, that they are still active, and that a few of the Barons themselves are in their sights. Their awareness of that uncomfortable fact may just stimulate an acceleration of the negotiations. If the CPZ are prepared to have faith, and if, in fact, both groups are trying to achieve some stability here, then I think they will agree to work together for the common goal of prosperity for Zimbabwe. What I am worried about is those SOBs in Washington. I don't think they would tell a straight story if it was the closest way to achieve what they want. I want to be able to tell Alexander Pope that one of the groups is holding the killers, so that he will be able to pass on that information to his contact, also letting him know that the killers signed affidavits regarding their activities. I would further like to pass on the information that, not only the Zimbabwe Government, but the Chinese Government, is negotiating for possession of them.

"We will get Gordon involved. We can package some of the information from Jim's reports and some from what Gordon discovered, while we get rapid possession of the two guys. This should give us sufficient leverage to negotiate with the Washington group to provide some financial help, to release the money being tied up from the diamond auctions and to obtain a promise to back off activities in Zimbabwe. Although it will be a soft trade, it's about all we will be able to get. We will know who they are. We will have a package of damaging information, and the other players will figure that out. It might just make allies of convenience.

"At minimum we need to be able to identify the two killers. Ideally, we will take them into our possession." Daniel continued exploring ideas. "We just need to be sure that we have them out of Zimbabwe for a few days."

"I'll gather the crew coming in and come up with a plan," Clive replied," no holds barred?"

"Try to stay legal, but if you can't, at least keep it defensible." Daniel replied. "Do you have any ideas?"

"I have a couple," Clive answered.

"Let me get on it and we will charge ahead."

"Good luck man! Don't get hurt!" Daniel looked up at Clive as he turned and left the room. 'They don't get better than that,' he thought.

'The two killers will be identified and taken out of action here. We will use the threat of arrest for murder in Canada if they refuse to cooperate and give us the information we need regarding the murder in Harare. Once we have resolved the Harare issue and been given the information about their activities over the past week or so, then I will pass the details to Scottie so that he can arrange for his client to be cleared.'

DANIEL MEETS WITH CPZ - HARARE - 08:00 I MAY 2014

aniel took the stairs down to the lobby to see what room had been assigned for his meeting with the CPZ. The Palm Court Room was set up with a breakfast buffet when he arrived. Jacobus and the other members of CPZ would be arriving within a few minutes. He hoped that the stenographer was at the hotel and ready to take notes for them. He walked over to the house phone and called the front desk to enquire. He was told that she would be there within five minutes.

"*Goeie môre*, Daniel," said Jacobus, as he led the group into the room.

"Good morning to you Jacobus, Petrus, Johnny. How are you guys today? Please, help yourselves to breakfast and coffee, and then we will get started. We will have a stenographer here soon."

Daniel was excited about getting things settled today. He was optimistic that the CPZ would buy into the idea of a united front, and he was excited about convincing the Barons that the plan was in the best interest of all. He hoped that Alex Pope would be successful in his negotiations with the American group.

DANIEL MEETS WITH BARONS -
HARARE - 12:30 - 1 MAY 2014

D aniel's car was driven through the front gate of the Nkosi Estate, up the driveway, and was stopped at the front door. Walter was standing under the portico waiting to greet him.

"Good afternoon, Daniel. Come on in and I will introduce you to my guests. We have a bit of lunch waiting to help us deal with our issues. I hope you have an appetite."

Daniel shook hands and replied, "Happy to be here Walter, quite a place you have. Actually, I have been eating all morning as we tried to get a position paper together, but I do look forward to meeting your friends."

Walter led Daniel through the grand entrance of the house and down a corridor leading to a large salon.

"Gentlemen, I would like to introduce Daniel Sonneblom, of Wilberson, Jonas & Sonneblom in Pretoria. For those of you who don't already know him, he is one of the best known South African lawyers. Daniel meet Dr. Brighton Chidarara, Minister of Mines, Mr. Goodwill Mashonga, Minister of the Treasury, Major-General Isaac Nkala and Brigadier Khuphe of the Zimbabwe Army, and my fellow industrialist, Fortune Makamba. A few members of our group are not in attendance for reasons which I believe you already understand."

Having completed the introductions, Walter then introduced Timothy, who politely described the buffet to the guests.

Walter suggested that they fill their plates and be seated so that they could get started.

"I know you are all busy men, so we will proceed as quickly as practical. We have some very critical business in front of us today and Daniel will present a proposal. I will say that we have a very special opportunity to make some noticeable progress if we are prepared to be flexible and decisive."

Daniel put very little food on his plate, just enough to be polite. It all looked quite delicious, but he was full, from having eaten two breakfasts earlier in the morning. He answered Timothy's offer of a drink by asking for a cappuccino, and then he sat at the table and prepared for his presentation.

Daniel began by describing the litany of abuses of the land tenure in Zimbabwe, beginning with the Charter granted to Cecil Rhodes and the purported fraud on Lobengula that had allowed the grant to occur. He went through the assignments of lands to the British military, the battles under Ian Smith and the Unilateral Declaration of Independence, the election of Robert Mugabe under the new constitution, and the different phases of the land rationalization program. He then identified the general background of his client, the group, CPZ, and what their objectives were.

"We are faced with is a situation that has culminated in murder, with two professional killers on the loose. We are certain that they have killed one man already in Harare. I believe that one of your members was involved with a group from the United States that contracted the killers. Some of you may be on the hit list. I believe that if we can put a package in front of the American group, we may be able to convince them to back off, release funds being held back from the diamond auctions, and provide some funds that will provide a new opportunity for progress with the land problems."

Daniel withdrew a folded paper from his pocket and began to go through his speaking points:

- My client, the CPZ, wants to be more proactive in helping the subsistence farmers get established and, once they prove themselves, either sell them some land or allow them to obtain long-term leases. They would also agree to stop pressuring white farmers off their lands.

- Support CPZ demands.
- Reinvest your wealth in Zimbabwe.
- Commit to accepting land tenure as sacrosanct and commit to expropriation limits.
- Turn over a share of land to subsistence farmers in return for modest rents and allow them to develop their skills. Rent unused lands, properly acquired, to farmers capable of farming profitably, whether white or black. This can be done by partnership or by lease agreements.
- Use all efforts to force the government to respect and implement legislation to achieve these objectives.
- Use all efforts to obtain functional budgeting, including appropriate royalties, on all mineral extraction.

Subject to financial assistance from the African Development Bank and the World Bank, and a release of the foreign sanctions.

"Remember gentlemen, if you wish to become honourable men and have your children live safely and without fear in a land of opportunity controlled by Zimbabweans, then it must begin with you. The great writer of ancient India, Kautilya Chanaka said. 'Low class men desire wealth; middle class men both wealth and respect; but the noble, honour only; hence honour is the noble man's true wealth.'"

DANIEL CONTACTS JACOBUS - 17:00 - 1 MAY 2013

"Jacobus, you and I will have to finalize our plan now, so that we can get moving on it. After we have finished, I will put in a call with Alexander Pope in New York and discuss it with him. If he has suggestions, I will add them into our plan, and then email the final document to him so that he can present it to his contact. Of course, now that we have two of their contractors in our custody, I think we will have some much-needed leverage. They have already provided a great deal of information that links them to both the Abrin Financial Group and the U.S. Government. We have a lot of sensitive material that neither of those bodies wants made public. If we do not get their cooperation, then it will be quite easy for us to arrange to have the information released by the Chinese Government. We have more than enough information to demonstrate the direct inter-ference of the United States in the internal affairs of Zimbabwe and the consequent compromise of Chinese investments there."

DANIEL TELEPHONES ALEXANDER
– 2 MAY 2014 – 13:00 NY TIME

"Good afternoon, Sullivan, Wachtel and Pope. How may I direct your call?" asked the professionally crisp voice on the line.

"This is Daniel Sonneblom for Alexander Pope."

"One moment, Mr. Sonneblom. I will see if Mr. Pope is available."

The next voice Daniel heard was decidedly more masculine than the last.

"Mr. Sonneblom, it's great to hear from you. Though we've not yet met, I feel as though I know you, thanks to our mutual client."

"It's Daniel, and I feel the same way, Mr. Pope."

"Alex to you, Daniel. Now, since time seems to be of the essence, shall we get to it? I will call you right back on a secure line."

Daniel outlined the plan and informed Alex that the killers were in custody and that they had already provided plenty of information that linked them directly to both the Abrin Financial Group and the US government.

"We have a great deal of sensitive material that those entities do not want made public. If necessary, we will have the Chinese Government release the information, and there is more than enough to demonstrate to the Chinese the direct interference by the United States in the internal affairs of Zimbabwe and the consequent compromise to Chinese investments there."

"That's certainly damning information, Daniel. The plan to ameliorate the interference is a sound one, in my opinion. I am confident that when I present it to my contact, he will take and seriously and will, in turn, present it to his people as such. It seems to me that this will force them to acquiesce to the plan.

"Incidentally, I am relieved on behalf of our client. From all perspectives."

"So am I, Alex. Now that we've finalized the details, I will email the plan to you immediately and let you work your magic. Let's be in touch as soon as possible."

ALEX NEGOTIATES A DEAL – 2 MAY 2014

Once they disconnected their call, Alex phoned the Senator.

"We need to meet," Alex stated without preamble.

"An item of extreme urgency has arisen, and it involves your group. We may have to do this by secure conference call, if you can arrange it. Otherwise, I'll charter a chopper and be down there in two hours."

"Slow down now, Alex," responded the Senator.

"The world doesn't move that fast. We can deal with whatever it is in due course. Why don't you come down tomorrow and we can chat then?"

"With all due respect, Senator, drop the supercilious tone and be assured that you will not like the outcome of tomorrow morning's news cycle. This is not in my control. I am calling you as a courtesy because I know you, and because I would rather not see our country dragged into a real mess, if I can help it. I have no obligations to your group, but you need to know that the information that will be released ties together the group and the government. I suggest you speak to your counterparts and get back to me immediately."

"Alright, Alex, but just stay relaxed," came the subdued response, "I will try to see whether I can get in touch with anyone. I will phone you back in a while."

The Senator hung up.

Alex was not happy with that response. How was he going to stimulate a reaction in time to meet Daniel's schedule? If he couldn't convince the Senator and the Abrin Financial Group to deal promptly with the situation, there was a definite risk that the Zimbabwe Government or the Chinese Government would become involved. If the Chinese became involved, Alex knew that they would not do anything precipitously unless Robert Mugabe went ahead. Then the Chinese would be required to choose a side, and it would most likely have to be Mugabe's side. That would be embarrassing both to the US Government and to the Abrin Financial Group. The sooner the Senator called Alex back, the greater the likelihood of success. Alex asked his assistant to phone the helicopter charter company to determine the availability of a chopper that could take him to Washington, D.C.

"Mr. Pope," Alex's assistant leaned through the door of his office, "you will be able to catch a helicopter at the Wall Street heliport on twenty minutes' notice. Since it will be only you flying, they suggest a Bell 406GX, which will get you there in about an hour-and-a-half. It will land at the South Capitol Street Heliport in Washington. Just let me know when you know, okay?"

Alex's phone rang.

"Alex Pope here," he stated clearly.

The Senator merely asked, "What time will you be at my office, Alex?"

"I can be there in about two hours. If you will have a car waiting for me at the heliport on South Capital in about an hour-and-a-half, it will get me there faster. Call my cell to confirm the car. I am on my way." With relief Alex hung up the phone, grabbed his coat and briefcase, and, as he rushed past his assistant's desk, he said, "Order the helicopter. I am on my way. I'll need them to be available to fly me back about four hours later, okay? I'll be on my cell."

Alex was escorted to the helicopter. It looked a lot like the old 206 he was used to flying, but as soon as the door opened, he noticed the differences. He sat in the rear seat, on the opposite side from the pilot. As soon as the doors were secured and the ramp personnel were out of the way, the rotors were wound up and the Allison 250 powered them off the pad, and they were on their way.

'This is very smooth,' Alex thought. He looked into the cockpit and saw the two large screens, and thought wryly, 'I hope they are more dependable than my computer screens,' but since it was a clear day he was not concerned. He settled back into the soft grey leather seat, surreptitiously putting up his feet on the facing seat, and opened his briefcase. Time to get to work.

It seemed as though no time had passed when the pilot turned the helicopter for its final approach into the Washington heliport. The pilot's voice came over the intercom, instructing him to secure his seatbelt. Minutes later he was on the ground, and he spotted a man at the edge of the heliport who was holding up a sign with his name on it. He turned to the pilot, whose door was open, and told him that he planned to return to New York in about three or four hours. The pilot handed him a card and suggested that Alex call twenty minutes before he was ready to leave. He was asked to call also if he was going to be longer than four hours.

Alex headed off with the driver and soon was in front of the Senator's office building. He walked through the entrance and took the elevator to the fourth floor. Before he even stepped toward the receptionist, the Senator intercepted him, taking him by the arm.

"This way, Alex. How was your trip?" he asked. "We have a couple of people who will sit in on our meeting, but I will not be able to introduce them to you. I hope that is okay with you."

"Fine, as long as they are decision-makers," Alex replied.

Alex followed the Senator into the meeting room. It was paneled in polished walnut, and dark green leather upholstered the eight chairs placed around the large mahogany table. Two men sat side by side with their back toward the window, leaving Alex to sit staring into the light. The Senator took his seat at the head of the table. The Senator offered coffee or tea. The two mean across the table asked for coffee, so Alex joined them.

The Senator opened the meeting.

"Alex, why don't you explain why we are gathered here? I have told these two gentlemen who you are and who you represent. Please proceed."

"Senator, gentlemen, this meeting is related to my client only partially. As the Senator has made me aware, your firm has…"

"Excuse me," interrupted the man sitting nearest the Senator, "please do not make assumptions about who we represent."

"I don't care who you represent," Alex rebuked him sharply, "the Senator has been kind enough to have you present and he knows what the issue is and what is at stake, so pardon my assumption that you also may know something about why I am here. Now, if there is nothing else, I will continue.

"There has been a flurry of activity in Zimbabwe, resulting from two independent investigations into the flow of funds, and other issues, relating to the diamond business. The action on these investigations has been brought to a head by the murder of an individual in Harare, who happens to have been associated with a Chinese investment firm with close connections to the Chinese Government. My contact has informed me that the assassins are now in informal custody and are telling interesting stories, including something about their involvement in a murder in Canada. They also seem to have some interesting revelations about who employed and supported them. Is that enough to capture your attention?"

"And just what is it that we are talking about?" asked the second man.

"I think that much of this can be shut down if it is resolved quickly," replied Alex. "The Chinese investors want their money and cessation of the interference in the diamond auctions. The Government of Zimbabwe needs to placate the Chinese investors in order to avoid upsetting the Chinese Government. There are two groups in Zimbabwe who want foreign interference in government policies eliminated, and assurance of suitable funding from the World Bank and from the African Development Bank to allow the continuation of the current land buy-back system, and more importantly, to fund start-up farmers. Does either of you have any suggestions?"

"Why would we?" asked the first man in a hostile tone. "And what would be in it for us if we did have any interest?"

Alex took a deep breath.

"First, in return for farm purchase funding commitments, the two groups who now possess the evidence of financial fraud and currency manipulation will agree not to release the information. Second, once you jump that hurdle, they will convince the Zimbabwe Government to provide rapid extradition to the United States of the two hired killers. Third, once all of the funds from the diamond sales at the two main auctions have been paid to the proper beneficiaries, the two men will be turned over immediately to U.S. custody. Fourth, the U.S. Treasury will announce support of the funding of the African Development Bank to cover the farming project."

"What amounts are we talking about, for the two financings?" asked the first man.

"In addition to the return of all monies relating to the diamond sales, the total amounts to about three-hundred million dollars, which will be funded in three equal, annual tranches, beginning immediately," was Alex's prompt and firm response.

"And what security will we have that this is not just the beginning of a blackmail campaign?" asked the second man.

"The two groups that possess the research have no desire of potential benefit beyond the objectives I've just presented. The Harare police have enough to do without getting tangled up in an international extradition fight, let alone a lone investigation. Since my client is the only person who has access to the information necessary for a quick conviction, they will likely agree without hesitation. My client has no interest other than seeing the deal formalized, the diamond monies released, the funding made, and the interference stop," Alex recapped.

"Senator, can you give us another room for half-an-hour, with a secure phone line, please?" asked the first man.

The Senator stood and said, "Follow me, please," and without further ado, they left Alex alone.

A few minutes later, the Senator walked back into the room and sat down.

"Well, Alex, you have balls, I'll give you that. You *are* aware that those guys could extinguish you and your client in ways that no one would ever know."

"I don't think you would want that to happen, Senator," was Alex's reply, as he looked the Senator in the eye, "I really don't think so."

For the next ten minutes a tense silence sat between them like smog. Finally, the Senator spoke. "Alex, do you trust your client and his cohort?"

"Yes, I do," he replied, "I understand what they are after, and it is not unreasonable. In fact, in my opinion, they are being very generous."

Again, the room was silent and remained so until the two men returned a few minutes later.

The first man spoke.

"Not interested."

Alex looked from him to the second man and then to the Senator. He rose from his chair, saying, "Okay, then, I will get back to my client and let him deal with things as he and his associates see fit. Thank you for taking the time to meet."

Alex reached out his arm to shake hands with the Senator.

The second man spoke. "How would you propose to keep the United States Government out of this?"

"I wouldn't. They put themselves into it."

"Could the funding be put through a local institution?" asked the second man.

Alex looked at the two men and then at the Senator.

"Did you say no, or did you say yes, subject to some negotiation of the details?"

Alex asked, staring hard at the two men.

"Well, perhaps we can negotiate somewhat," replied the second man.

For the next two hours, Alex, the Senator and the two men worked out the details of the arrangement in a way that Alex thought would satisfy the people in Zimbabwe. The deal was subject to the Americans' ratification within twenty-four hours. It was 18:00 in Washington by the time they completed their negotiations.

"I will let my people know that you will be back to us with a firm answer no later than 18:00 ET tomorrow."

Alex stood and offered his hand to the Senator.

The Senator stood slowly and looked first at the other men. The more senior of the two nodded. "That will be fine. I think we will be able to give you an answer one way or another by then."

The Senator grasped Alex's hand firmly. "For all our sakes, let's hope we can."

"Send the executed documents, without changes, to my office in New York," ordered Alex. He left the room, stopping at the reception desk to collect his overcoat before heading into the hall.

He called his assistant in New York and asked her to arrange a helicopter for him as soon as possible, and then he flagged a Yellow Cab from the street. Once Alex settled into his seat, he placed a call to his client, Gordon Zhong.

"Gordon, we are making progress, I think. I should know by tomorrow at this time if the diamond monies will be released. Just stay put and I will call you back tomorrow, as soon as I have heard something."

"Good news, Alex!" Gordon replied, relief obvious in his voice. "Is there anything else?"

"You might figure out where all your relevant documentation is and have a duplicate set prepared. I'll have more to tell you tomorrow," said Alex.

The next call Alex made was to Daniel to update him on the status of the negotiations. It was very early in the morning, but he knew Daniel did not want to wait.

"Hello?" Daniel answered sleepily.

"Hi, Daniel! Sorry for calling in the middle of the night!"

Alex took a breath as the taxi driver swerved up to the heliport.

"Just a second, Daniel. I've got to pay the cab driver," he said as he slipped a twenty to the driver and indicated that he was to keep the change.

"I am just catching a flight back to New York and I want to let you know that we are making progress. They will go firm or not by 18:00 my time tomorrow."

"Sounds great, Alex! Many problems?" Daniel asked.

"Just the normal negotiation bullshit," he responded. "I think they are a little uncomfortable about how they will explain everything to their bosses in a way that will save their asses."

"Good! Let them stew! I'll wait to hear from you in about twenty-four hours. Safe flight."

Alex said, "Good night." He hung up his phone and dashed to the helicopter. As the 406 climbed out and turned to the northeast, Alex nodded off.

EXTRACTION OF KILLERS – RIFA
HUNTING CAMP – 1 & 2 MAY 20

Rifa Hunting and Fishing Camp sat on the banks of the Zambezi River on the northern border of Zimbabwe. Upstream the magnificent Victoria Falls spills water from as far north as the Democratic Republic of Congo in the interior of Africa, over one hundred metres off the lip of a basaltic plateau to the chasms below, in an amazing spectacle of nature's beauty. The thundering mists rise so high they are seen from twenty kilometres away. From there the river meanders east then north into Lake Kariba, before swinging east to Lake Cabora Bassa in Mozambique.

Between Lake Kariba and Lake Cabora Bassa on the south shore of this river lies the spot where two men were having their photograph taken beside a huge but immobile hippopotamus. Their PH was on his belly in the sand lining up for the obligatory snapshot that most hunters retain as evidence of their success. The head tracker waited for the arrival of the recovery crew. They would drag the carcass to the edge of the clearing then separate the tusks and the hide from the large beast. Any locals wishing meat would be able to help themselves. Some of the carcass would be retained for the staff and the balance would be transported to a nearby safari camp for use as bait for lions.

The hunters walked back to the truck with the PH to enjoy a cold Zambezi beer. It had been a great day so far. The hunters had been up since four in the morning checking the lion blinds set up over the three previous days. They had elected to call this lunchtime. Folding chairs were pulled from the back of the Land Cruiser and set up around a small mopane fire.

Pieces of the hippo were put on the skewers and roasted over the fire. A large green cooler was brought from the land cruiser and sandwiches were laid out, along with some fresh tomatoes and the condiments. The warm sun made relaxing easy as they slowly sipped their ice-cold beer. Far away but unknown to them, decisions were being made as to their fate.

Clive had assembled his crew at the airport hangar as soon as they had arrived. Maps were tacked to a corkboard, photos were assembled, and sketches of the layout of Rifa Camp lay on the table. There would be eight men going into the two Zodiacs that would be launched from the beach on the south side of the Zambezi, just twenty-five minutes west of the Rifa Camp.

The night sky slowly pushed the remainder of the red orb through the indigo cushion behind the acacia trees and into its sleeping place below the horizon. Clive's team was moving efficiently. The two rented Bell UH-1 Hueys had returned to Harare. The men were sufficiently geared for light combat risk. Camouflage paint, watch caps on and dark pixilated combats completed the basic outfit. On their combat webbing they carried a camel pack, a Sig Sauer 9mm with four backup 10 round magazines, a Bussy Boss jack knife, and a Selex Communications H4855 Personal Role Radio (PRR) radio. Four members wore Gen 3-night vision goggles. Four of the team carried H&K 416 A5 - .556x45 carbines on a shoulder sling. Two had the Heckler and Koch MP-5 SD - 9mm with the built-in suppressor and 30 round magazines.

The two old Zodiac Mk2 Inflatable Raiding Craft arrived, one on each Huey. Each would hold four men, with room left over for their guests. They should be able to reach Rifa Camp within 15 minutes and then Stephen's Camp, just inside Mozambique, within 50 minutes after departure from Rifa. Once the Zodiacs were laid out with floorboards, the CO_2 packs inflated them quickly. Night operations in waters infested by crocodiles and hippos would inhibit the Zodiacs' top speed to 20 mph.

Clive's plan was to reach Rifa Camp by 21:00. The hunters would have returned from the field and have finished their dinner by then. Two men would remain in each boat and two from each would go ashore. Once the guests had been recovered, they would travel one each in the boats until they reached Stephen's Camp in Mozambique. They still had thirty minutes before departure to review the plan. The men were comfortable and busy making final adjustments and buddy checks of their equipment.

Clive took one more look at his watch and called out, "Mount up boys."

Within seconds of pushing away from shore, both Zodiacs were headed down the Zambezi River. Clive cautioned the lookouts to watch for signs of hippos. Most of the men were very familiar with Africa and knew what was needed to get them safely to the insertion target. The motors were barely above an idle as they rounded the last bend. The drivers found a spot of abandoned beach and nosed their craft to the shore. The men disembarked and scrambled up the hill. When they reached the top of the ridge, their stealth for the last fifty yards startled the men sitting around the mopane campfire.

"Hello," Clive opened in a friendly manner. He quickly spotted the two men and knew they were wise enough to avoid any confrontation if possible.

"You must be our passengers," he spoke directly to the black-haired man, whom he took to be the team leader. "We are here to get you guys out of harm's way," he continued. He received no response.

"Some guys in Washington are very concerned that the Zimbabwe military doesn't take custody of you. There are about forty on their way here, as we speak. Apparently, some policemen in Harare implicated you two in a murder there the other night." He paused, waiting for a response, before continuing, "if you have had your dinner, I would suggest you grab your gear and let's get mobile."

"Who the fuck are you?" the black-haired man demanded to know, showing no indication of getting up to go anywhere.

"I didn't ask who the fuck you are, so let's be courteous. I get paid whether you decide you can take them on yourself or you come with us," Clive replied calmly but firmly.

"We're not going to be here when they arrive. You call it."

The blonde guy looked over at his teammate as if to say, "What do you want to do, boss?"

The black-haired guy still didn't move.

Clive call over the PH and said to him, "Perhaps you can explain the alternatives to these guys before I head to the boat, but make it quick."

In the distance, a shot was fired, promptly followed by a few three-round replies. Another couple of shots sounded.

"Coming, asshole, or would you like to ride back to Harare?" Clive turned and ordered his guys back to the boats.

"Wait! We're coming," the man finally said and jumped up to head to his tent.

They were back within sixty seconds and followed Clive to the boats. Clive shouted over his should, "Jacobus will sort out any payments due you within the week."

"One into each boat, please. Sit midsection. Keep your body and your limbs in the centre of the boat unless you want to be someone's dinner," Clive ordered. "No round in the chamber, please. You can keep your mag full," he told the black-haired guy, who was carrying his .375. "Don't want an accidental hole anywhere."

As soon as the Zodiacs were loaded, they were off into the dark, floating silently down the river. The PH went to his tend and turned on the radio set.

"Rifa to home. Rifa to home. Over." He waited and soon heard the scratchy response, "Rifa, this is home. Over."

"Home, patch me to 'Lion' please. Over."

"Wilco. Stand by, Rifa."

A female voice came on the line, "Lion's den. Over."

"Message for 'Lion'. Mother has the two cubs. They departed five minutes ago. Over."

"Message received. Thank you. Out." And the radio clicked back to the station.

"Rifa out," the PH closed the conversation.

"Keep quiet," Clive whispered, "no lights, quiet power until we are a half mile downstream."

As the Zodiacs almost silently drifted to the middle of the stream, their occupants could hear drums from a village party near the shore in Zambia. It was just loud enough to drown out any sounds from the outboard until they were far enough away to be out of range of any troopers.

"Ok, let's get the hell out of here!" Clive told the driver, then turning to the black-haired man he explained, "We are going to head to a camp on the Mozambique side, once we get past the Zambian border. We will park there for a few days, and then fly you guys to Jo'burg, where the U.S. Embassy is going to get you out of Dodge. Hope that works for you."

"Why the hell are you guys involved in this?" the black-haired man asked again.

"Simply for the money man," Clive answered.

"This is our living," he added not letting on that he knew why the killers were there. "It's really crap that some SOB in Harare has decided that you guys would make likely candidates for a charge of murder. I guess since you weren't actually in Harare anymore, he convinced his boss that you had run away from justice. Seems it was an easy sale."

The two Zodiacs approached Luangwa, Zambia with power back. Once they were past and headed east, they fired up the engines. Things were going well.

"Lights on!" Clive shouted up at the lookout. "Maybe we can pick up a bit of speed. I am a land man not a sailor! The sooner I am off this thing the better."

The engines roared to life and, as the speed built, the stern of each Zodiac sank into the river.

Twenty minutes later they pulled to the west shore and watched for signs of the camp. Soon they noticed the light of a campfire flickering through the trees that lined the shore. Slowing, the sailors swung the bows of their Zodiacs into the current to make their approach. Soon the soft scrunch of the bottoms sliding onto the sandy mud of the shore indicated the end of the night's journey. A quick look about showed that any resting hippos or crocs had moved out, and the men began disembarking. The men on board passed gear to the men ashore and the last men out assisted the sailors in pulling the boats up onto the shore and securing them.

" *Oi como vai,*" an old voice came from the ridge above the shoreline.

"*Ola*, you old bugger," Clive replied.

"I thought you had died years ago." He laughed. "How the hell are you, Lourenço?"

"Just slowly dying away out here. If it wasn't for the endless supply of young wives out here, I would be dead already. Come on up and have some dinner. How many are you?" Lourenço called out.

"Ten," answered Clive, "we'll be right up."

He turned to the black-haired guy, looked him straight in the eye and said, "You Ok, Bud? You're awful quiet.

"We're going to have to split you guys up for sleeping for a few nights. I hope you won't mind. You see, now that we have you out of there safely, we have to deliver you safely to the Embassy guys or we won't get our full payday. You understand." Clive explained, "I know you guys know how to hunt, but the guys around here have a little more experience in this country and seem not to have anything to lose. Want some more dinner?"

"Well, maybe a drink if you have one," the black-haired man replied.

"We'll see what old Lourenço has," Clive smiled, "we didn't have much of a chance to go shopping."

They all took their seats around the fire. Clive had Lourenço get his men to move the bags into the tents. "Put this guy in with my gear in the second tent," Clive ordered, pointed to the black-haired man. "The rest of you guys get settled. Our other guest will be in the second tent from the far end. I want one man at each approach with one ready for backup. You will rotate on four-hour shifts, two to a shift."

Clive took a chair while Lourenço puled some extras from the mess tent.

"The cookie has some grub on the way," he said, sitting to join them.

"So, what brings you over here, my friend?" Lourenço asked.

Clive continued the fiction. "We just jogged over here to save the asses of a couple of our friends from your former friends in the Zim army. You know how pleasantly they treat guests in their prisons, eh?"

Lourenço looked at the two guests, smiled and said, "What the hell did you fellows do to stir the wasps' nest?"

"Don't know," the black-haired man answered, "I guess we pissed of a copper in Harare for some reason."

Clive was happy to see that he complied with the fiction.

"Do you have a phone or radio?" Clive asked the two men. "If so, I'd like to see them."

"We have a couple of phones, but they both need a charge," the black-haired man answered. "I'll get them for you before we hit the hay."

"Got something to drink old man?" Clive challenged Lourenço.

"Sure, but you might not like it much. I'll be right out with it." he replied with a grin.

It was ten before they headed off to bed for the first of three nights. Clive had been able to radio to the Lion with their coordinates before bed. There would be no hunting, no roaming; just card games on the mess tent table or joking around the campfire. The two guests seemed to be comfortable with the story perpetrated by Clive. Clive's men were happy to avoid discussions about the mission. They would await the results of Daniel's negotiations.

CLIVE NOTIFIES DANIEL AND DANIEL CALLS THE INSPECTOR - 3 MAY 2014 - 07:30

The morning after Daniel heard from Clive that the two killers were secure and out of the country, he placed a call to Inspector Butholezwe.

"Inspector, Daniel Sonneblom here. Do you have a minute?" Daniel waited for the reply.

"Yes, go ahead," the abrupt answer came.

"I want to let you know that the two guys that killed the oriental at the Meikles last week are out of the country and in the custody of a security company. Your Detective-Sergeant Sibangilizwe was not directly involved in the murder, but was aware of those responsible, and he was in contact with the firm in the United States that engaged and instructed them.

"That son-of-a-bitch! I had a feeling he had too many bosses," the Inspector retorted. "How soon can you get those two guys to Harare?"

"Well, that's where it gets a bit sticky," Daniel replied, "The U.S. Embassy wants them too. I think you might save yourself a lot of time and trouble if you let the Americans take possession of them in South Africa or somewhere other than Zimbabwe. You will be able to make an announcement that you have one of the parties involved, being the Detective-Sergeant, and that the other two have been sent to the United States where they will be dealt with. I do need you to send some evidence related to the murder to the RCMP in Canada, as it relates to a murder there. One of the Detective's acolytes assisted him in disposing of a piece of evidence. We don't know the constable's name. The Meikles front desk clerk can give you the records of the material Fed Ex'd to Washington by the Detective-Sergeant. He may be quite willing to speak if he knows that his employer has sold him as part of another deal."

"Let me bring in the Detective-Sergeant and I'll have a chat with him," the Inspector replied, "where can I get back to you?"

"Just call me on this number," Daniel explained, "I'll be bouncing around to meetings. Call anytime, but time is critical and please keep this quiet for now."

"I will talk to you later," the Inspector answered in a noncommittal fashion.

The next person Daniel called was Jacobus to let him know that the Barons had agreed in principal and were trying to get things sorted out with the Government. He asked Jacobus if he or his guys had had any problems since the last meeting.

"No," Jacobus said, "If it all works out Daniel, we will have taken a small but important step in the right direction. Godspeed. I'll inform the others."

It was after 15:00 when Daniel's cell buzzed in his pocket.

"Hello, Inspector," Daniel answered, "What's the news?"

"I spoke to the Detective-Sergeant, and he provided the information I required," he answered. "His helper let us know that he simply disposed of a bag in the dumpster. I have sent a few guys over to see if we are too late to retrieve it. Funny how quickly they respond when you ask questions nicely," the Inspector chuckled as Daniel cringed.

"How about the two guys?" Daniel asked.

"What two guys?" the Inspector replied, "I have my culprits."

Once he had cleared his mind, Daniel dialed Scottie at his office.

"Scottie, how are you?" Daniel asked allowing the two to adjust to the time shift in the call. "We should know by 15:00 your time today if we have made a deal on this mess. I have agreement from CPZ and the Barons, subject to the Americans' and Gordon Zhong's approval. I understand from Alexander Pope, the lawyer in New York that Mr. Zhong's demands were fairly clear and apolitical, and it appears they will be resolved. The Barons are going to apply whatever effort is needed to get the Zimbabwe Government onside, and I have spoken to the Inspector in Harare about the disposition of the two guys who were over in your country. I have asked the Inspector to provide a package of evidence that should allow you to get your client off the hook and explain, in part, the cause of Jim's death. The bad guys will be in custody of the U.S. on the understanding that they can deal with them as they wish. How does that sound to you?"

"Good work, man!" Scottie sounded pleased. "Let me know when you hear. I'll find out where the evidence should be sent and who the contact is, and I'll let you know. This is great news, Daniel!"

ALEX TELLS DANIEL OF AMERICAN'S AGREEMENT

The deadline was looming, and Daniel was becoming concerned about holding everything together. Clive had told him that the two men were getting a little nervous and were beginning to ask a lot of questions. Clive felt that if he had to keep them secure for more than one more day, he would need to change out some guys to keep up the cover. Daniel was sitting in the Explorers Club, having a cool beer with his sandwich, and waiting. The cell on the table beside him vibrated. It was Alex.

"Alex, how are we doing?" he asked with some trepidation.

"I think we have got something that works," Alex replied, "let me run the agreement past you while my assistant wires you a signed copy."

"Great! Go ahead," Daniel said eagerly, grabbing a pencil and pad from his case. "Ready."

Alex started, "Okay, both sides will agree to keep the information they have discovered confidential. The two men who are in custody will be released to the U.S. Embassy. Any necessary extradition papers will be signed post-haste in Zimbabwe so they may be returned to the U.S. from South Africa. They will agree not return to Zimbabwe. The Detective-Sergeant, under the watch of the Inspector, will remain in Zimbabwe to be dealt with, as long as there is confidentiality. Once the two contract men are back in the U.S., instructions will be given for the release of the currently frozen diamond funds. The investment bank agrees to back off interference in the Zimbabwean economy and cease currency manipulation. The U.S. Government will cease legal and financial interference in the diamond exchanges. The U.S. Government and the investment bank will provide support to the World Bank, and to the African Development

Bank to allow continued redevelopment in Zimbabwe. The Senator will use his best efforts to cause the U.S. Embassy to disseminate a press release covering the commitments for funding. The Abrin Financial Group will announce financing to back the farming program. It will be managed by the Standard Bank."

"What happens if they don't perform their commitments?" Daniel asked.

"They have two weeks to get everything worked out and the press releases distributed, after which we can start leaking our information, including photos of the two men and the Detective-Sergeant's testimony," Alex replied, "I think that will be enough to keep them in line, don't you?"

"Well done, Alex. I'll get in touch with the other guys and let them know where we stand," Daniel stated, "let me know when to expect the U.S. Embassy contact, and we will move the two guys."

A few hours later Daniel reviewed the documents and passed copies on to the Barons and to the CPZ. Then he phoned the Inspector and confirmed that everything was still onside with him. It was time to phone Gordon.

"Hello?" Gordon answered hopefully, "Is there anything new, Daniel?

"We've done all we can do for now. They still need a little time to get to a press release on all the issues. The good news is that the frozen diamond sale funds will be released shortly after we get the two killers into the custody of the U.S. Embassy in Pretoria. How do you feel?"

"I feel great," Gordon replied enthusiastically, "When may I return to Harare?"

"I would wait until the exchange is made." Daniel added, "I will have clearance from the Inspector by then, just a few days."

EPILOGUE

HARARE - 15 MAY 2014

For the first time ever, Mama Prudence was sitting at the dinner table with three of her sisters together. They were the guests of Daniel, Clive and Gordon. Veronica was very shy and quiet, Akatendeka was bright and brilliant, sitting across from Gordon. Prosper was having fun teasing Clive for being single and sooo old. Even though they were close to the same age, his hair was showing some grey. Mama and Daniel were presiding over them like two proud mentors watching their protégées.

Daniel stood at the head of the table and when the chatter had quieted down, said, "I would like to propose a toast tonight to the resolution of a major crime and thank each of you for the important part you played in resolving it. Cheers!" After an appropriate period of time Daniel stood once more.

"I would like to propose a toast and a moment of silence to Jim, to Gordon's assistant, whom we all called Sparkly, and to the other victims. We wish their souls Godspeed."

After a minute they all clinked their glasses and in unison replied, "Godspeed."

"I wish that I could tell all of you about the other people involved in resolving these matters, but I cannot. There were people in the United States who helped, like Mr. Zhong's attorneys; there were the people in Canada, whom I am not able to name; there were two groups of

Zimbabweans who have been in opposition for many years, and who have agreed to give each other a chance to show how they will make Zimbabwe great again. Once again, I cannot name names. There is also a sisterhood of wonderful witches, whom I will not identify. To all of them, thank you!" Daniel finally sat down, then promptly stood again. "...and to that little Chinese ghost who saved Gordon's butt on the way to the airport." They all laughed, and the party continued.

Mama stood and said, "People, I would like to tell a story tonight. As we Zimbabweans all know, one does not tell stories during the day, as it brings famine to the community. It is dark and I have drunk a beer, and now I begin my story. This story takes place long ago in the year when the Zambezi flooded it banks and all the rivers ran high. It is a story about a young woman. She had a bad husband who would return home and find some excuse to beat her. He was a poor husband and could not afford to have more than one wife, but he still expected her to do all of the work. She cleaned the house and cleaned the yard. She planted the cotton and planted the maize. She chased away the baboons and the elephants that wanted to eat the crops. She did his cooking. He could not make her have a baby, so he beat her more. She eventually found a lover and her tummy began to swell. The husband stopped beating her, thinking it was to be his child. She could not, however, remain happy, and for this he again began to beat her.

"As the time for the baby to come into this world she knew she needed help. Now it becomes a story of how the sisterhood was able to make one life better and, in doing so, to make many lives better. The baby needed surgical help to be born. The mother died during the operation and was given to a crocodile that returned her with a fresh soul and a young body. The beautiful little baby also *died* and was also fed to the crocodiles. They returned her soul and placed it in a new body. The bad husband never came to see his wife or her child. He was cursed for evermore and never could find a wife. He died while fishing. He was eaten by a crocodile but neither his body nor his soul was ever returned.

"One of the helpers on that night is here tonight, and we all see Veronica. She transferred from a bad life to a wonderful life and, ever since that night, has found things to smile about. The mother of the baby returned to live a good life and worked hard and learned to accept the loss of her baby. She completed a business degree and is about to complete her MBA and become a totally modern woman. Prosper stand up with Veronica."

The table cheered for Prosper and Veronica.

"I now want to introduce another beautiful young woman who graduated at the top of her class in secondary school, graduated summa cum laude at Witwatersrand University in Johannesburg, earned her black belt, and who now appears to be falling in love before our very eyes. Akatendeka, please stand up. Gordon Zhong, you are welcome to join our family, if you wish."

Another round of applause and cheering broke out.

"Now I would like to finish the story. Akatendeka, please come here. Prosper, you come here. Folks, for reasons I cannot reveal, it has been impossible until now to let these two women know that they are mother and daughter. A squeal came from Prosper as she leapt to hug Akatendeka. Akatendeka was equally excited, but in a state of shock. Veronica broke out in tears, as did Mama Prudence. Gordon Zhong stood and walked to Akatendeka's side and wrapped his arms around her. He whispered in her ear.

Gordon Zhong then took up his glass and said, "With the permission of this group and the consent of Akatendeka, I would like to take her to meet my family in Shanghai. After that, and assuming she doesn't run, I would like to ask for her hand in marriage. I propose to move to Harare and earn a part in this wonderful country, as we all try to make it great again. Cheers!"

Mama Prudence stood gracefully, paused, looked first at Gordon, and then at Daniel. "There is something I must tell you men. Even old women need a cuddle now and again. There was a day when I was also young and beautiful. I fell in love with a man I could not have. That man was a soldier, so to speak, and he travelled through the world doing favours for his country. He is old now and lives in a home for the aged in Pretoria. He helps me now and I help him. He is my man and I love him, even if we do not live together. He was the man who was in Hong Kong helping us to learn what Gordon was up to with his New York lawyers, and he was the man who saved Gordon's butt on the way to the airport to run away with Clive!" More cheers all around. "Now you know."

Mama Prudence sat down, lowered her head, then small tears spilled from her eyes. She felt the pain in her throat and the quiver in her breathing as she remembered days long past.

Zimbabwe Times - 15 May 2014 - writer

Two men arrested in the Dande Area will be extradited to the United States to face trial. Although they are believed to have committed criminal activities in Zimbabwe, according to Inspector Butholezwe, the President of Zimbabwe has decided to honour a request from the United States for rapid action based upon crimes believed to have been committed in that country.

On the front page of the Zimbabwe Times dated 15 May 2014, below a photograph of a smiling Mr. Walter Nkosi and Mr. Fortune Makamba standing beside Dr. Brighton Chidarara, the Minister of Mines and Mr. Goodwill Mashonga, Minister of the Treasury.

ZIMBABWE FARMERS STRIKE DEAL

Today the Government of Zimbabwe and the Council of Entrepreneurs and the Committee for the Preservation of Zimbabwe jointly announced a new initiative to assist farmers.

One major component will be funded by a group of private landowners, both black and white. It would make land available for the subsistence farmers for farming on various estates. It would provide training, supervision, and financing to assist these new farmers to raise and sell their crops.

A second component will be funded by the Federal government and would make loans available for the purchase of land to seasoned farmers. Financing would be made to equipment cooperatives to allow farmers easier access to expensive farm equipment for planting and harvesting on a contracted basis. Marketing boards would provide cash advances for production of crops and minimum price protection for the production for the first ten years until farm incomes stabilized.

Spokesmen for the CPZ stated that they would provide all assistance possible to ensure a successful outcome of the two programs.

The President of Zimbabwe thanked the World Bank and the African Development Bank for their support in providing funds for certain aspects of the initiatives. The balance would be funded from a share of modestly increased mineral royalties on precious metals and diamonds extracted in Zimbabwe.

KELOWNA - 15 MAY 2014

was released from the hospital and from custody on May 7, thanks to the great work of Tattoo, Scottie, Daniel and everyone else. After a full autopsy was performed, the cause of Jim's death was discovered. It matched the cause of death of Sparkly. Once the blood tests were back, the report from the Harare investigation was forwarded to the RCMP and that, combined with the work done here, provided enough information to have all charges against me lifted. The U.S. Embassy collected the two killers in Pretoria, South Africa as soon as they arrived there. The Inspector in Zimbabwe decided he would not prosecute them because he lacked sufficient evidence to try the two men for murder in Harare.

On the first evening after my release, Scottie, Tattoo and I met at the Keg downtown, for a good steak and a few beers. Once we had our steaks in front of us and a few beers inside us, Tattoo asked if I had ever been on a Safari.

"No, but it is something I have always dreamed of. I grew up reading Robert Ruarke's books. I have read all of the Wilber Smith books. I can't wait to see Africa, to smell the air and feel the breeze, and to spend an evening in front of an ironwood bonfire with a glass of vodka tonic and a good cigar," I replied, with a great smile on my face.

"What do you think, Scottie? Do you think he could make it?" Tattoo asked hopefully, jokingly.

"Well, not if every time something hits him his bones all break!" he laughed, pointing at my cast.

"Daniel's client, Jacobus, has invited us to go over and hunt from his place. He will arrange for a PH and we'll have a great time. We'll have time to visit with Daniel, Clive, Mama Prudence and the rest of the team. We won't be going until the fall, though. That should give you time to heal up. What do you think?"

I answered the only way I could, "I am in!"

I felt the strong camaraderie that develops among hunters. I also knew that it was likely to be the beginning of a long relationship with Africa.

"Maybe there will be things the three of us will work on together when we get to know one another better, man." Tattoo smiled, "Of course that depends upon whether you can get fit enough, old man."

They both had a good laugh - at my expense of course.

- THE END -

GLOSSARY

Xiàwŭ hăo, -Hello - Mandarin

Zàijiàn - Good bye - Mandarin

Hóngsè de tiānkōng - Red Sky Mandarin

Bhai, bhai ona iwe manjemanje - Bye Bye , See you soon Shona

Mangwanani - Good morning - Shona

makadini zvenyu?- How are you - Shona

Gukurahundi— 'the early rain, which washes away the chaff before the spring rains' Shona

Butholezwe (soldier of the nation) male Nkosi (king) male

Khumbulani (remember) male

Livuke njani? – (Good morning) – N Ndebele - One starts with Li when you are greeting an elderly person, a senior or someone who is older than you. The opening is used to show respect to an older person.

Ufunani? – (What do you want?) - N Ndebele

Tot siens, Ek sal môre by die huis wees - Bye, I'll be home tomorrow - Afrikaans

Kom hier Brutus, spring - Come Brutus, jump - Afrikaans

Hey, Brutus, dit gaan 'n lang dag wees vandag, né? - Hey Brutus Its going to be a long day, eh? - Afrikaans

Veldtschoens -Afrikaans - a type of simple boot worn by farmers in the veldt of Africa. Often used by hunters to allow quiet stalking of game.

Daniel, maak asseblief die deur oop - Daniel, open the door please. - Afrikaans

Hoe gaan dit met jou - how are you doing? - Afrikaans

Ja, goed - yes, good - Afrikaans

Goeie môre - Good morning - Afrikaans

ABOUT THE AUTHOR

Bob Gibson was born in Bentley Alberta, (pop. 800) in 1946. After a year attending the University of Alberta, he began his business career, initially as a seismic surveyor, but quickly moved on to become a district sales manager for thirty-one 7/11 stores. His greatest business success was in real estate development, where his association with the Jack Singer family took him to projects across North America and Europe. He learned sufficient Russian to conduct business there amidst the post-Soviet disorder. Gifted with an amazing mathematical ability and great insight into the character of his associates, he was a valued partner, director, and board member for several international resource and financial services companies in Calgary. He was an Honourary Colonel with the Calgary Highlanders and, having gained special admission, completed a Master of Strategic Studies at the University of Calgary in 2016. Bob was a certified offshore sailor as well as a fixed-wing and helicopter pilot, an accomplished fly-fisherman, and generous philanthropist. He was also an expert big-game hunter; many of his African experiences, as well as his inside knowledge of high-level international business practices, are reflected in *Hunting Trophy*. On top of all these manifold accomplishments, Bob was a successful cattleman raising purebred Angus at his beautiful Bobtail Ranch west of Penticton B.C. He died on the ranch in 2020.

Printed in Canada